MW00325062

BETWEEN THE RIVERS • BOOK II

BANDEAUX CREEK

Also by Carolyn Rawls Booth

Between the Rivers (Coastal Carolina Press, 2001)

Aunt Mag's Recipe Book: Heritage Cooking from a Carolina Kitchen (Winoca Press, 2004)

BETWEEN THE RIVERS • BOOK II

BANDEAUX CREEK

A NOVEL

CAROLYN RAWLS BOOTH

Wilmington, North Carolina
Winoca Press

Bandeaux Creek: A Novel
© Copyright 2005 by Carolyn Rawls Booth
All rights reserved

Published by Winoca Press
106 North 16th Street, Wilmington, NC 28401-3819 USA
www.winocapress.com
Available from the publisher or from the author:
P. O. Box 6, Cary, N. C. 27512 USA
carolyn@carolynbooth.com

Printed in the United States of America
07 06 05   10 9 8 7 6 5 4 3 2 1

Illustrations by Katie Anne McKendry
Book cover and interior designed by Barbara Brannon

Library of Congress Cataloging-in-Publication Data
Booth, Carolyn R. (Carolyn Rawls), 1936–
Bandeaux Creek : a novel / Carolyn Rawls Booth.
p. cm. — (Between the rivers ; bk. 2)
ISBN 0-9755910-3-7
1. Married women—Fiction. 2. Women novelists—Fiction.
3. Life change events—Fiction. 4. North Carolina—Fiction. I. Title.
PS3602.O66B36 2005
813'.6—dc22
2005015118

IF THE WRITER HAS USED THE CLAY OF LIFE to make his book, he has only used what all men must, what none can keep from using. Fiction is not fact, but fiction is fact selected and understood, fiction is fact arranged and charged with purpose.

THOMAS WOLFE
Preface to *Look Homeward, Angel*

CONTENTS

CONTENTS, *continued*

A Note to Readers

In these pages you'll find the long-awaited sequel to *Between the Rivers*. I wish to thank the many readers who urged me to continue my story of Maggie Lorena Ryan. As Aunt Mag would say, *there's more to it*—and here you have it.

Bandeaux Creek is the second book in a trilogy of historical novels modeled in part on links in my ancestral chain. For those of you who know me, especially my kinfolk, you will recognize family names, characteristics, and stories I've used to serve my purpose. But you'll only frustrate yourself if you try and put them into the context of your own knowledge or remembrances, for I promise you, this book is a work of fiction. Yes, I have used the clay of my life to flesh out characters, but their words and actions are straight out of my capricious imagination, as are the "newspaper clippings" meant to resemble social and funerary announcements of the day.

The story begins a dozen or more years before I was born, unfolding on a landscape that had changed little by the time I began to write. Even so, historical events have been embellished by one who sees what she wants to see and hears what might never have been said. Come along with me, then, sit back and enjoy my fanciful glimpse into life in the 1920s.

Credit must be given to all who have helped me: my editor, Barbara Brannon, and Winoca Press, who made the difficult task of bringing my book to print such a pleasure; Wilmington author and historian and writer Susan Taylor Block, for her encouragement and informative collections of historical matter; local history librarian Beverly Tetterton, who never failed to provide a resource; and Susan Sharpe, who allowed me to include her story. I must also thank the many booksellers who have taken such a special interest in my stories, especially Linda Maloof, Nicki Leone, Nancy Olson, Terre Oosterwyk, John and Carolyn Westbrook, and Gerry and Sue Kurowski.

And, once again, I am deeply indebted to my husband, for his tireless research of Bladen County history; to my sister, for the beautiful illustrations; to my mother, for her love of family; and to my children, for their steadfast encouragement. Without the love and support of each of the above, this writing might not have happened.

C. R. B.

for Millie

BANDEAUX CREEK

PROLOGUE

Davy's Journal

January 1925

THIS HERE IS MY STORY. *Dr. Cameron at Dix Hill said it would help me understand how I ended up in a place like this. He said it would help him and maybe he could cure me. I laughed because I know I'm not crazy. He said I might laugh now, but if I'm not crazy, they'll send me to the electric chair. I decided to do what he said because I don't want to die or spend the rest of my life in this loony bin.*

Patty Sue Jackson came into my life in August of nineteen and twenty-three. I'd just turned twenty-one and was helping my daddy farm down on Bandeaux Creek in Bladen County, North Carolina. She was the prettiest thing I'd ever laid eyes on. Sure, she was about thirteen years older than me, but that just made her all the more interesting. My cousin and best friend, Calvin McBryde, said she had a wild crazy streak in her. I had one too. I guess that's why she fell for me. Head over heels, I might add.

Calvin was about to start a new job working at the Coast Line down in Wilmington, when he'd come by in his daddy's old Crow-Elkhart automobile wanting me to take a ride up to White Lake where our crowd hung out. Just so happened I had a jar of white lightning I'd bought off a buddy of mine and hidden nearby in a stump. By the time we'd gotten to Melvin's Beach we'd belted down half the jar. There must of been fifteen or twenty cars parked along the water's edge on that late August evening. We'd just started out onto the pier when I saw this woman sitting in a black Chrysler sedan along with some city-slicker fellow. The car door was partly open and her foot was on the running board. I stopped in my tracks and grabbed hold of Cal's arm. "Listen to that," I said. "She sounds madder than a wet hen."

She was cussing the man out up one side and down the other. I said, "Let's go see what it's about," but Cal wouldn't budge, saying it wouldn't do to get involved in somebody else's fight. I kept on looking—I know trouble when I see it. The woman got out of the car and slammed the door so hard I thought it would come off at the hinges. She was wearing one of those little short dresses and a funny hat pulled down over her ears. Neither one of us had ever seen her before.

Then she got back in the car, tried to pull the door closed, and leaned towards the man like she was going to kiss him on the cheek. But the guy pushed her off and backhanded her across the face. When she screamed, he shoved her out the car door, tossing a satchel after her. "So long, bitch," he said, lighting a cigarette and flicking the match towards her. Well, she let out a string of cuss words you've never heard the like of, calling him every name in the book.

Calvin grabbed my arm, tried to hold me back, but I took off over there and jerked the driver's door open, intending on pulling the son of a bitch out of the car and beating the hell out of him. He was a scrawny little fellow, ugly as homemade soap, with patent-leather hair and a pocked face, but one look at the sawed-off shotgun lying across his lap aimed straight at my belly, and I backed off.

"You'll mind your own business, hick," the jerk said to me, "unless you want a load of buckshot coming out your ass." I did just what he said. He put the car in gear, stepped on the gas—with the door still open—and spun out towards the highway.

The girl wasn't hurt, just all to pieces, crying and carrying on. We led her over to Calvin's car, me on one side and him on the other. I reached in the car and got the likker for her. Told her she needed a drink to calm her nerves. She pulled off her hat and shook out a head full of yellow curls. Then she took a long swig out of the jar. Grinning like a Cheshire cat, she told me I was lucky he didn't kill me.

I grinned back at her and said that pock-faced goon didn't scare me, but I didn't take kindly to somebody pointing a shotgun at me. Cal opened the car door and she sat down on the running board, stretching her legs out. "You boys from around here?" she asked us.

"Bandeaux Creek," I said.

"I grew up over there near Cotton Cove," she said, twisting a curl down over her eyes. "Took off when I was sixteen. Haven't been back since." She asked us our names and she told us hers. Before long, she was cutting up— acting like she'd known us all her life. "Betcha won't swim naked with me." she said, rolling her hose down. Cal and I looked at each other. "Just you, big boy," she said, her saucy blue eyes on me. I could've died right then.

Cal sauntered off towards the pier, said he could tell when he wasn't wanted. Patty Sue got to the water's edge and shimmied out of that little green silk dress, showing off a pink brassiere and some matching drawers. She slipped out of those and into the water so fast, I didn't even get a good look. I stripped off my shirt and britches and dove in after her, naked as a jaybird, following her out to deep water. Now, if you've ever been to White Lake you'll know what I'm talking about when I say I could see everything she had in that clear moonlit water. She was twisting and turning, wanting me to look—swimming all around me, giggling and splashing me in the face.

I grabbed her arm and pulled her towards me. She wrapped her legs around my waist and squeezed hard. The lake was warm as bath water and my business so hard when I came inside her that she screamed like a banshee. I put my hand over her mouth and told her to shush, there were people on the pier. "They'll think you're drowning," I said. She tore away from me, almost turning me wrong side out, grabbed me from behind by the neck and tried to push me under, saying she'd show me who was drowning. God, she had a mean streak in her.

Getting out of the water where we'd left our clothes, I got a good look at her smooth round butt and little tits, not that I could tell how old she was, but right then it didn't matter. I grabbed her arm and tried to kiss her, but she pushed me off and put her dress on, wadding up her underwear and cramming it in her purse. When we got back to the car, ol' Cal was sound asleep, stretched out in the front seat with his feet propped up on the opposite door. I took the jar and told her we needed to go where we could get better acquainted.

We found a patch of sand under some scrubby oaks, away from the edge of the lake. She pulled me down on top of her, laughing that crazy laugh of hers. "So you want to get better acquainted?" she said. We got it on again and smoked about a pack of cigarettes before Cal woke up. She told me then how she'd been living up in New York and she'd asked this guy to bring her to Bladen County because she'd gotten word that her daddy had died and left her some money. When she got home, her mama wouldn't let her in the house, told her to go back where she come from. Tony, that was the guy's name, said he didn't want any more of her company either if she couldn't pay him for the ride. I think he might of been a gangster or something.

Anyhow, that's how we met. Daddy and Miss Geneva, my stepmother, didn't take kindly to Patty Sue, her being so much older and all, but they did let her stay at our house while she tried to figure out what she was going to do. Daddy even went over to Mrs. Jackson's house and tried to reason with her. Mrs. Jackson told Daddy that Patty Sue could go to the devil for all she cared.

Me and Patty Sue were wild about each other, and Daddy and Miss Geneva watched us like hawks. Patty Sue didn't seem to care, but sneaking around made me feel like a two-cent piece with a hole in it. She even made friends with my sisters Alice Ann and Jessie Rae. They just loved her. Miss Geneva sure as hell didn't. She said Patty Sue was a golddigger. Said it right to my face. Of course, Miss Geneva was four years younger than Patty Sue and I think she was a little bit jealous. She'd only been married to Daddy since last Christmas and I think she might of caught Daddy looking at Patty Sue a time or two. I know I did.

I'd had about all I could take of the bad talk and sneaking around, and I told Patty Sue I thought we should run off for good. But Patty Sue wouldn't hear of it, not until the circuit judge came to probate her father's will. That happened soon enough, and Patty Sue found out that her daddy left her everything—didn't leave her mama a pot to pee in.

———

So, that's how we came to get married. Mrs. Jackson had no choice but to let Patty Sue come there to live, and Patty Sue wouldn't go unless I went with her, scared as she was of her mama. I told Patty Sue we'd have to get married first, because I knew it was going to be hard enough on Daddy and Miss Geneva, them being churchgoing people and all.

Saturday night, right after Thanksgiving, I asked Daddy if we could use the truck to go to a movie in Burgaw. But we went to Dillon, South Carolina, instead—in Dillon you don't have to wait around to get married. It took us about two hours to get to the state line. We just pulled up in front of the first Justice of the Peace sign we saw, finding the J.P. in his nightshirt and his wife with curlers in her hair. They were real nice, giving Patty Sue a little white satin pillow after the ceremony with "Just Married" written on it.

We headed straight back to Cotton Cove. It was almost dawn and I figured we'd better show up at the breakfast table like always. I'd really started to worry on the way home that Daddy might kill me. I knew he put a lot of store in me, being the oldest boy and all. I dreaded like hell telling him the news. When I did, he was scraping up the last of his eggs—didn't even wipe his mouth, just gaped at me, his face turning red, then purple. "You did what?"

Patty Sue came over and held onto my arm, standing a little bit behind me. "We got married," I said, looking him directly in the eye. Angus McBryde wouldn't stand for you not looking him in the eye. Well, sir, he got up from the table and walked to the back door. Just stood there leaning on the door jamb like he was catching his breath. Miss Geneva, nervous as a whore in church, didn't say a word, and me and Patty Sue just looked at each other. Finally, Daddy pushed the door open a little—didn't turn around or anything. "I hope you haven't ruined your life, son," he said, real easy-like, then stepped outside. He didn't even slam the door. I'd seen him do that before—simmer down, you know, get his temper under control, because he knew if he let loose, he'd knock me in the head with the first thing he laid his hands on.

That afternoon, I asked Daddy if we could borrow the truck again to move some things over to the Jackson place. That's when he told me to take it and get the hell out of his sight. I almost died, knowing I'd done a terrible thing in his eyes. But what was done was done and I'd have to live with it.

While I got some of my things together, Patty Sue drove the truck over to her mama's to let her know we were coming. I took the opportunity to talk to Miss Geneva, to try and tell her how much I loved Patty Sue—ask her to talk to Daddy. She said Patty Sue was a golddigger, that any fool ought to have seen what she was up to, but I told her she was wrong. I was the one who wanted to get married.

———

The Jackson house was one of those plain little houses you see down in the country, set up on brick pillars with a porch all the way across the front. Even though the paint was peeling off, it was painted, which was more than I can say about some of those houses back towards the river. There were screens on the doors and windows too—which told me somebody had taken some pride in the house at one time—but the lane had grown up so thick you could hardly see the house from the road. Hard to get along with as she was, I reckon Mrs. Jackson liked it like that. I'd heard from some of the fellows at the store that she kept pretty much to herself.

As soon as we drove up, the old lady got up from a chair on the porch and went inside. I asked Patty Sue if she'd told her mama we'd gotten married. Patty Sue shot me a look that would kill. "Of course I told her," she said. "She probably hoped we'd stay at your place."

I thought surely that would make a difference, but Patty Sue said, "You let me handle her." I tried to reason with Patty Sue, said we shouldn't shove it down Mrs. Jackson's throat—maybe there was a better way. But Patty Sue put her hands on her hips and said, "This is my house and she may as well get used to it."

———

We set up directly in her daddy's old room on the front of the house. Patty Sue said him and her mother hadn't slept in the same room for thirty years. The old lady stayed in a little room tacked onto the back of the house with a separate door. She'd go off somewhere in an old beat-up Chevrolet for a day or two, then show up again out of the blue. Now and then I'd see her out in the yard feeding the chickens or hanging out the wash.

Patty Sue was pretty sassy to her mama. I didn't like that much, but Patty Sue said we had to keep the upper hand with her. Said her mama would leave sooner or later if we made her miserable enough. Now, I wasn't raised like that, and it didn't set well with me no matter how much Patty Sue hated her, but I went along just to keep from riling Patty Sue.

The place was in even sorrier shape than I thought. Absolutely nothing about the farming operation had been tended to for a long time. First thing I did was to sharpen an old sling blade and get after the grass that had grown up so high out back you could hardly see the barn, which was covered with vines anyhow. I looked for a tractor, but there wasn't even an old plow—not a harness to hitch up a mule, much less a mule to hitch it to. Patty Sue said her pa liked to ride horses, not work them. What he did for a living if it wasn't farming was beyond me at the time, although I should have known. I couldn't find a trace of a hog lot or a cow pasture, just a few scraggly old hens pecking around what looked to be the gate to a garden.

I worried a lot about my own daddy—what he was thinking about—how he'd acted. Before Mama died, he'd shown me a piece of paper with a drawing as to how he planned to divide his land up between the nine children. All of us would get a piece, even the two girls. I didn't intend to give that up, but I knew I'd have to work real hard to show Daddy that I could still amount to something.

———

Mr. Jackson not only left Patty Sue his house and land, there was about two thousand dollars cash in the bank. Not one red cent did he leave that old woman. She might have been mean as the devil, but at the time, I felt sorry for her. Patty Sue just rubbed it in. First she went out and bought an old Ford pickup—second-hand, but in real good condition, overhauled by one of the Ryan boys over in Colly that I think I'm some kin to. Then, that spring, she brought home a used Farmall tractor—just for me, she said.

That tractor gave me a new lease on life. I'd been trying to figure how I'd ever get some corn planted with just this old mule Mr. Dudley Cooper loaned me. The tractor cut the work in half and made me think more and more about the land my daddy had promised me. If I showed him what me and Patty Sue could do without his help, maybe he'd come around—give me my land. Then we could get away from the old lady.

I should've known Patty Sue wasn't going to be a wife who'd sit around in the kitchen all day taking care of young'uns and such. She'd been out in the world and she liked the feel of cash in her pocket. She said she wanted to own a store someday like Buck Wetmore's up the road, and she didn't waste any time getting her a job there. Wetmore's store had belonged to Uncle Rob before he and Aunt Eva moved down to Wilmington. Uncle Rob had gone broke trying to farm, run a small grist mill, and keep up his little roadside store where Aunt Eva had been the postmistress for thirty years. When they moved, Aunt Eva suggested Patty Sue take her job. I think she was trying to help us out since she and Mama were sisters. I was real proud to have my wife taking Aunt Eva's place.

———

For a while, things seemed to be going pretty good, with Mrs. Jackson staying to herself most of the time and me and Patty Sue acting like old married folks, frolicking around in the bed at night and working all day. But one day we came home and found the little satin pillow that Patty Sue always kept on our bed half-burned up under the washpot. Patty Sue was mad as hell, and she tore into her mother. I had to go out back to get away from it. The next day, we found WHORE written all over our bedroom wall with lipstick.

———

Then, one day in June, the big trouble started when Patty Sue handed me a blue steel revolver before she left for work. "Mama's out back doing her washing," she said. "Don't you leave this room as long as she's home. I'm sick and tired of her messing with my things." She handed me the gun. "If she tries anything, use this."

Where Patty Sue got that gun, I have no idea. I'd left my shotgun and an old Colt .45 at home, figuring I'd go back and get them sooner or later. Lately I'd been thinking I needed to have a gun around the house in case I saw a rat or a snake, but I sure as hell wasn't thinking I'd use it on Mrs. Jackson. Checking the barrel, I saw all six chambers were loaded, and I knew Patty Sue meant business. Making trouble was the last thing on my mind. No sir, it would have suited me just as well to camp out in the woods until the old woman left. I wasn't a damn bit happy about sitting around in our room with the door closed either, but it was about the hardest thing in the world to say no to Patty Sue Jackson.

I'd read all the old Wild West magazines in the house. Mr. Jackson must've been a nut about cowboys. There were stacks and stacks of magazines in the closet, along with two pairs of real authentic cowboy boots. Bored out of my skull, I picked up the pistol and stood in front of the dresser mirror, twirling the gun like Buffalo Bill Cody had done at the county fair. I'd always thought it looked so easy. Thrust your hand out and let the gun roll around your thumb. Over and over I threw it until finally I ended up with my finger on the trigger.

The old lady didn't make a sound when she opened the door, but I felt a chill come over me as soon as she entered the room. When I looked up, I saw her in the mirror. She was wearing an old feed-sack dress down to her ankles. The top part of the dress was soaking wet. It clung to her breasts, which sagged down to her waist. Strands of gray hair were pasted across her forehead, and long oily braids hung on either side of her round face. I was thinking how she looked like that old mama pig who'd charged me in the hog lot when I was only three years old. I fell in the mud when I tried to run, and Daddy had swooped me up, but not until I'd stared that pig straight in the face like I was doing Mrs. Jackson right now. It wasn't the first time I'd wondered how on earth Patty Sue could have come out of that lopsided old hag.

"What're you doing with my gun, Davy McBryde?" she growled, her eyes full of contempt.

I said, "I believe this is Patty Sue's gun, Mrs. Jackson."

"No, it ain't," she said. "It's mine and I can prove it." She spit on the floor and ground her shoe in it. "Let me have it."

I told her I didn't want any trouble. "Why don't you get on back to your washing and leave me alone," I said.

"Don't you be telling me to git along lil' dogie," she said, real sassy like, wobbling her head. I tried to tell her I didn't mean it like that. "Most men would've been out in the field by sunup," she said. "But you and Patty Sue been piled up in that bed there ever since you got married. You're as sorry as she is."

I told her again that I didn't want any trouble. "Soon as Patty Sue and me can get a little start, I'm going to build us a house over there near the river. You can have this old place. It don't mean a thing to me," I said. My finger was on the trigger of the gun I held down by my side. It startled me when it gave a little. "We won't be in your way much longer," I told her.

"You been here too long already," she said, taking a step back. She reached around the side of the door for a second, like she was checking for something. A loaded shotgun, was what went through my mind.

"You need to talk to Patty Sue about that," I said.

She puffed way up, red in the face. "You think I don't know you knocked her up? That's why you run off and got married. I'm no fool." I didn't say anything, wondering what was she getting at. "Why didn't you move in with your pa and Miss Geneva?" she snarled, her words full of venom as a rattler's bite. "Wouldn't they have you? I reckon not. Patty Sue's almost old enough to be your mama." She sort of sashayed back and forth, grinning at me with a mouthful of bad teeth. "Found her a young buck, didn't she? A sorry one at that. You ain't even dry behind the ears yet," she said, pointing a long gnarled finger at me. "Here you are piled up in bed with a thirty-four-year-old woman. Why don't you just go out yonder in the hog lot and wallow around with an old sow?"

I couldn't believe she'd say such a thing about her own daughter, but she was wound up. "Probably be just as good as Patty Sue. She's been with about every man between here and Wilmington since she was thirteen. I'll bet she's—"

I yelled at her. "Stop it, you old cow! Stop it right now! I won't have you talking about my wife like that." Shaking all over because I was so mad, I raised the gun and pointed it at her, just to scare her—not thinking for a minute that I'd shoot her.

Color drained from her face, and she sucked in her breath, glaring at me. "You haven't got the guts to shoot a hog at killing time, much less an old woman," she said, reaching for the doorknob. It was a goddamned dare. She was pushing me and I just knew she had a gun out there somewhere. Exactly what happened next, I'm not sure, but when she slammed the door behind her, Patty Sue's pistol went off in my hand like it had a mind of its own. I threw myself against the wall away from the door waiting for the shotgun blast that I knew was coming. I waited and I listened for five, maybe ten minutes, not moving a muscle—not until her blood seeped under the door, forming a scarlet puddle at the foot of our bed. The old lady fell against my feet when I opened the door, her eyes fixed on the ceiling. I don't remember much after that, but Patty Sue said she found me on the back porch passed out cold.

When I came to, she was yelling, "Davy, wake up." I remember think-ing she was the prettiest thing I'd ever seen. She was wearing my favorite dress, the one with big blue flowers with yellow centers the same color as her hair. Reaching up, I tried to touch one of her breasts. She'd let me kiss the two flowers over each of them before she left this morning. First one, then the other.

"What's wrong with you?" she said, pulling away. "Get up off the floor."

When I stood up, we both stared at my feet, at the bloody tracks on the porch floor. She pushed past me, stood in the kitchen door. "My God, you've killed Mama," she said.

Later I recalled that she didn't even scream, just walked back out onto the porch and looked at me. I told her I didn't mean to. I said her mama was talking ugly about her. "When she slammed the door, the gun went off," I said.

Patty Sue said I'd probably saved her the trouble. Then she told me we had to make it look like the old lady had done it herself. I thought she was crazy.

"You want to be charged with murder?" she said, looking about as mean as her mama had. When she turned around and walked back into the house, I hung back, not wanting to go look at that old woman dead on the floor. Patty Sue stuck her head out the door and yelled, "Get your ass in here and help me. Don't you see that cloud coming up?"

She headed for the bedroom, stepping over her mama's body like it was a dead squirrel. I stayed against the wall, sliding along it until I reached the bedroom door. Mrs. Jackson's shotgun was there, just as I'd figured. "Pile everything of ours on the bed," Patty Sue said, dumping out all the drawers on the bedspread. I tried to show her the shotgun—tell her that Mrs. Jackson was planning on using it on me. She told me to shut up my blabbering, all the while raking curlers, lipstick, perfume, everything off the dresser, into an empty drawer. "Take this out to the truck and wait for me. You look like an idiot standing there," she said. She'd never talked to me like that before, and under ordinary circumstances I might have hit her, but I was in no shape to do anything about it then.

Outside, the wind had picked up, and large drops of rain splattered all around me. I remember thinking that I wanted to lie down in the yard and let it wash me clean down to the river. But I kept going, dragging the heavy bundle behind me. When I reached the shed and tossed it into the truck, I smelled smoke. I turned around just in time to see Patty Sue using a straw broom as a torch, going from window to window, setting the curtains on fire. Flames were licking the kitchen walls and biting through the shingled roof.

Then the rain came down harder and I could barely see the house. Lightning flashed and thunder crashed overhead. I remember thinking that the Lord was sending his wrath down on us. It rained like I've never seen it rain before. Would you believe all I could think about my was new corn, barely up a few inches? For a farmer, there's such a thing as too much rain all at once. But when it comes to putting out a house fire, nothing can beat it.

———

Mr. Reuben Squires, the mailman, told everybody he stopped by to bring the mail since Patty Sue wasn't working at the post office that day, because she'd driven over to Atkinson to see Dr. Bayard. Mr. Reuben said he was running a little late since he'd had to sort the mail and all that before he delivered it. He figured she'd be back home by then, so he pulled into the lane and honked his horn. When Patty Sue walked around front to meet him, I hid behind the shed. "Afternoon, Mr. Reuben," she said, like it was any other day. He climbed out of his car carrying Mrs. Jackson's mail and looked at Patty Sue, then at the house, where steam was rising off the kitchen roof. "Did you get struck by lightening?" he asked her.

"Yessir, but that's not all," she said. "Mama's committed suicide."

PART I

Wilmington, North Carolina

Xo

Rob and Eva McBryde's Crow-Elkhart

1

A House on Princess Street

HUGH McBRYDE WAS TWENTY-FOUR YEARS OLD when he decided to take the bull by the horns. Wasn't it was his duty as the eldest son—the most level-headed one, he'd thought—the first of his siblings to find a job in Wilmington with the fastest-growing railroad on the East Coast? For weeks, Hugh had been mulling something over in the back of his mind. What if he and his brothers, Harry and Calvin, who also worked for the Atlantic Coast Line now, bought one of those old Victorian houses downtown and turned it into a boardinghouse? Half of the young folks he knew lived in rented rooms in town—his sisters Rebecca and Belle among them. A boardinghouse with decent meals and hot water could pay for itself in no time.

The day he'd decided, he'd left his office in the Freight Department of the Atlantic Coast Line Railway at precisely five-thirty in the evening, walked down to the Orton Hotel, picked up a newspaper, crossed over to Princess Street, then strolled back down to the Post Office, where he'd found a shady spot on the broad granite steps. The air was sticky and unseasonable, a warm front having moved up the coast earlier in the week. With the Gulf Stream nearby, winter never seemed to last long in Wilmington. He'd lived there for two years now and had yet to find the need for a topcoat.

Hugh rolled up his shirtsleeves and loosened his tie before pulling out the last section of the *Evening Dispatch,* opening it to the classified advertisements. He'd seen the house at 405 Princess Street the day before when he and his brother Cal were riding the beachcar out to the company's annual fish fry at Wrightsville Beach. The beachcar had stopped at Princess and Fourth Streets, waiting for a few Coast Line stragglers who'd run up the street to catch the last trolley. Opening the window to get some air, Hugh had looked directly at the large board sign nailed onto a porch post. FOR SALE FOR BACK TAXES. "Look at that, Cal," he said.

"What?"

"That beautiful old house across the street. It's for sale."

"Used to be a pretty one."

A brief comment was about all Hugh could expect from his brother, who was sitting slumped on his tailbone eating an apple, his knees on the seat in front of him. Calvin McBryde was as different from Hugh as night from day, in looks as well as disposition. Cal's interests leaned more towards cars and aviation, things that Hugh didn't care a thing about. In the freight department where they both worked, the tall, lanky younger brother, with his boyish face, was known as a prankster who was seldom at his desk and more often seen at the water cooler, tie loosened and shirtsleeves rolled up above his elbows. Hugh, on the other hand, seldom left his desk just outside his boss's door; instead, he sat poised in coat and tie, ready to jump when called or follow when needed.

Just as well, Hugh thought. Until he'd had a chance to look into the business end of running a boardinghouse, there was no need to take the conversation further. Foolish thinking was not one of his shortcomings, and he didn't intend to start now. He scanned the long column of advertisements until he found the listing he was looking for. *Yes!* There it was! For two thousand five hundred dollars, he could have his boardinghouse.

That night, in the room they shared in Mrs. Bloom's home on Third Street, Hugh had been awakened by Cal's loud snoring. Unable to get back to sleep with thoughts of the new business venture somersaulting in his head, he wondered how they would come up with the money. All three brothers worked at the Coast Line, each bringing in enough to put a little away every month. But the bank might not go for it—none of them had much collateral.

And there was the problem of who'd run it. *Mama and Papa would be perfect*, he thought, drifting off to sleep.

———

WOP! A PILLOW CAME OUT OF NOWHERE, catching Hugh, still sleeping, on the back of his head. "Better get up and at 'em, big guy, unless you want scraps for breakfast," Calvin said.

Hugh slid out of the narrow bed, rubbing his eyes and shaking his head. "Man, I was sound asleep—dreaming about something."

"I'll see you downstairs," Cal said, closing the door softly.

Hugh slid out of bed and pulled on his pants and socks before stepping into the hall. Another boarder stood waiting just outside the bathroom. Hugh nodded and closed his door. In the small mirror above his dresser, he studied his reflection. *Not a bad-looking fellow*, he thought, smoothing the dark brown wavy hair he and his brother Harry had inherited from their McBryde ancestors, most of whom had been tall and favorable like him. Cal and their baby brother, Rodney, had inherited an altogether different look, with their glossy black hair making a distinctive widow's peak on their foreheads above playful eyes. Hugh rubbed his hand over his morning's beard and wished the other boarder would hurry.

One by one, four of the eight children of Robert and Eva McBryde had rejected their inheritance of fertile farmland in Bladen County in southeastern North Carolina, moving to the port city of Wilmington, where they'd hopped upon the prosperity bandwagon that was sweeping the country. Hugh McBryde had led the exodus from the farm on Bandeaux Creek, followed by Cal, Harry, and then Rebecca and Belle. If he'd stayed, they might all have stayed, been farmers or storekeepers like their parents. As it was, the last three—Millie, Rodney, and Vera—in due time would likely do the same as their elder brothers and sisters.

Hugh was worried about what would become of his parents. Small farmers like Rob McBryde, with their antiquated farm machinery, were losing out to big mechanized operations, and his father was too old and too set in his ways to change even if he could afford to. Neither Hugh—nor his brothers and sisters, he was pretty sure—would ever go back. Would never *want* to go back. In Hugh's mind, the only way to care for his aging parents and younger siblings was to move them to Wilmington. A boardinghouse would make that possible.

———

FLETCHER PIERCE'S REAL ESTATE OFFICE was on the second floor of the Southern Building at the corner of Front and Chestnut Streets. The stairway was hot and airless, Hugh's hands sweaty on the worn banister, as he took the steps two at the time. He knocked, half expecting the office to be closed that late in the day. "Come on in," a deep voice called out. Hugh turned the knob and peered into a room thick with cigar smoke. Books, papers, and placards of every description touting past *For Sale* properties were stacked on either side of the room. "Secretary's gone for the day," said a stout, balding man from behind a cluttered desk. "What can I do for you?"

"I'd like to take a look at that house over on Princess Street. I believe it's number 405."

"What'd a young fellow like you want with a big old house like that?"

"I'd like to take a look at it."

"You'll have to give me a better reason before I'll haul my ass all the way over there. 'Just looking' won't get it."

Hugh explained his mission, and Fletcher Pierce guffawed. "You're not the first one to think of that. I suppose you've got the money sitting there in the bank," he said, lighting a half-burned cigar. "Old lady's family couldn't pay the taxes and the tax man won't wait any longer."

"I'd like to see it. Might not be interested after that."

Mr. Pierce peered at him through smudged glasses. He shifted his heavy frame in his chair, doused the cigar in a dirty ashtray, and opened a desk drawer full of keys. "I reckon one more looker today won't kill me. C'mon, let's go."

———

THE EXTERIOR OF THE GRAY TWO-STORY HOUSE on Princess Street was chipped and peeling, and the white porch railings were covered in layers of bird droppings where pigeons and gulls had found a roosting spot in the recessed molding above. At one end, an old swing moved slightly, as if to remind the callers of warm summer days when lemonade was served against a backdrop of tangled wisteria vines. Hugh pictured his own mother, a glass of iced tea in her hand, one foot on the floor, swinging back and forth.

Pierce unlocked the front door with its tall panels of beveled glass set into thick wood. Hugh reached around him to turn the key of a large bell mounted into the center panel. "That'd be electric this day and time," Pierce noted. "Old man Ainsley had most of the house wired back when the electric plant first opened." He pointed to a small chandelier overhead in the foyer. "But he left some of the gas fixtures 'cause he said the lady of the house liked the light they gave off better. After he died, I don't believe she ever turned a light bulb on again. Stayed in one or two rooms with gas heaters in the fireplaces."

Pierce opened a door off the main hall that led into a large, high-ceilinged room rank with the musty smell of closed-up upholstery and drapery. Hugh could tell the house had not had a breath of fresh air in years. Running his hand up the wall beside a tall window, Pierce found a cord and pulled it. Light flooded a room filled with red velvet high-back settees and chairs arranged around the edges. In the center was a large galvanized bathtub. "Don't know how that got in here," he said.

"How long has the house been for sale?"

"There's a kitchenette over there," the agent said, ignoring Hugh's question. "Through that door is a bedroom." Hugh waited for him to start towards the door. When he didn't, Hugh turned the knob, letting out a pungent, unmistakable odor.

"The widow had a lot of cats."

"Was Mrs. Ainsley the last person to live here?"

"Actually, there was a woman, uh . . . an entertainer rented out this apartment for a while. She might've had a few cats too."

They wandered into the kitchen on the back of the house, where Pierce opened an outside door to let in some daylight. "Reach up and turn that on," he said, indicating a bare bulb that hung from a long cord in the center of the ceiling. Wall cabinets were arranged above counters on two sides of the kitchen. In the corner, below four high windows, a large enameled sink dressed in a ragged flowered skirt was filled with pots and pans. A glass-front china cabinet ran the length of another wall. Hugh opened the cabinet door, revealing a jumble of plates and bowls in all sizes and shapes, most painted with a delicate pattern of blue flowers. He picked up a plate and turned it over. The word *Limoges* was stamped on the bottom, below it MADE IN FRANCE.

"Just a bunch of old dishes," the agent said. "Probably get someone to take 'em off your hands."

"Might come in handy for a boardinghouse."

"Hey, that's right. You might be onto something. Here, look in this pantry."

Hugh ducked into the pantry and pulled the light string, illuminating floor-to-ceiling shelves filled with mason jars of preserved vegetables. On the very top shelves, large serving platters and tureens were draped with what looked like tea towels. "Old lady never cooked, I hear," Pierce said. "When her housekeeper died, she walked down to that diner at the end of Fourth Street every evening except Sunday to get her supper."

"Doesn't her family want any of the furnishings?"

"Nope. Her niece said the house was to go 'as is.' You know how these young moderns are. They want all new stuff. Bought on time, I might add."

"Just needs a good cleaning, I'd say. How many bedrooms does it have?"

"Sleeps ten, including that porch upstairs. It's got four bathrooms, too. Running water and all that."

Upstairs, Hugh turned one of the faucet handles at a pedestal sink. "Water's been turned off," Pierce said. "I'm paying to keep the electricity on, but there's right much built up in back bills. Whoever buys it will have to pay those bills. Better keep that in mind."

"How much is that?"

"Right fair amount, I expect."

"Don't you know?"

"Look here, young fellow. You're asking a lot of questions for a *looker*. How do I know you're not just wasting my time?"

———

BACK IN FLETCHER PIERCE'S OFFICE, Hugh elaborated on his idea.

"A boardinghouse might work," Pierce said. "Old place is going to be torn down otherwise. Property's too valuable to let it just keep accumulating debt. City'll condemn it sooner or later."

"I'll talk to my brothers tomorrow."

"You might have trouble getting the bank to put up money on an old house like that. You'll need some extra for repairs."

"You let me worry about that, Mr. Pierce," Hugh said.

———

THE NEXT DAY, HUGH ASKED CAL AND HARRY to meet him at the New York Café on Front Street. The eatery was a favorite of the boys, who thought the stew beef and fried chicken served there were worth waiting in line for. "Not as good as Mama's, that's for damn sure," Harry said. Only twenty-one, Harry was the youngest of the three McBryde brothers who worked for the Coast Line, and that was only until he could save up enough money to get into law school.

"You're not fooling me," Cal said. "The food's not what you come here for, you're looking for future voters."

Harry lit a cigarette, blowing the smoke towards the open door. "Can't blame a man for thinking ahead, son," he said, displaying a devil-may-care attitude that he'd picked up the one year he'd attended Wake Forest College. Cal and Hugh often remarked to themselves that Harry should have been a movie star, with his good looks and the flamboyant suits and ties that he somehow managed on the small salary he received from his job. There was another side to Harry, a serious side that had convinced his uncle, Judge O'Kelly, to send him to Wake Forest. But Harry had been prideful like the rest of the McBrydes, and when his first year was up, he moved to Wilmington, deciding that he'd rather not be beholden to any man, not even his mother's wealthy brother.

"There's a table," Hugh said. "Grab it. I need to talk to you guys about something."

"Why do I get the feeling it's about a house?" Cal said.

His brothers listened intently, especially the part about who'd run the boardinghouse. "Papa's never said it, but he's bound to be disappointed that not a one of us took up farming," Hugh said.

"I've always told him I wanted to be a judge," Harry said.

Calvin smiled. "There's little brother Rodney. He might still grow up to be a farmer."

"Papa'll have one foot in the grave by then," Harry commented.

"Don't be talking like that," Hugh said.

Calvin was somber. "Do you really think they feel like we've abandoned them?"

"No, Cal. They don't think anything of the sort," Hugh said. "You know they don't, but I feel we have an obligation to them."

"I worry about those three young'uns more than Mama and Papa," Cal said. "Millie is so sweet and cute. You know she's about fourteen now, and some hick farmer is liable to come along and want to marry her before you know it."

"The hell you say. That'd be over my dead body," Harry said, squashing his cigarette in a tin ashtray.

"Well, how about it?" Hugh asked.

"I've got some cash I was going to invest in the stock market," Harry said. "Couldn't do both."

"I've been saving for a new car," Calvin said. He looked at Harry. "Guess it could wait a little longer."

———

HUGH MCBRYDE PRIDED HIMSELF on his head for figures. He'd been sent off at an early age for his schooling, first to the Boys' Academy at Delway over in Sampson County, then to Oak Ridge Military Institute in Forsyth County, where he'd graduated with honors in 1922. At the Ridge, he'd excelled in numbers, advancing through the school's business program and catching the eye of one of his professors who came from a family of trainmen. "The Atlantic Coast Line in Wilmington is a natural for you, Hugh," the professor had told him. "I'll write a letter of recommendation if you like."

His bother Calvin had followed Hugh to the Coast Line in 1923 after also graduating from Oak Ridge. They'd shared a room in Mrs. Bloom's boardinghouse on North Third Street ever since. When Harry had come to Wilmington needing work and wanting to enroll in night classes at Wilmington Law School, Hugh had gotten him a job in the Coast Line's receiving department, and a third McBryde had taken up residence in the same boardinghouse. Hugh guessed that the sum of what they were paying for room and board would go a long way toward a mortgage.

That evening, the three McBryde boys picked up the key from Fletcher Pierce's office after work and walked over to look at the house on Princess Street. "I think you're onto something, brother," Cal said. "This old house has a lot of character. At least it'd be an investment. Rent money goes right down the drain."

"Anybody got friends at the bank?" Hugh asked. "We'll have to draw up some kind of paper. The bank will help us figure it out."

Harry perked up. "The hell, you say. I'll get a friend of mine to do that," he said. "We don't want some banker controlling everything. This could be a real money-making project for us."

"Now you're talking," Hugh said. The first part of his plan, at least, was falling into place.

————

THE FOLLOWING WEEKEND, HUGH INVITED his adult brothers and sisters to eat oysters with him out on Masonboro Sound, where old man Henry Kirkum served oysters to about half of Wilmington every weekend during the "r" months.

The three boys picked up Rebecca and Belle in Calvin's car, an old 1913 Model T Ford he'd recently acquired from their landlady, Mrs. Bloom, who'd never learned to drive. Her deceased husband had parked it on the street shortly before he died. There it had remained, filthy, its tires flat and rotted, ever since. "You can have it for twenty-five dollars," Mrs. Bloom said when Cal asked about the car, "but you can't leave it there on the street." Cal had to rent a garage down on Front Street where he'd worked on the car every evening for a month, mighty glad not to have to depend on his papa's Crow-Elkhart any longer. Both cars were ancient and out of fashion, but three boys learning to drive in the Crow-Elkhart had put some serious wear and tear on its gearbox. The old car had barely made the trip to Wilmington.

"I wish I had me a car," Belle McBryde said. "All you'd see would be my dust."

Cal looked over at his sister and thought she didn't have the temperament to drive a car. He was sure she'd drive the way she walked, in jerky little moves, dodging and darting this way and that. "Better get somebody else to teach you."

Rebecca, sandwiched between Harry and Hugh in the back

seat, snickered at the remark. Harry elbowed her. "I'll teach you, darlin', but you'll have to get the car first," he said to Belle.

"Turn in up there," Hugh said, indicating a lane off the Wrightsville Beach road that led to a tarpaper-covered fishing shack surrounded by cars parked among piles of discarded oyster shells. Cal maneuvered the car into a narrow space between two other automobiles. "Better back up and let us out unless you want a few more dents in your doors."

"Would it matter?" Belle asked in retaliation. Cal ignored the comment. Belle would argue with a damned doorpost, and he'd been the victim of her sharp tongue too many times. "Phew!" Belle said, getting out of the car. "This place smells like dead fish. Whose idea was this, anyway?"

"Oh, c'mon, Belle, quit acting up. There's a breeze off the sound out back. That's just the shells you're smelling," Harry said.

"I hadn't even noticed," Rebecca said.

"You wouldn't after emptying all those bedpans and—" But before she could finish, Harry swept her along and up the rickety steps of the porch, where several boys were hosing off freshly harvested oysters.

Inside, the narrow room was jam-packed with oyster lovers at long, newspaper-covered picnic-style tables with benches on either side. The boys sat on one side of the table, the girls across from them. A tin can full of oyster knives was passed around, and the siblings all tied red bandana napkins under their chins.

"Kin I git y'all some root beer?" a server asked.

"Is that the best you can do?" Harry said, with a wink of his eye.

"Yassuh, dat's de law. 'Course, I been known to break the law befo', but not at Mr. Kirkum's place." He slapped his knee and cackled. "Root beer's the best I kin do t'night."

When their server had gone, Hugh cleared his throat and leaned forward. "We've been talking about something. I wanted to throw it out to you girls," he said. "One of those old houses on Princess Street is up for sale. Back taxes is all they're asking for it."

"Yeah, about twenty years' worth," Harry said. "Still, it's a bargain." He reached into his coat pocket and pulled out a flask. "Anybody wanna wet your whistle?"

"You better watch it, Harry," Rebecca cautioned. "I hear the sheriff keeps an eye on this place."

Harry squinted his eyes and looked around the crowded room. "I know the sheriff. We'll ask him over. Prohibition never stopped Mac Beasley from having a drink."

Calvin laughed. "He's probably out there in his car nursing a bottle of his own."

"Listen, y'all, here's my idea," Hugh said. "This is a fine old house. It's full of furniture. Make a great boardinghouse. If we went in together, took a loan from the bank, we could all live there and chip in for the payment every month."

As usual, Belle's dark eyes were searching the room for any eligible young men. A petite brunette with a pretty face and smart-looking clothes, she seldom had to look far before someone flashed her a smile. "That's crazy, Hugh. Why'd we want to buy some old house on Princess Street?"

Before he could answer, the server returned with a tub of steaming oysters. "Better eat 'em while dey's hot."

"Bring 'em on!" Cal said. "I've been looking forward to this all day."

Belle slid the knife into the rim of an oyster, forcing it open. Daintily, she slurped it out of the shell, careful not to smear her painted lips. She didn't really like oysters, but no one had asked her. "I don't intend to be in this one-horse town any longer than it takes me to get my business certificate," she said, annoyed that she had to eat the slimy sea creatures or be ridiculed by her siblings. "I'm moving up to Washington, D.C., where I have friends."

Rebecca frowned. "Better not count on it, Belle. You'd need to get a job first. Wouldn't be any family up there to fall back on if things didn't work out."

"Always the nay-sayer, Becca," Belle replied in a mocking tone.

She tossed back the long wave of hair that hung over her right eye and looked at her sister. "I guess you think I should stay around here and be a nurse like you? Well, let me tell you something, dear sister, it'd be a cold day in hell before I'd take care of a bunch of sick people—watch them die and all that."

Rebecca smiled. "You mean help them get well, don't you?" The smile faded. "But what would you know about helping anyone but yourself."

Hugh shook his head. "You two, quit your arguing."

"Who wants to be saddled with a big old house in Wilmington for the rest of their lives?" Belle continued. "Don't count on me." She lit a cigarette, blowing the smoke from her draw towards Hugh.

"All right, Belle, you don't have to buy into it if you don't want to. Calvin, Harry, and I will make the payments. You girls could just pay us the same rent you're paying now. Could we count on you for that?"

"Sounds all right to me," Rebecca said. They all looked at Belle, who refused to reply.

"We've got a bunch of cousins living in town, too," Hugh said. "I don't think we'd have any trouble renting out rooms. The place has five bedrooms, plus a small apartment with a kitchenette made out of a big closet."

"I'd want that one," Rebecca said. "I love to cook."

"I'm sorry, Becca, we'll need to rent out the best rooms. They'll bring in the most money."

Belle wadded up her napkin and threw it on the table. "Humph. I'll probably get a closet for a bedroom."

Hugh looked up at her over his glass of root beer. "Does that mean you'll go along?"

"I guess so, but I still say it's a crazy idea."

"I don't think it sounds so crazy, sis," Cal said. Despite her argumentative nature, he adored his sister and wanted her to support the boardinghouse.

"I talked to a lawyer friend of mine today," Harry said. "He thought we could get the money. He'll draw the papers up for free."

"There's one other thing." Hugh hesitated, looking at his sisters. He had the habit of pursing his lips before smiling, an effort not to give away his joke too soon. "We'd need to hire a cook, unless you'd want to quit nursing school and cook for us, Rebecca. Belle, you could do the cleaning." All three of the boys burst out laughing, causing heads to turn.

"Wild horses couldn't drag me away from nursing school, and you know it, Hugh McBryde," Rebecca said. "Quit teasing."

Belle gave him an icy look. "I won't even dignify that with an answer."

Hugh became serious again. "We'd need somebody to run it. Might be a good way to get Mama and Papa to Wilmington where we could look after them."

"What's that got to do with it?" Belle asked.

"They'll soon be all alone," he said. "McBrydes have been leaving the nest at a pretty fast clip."

"We sure couldn't make a living farming," Belle said.

"Me and your brothers are worried about the rest of the family. They'd be better off here in the city too. We could be a family again. Children need that."

Rebecca beamed. "Hugh, that's a perfectly wonderful idea. You're a genius."

"Mama and Papa will never come," Belle said. "Mama won't leave her little post office."

Harry had kept quiet, letting Hugh do the talking, but he'd been thinking and was convinced that bringing his parents to Wilmington was the best thing, too. "If Papa wants Mama to come, she will," he said.

"Don't be too sure," Rebecca cautioned. "Mama's been the postmistress in Bandeaux Creek since before she married Papa."

Harry smiled. "Your mama grew up in a different generation. She'll do what Papa wants her to do."

Belle choked up. "All Papa knows is running that store and

farming. He used to tell me I could run it for him someday."

"Now look who's the nay-sayer," Rebecca said.

Instead of firing off the usual retort, Belle pulled a handker-chief from her purse and wiped her eyes. "Papa would never sell his land, and all Mama talks about is . . . "

Rebecca stood up, flailing her long arms. "Don't be so morbid, Belle," she cried. "A stroke is just a warning sign. There's all kinds of new medicines. If she were here, we could get her to a good doc-tor."

"Sit down, Rebecca," Hugh said. "Before we go any further with this, let me talk to Papa."

Belle sent a coy smile Harry's way. "You'd better let Harry talk to him. He's the politician." She'd always been Harry's pet. He humored her—thought she was sassy and cute, things he liked in a girl.

Rebecca nudged her arm. "Quit flirting with your own brother, Clara Bow."

"Be serious, y'all," Hugh said.

Rebecca sighed. "Wouldn't it be fun to all live together again? Mama could have a cook and Papa a little garden out back. We could take the children to the beach on Sundays."

Belle stood up, shaking her head. "Rebecca, you make me sick. I have no intention of taking children to the beach on Sundays. I don't want anyone to think I'm an old married woman." She stomped towards the door. "C'mon, Cal. It's time to go."

2

The Rest of Our Days

THE PREACHER AT BANDEAUX CREEK Baptist Church was off on rounds once a month, taking the Word to the small backwoods congregations scattered about the county. No worship services that week meant it was an ideal time for a carload of McBrydes to drive up to the country for a good Sunday dinner. Never knowing how many she could count on, Eva McBryde had gotten up at dawn to start cooking. She could expect at least one or two of her sister's grown children. Kathleen had died a few years ago, leaving nine children. Eva had eight living of her own, so the cousins found Aunt Eva's table a familiar and comforting place to be.

It was too early in March for fresh vegetables. But Eva, like most farm women, could always pull a meal together. She'd have chicken and pastry, turnip greens and cornmeal dumplings, a big bowl of hominy, and some sliced country ham. Fourteen-year-old Millie had volunteered to make potato salad and deviled eggs. Mother and daughter worked together in the farmhouse kitchen while Rob McBryde kept the younger children busy outside.

"I had to throw out about half of the potatoes because they'd sprouted, Mama," said Millie, typically cheerful no matter the task. Early this morning she'd rummaged through what they called "the girls' closet," wanting something more grown-up to wear, and found a white middy blouse and a gray tissue wool pleated skirt that both her older sisters had outgrown. She'd tied her thick, wavy black hair back with a white ribbon, leaving the sides loose to cover her ears.

"Well, it won't be long before we'll have new potatoes," Eva said, pulling the hot chicken from the bones. "My garden peas are already up." She stabbed a fork into the boiling potatoes. "Better pull them over to the side. They'll finish cooking on their own."

"Before Rebecca went to nursing school, I never got a chance to help you in the kitchen."

"You've had plenty of chances since she left, haven't you?"

"I guess so," Millie said, wanting to add that her other older sister Belle had certainly never been any competition in the kitchen. But Mama didn't like to hear that kind of talk.

"Ask your papa to bring in a few more sticks of wood, honey. This stove's not hot enough to bake my biscuits."

"I'll get the wood. Papa's got Vera and Rodney out there helping him sweep the yard. The Wilmington crowd ought to be here soon."

"Leave the door open," Eva said, brushing her dark auburn hair back off her face. "The stove might not be hot enough, but *I'm* hotter than a firecracker."

Millie returned directly, carrying an armload of wood. "Hugh's here," she announced. "He borrowed his boss's car."

"I didn't hear him drive up, did you?"

"No, ma'am. He told me to run along, he needed to talk to Papa about something. Said it wasn't any of my business."

"What in the world could that be about?"

WHILE HUGH PRESENTED THE PLAN to Rob McBryde, his father puffed wordlessly on his pipe, looking out across Bandeaux Creek. Hugh was suddenly overcome with guilt. What was he asking of his father, who'd played in that creek as a boy? What was he asking of himself? Someday he'd have sons of his own, and they'd never know the joy of catching crawdads and tadpoles in the cold, clear, spring-fed stream.

"Papa?" he ventured. "You think it makes any sense at all?"

"Spring's late this year. Creek's high." Rob took a deep breath and led Hugh around behind the barn, where they sat on a rough-hewn bench, their backs against the sun-warmed cypress boards. "I reckon there comes a time in every man's life when he has to face up to the fact that what used to work, don't work anymore," Rob said. He opened a can of Prince Albert tobacco, repacked his pipe, and struck a wooden match to the bowl. After a few puffs, his eyes wandered across the bare cornfield. "I'd hate mighty bad to leave this land. Farmed it over forty years, just like my daddy did before me."

"Your way of farming has been good for a long time, Papa, but unless you have modern equipment, tractors and such, you can't make much on a farm anymore," Hugh said.

"Governor Morrison spent all our taxes on new roads," Rob said, sending up little puffs of smoke from his pipe, "and he hasn't done a damn thing for farmers."

Hugh moved to the seat of a rusted harrow. He picked up a chip of wood and began peeling it apart. "Didn't you work in Wilmington when you were young, Papa?"

"Yep, my daddy wanted me to see a little bit of the world before I settled down. Sent me to work on the dock, loading ships. I almost signed on one so I could see the world." He puffed on his pipe, looking up to watch a red-tailed hawk circle its prey. "What would I do in Wilmington?"

"I'm sure you could get on as a carpenter at Alexander Sprunt and Sons. I know a lot of guys who work there."

"I reckon I could do most anything I wanted to, Hugh, but who's going to hire a man my age?"

"They'd be glad to have a man who knew how to measure twice and cut once. You ought to see some of the shoddy construction going on in Wilmington. They're tearing down these beautiful seventy-five-year-old homes and putting up things that won't last ten or fifteen years."

"Who'd want to buy my land when farming's not a going thing?"

"You told me that a surveyor from Lumberton said he'd make you an offer if you ever wanted to sell."

"Yes, he did. Buck Wetmore wanted my land for the timber." Rob stood and walked towards the woodpile, stooping to pick up some scattered pieces of kindling, stacking them on one arm. The hawk screeched, and they looked up in time to see it dive into the grass and come up with a field mouse. "Said he wanted my store too. Said he'd put in gasoline pumps. I was gonna do it myself once they paved the road." Rob appeared to be in a trance, thinking out loud.

"Think he might still be interested?" Hugh asked, breaking the spell.

"Might. But I reckon I'd better talk to my brothers first. I think your uncle Angus would have a heart attack if he thought some of this land was going to go out of the family."

Hugh knew he should give him an out, say something like *Just be thinking about it*, but he'd gone too far to back away. "It won't be easy to leave this place, Papa. Been home to us all our lives. But we think it could be a good thing for you and Mama. We could take care of you in Wilmington."

"We take care of ourselves pretty good right now."

"I know you do, but I'm talking on down the road. Mama's heart is a big worry to us."

"The Lord will take us all when it's our time. Don't matter where we live." He picked up a few more sticks of wood, tried to straighten his hunched back. His hair suddenly seemed whiter, his step slower.

Hugh felt confident again. Why hadn't they thought of this before? Even two years ago, Papa had seemed as spry as a twenty-year-old. But now . . . "How old are you, Papa?"

"I'm getting on up there, I reckon."

"How old?"

"Old enough to know better, son."

"C'mon, Papa. I really don't know how old you are."

"Fifty-eight. Your mama's still a spring chicken, though. She's only forty-nine or so."

"You're not opposed to the idea?"

"Like I said. . . . Here, take this kindling up on the porch and go in and speak to your mama. I'll talk to her tonight."

———

NO, ROB HADN'T BEEN OPPOSED to the idea. He reckoned if five of his eight children had found a better life in Wilmington, there ought to be something there for the rest of them. When a door closed, you had to open a window. As each of his older children had left the farm, Rob had become more accepting of the fact that he'd probably be the last of his line to tend the family's farm. Farm prices couldn't get much lower. And the grist mill and general store that he'd operated most of his life would not sustain his family much longer, not with hard-surfaced roads making towns like Atkinson and Burgaw seem closer. But could he give up his land?

The O'Kelly and McBryde clans had settled in northeastern Bladen County two centuries ago or more, acquiring over time large tracts of the rich bottomland on Bandeaux Creek between the Black and Cape Fear Rivers. They were industrious landowners, producing abundant yields from their flood-prone farms, building sturdy homes from the plentiful oak and cypress. They were store-keepers, mill owners, loggers, lawyers, and politicians—but the land was what had sustained them.

Around the turn of the century, Rob McBryde and his brother Angus had married the O'Kelly sisters, Eva and Kathleen, both love-ly and fair with the deep russet hair characteristic of their clan. The girls had been orphaned by a house fire that claimed their parents' lives and their home as well. Until wedding the McBryde brothers, they had lived on Bandeaux Creek, subsisting on the income from their father's small country store and living above it. But they brought into their marriages a commodity worth much more than the dressed timber of a fine home or the store: they brought land.

Once the McBryde brothers had started families, it was like a competition to see who was the most prolific. One year Rob and Eva would have a baby, the next year, Angus and Kathleen. By 1919, they each had nine children, and hardly a day went by that Eva didn't have one or two of Kathleen's children to visit or vice versa. They were like one big family, sharing their blessings right down to the clothes they wore.

But in that same year, Kathleen had died of breast cancer. A month later, Eva's year-old baby died of pneumonia. The birth of another baby the following year eased Eva's heart somewhat, but she thought she'd never get over missing Kathleen. Her sister had been her best friend.

———

THE ARRIVAL OF THE YOUNGER GENERATION created a commotion, as usual. Rebecca, Belle, and two of Eva's sister's children, Jessie Rae and Alice Ann, had ridden with Cal from Wilmington up to the country. Jessie Rae and Alice Ann were the eldest in their family, born along the same time as Hugh and Cal. Both had gone to business school in Wilmington and taken jobs at the Coast Line, where they dressed in the required secretarial uniform of white blouse and navy skirt. But today they were both wearing fashionable short dresses, belted below the waist, and elegant suede pumps. Belle and Rebecca were dressed similarly, all having benefited from recent gift boxes sent by their Uncle Dick's wife, who had no children of her own to spoil.

"I declare, you girls look like you just stepped out of a bandbox," Eva said. Young Millie looked on, wondering if she would ever be so grown-up. When she'd watched her reflection in her mother's oval dressing mirror that morning, Millie was sure she saw a more mature girl, a girl who'd just recently come of age. Rebecca had warned her not to be alarmed when she saw the dark spots in her drawers. *It means you're almost a woman,* she'd said.

"We went to Sunday School together before we came up here,"

Rebecca said. "I had to drag Belle out of bed, but Papa made me promise we'd go to church every Sunday."

Belle yawned. "Sunday School's not the same as church and you know it."

"It's better than not going at all," Jessie Rae said.

They sat around the dinner table laughing and talking for an hour or more before the men went out on the porch for a smoke. The girl talk turned to the most recent gossip, about Davy McBryde running off to South Carolina and marrying Patty Sue Jackson, a woman thirteen years his senior.

"And a floozy to boot, I heard," added Rebecca, though she wasn't exactly sure how Jessie Rae and Alice Ann felt about their brother's new wife. Eva peeked out the door to make sure the men were out of earshot. "Calvin is just sick about it," she said. "He and Davy were so close. Now they never see each other. Ordinarily, Davy would have been right here at this table today."

"I could've jerked a knot in him," Jessie Rae said. "It liked to have ruined Christmas for us. Since Mama died, Davy and I had done Santa Claus for the younger children. This year, Miss Geneva had to help. It just wasn't the same."

"Why's that?" Eva asked.

"Oh, Davy liked to get up on the roof and jingle the harness bells. You know, things only a boy can do. Daddy never got into Christmas much, and Miss Geneva never had any children of her own. We just filled the stockings and wrapped the presents, and left it at that. Like I said, it wasn't the same without Davy."

"I'll bet he would've come if you'd asked him," Rebecca said. "He probably didn't think about it."

"No, sir," Jessie Rae said. "Patty Sue won't let him out of her sight. I think they're both afraid of that old hag, Mrs. Jackson."

"Jessie, honey, don't say such things," her aunt said. "I never met her, but I'm sure . . . "

Alice Ann laughed. "Don't give her too much credit, Aunt Eva. "She's pretty rough around the edges."

Her sister frowned at her. "We liked Patty Sue, though, didn't we, Jess?"

"At least your mother has been spared this, God rest her soul," Eva said, lowering her eyes.

Rebecca had cleared most of the table, and Millie had gone to the kitchen to wash the dishes. "I heard Patty Sue was in cahoots with a bunch of gangsters in Chicago," Belle said. "One of them brought her down here. The only reason she came back was to see if her daddy had left her any money."

"Belle, please honey, don't let Millie hear that kind of talk," Eva whispered, concerned that the clinking of silver and china from the other side of the door was not sufficient to mask the conversation of the older women.

"Well, it's true, Aunt Eva," Jessie Rae said.

"Miss Geneva is not even as old as Patty Sue Jackson," her sister said. "She and Daddy get along so good. They'd only been married a year and Davy runs off." She shook her head. "I still can't believe it."

"Just say a little prayer that things will work out," Eva said.

———

NOT A WORD HAD BEEN MENTIONED at dinner about the boardinghouse. But after the dishes were done and the Wilmington crowd had left, Millie took Rodney and Vera to play by the creek while Eva and Rob rested on the front porch. "Don't get your feet wet," she called to the children. "This is pneumonia weather." She put her hand on Rob's arm. "It's our turn to clean up the cemetery."

Rob had closed his eyes and propped his feet up on the rail, pretending to nap until she settled down. "What made you think of that?"

"Pneumonia weather. Clarence took sick in March."

"I declare, I never can tell how your mind's working."

"I'd like to go over there, see how much needs to be done before May."

"I'll go with you," Rob said.

"No need, unless you just want to."

"Don't you think you should rest, shug? That was a mighty big dinner you put on the table. Dr. Bayard said getting all tuckered out might bring on another little stroke."

Eva stood up. "Phsaw! I'm not going to sit around and wait for something to happen. Not on a pretty day like this."

"I thought we might just sit here and talk a little bit."

Even at almost fifty years old, and after nine children, Eva stood tall and slender. She wore her auburn hair in a loose roll, piled on top of her head. Her navy crepe dress and matching cardigan were stylish, thanks to Lilibeth, her brother Dick's wife, who sent all the women in the family boxes of hand-me-down dresses and undergarments from time to time. She leaned across her rocking chair arm to kiss him on the cheek. Theirs had been a close marriage, lasting all this time because of their deep affection for one another, something not all women could brag about. "Come go with me, Rob. We'll talk there. I'd love that."

"I'll crank up the automobile. March wind pinches and bites this late in the day."

She put her hands on her hips. "Listen here now, I want to walk. Spring is in the air. Can't you feel it?"

"I don't have to feel it. I can see it out across the pasture. Soon it'll need mowing."

"Bring your pocket knife and we'll cut some yellow-bell switches. They'll root in no time, as wet as it's been."

———

THE MCBRYDE FAMILY CEMETERY was on a piece of high ground, probably the rim of an ancient bay in the sandy lowlands of Bladen County. Rob's ancestors had long ago designated the site for the burial of their people. He and his four brothers had built their homes in close proximity to it, with five spokelike woodland roads leading mourners to the axis. Yearly, one family took a turn cleaning the cemetery, clearing branches and fallen leaves, straightening stones when they needed it. After church on the first Sunday in May, all of the families came with pots of fern and flowers to place upon the graves. The oldest living member of the family led them in prayer, followed by individual petitions to the Lord to bless certain loved ones. When tears were dry and the children had run off to play, the women spread their platters of chicken and country ham, potato salad and deviled eggs on tables under the moss-draped trees. A separate table held nothing but cakes, pies, and other desserts, more than enough to feed the passel of McBryde kith and kin who came from far and near for the yearly gathering.

———

ROB PUSHED THE YELLOW-BELL CUTTINGS deep into the sandy soil while Eva brushed the leaves off Clarence's small grave. Atop the marker, carved in stone, a baby lamb rested in a bed of flowers. The inscription read, *Planted on Earth to Bloom in Heaven.* "Don't you wonder how Clarence would have turned out?" Eva asked.

"He was a good baby."

She took a few steps towards her sister's gravestone. "Maybe he's in Kathleen's arms this very minute."

"Probably so."

"Let's sit down over there on the bench and say a little prayer for them—all our loved ones buried here," she said.

Reluctantly, Rob joined her on the bench where they looked out over the family headstones, some worn down by rain and weather until they were hardly legible. Rob knew his mother's epitaph by heart. *Here lies Mary Carter McBryde, Dearly departed wife of Peter McBryde, Mother of ten precious angels whom she will welcome in heaven on Judgment Day.* As a child, Rob had grieved that he would have to die before he would see her again. "After you get finished, I'd like to have that talk," he said.

She gaped at him. "After *I* get finished? Aren't you going to say a prayer with me?"

"Look here, shug, I've got a lot on my mind. Can't the prayers wait?"

Eva thought he was acting mighty peculiar. "What is it, Rob?"

"The boys are buying a big old house on Princess Street in Wilmington."

"They are? Hugh didn't mention it to me today. Isn't that funny?"

"He wanted me to tell you about it first."

"What's going on, Rob?" Eva knew her husband well and was quick to detect the seriousness of his tone. "You're beating around the bush about something."

"It's a good investment. They want to turn it into a boarding-house. Want me and you to come operate it for them."

"Well, that's ridiculous, isn't it? We could never leave our home on Bandeaux Creek. We have a farm, the store—the post office. We couldn't just pick up lock, stock, and barrel. Could we?" He didn't reply. "Could we, Rob?"

"I expect there's some things we could leave behind. Every year I've had to sell a piece of land to pay our taxes. I'm sick and tired of seeing everything I've worked for go down the drain."

"We've always managed. My brother would help us."

"I'm not asking Dick to take on my family to raise. He's done enough for us already."

"But Dick promised my papa that he'd always look after Kathleen and me. Now that Kathleen is gone . . . "

"I'm not going to live hand to mouth, Eva. Have Dick pick us up every time."

"You've made up your mind, haven't you?"

"I didn't say that."

They'd never had a cross word in their marriage, mostly because she'd never stood against him. Wasn't right for a woman to go against her husband. The Bible said so. Nowadays, people were getting divorces left and right. The preacher said that divorce was the devil personified. Just recently, Eva had heard of a man in

Atkinson leaving his wife and children for another woman. Rob McBryde would never do that. He'd never have reason to.

She did not pause for long. "Whatever you say, Rob."

He pulled her towards him, put his arm around her. He knew her heart would always be here, in and on the land where she had been raised, where she had laid her parents, her sister, her infant child to rest. "I'll keep that piece of land over towards Colly," he said. "When the rest of the children are grown, we'll build us a nice little house—something just big enough for a garden and a few chickens. We'll live out the rest of our days right here between the rivers. I promise."

3

Things Left Behind

T HEY MOVED TO THE CITY IN LATE APRIL, just after the garden peas were finished. Mr. Wetmore had bought their home in Bladen County, and along with it the store and five acres of land. Angus McBryde had bought the rest. The boys had rented a big truck and brought it to Bandeaux Creek on moving day while Rebecca, Belle, and Millie stayed in Wilmington to sort things out in anticipation of the truck's arrival on Princess Street.

Eva had cried all night. "I can't believe we have to leave Mama's pianoforte here," she said between the tears. "It's been in my family over a hundred years."

"We can come back and get it, shug, but you know there's a perfectly good one at the house in Wilmington. That old thing of your mama's hasn't sounded a note in twenty or more years."

"Did you empty out the packhouse? Our first dishes are in there, the ones Aunt Nancy gave us. I couldn't bear it if anything happened to them."

"Half of them were broke, shug. That's why you put them in there, remember?"

So it went, Eva begging to take with them everything they had accumulated in their twenty-five years of marriage, Rob wanting to leave most of it behind. "We won't have a packhouse in Wilmington. We'll have to put it all somewhere in that house on Princess Street. It's full already," he said.

Finally, Rob had gotten Calvin to take his mother on to

Wilmington. "We'll be along as soon as I check around and see what's left," he told his son. "We may have to come back for another load."

Eva climbed into Calvin's car, and Rob handed her a pot of ragged-looking wandering Jew. "You won't leave anything, will you, Rob?"

"Will you stop worrying, shug?" He closed the car door and leaned in the window to give her a kiss. "Just be sure you have one of the girls pour some water over those plants we dug up yesterday. We particularly don't want to lose that rosebush."

The climbing rose was but one of the many plants Rob had helped Eva set out around the Bandeaux Creek house in the years they'd lived there. In the spring, clusters of bright red blossoms practically covered the smokehouse. Yesterday they'd walked around the yard and dug up clumps of this and that—iris and cosmos, some dusty miller—potting them up temporarily in discarded pails and pots whose holes and dents would long remind Eva of their former use.

The house on Princess Street had a tall board fence that separated the back yard from the neighbors' lawns. Eva had seen signs of a neglected formal garden, but there was little sun and no place for vegetables among the small trees and shrubs. She'd be lucky if Rob could find a place to string her a clothesline. Down the street, there were plowed garden plots on several vacant lots. Rob would surely locate one where they could grow a few tomatoes and hot peppers. The rest of their vegetables, they'd have to buy at the city market like other folks. It was an idea so foreign to her, she felt they might as well be moving to China.

———

THE GIRLS DID THEIR BEST TO CLEAN the neglected house. Harry hired the janitor from the courthouse to wash the windows and take down the heavy drapery and cornices that had likely been hung when the house was built seventy-five years earlier. Some of the curtains had been shredded by the cats, but Harry insisted that they be boxed and placed in the attic in case Eva found some use for the upper parts in the future.

Rebecca's friend Lela had come to help, and the two girls stood behind the door watching the plumber dismantle the large galvanized tub from a rectangular dais in the center of the parlor. "What do you think they *did* in that tub?" Lela asked, grinning and raising her eyebrows.

Rebecca put her hand over her mouth to stifle a giggle. "Imagine, with everybody watching!"

"It's certainly big enough for two!" Lela said.

When the plumber had disconnected the plumbing apparatus, he laid out an old quilt on the floor and heaved the tub onto it. Struggling with the weight of it, he dragged it through the double doors of the parlor and into the hall. "What're you going to do with it?" Belle asked.

"Mr. Hugh said I could have it for getting it out of here, but it won't be no bargain if I can't get it out that front door," he said, looking from the tub to the door, gauging the size of both.

"I mean, what are you going to do with it *if* you can get it out? Is your bathroom that big?"

He was leering now, aware of what the girls were thinking. "I think me and the wife might have some fun in it," he said, obviously enjoying his sport. "Want let's me and you try it out for size?"

Lela, ignoring his suggestive look, measured the tub against the dust-mop handle and quickly showed the plumber that the fixture was too large to go through the door. "Looks like you'll have to take it apart at the seams," she said. "C'mon Becca, he doesn't need our help."

Belle had shown up late in the morning, her face made up and her nails freshly polished. "I've got a date tonight, so give me something to do that won't chip my nails."

"Give me something to do that won't mess up my *hair,* my *nails,* my *dress,*" Rebecca mocked. "Why'd you even come, Belle?"

Belle gave her a sharp look. "Let me have that Hoover." She dragged the vacuum cleaner from room to room, searching for electrical outlets. "I hope somebody bought some drop cords," she yelled to no one in particular. Harry had purchased the appliance from a client who'd given him a good deal on it. Belle was amazed, watching the old oriental rugs come to life again after they were vacuumed. "I was ready to throw them out, but they're hardly worn at all," she said.

Rebecca was dusting the walls and baseboards with a dustrag attached to a long stick. "I guess not—most of them were rolled up. The widow Ainsley wasn't much of a housekeeper in her latter years. She probably forgot about them."

Tall windows glistened, letting in daylight for the first time in years. "Mr. Rehder said he'd let Mama have some lace curtain material at a good price. You and Millie can help her make them," Belle said.

"When are you going to learn to sew, Belle?"

"Never," she answered emphatically. "If I can't find a man to buy me pretty things, then I'll just do without."

———

ARRIVING AT THE HOUSE MIDDAY, Eva eyed the Hoover, wondering at the miracle of a machine that could eat dirt. "Everything is electric now, Mama. You'll never have to use a broom again."

"We'll see about that, Rebecca."

"We've set your room up for you. You'll love the big bed. It was in the downstairs apartment, but the boys moved it upstairs for you. It's much nicer than that old iron bed you had at home."

"I liked that iron bed," Eva said, smiling at the memory of the nine children that had been conceived in it. "Were the mattresses in good shape?"

"Only the one on your bed. We put your feather mattress on top of it. Papa thought of that."

"Um-hmm. Papa's real thoughtful." She stood at the bottom of the staircase in the front hall. "Lots of steps to climb."

"I know, Mama, but Hugh says we'll get more for the downstairs bedroom with that little kitchenette."

"Oh, I wouldn't have that big old room. I know what went on in there. Besides, the stairs will be good for me."

Rebecca picked up a stack of linen. "A washerwoman stopped by the day we were cleaning things out, and I gave her all the linens I could find. She brought them back this morning, fresh and ironed."

"Well, we certainly won't need a washerwoman after Rob gets my clothesline up. Can you imagine a house this size with no clothesline?"

"Mama, you're going to need some help running a boarding-house. Harry says he's found you a cook."

"A cook!" Eva exclaimed. "For heaven's sake. I don't need anybody to cook for me. You used to be a big help in the kitchen, and Millie is smart as a whip when it comes to cooking. She can make a better pan of biscuits than me."

"Harry knew you'd have a fit about him hiring a cook. That's why he hasn't told you yet," Rebecca said, laughing. "Her name is Mae. I bet you'll really like her when you get used to it."

"Well, I never . . . "

"Come on, Mama, I want to show you your room. Belle, put your things out on the dresser."

Eva took a firm grip on the banister, struggling to lift her weight with each step. *Yes, I'll get used to all of it,* she thought, longing for the simple farm home she'd left behind in Bladen County. She'd always had help, but it was just that, *help.* No titles like *cook* or *washerwoman.* Old July, the colored tenant who lived across the road, had two wives who'd helped her out. Aunt Rhoadie, the first one, had delivered all but the last two of her babies, staying a night or two each time. Eva had told the children that the old midwife had pulled the babies out of a stump. July's second wife was younger, able to do more, washing and ironing and scrubbing the oak floors with lye soap. But nobody—*nobody*—had ever been in charge of Eva's kitchen.

"I wish you'd wear those elastic stockings I got for you," Rebecca called over her shoulder. "You ought to have them on right now."

"I know, honey, but they are so hot."

"Dr. Sidbury makes the student nurses wear them. He told my class that most nurses have varicose veins because they're on their feet so much," Rebecca said.

"Mine came from having so many children. My mama had them, too, but I wouldn't trade a single one of you," Eva said, reaching the top step. She took a deep breath. "You run up those steps every chance you get, Becca. I don't want your legs to ever get as bad as mine."

Rob met them coming out of the hall bathroom. "Sure is nice having an inside toilet," he said, drying his hands. "You'll never have to empty chamber pots again, shug."

Eva put on a mock face of indignation. "Imagine, we didn't have even one bathroom in the country. How on earth did we ever manage?"

"Tile floors, too."

"I'd say some mighty rich folks built this house, wouldn't you?"

"Would've been a shame to tear it down," he said.

Yes, she thought. *It would have been a shame. Houses were made for families to live in. When one family moved or died out, another should come in to fill it with life and laughter.* But why did it have to be her, Eva McBryde, who wanted nothing more than to finish out her life in the home that Rob built for her in the country? In a few years the children would all be gone, and what would she and Rob be left with? A house on Princess Street. An old house for old folks. The more she thought about it, the more determined she was to make her way back to Bandeaux Creek. One way or the other, she would.

ROB MCBRYDE HAD GOTTEN ON RIGHT AWAY as the night watchman at the old Solomon Bear Winery, closed since nation-wide Prohibition took effect nine years before. The owners had been so sure the Volstead Act would be repealed that they had kept all their winemaking machinery, filling the huge wooden casks with water so they would lose no time starting up again. But after the place was broken into a couple of times, the Bear owners had decided that a watchman on the property was a good idea.

The upstairs sleeping porch of the Princess Street house, enclosed by windows on three sides, became Hugh and Cal's quarters. Each brother had a double bed and a dresser, and there was a small area for Hugh's desk out on the large landing at the top of the steps. Every afternoon, sun streamed through high windows that overlooked the front, lighting up the dark halls throughout the entire house.

There were three other bedrooms on the second floor and a back stairway to the kitchen. Rebecca and Belle shared a room, as did Millie and Vera. Rob and Eva had the only bedroom upstairs that had its own bathroom. Rodney was awarded a little room off the kitchen that had once been a maid's quarters. He shared a bath-room with the boarders in the apartment that had been separated into two rooms. Their cousins, Jessie Rae and Alice Ann, took one of the rooms, and a young couple who worked in the shipyard took the other with the kitchenette.

Harry, although pitching in his share of the house payment each month, opted to keep his room near the Lawyers' Building, claiming that he kept such odd hours he was afraid his comings and goings would disturb everyone in the house. Actually, it was no secret that Harry was doing some heavy courting and he didn't want anyone keeping tabs on him. He'd soon finish his law studies, and a young attorney with his eye on a political career would do well to be thinking about settling down and starting a family.

The boardinghouse concept had worked out perfectly by all accounts. All the rooms were soon taken, and the dinner table seldom had an empty place. Two meals a day for the boarders were included in the rent, but the noon meal was open to the public between the hours of eleven-thirty and one o'clock. Cal saw to it that just about everybody in the Freight Department at the Coast Line put their feet under Eva McBryde's dinner table at least once a week. He loved the camaraderie of walking to his home in the middle of the day with two or three of the fellows who worked beside him. Sometimes a couple of the secretaries came, too. He'd never had many friends, didn't much like the idea of a bunch of rowdies riding around in his car, drinking and smoking. The boardinghouse afforded him an opportunity to be sociable without all that.

Mae soon endeared herself to Eva, stretching two nickel boxes of vanilla wafers and three or four bananas into a bowl of banana pudding big enough to feed a crowd. The heavy-set black woman shuffled around the kitchen in a pair of slippers that she left by the back door each evening. Her good shoes and a wide-brimmed hat were a part of her attire when she arrived and when she left at the end of the day.

Hugh assumed the business end of running the house as he'd planned, collecting the rent and paying the mortgage and taxes. He'd worked his way up to assistant manager of the freight department under Mr. Jack Baldwin, a respected figure in the Coast Line organization and a valuable mentor for an ambitious young professional. Occasionally Hugh brought his boss to the house for dinner, where Eva might catch a glimpse of Mr. Baldwin's hand on her son's shoulder.

"You don't charge him anything, do you, son?"

"No, ma'am. But I've seen him slip a coin or two into Mae's apron pocket."

"Well, he's your boss and Calvin's too. We need to favor him. You know what they say—the way to a man's heart is through his stomach."

Hugh laughed. "I thought that saying was about marriage."

"Well, think again. There's been more than one boss or supervisor won over with a good meal."

"Mr. Baldwin is too smart to be bribed, Mama. But he says the food is good and coming here makes him forget about business for an hour or so. Running the freight department at the Atlantic Coast Line is no easy task."

Eva had to stand on her tiptoes to give Hugh a kiss. "You could run it, son. Maybe someday he'll retire, and you—"

"No, I don't want to do what Mr. Baldwin does. I practically run the department already, but I don't want to have to do that political hobnobbing, running up and down the East Coast, fighting with the union organizers and all that. Every time there's an accident in the freight yard, he gets blamed for it."

Eva winced. "I declare, son. I had no idea. You certainly don't want to get blamed for any accidents."

4
A Heap of Trouble

IN THE BRIEF TWO MONTHS THE MCBRYDES had been in Wilmington they had become accustomed to the rhythm of city life. The end of the week brought a flurry of energy as cleaning and preparation for a restful Sunday were completed. Saturday mornings were reserved for a trip to the market down on Front Street to restock the larder with meats and fish for a few days.

Eva knew it was something far out of the ordinary, then, when her husband's brother, Murdoch, last-born of the McBryde siblings and now a butcher with a thriving shop on Front Street, appeared at their door on a morning when he should have been busy serving customers.

"Something's happened," Murdoch said, winded from the climb up Princess Street. "You won't believe it," he said to Eva and Rob. He stepped into the foyer, still clad in his blood-smeared butcher's apron. Eva, drawn as she always was to the sight of the stub on Murdoch's right hand, remembered the family story she'd heard about him once cutting off his finger while making sausage—the missing digit never found.

"Up in Cotton Cove," he said, short of breath. "It's Angus's boy, Davy. He's been arrested for murder."

"Davy's been what?" Rob asked.

"Arrested for killing his mother-in-law, Gladys Jackson."

Eva clasped her hand to her mouth. "I don't believe it!"

"Angus called me from Lyon's store," Murdoch said, still catching his breath. "Told me Davy didn't do it on purpose. They've got him locked up in jail at Elizabethtown anyhow." Removing his cap, he ran his fingers through his thinning hair. Rob beckoned to his brother to follow them into the parlor, where Eva took a seat in a large upholstered chair that still reeked of smoke from a small fire set by a boarder earlier in the week.

"Patty Sue told the sheriff at first that her mama had committed suicide," Murdoch explained. "A bullet to the forehead."

"Well, I never . . . . Maybe she did," Eva exclaimed.

By then Hugh and Harry had heard their voices and come downstairs. Cal was not far behind. Rob filled them in briefly and urged Murdoch to continue.

"They don't think so now," his brother said. After the coroner examined the bullet hole, he said the bullet entered from the *back* of her head."

"But how was Davy implicated?" asked Harry, his legal mind in a whirl.

"Coroner said it would've been impossible for Mrs. Jackson to shoot herself in the back of her own head. That's when Patty Sue changed her tune. Said Davy *accidentally* shot her mama while he was cleaning his gun."

"I knew it had to be an accident. Davy wouldn't shoot an old woman like that," Cal said. He flashed back to the the night the previous summer at White Lake, when he and Davy had met Patty Sue Jackson. Davy could be reckless and wild, sure, but never violent.

Cal knew his cousin well. They were the same age, born only six months apart. They'd been closer than brothers ever since they were little fellows. But things had changed when Davy got kicked out of Oak Ridge, not long after his mother had died. When he'd been lined up to enroll at the Ridge, Calvin had begged his Uncle Angus to let Davy come too. Angus had finally given in and agreed to send his son. Davy hadn't lasted the year. Hiding a firearm in your locker might not have seemed so serious for a country boy, but it was one of those rules they were hard and fast about at the Ridge. Cal had known then that he and Davy were headed down different paths.

Rob scraped the bowl of his pipe with his pocket knife and tapped the ashes out into an ash tray. "What does Davy say?"

"He told his daddy that the old woman tried to claim a gun Patty Sue had given to him. She slammed the door in his face when he wouldn't give it to her." Murdoch threw up his hands in despair. "He said the gun went off, just like it had a mind of its own."

"See, I knew it was an accident," Cal said, sounding relieved. But in his heart, he also knew that his cousin could handle a gun better than that.

"Wait a minute, Cal, there's more to it," his uncle cautioned. "Patty Sue told the sheriff that Davy tried to set the house on fire to cover up the murder. That don't sound like *she* thought it was an accident, does it?"

"She probably did it herself," Cal said.

"That's what Angus thinks."

Eva was having a hard time believing her own ears. "Does anybody around there *know* the Jacksons? Surely, they don't think that a nice boy like our Davy—"

"Angus said there was only that one family of Jacksons that he knew of. He remembered when they bought the old Colvin place over near the canal. Said they kept to themselves. Not churchgoing people and all."

"Well, that explains some of it," Eva said.

Rob eased himself onto the sofa. "Sit down, Murdoch."

His brother plopped down on the opposite end of the sofa, wiping his brow on his shirtsleeve. He was solidly built, only forty-two years old, but his hair was snow white and he wore a long mustache that he twirled from time to time. Off his feet, he was more relaxed, even considering the situation. "Not a soul knew Patty Sue until she showed up after her daddy died," he said. "He must've told her he was going to leave her a lot of money. They say she'd left home a long time ago, gone up north where she'd gotten mixed up with a rough crowd. When she came home, Angus said, her mama wouldn't let her in the house. Next thing everybody knew, Davy had run off with her to South Carolina and gotten married."

That part Eva remembered well. Calvin said Davy had been drawn to Patty Sue like a magnet. Eva had grieved about it because Davy was still just a boy to her. Why didn't Angus do something? Why didn't he see it coming? But Angus had been squiring a new wife around, and she'd been busy making a new life in Wilmington. No wonder the boy had found an older woman to make over him. Eva stifled a sob. "What's he going to do, Murdoch?"

"The sheriff said Davy was in kind of a trance when he arrested him, only half his wits about him."

"That the same sheriff that arrested him for being drunk and disorderly up there at Melvin's Beach last year?" Rob asked, glancing at Cal.

"I don't know, but Davy sure has got a reputation for being a rounder."

Eva popped up out of her chair. "But not a murderer!" she wailed.

"Sit down, Eva," Rob said. "You're pale as a ghost."

"This is too much for her, Papa," Hugh said. "Let me take her upstairs."

"You'll do no such thing, son," Eva said. "We're talking about my poor dead sister's son. She would want me to be here."

"Dr. Porter said you weren't to get upset, Mama. At least sit down."

Rob McBryde lit his pipe, sending little puffs of smoke into the room. "I imagine Angus is taking this pretty hard. We'd better get on up there tomorrow and see how we can help out."

———

AS USUAL, EVA AND ROB ROSE AT FIVE. Although they now had an electric stove and steam heat, the old habit of getting up early to start the fire in the cookstove was hard to break. Eva cracked two eggs into the hot grease. "I wish we had a few laying hens," she said. "Remember how good those eggs tasted right out of the nest?"

Rob had brought his shoes down to the kitchen and was putting on his socks. "We're better off here," he said.

Eva was wearing a peach-colored quilted satin robe her sister-in-law had sent her, inappropriate for a boardinghouse matron, but she loved it nonetheless. Her long auburn braid lay across one shoulder. She smiled. "I can wishful think, can't I?"

But he was irritated, his mind more on the chore before him that day. "How about that refrigerator? You wouldn't have that down in the country," he said. Walking across the kitchen to the sink in his stocking feet, he turned on the water. "And look at this, running water. It may be years before they string wire out in the country so's you can have electricity for a pump. You ought to count your blessings, shug."

"I know. It's just that Cousin Maybelle said that Jasper Corbinn has built a new house and put in a Delco generator. He has a little hydraulic ram pump down in the spring that pumps water into a tank." She poured him another cup of coffee, putting her hand on his shoulder. "I just thought it was something to have toilets that flush and everything, right out there in the country."

"I still say we're better off here in Wilmington where the children are," Rob countered, glad to have his own family close at hand.

She sat down at the kitchen table and buttered a biscuit and spread strawberry jam on it. Millie had worked at the cannery two Saturdays in a row capping strawberries, and the jam was part of her earnings. "I guess this business with Davy got me to thinking that it might not have happened if we'd been there. Davy just hasn't been right since Kathleen died. He was her oldest boy. She had so many hopes for him. Maybe he would've come to me if I'd been there. I could've talked to him."

"Eva, there's nothing you could've done. Davy's who he is and we can't change that."

She took a shallow breath, stroking the long braid as she might have a kitten. "You will take me back someday though, won't you, Rob?"

"I said I would."

There was a light tap on the kitchen door. Alice Ann peeked in through the swinging door, Jessie Rae right behind her. "What're you girls doing up so early? Come on in, have some coffee," Rob said.

"We want to go to Cotton Cove with you, Uncle Rob."

"Sit down and I'll fix you some eggs," Eva said. "The grease is still hot. Nothing seems quite so bad on a full stomach."

Jessie Rae sat down at the table and put her head in her hands. "What in the world has my brother gotten himself into this time? Mama will roll over in her grave." She lit a cigarette. "He was always getting in trouble, but he'd never murder someone, especially an old lady."

"Calvin said Patty Sue was a bad influence on him from the start," Rob said.

"I liked her," Alice Ann said. "She was sweet as she could be to me."

"There's two sides to every story," Jessie Rae said. "I don't think she was really a bad girl. She just left home when the time came, like the rest of us."

Alice Ann got up and poured herself another cup of coffee. "Old Mrs. Jackson was really hateful to her—wouldn't even let her in the house when she came home."

"You taking up for her?" Rob asked.

"No, sir, I'm just saying that's how Davy got mixed up with her. He felt sorry for her."

"I think there was a little more to it than that, shug." Rob got up and pushed his chair in. "Eva, I reckon you ought to call your brother in Oklahoma. Sounds like Davy's going to need a good lawyer."

5

The Situation

THE NEXT DAY, AS HE PULLED INTO the sandy drive at the old home place in Cotton Cove, a wave of nostalgia nagged Rob into a dark mood. His brother Duncan's car sat under the trees. Rob wondered if Duncan and Murdoch sometimes felt the same way he did. Angus had taken the homestead when their mother died, his right as the eldest brother, but his inheritance had given Angus a head start on his other brothers who'd had to cut trees and burn stumps in the flood-prone woods before they could plant the first hill of corn or cotton. Without that head start, Angus might have been the one who'd gone broke years later and had to move to Wilmington.

The air was warm for June, but the live oak trees surrounding the house had put on new growth and lent a shady, greenish tint to the freshly painted house and outbuildings. That would be Geneva's doings. Angus was bent on keeping his young wife happy, and a little fresh paint went a long ways. This would be the second year for her roses and peonies that graced the walk up to the side porch, where a large dinner bell had been mounted strictly for decorative purposes.

Geneva opened the door before they got to it. She hugged Jessie Rae and Alice Ann, blinking back tears. "This is just awful for you all," she said. "And my heart's broken for your daddy."

She turned to the men, offering her hand to shake Rob's at the same awkward moment he reached out to hug her. *Probably worried that Angus would be jealous, the old coot,* Rob thought resentfully. Geneva blushed. "Angus is all to pieces back there in the kitchen," she said. "I don't know how much longer I can keep him from going after Patty Sue. He blames her." Rob marveled to himself that his brother at his age had been able to catch the young schoolteacher who'd come to Cotton Cove shortly after his first wife died. The aroma of something stewing on the stove reminded him that she was a good cook too.

"That's what Eva says. She gave him the gun, for one thing."

"Well, please go on in there and see if you can calm him down. I'll put on another pot of coffee."

Eva and Rob had been pleased as punch when Angus remarried. He was moving on up there in years—almost sixty—and had been looked after by a loving wife most of his adult life. There were three other boys besides Davy, plus the two girls who lived in Wilmington, but it was the little ones who needed the guiding hand of a woman about the house. Geneva McBryde was still in her thirties. Rob didn't doubt that she'd have other children of her own.

Angus paced the kitchen floor like a mad bull, his white hair a sharp contrast to his reddened face. He was the eldest of the McBryde brothers, and his temper was well known to them all. "Patty Sue Jackson is a goddamned whore! That's all she is! That's what her mama called her and I reckon she knew her better than anyone else."

"How in the hell did he get tangled up with her?" Murdoch asked.

"It was cunt, nothing in the world but pure *cunt,*" Angus said.

"Hold on here, Angus," Rob said. "There's ladies present."

Jessie Rae glanced at Alice Ann. "It's all right, Uncle Rob, Papa's got a right to be upset. But we'll go on upstairs and let y'all talk."

"He got one whiff of her and that was all she wrote," Angus continued. "I've seen it before, like a bitch dog in heat. She sashayed around him and he couldn't keep his hands off her."

"Calm down, Angus," Murdoch said. "You're going to have a heart attack."

"To hell with me! That's my boy sitting in that jail up there in Elizabethtown."

"I know, and he's going to need his daddy. We've got to think of some way to get him out of this," Rob said.

"It would take a miracle, a goddamned miracle," Angus said. He suddenly grew calm. Staring out the window, he slapped his hand against the frame three times in succession. "You know the hell of it, the absolute hell of it?" The three brothers looked at each other, then at Angus. "Geneva thinks Patty Sue's pregnant."

"My God, does Davy know?" Murdoch asked.

"Not that we know of, and I'd just as soon keep it that way. I don't want anything to do with that woman—ever again!"

"Now, Angus, you might need to think about that," Rob said. "Might not be fair to—"

"Look here, Rob, I'm just asking the three of you to keep this under your hat. If she is expecting, there's no telling whose young'un it is, and I don't intend to raise somebody else's . . . not like it was my own."

Rob couldn't imagine that his brother was so callous about what might be his own blood, but nothing good would come from arguing with him. "I told Eva to see if she could get hold of the Judge," he said.

IT HAD TAKEN A DAY OR TWO TO GET THROUGH to Dick O'Kelly in Oklahoma, where he served as national attorney for the Creek Indians. Oklahoma was still a territory of the United States when O'Kelly had taken the job, and he was only twenty-eight years old when he'd been appointed a federal judge. At the time of his nephew's troubles, the Judge, as the family called him, had been attending a large Indian powwow where they'd given him a full-length feathered headdress.

With all he had pending in Oklahoma, the Judge told them, the soonest he could schedule a return to Bladen County would be early fall. He thought it best to let things die down a little, in any case, and as inauspicious as it might seem, he also wanted to be home in October for the church's community homecoming. Angus hired a local lawyer to do the preliminaries, and once he knew the Judge was coming, the lawyer said it was in Davy's best interest to wait for his uncle before they set the trial.

————

THE FIRST WEEK OF OCTOBER a Nashville-bound train pulled out of the Oklahoma City depot carrying Judge Dick O'Kelly, on an extended leave of absence; his wife, Lilibeth; and half a dozen trunks and valises containing everything from the Judge's best three-piece suits to an array of his wife's fashionable gowns—this year's and last's—to an ornate Indian headdress that required a trunk all of its own. In Nashville the couple and their luggage changed trains, taking the Dixie Limited into Atlanta, where they once again changed trains, this time for the comfort of a Pullman car on the eastbound route. They would be in Wilmington first thing in the morning.

The Judge's wife slept comfortably while the Judge himself watched the lights of small Southern towns pass by and listened to the comforting clatter of the rails. Thoughts of his Bladen County home crowded his mind—the fate of his unfortunate nephew, now in his hands, and that of the kinfolk whose own lives and prayers were caught up in Davy McBryde's future.

He thought with an unexpected nostalgia of his departed sister, Kathleen, and found reason to be glad she had not lived to see this trouble. He thought of Eva, who was bearing the burden for both of them, and whose health was being taxed even further by the situation.

And he reflected on his cousin he'd never met, Maggie Lorena Corbinn, who a few years ago had sent him a book she'd written.

Somehow, she'd confused his work with the Indians as that of missionaries, and suggested that he promote her book among the various tribes. *Little Pearl*, that was the title—a tale about a Chinese missionary. The story had appealed to him, and he planned to show her his recent acquisition, the headdress, while in the area. Perhaps Cousin Maggie would be inspired to write a story similar to *Little Pearl*, this time showcasing the Creeks, whom he was extremely fond of. He'd find a way to straighten her out tactfully about the mistake, too.

Home . . . it would be good to be home, mused the Judge.

———

THE SAME WEEK, THE FIRST OF OCTOBER, a local train pulled out of Burgaw, North Carolina, a train that would take Maggie Lorena Corbinn Ryan to Petersburg, Virginia, and on to points north. She carried with her a heart heavy with grief over the death of her young son, Yancey, a grief so terrible it had rendered her numb and senseless, nearly oblivious to the currents swirling around her home in Bladen County throughout the long, eventful summer. Her single trunk contained only a modest assortment of clothes she hoped would be suitable for autumn in Boston, and a half-completed manuscript. The only other thing she carried was the slightest glimmer of hope that she could change her life. How? Only time would tell. Until then, Tate and the boys would just have to make do.

———

UPON THEIR ARRIVAL AT THE WILMINGTON STATION, the O'Kellys had taken a cab straight to the Princess Street house, where Eva and her girls served a large meal consisting of all the Judge's favorite dishes. After he had finished off his second piece of caramel cake, the girls cleaned the kitchen, while the rest of the McBryde family retired to the living room to listen as the Judge expounded on Davy's situation for over an hour. "Now I know this sounds like the end of the world, Eva," Dick O'Kelly said finally. "But the boy just needs some good legal counsel, and I'm here to see that he gets it."

"Our dear sister in heaven is smiling right now, Dick."

Her brother strutted back and forth in front of the living room mantel, his thumbs behind his suspenders, stopping now and then to study the collection of family pictures Eva had assembled beneath the mirror. At forty-two years of age, her younger brother was not only one of the best lawyers in the nation, he was a millionaire, having made some good investments in the oil industry himself. "Calvin has agreed to take me to Elizabethtown tomorrow. Harry, I want you to go up there with me." He winked at Eva. "I'll show him a thing or two about lawyering." The Judge turned to his wife, Lilibeth, who lolled on an overstuffed horsehair chair, her gold-lamé-slippered feet daintily crossed on the ottoman. "Darling, you can go with me or stay here with Sister," he said.

Lilibeth had long ago been dubbed "Mae West" by her husband's family. Well endowed in the bosom department, she wore fancy satin lounging pajamas about the house and velvet ribbons in her bleached-and-permed blonde hair. "Sweetheart, you know how I detest all those flies and the lack of conveniences," she said. "You go, and Eva and I will do some shopping." Eva glanced at Rob, who detested the word *shopping* as Lilibeth used it. "What's the name of that little shop on Front Street, Eva, dear? They have the most adorable hats."

"Beau Monde. Yes, it's very nice. Just a short ways from here, if you don't mind walking," Eva said.

"Darling, you have cabs, don't you?"

"Maybe one or two. But it's a nice walk. I can show you Rob's garden on the way."

Lilibeth smiled and looked over at her nephews sitting three abreast on the sofa. "One of the boys will take us," she said.

"They'll be at work, Lil," Rob said, already dreading the next few weeks.

THE JUDGE ESTABLISHED A TEMPORARY law office across the street from the courthouse in Elizabethtown. Each morning he drove the nineteen miles to Cotton Cove in his brother Angus's car, one of a pair of Crow-Elkhart touring cars he'd bought for his sisters when his first Oklahoma well struck oil in 1913. He parked the car a mile outside of town and walked the dusty road in his cream-colored cotton cord suit, speaking to every man, woman, and child he encountered along the way. Calling it his "constitutional," he would sooner have missed his dinner than to have missed his walk.

A large, portly man, Dick O'Kelly stood six foot three, with auburn hair and a coarse, gargantuan nose that reddened when his temper flared. Although well educated, he had a demeanor like that of ordinary North Carolina country folk, earning him high favor with his potential jury pool. "I believe I knew your mama and daddy," he'd say. "Fine people, fine people." Most of the potential jurists understood that he was also calling their attention to the fact that he was a member of one of the oldest and most respected families in the county, lest they forget that the accused was his nephew.

The elder McBrydes watched closely as O'Kelly went about preparations for Davy McBryde's trial. Not a one doubted the Judge would find a way to erase the terrible blight on the family name. But the whole business was kept from the younger children as much as possible. When *the situation*, as it was called, was discussed, it was out behind the barn or in the privacy of a bedroom. One by one, the Judge had cautioned them not to talk about Davy's troubles or risk jeopardizing his case. "Won't do any good to hang out the family wash," he said. "One of you might want to run for public office someday."

DAVY McBRYDE'S INSTINCT FOR SURVIVAL had rebounded immediately upon seeing his legendary uncle. "That old lady made me crazy, Uncle Dick. She was leering at me and taunting me like a yard dog." The words were exactly what Dick O'Kelly wanted to hear—not pleasant to consider, but likely the only way to keep the boy out of the electric chair.

The Judge paced back and forth in Davy's jail cell. "Yes, go on. She was threatening you?"

Davy jumped up from his cot, maintaining a stance like he had assumed the morning of the murder. "Yessir, she was wagging her finger at me and telling me I was no good. I saw her in the mirror come in through the door. I'd been practicing twirling this pistol Patty Sue had given me—you know, like they do in those Wild West shows."

"You had the gun in your hand from the start?"

"Yessir."

"Did she have a weapon?"

"I couldn't see it, Uncle Dick, but I knew it was there," Davy pleaded. "Afterwards . . . after she . . . I saw it outside the bedroom door."

The Judge thought his nephew bore considerable resemblance to a deranged person. After four months in the county lockup, his hair was down to his shoulders, and he wore a beard that had been shaped with a pair of dull jailhouse scissors. "She was yelling all kinds of ugly things about Patty Sue," Davy cried. "When she slammed the door, the gun just—went off."

"In her deposition, your wife says that you tried to set the house on fire to cover up the murder," his uncle said.

"I did not! She's the one who started the fire. Why would she say that?"

"I think it's obvious, son. She doesn't want to go to prison either."

"I figured that's why she hasn't been to see me. She wants me to take all the blame."

"You pulled the trigger, didn't you?"

"No, not on purpose! The gun went off. Patty Sue put it there, told me to use it if her mother . . . but I never meant to—never intended to kill her."

"That's it, son. You're not guilty of murder. No McBryde is capable of murder. We are not that kind of folk," said the Judge soothingly, sympathetically. "But someone can push us, drive us crazy, can't they?"

———

THE JUDGE'S NEPHEW WAS NOT CONVICTED of cold-blooded murder. Several mitigating circumstances led to the jury's reasoning. His wife, Patty Sue McBryde, could not testify against him. Mr. Reuben Squires, the mailman, who said he had known Davy all his life, swore he had never seen or heard of any violence from the young man. And the sheriff testified that Davy's behavior at the time of the arrest was mighty peculiar, like he was out of his mind.

Arguments had gone back and forth, but in the end Dick O'Kelly convinced the jury that Davy McBryde was guilty only of house burning, an irrational act brought on by a madwoman who'd driven him insane—temporarily insane. Convicted of first-degree murder, Davy would have faced the death penalty. But a murder charge alleviated by temporary insanity called instead for internment at the state insane asylum, where a psychiatrist would determine Davy's state of mind at the time of the murder.

After the trial, the talk outside Davy's immediate family was not of the young man's innocence or guilt, but of the terrible tragedy that had befallen the Angus McBryde clan, all of whom had been silenced by the old man with a threat of disownership if they ever mentioned his eldest son again.

"Angus never had much patience. I believe he's satisfied that Davy got his just reward," Rob said.

"He might even be glad Davy's far enough away that he doesn't have to think about him," Cal said. "He's hoping that Cotton Cove will forget Davy, too."

"The boy could've been sent to the electric chair, son."

The mention of Davy's name set Eva to weeping. "The criminally insane ward at Dix Hill would be a death sentence for a sane man."

"Now, Eva, don't go getting upset again. The Judge said he had a lot of faith in psychiatrists. They might straighten him out."

"Patty Sue's the one that needs straightening out," Cal said.

"Well, I dare say she was the cause of all this," Eva cried. "Just ruined that sweet boy's life."

Cal decided he couldn't hold the information back any longer. "Mama, there's been some talk," Cal said. "I guess you ought to know about it. I'm sure you won't hear it from Miss Geneva."

Eva prepared herself for a shock. *Talk* was something every family dreaded. It went on behind your back, where you could neither affirm nor deny it. "Then you'd better tell me, son."

"Patty Sue was gone long enough . . . they say she might've had a baby."

Henry Montgomery's Buick

———

—BOSTON, MASS. Master R. Lendon Ryan
arrived in Boston on the 9th of this month to
visit his mother, a guest in the home of Mrs.
Henry Montgomery at No. 7 Upton Street in
the South End. Young Ryan's mother is Mrs.
Tate Ryan, a native of Bladen County, N.C.,
and a former student of Mrs. Montgomery's
at the Baptist Female Institute in Raleigh.
Mrs. Ryan is spending the winter months in
this city with her former teacher and mentor
while revising a novel she hopes will be published within the year. (Reprinted from the
Boston Herald.) *Wilmington Morning Star,
Feb. 14, 1925*

———

6

Little Cemeteries

FIFTEEN-YEAR-OLD LEN RYAN STEPPED OUT of South Station onto Summer Street, taking a deep breath of the frigid Boston air before turning the collar of his jacket up against the wind. He gripped his leather satchel and looked first up one side of the street, then down the other. A crowd of people, three or four abreast, hurried past him, while out on the thoroughfare checkered taxicabs darted between horse-drawn carriages, setting up a cacophony of blaring horns. Len studied the skyline, marveling at the tons of stone blocks stacked floor upon floor to form the tall buildings. Shoving past Len, a man in a long fur coat the color of a red fox stepped into the street, yelling, "Taxi!" The smoke from the man's cigar was the only thing remotely familiar to the boy. Everything else reminded Len that he was just a country hick from Colly, North Carolina, who'd come to Boston to find his mama.

Len stopped at the corner, looking this way and that, studying the map Mr. Henry had drawn for him on heavy brown paper. A row of small arrows end to end directed him to turn left onto Atlantic Avenue, then right onto Kneeland Street, then over to Tremont. Mr. Henry had made little pictures of things to mark Len's way.

Cold wind whipped around the tall, gangly youth, finding its way through his pants and long underwear, causing him to break out in goosebumps. Without a cap or hat of any sort, his flame-colored hair did little to retain his body heat. He swore under his breath, something he'd have to remember not to do around his mama, but he'd never been so cold in his whole life. Without Uncle Archie's coat Aunt Mag had saved all these years in camphor balls, he was sure he would've frozen right where he stood. Stepping carefully over the high ridge of dirty snow piled along the edge of the street, he found his leaky brogans no match for the icy mush. As he slipped and slid he wished he'd taken time to put on the rubber galoshes Aunt Mag had stuffed into his satchel.

Several cars passed, spraying rooster tails of muddy water his way before he could cross the street. The sun was warm, but the gale that blew down the narrow street took his breath away. Chased by the wind, he raced for the other side. Following the map, he passing house after house with tiny front yards enclosed by iron fences. *Like little private cemeteries*, he thought. *Might as well be— everything's dead as a doornail!* When he'd left home day before yesterday, branches on the trees beyond the pasture had already taken on a tinge of color. They'd be leafed out in another month or so.

Two weeks earlier, his mother's letter had come addressed to him. Pa had put it on the kitchen table to await Len's return from school. "Hurry up, son," his father had said with a big grin. "I have a feeling your mama's ready to come home."

Len was excited. Pa hadn't had this lilt in his voice since his mother had left for Boston last fall. "You reckon?"

Tate Ryan scooted his chair closer to the table. "Yep, she was just waiting until I was ready for her. You know how your mama likes things real nice." Len had opened the letter and begun to read, but he held the page up to prevent Tate from seeing the enclosed train ticket. "Well, what does she say? When's she coming?"

"She's wanting me to come up there, Pa—see about going to college." Len could've died right there, seeing the color drain from Tate's face, his jaw go slack. "Maybe we could all go," Len said.

Tate slumped back into the chair and stared at the floor. "No, son, I can't leave with spring planting right around the corner— your ma knows that—and Will's got all those cars out there to work on. You go—maybe find out what's keeping her."

———

STANDING IN FRONT OF NUMBER SEVEN Upton Street, Len folded the map and studied the three-story townhouse. Mama said there was also a basement where a coal-burning boiler sent hot steam up in pipes to radiators all over the house. *Mmm,* he'd like waking up in the morning to steam heat, especially when there was two feet of snow on the ground.

A stout horse hitched to a small buggy parked directly in front of the house chewed in a bag of oats while steam rose from a pile of manure deposited on the packed gray ice behind him. Looking out over the street, Len saw that there were automobiles parked in front of some of the houses, and he thought of Will. There'd be plenty of work up here for a mechanic, if he was of a mind to come. *Wonder if Mama has thought about that?*

He took the steps two at a time and turned the door bell, liking the sound it made. Someone inside was running down a long flight of steps. Mama had said she could see the boats in Boston Harbor from her windows up on the third floor. The door opened and Maggie, flushed and out of breath, reached out for him. "Lenny, son—I just can't believe it." She pulled him into the vestibule and hugged him tightly around the waist, unable to reach his shoulders. "You've grown a foot, a whole foot!" she said, ruffling his red hair and patting his cheeks, so reddened and chapped by the cold air she could hardly see the mass of freckles she remembered so well.

"Not quite. Papa measured me last Saturday and I've just grown four inches since the last time."

"How's your papa?"

"Pa's just fine. He sent you a present. I've got it somewhere," he said, digging into his coat pocket.

"Look for it later on," Maggie said, pulling him inside. "Miss Abigail's been dying to see you."

"Wait, Mama. Where's that yellow Buick Mr. Henry drove down home? Don't tell me he's traded it in for a horse and buggy." He laughed, tossing his head towards the street.

"No, it's parked in back in the alley. That's the doctor's buggy. Mr. Henry's been feeling poorly for the last week or so. The doctor stopped in to see him." She reached for Len's coat. "C'mon, we'll go upstairs and I'll show you your room. You need to freshen up."

She hung Len's coat on a hall tree alongside several others. There were two pairs of heavy boots and some umbrellas standing in a large pan on the floor. "You'll have to take off those wet shoes, son. Marcie gets upset when we track up her floors."

"Who's Marcie?"

"She's the housekeeper who lives in the basement. That's where the kitchen is."

Len thought about the elderly colored woman who'd kept house and cooked for his family for as long as he could remember. "Like Lizzie?"

"Well . . . yes, kind of."

The foyer was dark except for the yellow light coming from a small chandelier that hung above on a long chain. A stairway ran up one side of the hallway, its newel post heavily carved and polished. Len rubbed his hand over the dark wood, wondering how long it had taken someone to make it.

Mama looked different. Following close behind, Len noticed her silk stockings and low-cut black pumps below the hemline of her satiny blue dress. Most of the ladies in Colly still wore high-topped shoes and long dresses. She'd changed her hair, too. It was cut short and pinched into waves, instead of the twisted bun he'd always known at the back of her head.

On the third floor, Maggie opened the door ceremoniously into a large corner room. "Here you are, son. Abigail thought you'd enjoy this room with lots of windows." Pulling the curtain aside, she looked down to the street. "Oh, there's the doctor now, getting in his buggy." She took Len's arm and led him back into the hall. "Freshen up a little before we see Miss Abigail. There's a washrag and soap in the bathroom." She reached up to pat his cheek. "We'll get you a tub bath in the morning."

7

An Invitation to Boston

M AGGIE LORENA RYAN HAD BEEN IN BOSTON for three
months when she'd sent the letter inviting her younger son to
come and visit her in the city. Yes, her purpose was twofold. She
longed to see her children—at least one of them—and she was
looking for an excuse to prolong her stay. If Len decided to stay
with her in Boston, she'd have more time to reason things out—
perhaps remain a little longer as a guest of Abigail Adams
Montgomery, whose husband, Henry, was publishing her novel,
Evangeline. Then maybe she'd be able to give more thought to the
future.

In Maggie's mind, her departure to Boston was no different
from that of the many others who were leaving their farms in rural
Bladen County in 1925 to seek a better way of life in towns like
Wilmington, where opportunities were far greater. But to her husband, Tate, she knew that excuse didn't amount to a hill of beans.
He'd begged her not to go. Told her that Abigail and Henry
Montgomery were putting big ideas into her head, luring her away
with their promises to publish her book. "No, they're not," she'd
insisted. "You just don't want me to go."

"What about your young'uns?" he'd said. "Don't they matter
one bit to you?"

Even her old Aunt Mag had lit into her with the remark that
she'd lost her senses. "What in the sam hill do you think you're
doing?" she'd asked at the top of her voice. "A grown woman with a

husband and children going off like you didn't have a care in the world."

"What about *me?*" Maggie yelled back. "Why can't somebody think about me sometime?"

"You do enough of that yourself," Aunt Mag had said.

"You of all people," Maggie sobbed. "You know how much I've suffered. Lost my precious child." She threw herself onto the bed and covered her face with a pillow. "And the fires," she wailed, "*two* house fires!"

"Brought most of it on yourself," Aunt Mag had mumbled.

Lizzie, the black midwife and housekeeper who'd brought Maggie and her children into the world—the one who'd practically raised them—had her say, too. She was ironing at Aunt Mag's house when Maggie came to visit. "Won't do to leave Mr. Tate by hisself too long. Mens don't tolerate a gallivantin' woman much."

Maggie had sat at Aunt Mag's dresser combing her long red hair, frowning at the gray streak that had begun to show at her widow's peak. She was forty-two years old and the thought of becoming an old woman frightened her. "Gallivanting?" she said, whipping around on the stool. "That just shows how much you know about getting a book published, Lizzie. I'll bet you've never even read a—" But she'd stopped short, hanging her head. "I'm sorry, Lizzie."

"Sticks and stones'll break my bones, but words can't hurt me. You better lissen up, Missy. Mens, dey need a woman t'look after 'em." Maggie twisted her hair up in a knot and shoved the pins in. Why were they all giving her such a hard time? Lizzie spit on her finger and tested the hot iron. "Those young'uns is growin' up, but dey needs a mama. Mr. Tate can't do everything for 'em."

Maggie had taken hold of Lizzie's hand. "But you'll help me, won't you, Lizzie?" she pleaded. "I need to go. It's my big chance to get my book published. You'd be proud of that, wouldn't you?"

"Missy, I were proud of you the day you wuz born. You don' need to have no book printed up to 'press me."

———

SHE'D LEFT HOME IN OCTOBER, weeks before the first frost, arriving in Boston to find a light snow on the ground. Since then, there'd been several heavy snows and nightly freezing temperatures. Even steam heat was no match for Boston weather. The three-story brownstone, built right after the War between the States, was like many of the houses in the South End, antiquated and in need of repair. Abigail said that when her mother had bought the house, the South End had been the best neighborhood in Boston. But when they filled in Back Bay, many of the wealthiest people moved over to Commonwealth or Newbury Streets.

In 1905, Abigail Burchart Adams had taken a professorship at Baptist Female University in Raleigh, North Carolina, and her mother, Vanessa, had decided to go south with her daughter rather than remain in Boston. The two women had taken up residence in one of the cottages on campus in Raleigh, which was where Maggie had met them during her freshman year. In Boston, the house-keeper, Marcie, had rented out a few rooms in the brownstone to boarders while maintaining the private quarters for Mrs. Burchart and Abigail when they returned for the summers. Each time they'd come home to Boston, Abigail said, they'd found the neighborhood a little more run down. Immigrants of all nationalities had taken over the once fashionable brownstone houses.

After Maggie left BFU, Vanessa Burchart had become serious-ly ill. She returned to Boston with her daughter for good and lived with her in the brownstone until her death. Abigail had taught at Radcliffe College for a while after that, but she wrote Maggie that her world was torn apart when the invincible Mrs. Burchart passed away. She'd gone to Newport to spend time with old friends in the fashionable Rhode Island resort town, and Maggie lost touch with her—that was, until Abigail and her new husband, Henry Montgomery, had turned up in Colly six months ago with an offer to publish her novel. The enticement included an extended stay in the old brownstone on Upton Street and a whirlwind of activities on the Boston social scene. As grand as it all seemed when she left Tate and the boys behind, there had been times when, caught up in their ideas and plans, Maggie felt like a helpless pawn in the lives of the Montgomerys.

8

Lady Rowena

L EN RYAN TAPPED ON THE DOOR of his mother's room. Maggie shook away her reverie and rushed to open it. "I'm sorry, son. Come on in. I'll only be a minute. Sit there by the fire and tell me about Will and your papa while I finish up."

Maggie dusted her cheeks with rouge and painted her lips while Len told her all about Will's garage. He watched her, thinking he'd never seen his mama looking so pretty. He'd noticed immediately that she wasn't wearing the eyeglasses with their one dark lens, but said nothing. She tied a colorful scarf around her head. "Papa's fine, too," he said. "He's almost done with the house."

Maggie fixed her gaze on the row of perfume bottles on her dresser, trying to picture the house Tate had been building when she left. When she'd last seen it, the house had been an empty box. *Almost done* in Tate's fashion meant *half done* in her mind. She changed the subject. "How about Aunt Mag, is she doing all right?"

"She's fair to middlin'. She misses you too, Mama."

Maggie laughed, picturing her bossy aunt. "I'll bet she's having the time of her life, being in charge." But Maggie knew her Aunt Mag was lonely without her. She'd been like a daughter to her aunt, and hardly a day had gone by without them seeing one another. She missed Aunt Mag too.

Len sat down in a chair next to the fireplace and picked up an open book that had been turned face down on the footstool. "Don't see much of Aunt Mag," he said. "She keeps to herself right smart.

Sits around reading her Bible a lot."

"Aunt Mag reading the Bible? My stars, I never knew her to sit around doing anything." She straightened her skirt, glancing in the mirror behind her. "She's the one who always said it was better to wear out than to rust out."

"Maybe she did," he said in a distracted tone, before changing the subject. "I liked that book *Ivanhoe* you sent me for Christmas."

"Did you read it, son?"

"Yes, ma'am. The lady Rowena made me think of you. You know *Rowena* sounds like *Lorena*."

But Maggie was unsettled by thoughts that her aunt was unwell. "I declare, you make it sound like Aunt Mag is bad off."

"Papa says she's just getting old."

"Well, you tell Papa I said *that* will be the day!"

Len dug into his pocket. "Here's his present."

The small package was neatly wrapped in tissue paper that she figured Tate had found in the bottom drawer of her chest where she saved scraps of paper and ribbon from year to year. *No! That couldn't be!* Her chest of drawers, like everything else except her trunk, had been gobbled up almost a year ago by the flames that destroyed the house in Colly. The thought opened up her old wounds, and it was all she could do to unwrap the gift with mock enthusiasm. "I declare, it's an arrowhead."

Len stood over her, looking at the sharpened stone. "It's the one he gave you a long time ago."

"You reckon?" *I don't think so*, she murmured under her breath, wishing she could remember when she'd last seen the memento Tate had found along the river when he'd come for the new teacher, taking Maggie back to Onslow County for the first time.

"I haven't seen it since me and Will were tiny."

"I haven't either," Maggie said, her thoughts churning. Before the last fire, she'd kept it on the windowsill above the sink, where she'd often shown it to the children as a distraction, telling them how their papa had given it to her before they were married. She turned the arrowhead over in her hand and stared at it, stung by memories of the past difficult year. "Must be one he found recently." "No, Mama, it's the same one. See the cross there? Remember, he told you how the settlers brought Christianity to the Indians."

———

At dinner that evening, Maggie had to choke back her tears. Len was out of place in the Montgomerys' dining room, awkward handling the heavy silver and passing the delicate china. "Watch me," she whispered to him. Although she'd insisted on good table manners when the boys were growing up, she hadn't paid as much attention since the fire. Even more embarrassing, she saw that Len's clothes were ill-fitting, there was a fuzzy stubble on his cheeks, and his red hair badly needed trimming.

Sleet beat against the tall glass windows and the wind howled around the narrow building, sending cold drafts about their feet. "I apologize for this horrid weather," Abigail said. "If I were a muse, I would have petitioned the gods to bring us a breath of spring for your visit, Len."

Len looked at her a moment before the jest set in. "Well, let me check my pockets, I might of brought a little along." They all laughed, and Maggie began to feel more at ease. "I'm surprised Mama has stayed up here this long," he said, glancing at Maggie. "She's always hated dreary days in Colly. I can't imagine she likes them any better up here in Boston, Massachusetts, where it's so dang cold."

"Lenny!" Maggie reprimanded.

Henry cleared his throat before retorting. "Now, look here, sport, Bostonians love this kind of weather." A smile rippled his mustache. "One learns to do other things, like ice skating and hockey. Have you ever played hockey? Darn good fun." Len looked puzzled. "Hrrump! Well, yes, maybe you haven't, since the rivers and lakes down there never freeze over." Henry took a sip of wine and wiped perspiration off his pale upper lip.

Abigail pushed her chair away from the table. "Henry, darling, don't you feel well?" She gave him no chance to reply. "Marcie," she called. "Bring Mr. Montgomery's plate up to our room."

"No, dear, I won't have it," Henry said. "Not when we have guests. I'm fine. Let us finish our dinner, and we'll go into the parlor and I'll have my cigar as usual. Stoke up the fire, Marcie. I want to hear the news on the radio, too."

Marcie stood in the doorway to the butler's pantry waiting for further instructions. Abigail gave her a little wave. "All right, dear, if you're sure, but you know Maggie and Len would understand," she said.

"We do, Mr. Henry," Len said, rising from his chair. "I'm going to turn in myself as soon as y'all finish. Mama said she'd run me a bath in that big tub."

"Sit down, young man. Marcie has made us a pudding and I'm not about to miss it."

———

According to Abigail, too many puddings were part of her husband's problem. "It's his weight," Abigail confided to Maggie, slipping into her room just before bedtime. "I don't want anything to spoil your son's visit, but I'm really worried about Henry. Dr. Conrad said that his blood pressure is way too high and his preference for rich foods is killing him."

Maggie had seen the difference in Henry just since she'd first met him the previous September. Except for his balding gray head, he had been as spry as a chicken. She laughed when she remembered him in the oak grove in Colly, holding the Spanish moss up to his chin, making a curly beard. Now he showed signs of the same pallor that Tate's mother had along towards the last. "Tate's mother was stout," Maggie said, "but Miss Sally Catherine insisted that she was too old to change her habits. Then she developed sugar."

"You mean diabetes."

Maggie laughed. "Well, she just called it *sugar*."

They sat side by side on a narrow settee, Abigail on the verge of tears. She clasped her hands together. "I've been terribly worried about him. I'm so glad you're here. Promise me you'll stay."

"My stars, Abigail, of course I'm here to stay. I've barely gotten started on the revisions. Wild horses couldn't drag me away."

"I know, but one day you'll . . . ." She stopped, her furrowed brow betraying her deepest feelings.

Maggie was astounded. Abigail had always seemed so in control of her emotions. Now, it seemed that she was afraid of . . . something. Maggie couldn't put her finger on it.

9

A Headless Horseman

FOR THE NEXT THREE DAYS, LEN AND MAGGIE walked as far as their legs would carry them. Henry had taken the boy to Brooks Brothers and bought him some sturdy shoes, a beautiful brown wool suit, a dress shirt and tie, a heavy jacket, and several pairs of long underwear. When Maggie protested, Abigail had shushed her and told her that Henry was going to do it anyway. "It's part of his plan. He wants Lenny to come up here and go to school as badly as you do."

"Why in the world would he?"

"That's just Henry. He feels he had more than his share growing up. He's helped all of his nieces and nephews," she'd said.

On their first round of excursions, Maggie showed Len Boston Harbor, where the famous "tea party" had taken place. She took him to the Old North Church, the State House, and Faneuil Hall, telling him as much of the history as she could remember from her own tour with Abigail and Henry. Next, she pointed out the huge granite Trinity Church in Copley Square, with its red glazed tiles and knobby rolls and crockets all along the tower ridges. Inside the church, they warmed themselves in the quiet beauty of the nave while Maggie explained to Len how the church was built on land that had been marsh before Back Bay was filled in. "They say the tower weighs about ninety million pounds, and there are two thousand pilings underground, holding up the church."

"Who told you that?" Len asked in disbelief.

"Mr. Henry. While they were building it, he used to come down here every day. He said he stood right over there behind a fence and watched them drive the pilings in."

Len was eager, intent on absorbing every detail. He had grown so much, thought Maggie, but still he was the little boy who had always made her smile with his inquisitive mind. She was convinced that, given an education, that mind could achieve most anything.

Across the street from the church they stood on the steps to the Boston Public Library, where Maggie pointed out the handsome bronze doors. Inside, they sat at one of the long tables in the reading room. Len followed the barrel-vaulted ceiling with his eyes, counting the arches. "Man, this is bigger than that church."

Maggie thought the library was one of the most special places in the city. The closest thing to it she'd experienced before was the small library at BFU. The Boston library was only a short walk from Henry's office, just far enough for Maggie to stretch her legs. The thought of all those books from floor to ceiling that she had not read drew her time and again, and the smell of literature was every bit as irresistible to her as that of an apple pie cooling on a windowsill. "Those pictures on the wall are called murals. They tell a story." She pointed to a huge painting behind the delivery desk. "That one's called 'The Quest of the Holy Grail.' If you study it you can see it's a story."

"What about?"

"Some knights in medieval times who went to look for the cup that Jesus drank out of before he died. They believed it had some very special power."

Len looked at the painting, then back at her. "You used to tell us the best stories, Mama. Will you tell me that one sometime?"

"Why don't we get you a book about it and you can read it for yourself," she suggested.

"Not now, there's too much to see and do."

———

IN THE SPACIOUS PARK CALLED THE BOSTON COMMON, Maggie told Len how originally it had been a parade ground where soldiers practiced their marching. "It was like a big pasture. People grazed their cows there, too."

"A cow pasture right in the middle of the city? I don't believe it."

"Just watch where you step," Maggie said, laughing.

Len looked down at his feet, then back at her. "Aw, they don't do it now, do they?"

The wind was merciless, and snow covered all the flower beds as they walked through the Public Garden and around a small frozen lake surrounded by naked weeping-willow trees. Len gawked, unaccustomed to the winter scene. "Look, Mama, they're ice skating. Just like Hans in the storybook."

"I know. In the summer, you can ride in boats shaped like giant swans."

"Where are they?"

"Put up for the winter, I guess. Maybe we'll come back in the summer and ride in one."

"Let's do, Mama, and bring Papa and Will, too! Papa'd just love this."

"We'd never get him up here in a million years."

Len stopped dead in his tracks. "Wait, Mama. I almost forgot to tell you. Will said he was going to fix up an old car for Papa. Maybe he'll drive us up here!"

Not hardly, Maggie thought, remembering the time Tate had borrowed Jasper's car for his mother's funeral in Onslow County. He'd scared the daylights out of her on the sandy roads, weaving back and forth, nearly running into a bridge railing over the dark Northeast Cape Fear River.

But before she could answer him, Len ran up the steps to a spacious bandstand. "Look at this," he called out, making a sawing motion like he was playing a fiddle. "Wouldn't this make a good place for a square dance?"

―――

MAGGIE WAS SURE LEN WAS HAVING a wonderful time. Every morning he'd rush down to the breakfast table, asking what they were going to do next. "Mr. Henry wants you to spend a day with him," Abigail said one morning. "He'd like to show you where he went to school—where you might want to go. He said he'd let you do the driving."

They drove in the yellow Buick roadster up to Andover, where Henry had attended Phillips Academy long ago. Len was turned off from the time they parked the car and Henry Montgomery led him up the frozen walk to the brick administration building. The musty smell of closed-up rooms and dark halls hit him when Henry opened the heavy door and beckoned him inside. Len hung back, a feeling of dread coming over him like sudden nausea. "Come," Henry said, holding the door for his young friend. "The headmaster is expecting us."

Dr. Walton extended his hand to the boy, sizing him up with a look that covered every inch of Len's exterior in one brief glance. "So, we're from North Carolina, are we?"

"Yes, sir, Bladen County to be exact."

"Is that anywhere near Charlotte? I have a sister in Charlotte. Married into a fine family. The Davidsons."

"No, sir. Bladen County is nowhere near Charlotte."

"What major city is it near?"

"Wilmington."

"Ah, Wilmington," Dr. Walton said, taking his seat behind a large desk. "We'll just put that on the application, Henry. The present board is very fussy about the origin of its students," he chuckled, making a note on a piece of paper.

Henry began to shift uneasily in his chair, clearing his throat.

"I'm well acquainted with the present board, Dr. Walton. I appointed several of them when I was chairman."

"Yes, yes, of course you did, Henry."

Henry sniffed loudly and looked at his pocket watch. "I'd like to show Master Ryan the campus today. We're looking at several other schools. He needs to have some references before he makes his choice."

Now it was the headmaster's turn to shift uneasily. "Well, we certainly hope he chooses your alma mater, Henry. We'd love having you drop in from time to time to check on him."

Len had watched the conversation between the two men with interest. They were talking over him and he didn't like the feeling. When they were out in the fresh air again, Len spoke his mind. "He's kinda stuck-up, isn't he, Mr. Henry?"

"Not at all, son. A headmaster has to present himself as an authority figure, or else the boys won't respect him."

"He scared me in that black frock coat. All I could think about was the headless horseman."

"What on earth?"

"Oh, just a picture in one of my story books," Len said, beginning to laugh. He galloped a little down the walk, slapping his hind side and cupping his arm about an imaginary head. "This tall skinny man in a long black coat flying out behind him, riding a tar-black horse with wild eyes, tearing across a hilltop, with the moon overhead."

Henry couldn't help but laugh as he pictured Irving's "Legend of Sleepy Hollow." "My goodness, you certainly have a good imagination, son."

In the dining hall Len put away the food on his plate in no time. "Kind of skimpy with the victuals, aren't they?"

"Meals are a little heavier at dinner, son," Henry said, watching him in awe. Len had approached his meal with the enthusiasm of a ditchdigger after a long, hard day. His manners were acceptable, but his pace unquestionably was not. Henry looked at his watch.

"We're not going to be here for supper, are we?" Len asked.

"I've arranged to stay in the headmaster's cottage tonight. Thought you might want to stay in the dorm, see how the boys live."

Len threw his hand up. "Whoa! No way, Mr. Henry. That is, if you don't mind, I'd like to get back to town, talk to Mama." He started off in the direction of the car. "Wait here, I'll come pick you up."

ON THE WAY HOME, HENRY PUSHED the point a little more. "I've arranged for your entrance exams. You'd be starting midterm, but the headmaster said he'd tutor you himself."

Len pictured himself closed up in a room with Walton. That's when he decided he might as well get it over with, once and for all. "Look, here, Mr. Henry, I'm much obliged, but I can't stay up here now and go to school. Papa needs me at home." He was trying his best to sound grown-up. "Besides, when the time comes, Pa wants me to go up to Raleigh to the Agricultural School—if I go anywhere."

"I think your mother wants to have a say in that, Len." *I'm not a bit worried about Mama,* Len thought. "Let's not make any rash decisions," Henry continued. "You won't have another opportunity like this. Your mother here, working on her revisions."

"I can't stay . . . "

"You'd spend your holidays with us."

Len was pensive, not wanting to be disrespectful to his mother's benefactor. He had to admit it, he'd like to come back for another visit. Driving the yellow Buick roadster was like a dream come true. He loved cars. Not in the same way Will did—he didn't like to work on them—but he loved driving that car as good as anything he'd ever done. "How long you figuring Mama's gonna be up here?"

Henry was about to doze off. "Long as it takes, would be my guess."

They drove on another mile or two before Len got up his courage again. "Mr. Henry? You awake?"

"Wh . . . what? Yes, son. Pull over if you want me to drive."

"No, sir. I've been thinking, and I just wanted to say no thank you for your offer of sending me to school. My place is back home. Mama's is too."

———

AT LUNCH THE NEXT DAY, ABIGAIL SET the table with a Valentine's Day motif. On each of their plates she had placed an elaborate handmade valentine.

"Oh, Abigail, they're beautiful," Maggie said. "Did you make them?"

"No, dear, I found them among Mother's things. She had bought them in Paris on her last trip. For just such an occasion, I suppose."

Henry slipped into his chair after the ladies were seated. "There's a little something from me, too, under each of your plates."

In turn, they each lifted their plates and found shiny five-dollar gold pieces. "Henry, you are such a darling," Abigail said.

"Mr. Montgomery!" Len said, pushing his chair back and rushing over to Henry. He extended his hand. "I'm much obliged, sir."

Maggie caught Henry's eye. "I'm much obliged, too, Mr. Henry."

Henry stood and shook Len's hand. "You're both welcome. It's a pleasure to have you with us." He seated himself again. "Now, let's get on with lunch before Marcie's ice cream melts out on the back stoop."

Abigail was aghast. "Henry, you know what the doctor said!"

"Yes, I do. Conrad says there's not a thing wrong with me that a few days down at the Greenbrier won't cure. As soon as the weather warms, we'll go for a month and take you with us, Maggie."

Abigail turned to Len, seated on her right. "And maybe you'll come, too, young man."

"Oh, no, ma'am. I've got to get on back home to help with the spring planting."

When they had finished their ice cream, Henry cleared his throat and lifted his glass to Maggie. "Here's to talking some sense into that boy. I've offered to send him to one of the best preparatory schools around Boston, but he says his pa is depending on him. Admirable, I must say, but Maggie, dear, I've told the boy he needs an education if he is to get about in this world. The agrarian scene into which he was born has seen its day. The city is where things are happening. I can get him employment in one of the finest banks or warehouses."

"Thank you, Henry, it's what I want more than anything, but I'm afraid that's up to Lenny."

"Mama, you said it didn't matter to you one bit."

Maggie looked in her son's direction. "I know what I said, son. You mustn't do it for me, though. I want you to be the best that you can be, but you've got to do it for yourself—not your mama."

Len stood, almost upsetting his chair. "Papa needs me, Mama. You know that." He walked to the large bay window in the back of the brownstone that overlooked a small garden. There was a double iron gate enclosing it and a brick wall separating it on one side from the adjacent building. On the other side was a vacant lot, where children chased and played on the frozen soil. *How could she ever think that he'd want to live here, all closed up in buildings, the ground outside frozen hard?* He turned and looked at his mother, challenging her. "Papa needs you, too. When are you coming home?"

"Here, now," Henry said, walking over to Len, his hand out. "No one wants to rush you into this decision. The offer stands, but perhaps you need to return to North Carolina first and settle your affairs. You can always come back to Boston." He looked at Abigail. "Right, dear?"

Abigail slipped out of her chair and hugged Len. "Of course." She brushed the boy's cheek with her hand. "You see, you have lots of options. Just remember the importance of your education." She glanced at Maggie. "Your mother will tell you that it changes your life, opens up a whole new world."

———

THE NEXT DAY, HENRY DROVE THEM to South Station, waiting in the car while Maggie bought Len a ticket and walked him through the station to the train. When she had found the platform for the New York Special, she searched for the right words to say. "Tell your papa I'll write to him."

But this was not what her son wanted to hear. He sighed heavily and put his bag down on the sooty boardwalk. "It's not your letters Papa's missing."

"I know, son, I'm just not quite finished with my revisions. As soon as . . . as soon as . . . ." She was looking over his shoulder at two young women who were waiting to board the train. "I declare, I believe that's—"

"Papa said you need to tell him *when*," Len insisted. "He said you owed him that much."

"Lenny Ryan, what in the world! I'm your mama and I don't like you talking to me like this!"

"Okay, I'm sorry," he said, picking up his satchel. "But Papa's real sad."

She touched his cheek. "Listen, Papa and I have an understanding. He knows how much this means to me. You tell him I'm working very hard to come home before Easter, but I can't promise. Now, go on. The conductor just made the last call."

Watching the train pull slowly out of the station, she knew she had lied. Right now, she had no plans whatsoever to go home to North Carolina. She didn't want to go home, didn't want to be stuck in the same old rut of raising field hands and . . . *I'm sorry, Lenny,* she thought. Through the dimly lighted window, she saw him take his seat. Just behind him were the two young women. The girl beside the window turned and looked directly at her. Maggie could hardly believe her eyes. She was certain it was Agatha Evans who lifted her hand as if to wave, before her seatmate said something and she turned around again. The other girl got up out of her seat, pointing to Len, then disappeared down the aisle. Agatha—if it was Agatha—reached through the gap between the seats, getting Len's attention. At the same time she caught Maggie's eye and smiled.

For days Maggie would be discomfited by the memory of the girl's face. Had the young woman recognized Maggie? Perhaps not, without the telltale dark glass. One of the first things Maggie had done when she arrived in Boston was to replace her glasses. The little German optician had reprimanded her severely. "You are not blind. Why would you want your friends to think so?" There was no doubt she needed her glasses for close work, but not for distance. She was sure she had seen Agatha Evans. Would Lenny make her acquaintance on the train? She dared not write and ask him. A letter for *all* to see? Letters were read aloud or passed around. That's partly why her trunk had always been such a mystery. Maggie preferred to keep her correspondences private, but it had earned her a reputation of being possessive about her things.

Obligations

L
EN HAD COME AND GONE, AND MAGGIE KNEW she'd
acted too soon. But his rejection of her foolish ploy to get him
to stay was not the first of her disappointments. She'd thought by
now she'd be in a place of her own. She had her advance in hand.
Hadn't she seen rental signs go up in the windows of apartments in
the old brownstones? That's where she hoped she'd be by now. But
until *Evangeline* was ready to be published . . . Although Abigail and
Henry had welcomed her into their home as a guest, neither had
seemed anxious to pick up the pace towards that end.

First, Abigail had insisted that they take time to catch up
before Maggie began to work. They'd walked the downtown streets
arm in arm, stopping in dress shops and taking tea in the numerous
tea rooms. "I've thought of you so often, Maggie—how much you'd
love it here with me, but I knew you'd never leave Tate or your children," Abigail confided. "When you were in Raleigh that time, I
heard . . . " She stirred her tea and gazed out the window of a small
tearoom on Newbury Street.

"Heard what?"

"Nothing, dear. Reece Evans was never one of my favorite per-
sons either."

Maggie blushed. "I knew him from Onslow County." *Careful*,
she thought, unsure how much Abigail knew about her romantic
liaison. "Before Tate and I were married. In Raleigh, Reece recog-

nized me at one of those concerts. Came up to me. I believe I was with . . . "

"Then so be it."

"Why'd you ask? Was there some talk?"

"Maggie darling, you must know from all your years of having help, there's always *talk*. The help delight in a little tête-a-tête." She raised her eyebrows, nonchalantly flipped her hair. It was a gesture her mother might have made—something expected of a stage queen, but not of Abigail. "I didn't mind at all, dear. I rather enjoyed the thought of your having an affair."

So, Abigail *had* known all these years that she'd been with Reece that night in Raleigh. And if it had been no secret to Abigail . . . Maggie cringed at the thought. Best not to dwell on it.

Another day, Maggie had asked how Abigail had come to meet Henry Montgomery, a partner in one of Boston's most distinguished publishing firms. "Henry was in love with himself," Abigail said, laughing. "Thought I should be, too." She brushed her hair back again with that same air of nonchalance. "Henry is a darling." Reaching across the table, she'd taken Maggie's hand and said confidentially, "A woman needs a man in her life . . . to be respectable, if nothing else."

"Aunt Mag seemed to get along all right without one," Maggie said. *That's it,* she thought. Abigail was playing a part, the role of Henry Montgomery's wife. Her fashionable dress, the airs she put on—all so different from the straightforward professor she'd known at BFU. But why?

"Yes, but Aunt Mag had you and your family," Abigail said.

"Don't you have any family up here?" Maggie asked, the question pricking her own conscience. Here she was, with no family within eight hundred miles. Thinking of staying.

"None. Friends, but no family. Anyway, Henry wanted to marry me. He had his own brownstone in the South End—a much nicer house on the next street over in Union Park. But I couldn't bear to sell Mother's house—see it divided up into apartments like so many along Upton Street. So Henry agreed to sublet his own home to his nephew, Jonathan McNamara, a young doctor who is finishing his medical training."

"Well, there now, I'd say you *do* have some family," Maggie said.

CHRISTMAS BECAME THE NEXT IMPEDIMENT to the editing process. Abigail had easily dismissed the thought of work with visions of parties and holiday fun. "We'd hardly get started," she said to Maggie, "and Jon would come home for Christmas."

"You're expecting him?" Maggie asked.

"Yes, of course," Abigail beamed. She paced from one end of the parlor to the other, apparently composing a plan as they spoke. "He's away doing his residency right now, but he always comes," she said, absently tapping her forefinger against her cheek, a gesture Maggie remembered from the classroom. "Yes, I'll invite him to spend more time with us now that you are here."

"That'd be nice. I'd like to make his acquaintance."

"You'll adore Jon. He plays the piano, and we'll sing carols." She stopped in front of Maggie and hugged her. "Oh, darling, this will be a most wonderful Christmas with you here. I'm afraid it would be very dull here in Boston compared to being with all of your family for the holidays. If not for you, Henry and I would just rattle around in this old brownstone by ourselves. Most of our friends go to the Cape or Newport for Christmas and Thanksgiving. We give Marcie several days off." She reached into her desk for a pad and pencil. "I'll ask her to roast a duck for us before she leaves."

Maggie almost laughed. "I can cook, Abigail," she said. "I've never roasted a duck, but it surely can't be any harder than roasting a tough old turkey hen."

"Wonderful, Maggie! We'll all help. Jon loves to cook," she said, with such enthusiasm that Maggie forgot about the manuscript and joined in.

"I'll make cornbread dressing and gravy, just like back home. We'll need sweet potatoes, and . . . do you think we could find cranberries for sauce?"

Now it was Abigail's turn to be amused. "Cranberries? My dear, where do you think cranberries come from? New England, of course!"

Until then, Maggie had not even considered how much she'd miss Christmas in Colly. Her brothers and their wives, all the children, Katie and her family. They'd all gather at the old home place as usual for Christmas. Aunt Mag wouldn't have to do a thing. To assuage her guilt somewhat, Maggie sent small gifts to everyone—woolen socks for Tate and books for the boys, a lacy handkerchief for Aunt Mag. For the rest of her relatives, she bought small ornaments that reminded her of each one. For the men and boys, there were tiny cars and trucks hung by gold cords; for the women and girls, shiny glass baubles in red and green; for Katie, a more special one, a tiny, gleaming silver teapot ornament with a removable lid.

After spending several afternoons in the shops on Newbury Street selecting gifts for her family, Maggie was concerned that she had not bought a thing for the Montgomerys or for their anticipated guest. She hastily wrote to Aunt Mag to go into her room and find the two copies of *Little Pearl* that she had saved in a box under her bed, and send them to her.

"Will you put up a Christmas tree?" Maggie asked a few days before Christmas.

"Certainly, if you like."

"I'll help," Maggie offered. "If Mr. Henry's nephew comes, maybe he'll string some lights. We've never had them at home."

Abigail's face had lit up. "Yes, of course. I should have thought of that. Jon would love it." She smiled, glancing at Maggie. "He's tall, handsome, very intelligent . . . "

"And very engaged or married, to be sure."

"No, dear, Jon is a widower. I'll tell you about it sometime."

———

CHRISTMAS HAD COME AND GONE before Maggie had delved into her revisions. In early January, Abigail had finally taken her to the offices of Warren-Montgomery on Boylston Street, where she'd introduced Maggie to her editor, Eugenia King, explaining that Eugenia had just finished editing another manuscript and was ready to begin work with Maggie. *Why hadn't she said that before?* Although Maggie had loved the special attention she'd received as a visitor, she'd been ready for some time to go to work. A certain anxiety had set in, and her nights were restless. Tossing and turning, she'd wondered how long she could remain a guest.

A young brown-skinned girl half Maggie's age extended her hand. "It's a pleasure to meet you, Mrs. Ryan," the editor said, looking Maggie directly in the eye. "Abigail has told me so much about you. I really love your story." Though Abigail had prepared Maggie, still it was a shock to think that a Negro girl was to be her editor. It was even more of a shock to Maggie to think that Eugenia King had far more education than she did.

"You'll love her, dear," Abigail had said. "She was my brightest student at Radcliffe. She has some Southern in her background; she will be wonderful to work with."

"Yes, I'm sure I will. I've just never . . . "

"Never worked with a Negro? Of course you have, Maggie. You and Lizzie worked together every day for the good of your family. It's really no different."

———

MAGGIE DID COME TO APPRECIATE GENIE, but it had taken some time to adjust to her editing style. The first time Maggie saw her manuscript marked up, she'd thumbed through the pages in disbelief. Almost every line was marked with a red pencil, and she needed a list of proofreader's marks to decipher some of the strange-looking signs. "I have a lot of work to do," she said.

Genie pushed her glasses back on her nose with long fingers that looked as if they belonged on a piano. "I know. I tried to tell Mr. Henry, but he didn't want to rush you." She attempted a smile. "He said you and Mrs. Montgomery were having such fun getting reacquainted." She shifted the waist of her skirt and pushed up her sleeves, then sat down at a small desk. "You can work in here, or there's an empty office down the hall."

"I'd like to work in my room at Mr. Henry's house, if that's all right. I have my typewriter there."

"Suit yourself, but there's a good typewriter in the other office, and I just put a brand new ribbon on it. You might get more done here without any distractions."

"I reckon I might," Maggie said, silently agreeing that Abigail could be distracting. As much as she loved and admired her former instructor, Maggie felt that Abigail had been quite willing to let her drift along with no deadline in sight. On occasion, she'd felt that Abigail had completely forgotten why Maggie had come to Boston. Always before, especially back in Raleigh, Abigail seemed so purpose-driven, always doing a task of some sort, her time far too valuable to waste chitchatting. Maggie would have thought she'd find the life of a busy publishing executive's wife boring, but Abigail seemed perfectly content as long as she had someone to share her time with.

What bothered Maggie most was that over the Christmas holidays, they'd attended several parties in the neighborhood for eggnog or wassail. Abigail had held her arm and introduced her to neighbors as her friend and former student from North Carolina. Not once had she mentioned that Maggie was there to work—to *write*.

———

EVEN AFTER MAGGIE HAD GOTTEN INVOLVED in reworking her story to suit Genie, she began to miss her children. She'd see young boys playing ball on a frozen lot and her heart would skip a beat. Len and Will would be grown up before she knew it. Her boys would soon be men, and she was not there to watch them grow. That's when she'd come to her decision to invite Len, thinking he was the one most likely to stay. How foolish she'd been. Len was right. She owed Tate something—just what, she wasn't sure.

11

Horseshoes

LEN RYAN SETTLED INTO A COACH SEAT next to the window, waving to his mother with his left hand. His right had hardly been out of his pocket since Mr. Henry had given him the gold piece. He rubbed the coin between his fingers, turning it over and over. *A five-dollar gold piece!* He couldn't believe it.

"Excuse me." Someone in back of him touched his arm. "Could you help me a moment?" Len stood quickly, bumping his head slightly on the overhead luggage rack. The young woman sitting in the seat directly behind his looked like a picture out of one of his mama's magazines. A ribbon that matched her greenish eyes held a thick roll of wavy brown hair at the nape of her neck. She was older than him, but not by much. Girls up north painted their lips and wore rouge, he had learned, making them look a lot older than they were. Mama said it was the way they dressed too. Len was glad he was wearing the Brooks Brothers suit.

"I'm sorry to bother you," she said. "I've broken the heel on my shoe. I need my valise. My friend has gone to look for a porter, but I'll bet you could get it down for me." She flashed a broad smile.

Len thought he had never seen anyone so pretty. Color rose in his cheeks and he felt like his vocal cords were in a vise. "Sure, ma'am. I'll be glad to," he squeaked out.

"It's black cloth with tan leather straps. Do you see it?"

Tugging at the handle, Len wiggled the heavy bag until he could pull it down to the empty seat beside her. "Whew! You must have some horseshoes in here," he said, recovering a little. What was it about girls that took hold of him like that? He'd never heard a grown man squeak.

"Horseshoes? Not really, but I do have a lot of girl shoes," she laughed. Unbuckling the straps, she opened the valise, letting out a scent kin to that of the wild roses that grew along his mama's garden fence. "Just a minute," she said, lifting the inside cover. She'd removed her hat and he looked down on her dark curls, wishing he could touch them. "It'll only take me two shakes of a lamb's tail to switch my shoes," she said. "Here they are, right on top. Good thing I always put my shoes in last. Do you do that?" She looked up at him, fluttering her long lashes and smiling.

His knees buckled slightly and the vise grip held sway over his larynx again. He'd never given a thought as to where he put his shoes in his valise. "I guess so. Sometimes."

She took off the shoes with the broken heel and placed them in a soft cloth sack. Slipping on a pair of brown leather pumps, she looked up at him again. "There, that's much better. I told Belle that you'd help. You have a nice face."

He ducked his head and looked over his shoulder, his face scarlet. How come he couldn't behave right? "M-much obliged, ma'am." *Damn!* He'd almost stuttered. "I didn't mind a bit," he said, hefting the valise back onto the overhead shelf.

"Sit here and talk to me," she said, patting the seat. "There's no telling where Belle is. Probably smoking a cigarette."

Smoking a cigarette? A girl? "Maybe I'd better sit in my seat. Your friend might not like it if she found me in hers."

"Oh, come on. I won't bite. How old are you, anyway?"

"I'm . . . I'm fifteen," he said, sweat pouring down his cheeks and armpits. If he could just open a window for one minute, he might get hold of himself.

"Fifteen! I thought you were much older. Now sit down and tell me your name. I'm getting a crick in my neck looking up at you."

"Len Ryan," he said, wiping his brow with a clean handkerchief his mama had stuffed in his back pocket. He slid into the seat beside her, still feeling uneasy about it.

"Ryan? Sounds familiar. Where're you from?"

"North Carolina. Bladen County to be exact."

She smiled. *I thought so.* "Me, too. Onslow County, near Jacksonville."

"My daddy was born in Onslow County," Len said. "What's your name? I'll tell him. Maybe he knows your folks."

"Agatha Evans, but I don't live there anymore. Let's talk about you. I'll bet you go to Phillips Academy and you're going home on spring break."

Spring break? Len looked down at the brown wool suit, just right for a Phillips boy. Mr. Montgomery had said he'd get a two- or three-week break at Easter. It would have been so easy to lie, but he couldn't. "I was up there in Boston to look it over, but I don't think I'm gonna go there."

"Well, that's good. I'm at Wellesley, and I know some boys who went to Phillips and they are *such* snobs. You don't look their type."

The train lurched and began to roll. He could feel her looking at the side of his face, and he wished he hadn't shaved off the little bit of beard he'd been growing for the last year. "I might go to State College in Raleigh," he said.

"N.C. State College? Are you sure?" she asked, reaching over and touching his arm. "If I was a boy, I'd go to Carolina. I almost went to Meredith College in Raleigh, but my Aunt Emily thought it would be better for me to go up north to college. The schools are better up here, you know."

He was feeling a little more comfortable now, soothed by her friendliness. "My mama went to Meredith College when they called it BFU."

"That was her on the platform with you, wasn't it?" Agatha asked, already sure of the answer.

"How'd you know?"

"Wasn't hard to figure out," Agatha said, smiling. "You favor her, especially the red hair."

That was nice, he thought. Agatha Evans might have been one of the girls he went to school with, except she was prettier than any he'd ever seen in Colly, or anywhere else for that matter. "Mama's in Boston right now working on a book she wrote. She wants me to go to school up here, but I don't want to. It's too cold for one thing."

"You don't mean it, Len Ryan! I love cold weather. I'll bet if you learned to ski and skate, you'd love it, too."

"No, ma'am. I don't think so."

"Oh, here comes Belle. She's my friend from Wilmington. She has just been up to visit me at school. We're going home now— spring break, you know. Let her sit in your seat."

Len rose hastily. "No, ma'am. That wouldn't be right," he said, standing in the aisle, meeting Agatha's friend face to face.

"Oh, come on. We've been together for a solid week, haven't we, Belle?"

"Sure, whatever you say." But Len remained standing, confused by the unspoken language the girls seemed to share.

"Where've you been, Belle?" Agatha asked "I want you to meet Len Ryan. He's from Bladen County, too."

Belle eased into her seat, twisting her bottom seductively over the armrest, never taking her eyes off Len. She was tiny for a grown girl, but she was dressed up to beat the band in one of those skinny little dresses like his mother had been wearing, and she had on a hat with the brim turned flat up just over her eyes. "Where in Bladen County?" she asked, wiggling her little finger, flashing a shiny ring.

"Colly."

"Colly Swamp?" she teased, clicking her chewing gum noisily.

Len knew a couple of girls like her. Real smarty-pants. "Yeah, I live down 'air in the swamp with a bunch of alligators and possums." They all laughed. Being a comedian had gotten him out of stickier situations. "I only get dressed up like this once every year or so to run up to Boston and see my momma." The girls laughed again.

"I'll bet you're so backwoods you don't even know where Bandeaux Creek is," Belle said.

"I'll bet I do. It's just the other side of Cotton Cove."

"How about that. What're you doing on the train?"

Len grinned. "Like I told you, I come out of the swamp once a year to go up to Boston. Momma wouldn't have it any other way."

Belle studied him for a moment. "Who's your mama?"

"She's a Corbinn. Married my pa, Tate Ryan."

"You're Cousin Maggie Lorena's boy, aren't you?" she asked, unaware that Agatha Evans was staring incredulously at her.

"You two are related?" Agatha asked Belle.

Len answered. "She's my mama, if that's what you mean."

Belle didn't remember the exact details, but she'd overheard the talk. Her mother, Eva McBryde, and Maggie Lorena Ryan were second cousins who'd gone to Salemburg Academy together as young girls.

"How'd you know?" Len asked Belle. "Are we kin or something?"

"On the Moreland side, I think. I'm Belle McBryde."

"Well, I'll be."

"Your mama *is* the one who was burned out twice and the only thing they salvaged both times was her trunk, isn't she?"

Len was aghast. *What was she getting at?* "'Scuse me. I'd better get back to my seat," he said.

"*Sorreee.* I didn't mean to bring up something unpleasant," Belle said.

The train lurched suddenly, sending Len tumbling down the aisle, grabbing for something to hold onto. Several passengers reached out to catch him, but he hit the floor with a thud. A man helped him up. "You'd better stop courting and get back in your seat, young man," he said.

Agatha and Belle were unable to stifle their giggles. "It's not funny," Len said, getting into his seat.

Agatha reached through the gap in the seats and nudged him. "I'm sorry, Len."

"Forget it. I'll talk to y'all later." He closed his eyes and thought how wonderful it would be to be home again. The first thing he intended to do was ask his Pa what Belle McBryde was talking about. Len hadn't even been born when the first house burned, but he remembered the second time—the pretty little house Aunt Mag had given them burning to the ground. They'd stood out in the oak grove, helplessly watching. He could remember how hot the fire was, how brightly it lit up the sky—how sad Mama was. Lizzie had come and gotten him and Will, taken them across the field to her house and made them pallets on the floor out of quilts. She made them stay there while Mama went to Aunt Mag's house and Papa slept in the barn. Lizzie said Mama had gone all to pieces. Was it because she loved Aunt Mag's house so much, or was it because she'd almost lost her trunk? He'd never thought much about it— not until now.

Len made his way back to the men's room, barely glancing at the sleeping girls as he passed. In a small tin mirror above the basin, he rubbed his hand over his face, hoping that his whiskers were starting to grow out again. He bared his teeth and wiped them with his handkerchief, smoothed his tousled hair. The prettiest girl—the one named Agatha—had liked him. He could tell. And he'd felt that stirring in his loins that signaled something new in his life. Only a girl did that to him. Back in his seat, he settled in feeling tired but older than he had when he left Colly. Was it the new clothes, or had he really grown up?

12

Affairs of the Heart

E VANGELINE OPENED THE DOOR, EXPECTING TO FIND
one of the traveling salesmen who stopped by the plantation every week
or so. They'd found her husband, Lance, to be a willing customer for their
fine silks and beadware. Was there nothing too good, too costly for her? But
to her surprise, the young farmer who stood in the doorway with a basket
of strawberries was the young man who lived on the small farm adjoining
Cranewood. "I brought you some strawberries from Mama's garden. She
said you might want to make some jam with 'em."

How could she tell him that she no longer "made jam"? Her servants did
that while she rested and whiled away her days reading and sewing on
the large veranda overlooking Lake Catherine. Carrying Lance's child was
all that he required of her—that and the warmth of her body in the rice-
planter bed.

Greeting the young farmer at the door, she was reminded how close she'd
come to living in the log cabin where he now dwelled alone, a cabin he'd
never admit he'd built for her, but she knew he had. Oh, yes, he'd vied for her
attention, but he was no match for Lance Perdeau, who on their wedding
night had ravished her to her heart's content on the finest linens from
England. They'd bathed first by candlelight in the porcelain tub, then,
smelling of lilac water and sweet soap, fallen into the down-filled bed and
explored each other's deepest secrets . . .

Snapping out of her reverie, she thanked the farmer and asked him in,
politely steering him back towards the kitchen to keep his muddy shoes off
the parlor rugs. "Mama said she'd make you a squirrel pie the next time I

bagged some," he said. "Weather's too warm right now. Need cold weather to go squirrel hunting," he said. As if I cared, thought Evangeline.

~~*Suddenly*~~ *Unexpectedly, Evangeline heard the jingle of Lance's livery.* [Not his but his horse's livery!] *But he was not to arrive before the following Monday. He would be furious to find the farmer here. They had been childhood enemies. Oh, dear, sighed Evangeline. Her heart could not bear to hurt the farmer more. "Quickly, Lance is home, you* must *go!" she said. Thank goodness he had not brought his wagon, she thought, as he dashed off into the woods along the lake. Lance might have . . .*

Maggie plugged away at the revisions, while Genie continued to turn up more and more corrections and additions. "This could go on forever," Maggie said. "It doesn't even sound like me anymore."

"Of course it does. No one but Maggie Lorena Ryan could have written *Evangeline*."

"I should have seen all of these things when I was writing it."

"No, that's my job. I'm the editor and you're the writer," Genie said, looking every bit the part, dressed in a white starched shirt and a long tan skirt, dark braids pinned loosely up on her head and a yellow pencil stuck behind her ear. She obviously loved what she was doing, and at times Maggie felt like turning the manuscript over to her and saying *here, you do it!* "We need each other, don't we?" Genie said, bringing Maggie back to the moment.

"Genie, have you ever been down South?"

"No, I haven't. And from what I hear, I wouldn't like it very much. They don't cotton to niggers down there, do they?"

Her words stung Maggie to the core. She'd never seen Genie riled up. "Some of my best friends are Negroes," she said.

"Oh, you mean the ones who work for you, the old black Joes?" Genie's hands were on her hips, and she wagged her head back and forth while her wiry hair held firmly in place. She was beautiful, Maggie thought, truly beautiful with her nutmeg skin and flashing eyes.

Maggie blushed. "Yes, I mean people like Lizzie and Uncle Freddie."

"See there! 'Uncle' Freddie," she accused, pointing her finger close to Maggie's nose. "Is he your uncle?"

"No, it's just a show of respect."

Genie turned away. "Respect? Hmmph!"

"Wait, you don't understand, it's all changing, Genie. It really is," Maggie said, trying her best to think of a reasonable argument.

Genie smoothed her hair and patted the bun at the nape of her neck. Evidently she'd heard that before. "No, honey, the only changing that's being done is here, up north, and that's where I intend to stay. Maybe in another hundred years—but I'll be dead then."

———

BY THE FIRST OF MARCH, MAGGIE WAS ONLY halfway through her manuscript. The process of rewriting was not only exhausting, it undermined her confidence in her work. The story had flowed out of her like molten lava at the outset; now it seemed rigid and forced. Genie had crossed out many of her favorite paragraphs and suggested she insert others that Maggie felt did not sound like her. To make matters worse, Henry brought home a newly published novel several times a week, explaining to Maggie that he wanted her to know the competition. In addition to Willa Cather's latest, she'd read Sinclair Lewis's *Main Street,* and Henry had promised that she'd be one of the first to read Scott Fitzgerald's new novel that was due out soon. Why would anyone want to read her book when there were so many good books already out there?

———

EVERY WEEKDAY MAGGIE WALKED with Henry to the Warren-Montgomery office on Berkeley Street. Henry was determined to lose weight, and Maggie found that stretching her legs had helped trim down her figure too. The walks were invigorating to say the least, the temperature hovering around freezing even in the early spring. With her advance Maggie had bought a long, fur-collared woolen coat and a pair of high-topped boots with thick rubber soles. She felt that she looked like the typical Bostonian instead of the county woman who'd arrived in late October. Abigail had invited her to her bedroom one afternoon and given her several dresses and a suit that she said no longer fit. Another stack of clothes lay on the bed. "Go through these and see what you can wear. I'll give the rest to Marcie." The good life, it seemed, was affecting Abigail's figure as well as Henry's.

"I declare, Abigail, these things are hardly worn. Are you sure you want to give them away?"

"Of course I do, dear. Henry is such a spendthrift. Every time he goes down to New York, he comes back with boxes of things from those exclusive stores along Fifth Avenue. There is no way that I could ever wear them all."

Maggie held up a satin blouse that still had the tags on it. "But you've never even worn some of them. Won't he mind that you're giving them away?"

"He suggested I give you some things. Henry knows I'll never wear everything in my closet, but he adores shopping for me. Every now and then he brings something I really love."

"You sure are lucky. I don't remember Tate Ryan ever buying me a thing."

"Yes, I am very fortunate," Abigail reflected. She took Maggie's hand, leading her over to the settee in front of the fireplace. "Come and sit down. I've asked Marcie to bring us some tea. You know, I've been thinking how I wish the same for you. That you might find someone you truly adore—someone who worships you. Tate is a wonderful man, but you two don't belong together."

"What in the world are you saying, Abigail?"

"I'm not just thinking of you, Maggie. Tate needs a strong farm woman who really wants to work beside him. And you belong in the city where there are people like you who love music and books."

"I do love music and books, but I'm still just a country woman. There's no way I'll ever change that."

Abigail grabbed her by her shoulders as if she were a stubborn child. "Darling, you're more, much more than that." Maggie tried to look away. "No, look at me! There's divorce. Have you considered it?"

"My stars! I could never get a divorce. Aunt Mag would kill me for one thing," Maggie chuckled.

Abigail sat back on the settee, but she did not give up. "I'm serious. People do it all the time—for lesser reasons. Evelyn Armstrong divorced her husband, Terry, years ago."

"The writer? Do you know her?"

"Oh, yes, but Henry knows her better. They spent their summers together as children in Newport. She was Evelyn Smithson then, a product of old New York society. I mean *old* New York society." Abigail pushed the end of her nose up and sniffed loudly.

"How did you know her?"

"Let's just say that Terrence Armstrong and Mother were well acquainted."

"Mrs. Burchart?" Maggie's thoughts turned to the elegant older woman who had taken her on as her protégée when Maggie played the role of Olivia in *Twelfth Night* at BFU. Although they'd spent many afternoons together on her porch, Abigail's mother had revealed little of her personal life to Maggie. "They had an affair?"

"On the society page they referred to Mother as his consort, not unflatteringly, I might add. Mother *was* a stage actress, and a beautiful one at that."

"Mrs. Burchart never mentioned him to me."

Abigail smiled. "There were lots of things Mother never mentioned. We all put some things away—just as you put things in your trunk."

Outside, the wind howled, causing Maggie to shiver. "Why are you telling me this, Abigail?"

"Because there's more to it, as your Aunt Mag would say." She slipped closer to Maggie. "Look, I've never told Henry about Mother and Terrence Armstrong. Don't ask me why, but it never seemed right. Maybe because he absolutely dotes on Evelyn. He's sent your first three chapters to her and asked her to comment on them."

"He did what?"

"Henry wanted an opinion from someone who did not know you personally, someone who would give him an honest evaluation."

"But Genie . . . . What about Genie? She loves my writing."

"Yes, she does, dear. I do too. But Henry wanted Evelyn Armstrong to look at it. She's very supportive of new writers. You've read her essays on the craft of writing."

Maggie reflected on a day last week when Henry had proudly presented her with a small book. "You read that," he'd said, "and you'll know everything you need to know about writing a story." She turned to Abigail. "Henry loaned me a copy last week."

"You've learned a great deal since you've been here, but Henry is right. There is always more."

Maggie felt her confidence slipping again. Was Henry disappointed in her? Had *he* even read her manuscript? Didn't he trust Abigail and Genie? Nothing was making sense. "I suppose I have, but I thought I was just about finished," she said. "What if she doesn't like it?"

Abigail had left her seat on the couch and was flitting about the room, rearranging trinkets on the tables, straightening books. "You're taking this far too seriously, Maggie. Henry knows what he's doing. Let's just see what Evelyn Armstrong has to say."

1 3

High Cotton

A LATE SNOW WHITEWASHED THE CITY near the end of
March, the glare of it somewhat brightening the dark, dreary
days. Maggie wondered if she would ever become accustomed to
the weather in Boston. Back home it would already be warm, the
pastures lush with bright green wheat and rye, the woods lit up like
Christmas trees with yellow jasmine. Here in Boston there wasn't
enough sun to warm the poor little sparrows, much less bring spring
along. On the occasional day that the sun burned through the over-
cast, the streets turned into a slushy mess, only to refreeze the following night into the same dark gray as the sky. Maggie hated
Boston weather as much as she loved the city.

Every weekend Abigail planned at least one festive occasion
out. They attended a musical concert at the Majestic Theatre, several plays at the Shubert, and, most thrilling of all, moving picture
shows at the new Metropolitan on Tremont. The Met was like a
huge palace, with four theaters, each with a marble lobby where
patrons could amuse themselves with table tennis, bridge, billiards,
even dancing.

Maggie gazed up at the pink marble pillars and gold chandeliers
while they waited to see Charlie Chaplin in *The Gold Rush*. "Gosh,
this must have cost millions of dollars to build. I never imagined
anything like it."

"Isn't it wonderful?" Abigail said. "Mother would have loved it."

"Yes, she would have, dear," Henry said.

"Did you know Mrs. Burchart?" Maggie asked.

"Only on the stage. My father was a great fan of the theater, and he took me to plays from the time I was old enough to sit up. I saw the dear lady perform many times." Henry slipped his arm around Abigail. "Had I known then that I would marry her lovely daughter, I would have paid better attention."

Abigail fluttered her eyelids and smiled. "Really, Henry. You are such a romantic. Mother would have adored you, too," she said in a honeyed tone. Maggie thought how strange it was to see Abigail around a man. Fetching and flirtatious, she was out of character from the Professor Adams Maggie had known at BFU, a no-nonsense teacher who dressed in man-tailored suits and sturdy shoes. Had she been playing a role there, or was she playing one now?

———

AFTER BREAKFAST THE NEXT MORNING, Maggie and Abigail sat in the sunny breakfast alcove overlooking a small corner of the back yard, where snow still covered the shrubs and a small mulberry tree. "Before long, the robins will be splashing around in that ice-covered bird bath," Abigail said. "It may not feel like spring, but Henry says all the stores are showing their spring finery. Why don't we go down to Newbury Street and window-shop?"

Maggie was pensive. "Abigail, you seem so happy with Henry. Did you miss having a man around when you were teaching?"

Abigail laughed out loud. "Oh, there were always men around. I just didn't let my students know about my love affairs."

"I don't mean that. I know you went to concerts and things, but your mother was usually with you. After your husband died, did you miss . . . ?" Abigail waited. "Oh, you know what I mean!" Maggie said.

Abigail slipped into the chair closest to Maggie. "Yes, I do know what you mean. I did miss the intimacy of marriage. But, darling, I have friends whose closeness I value more than any husband's. Henry fills a void in my life, but being kissed and embraced is *not* it." She reached for Maggie's hand. "There's something missing in your life, Maggie. I told you how we could change that."

"I don't think you understand. I can't divorce Tate."

"There are other ways."

Maggie blushed. *An affair?* Was Abigail referring to the young Dr. McNamara? Had she seen how he'd looked at Maggie during Christmas? Pushing her chair away from the table, she picked up her breakfast plate and carried it to the butler's pantry. *So, it was not my imagination*, she thought. And she'd felt an attraction to Jon, such an attraction that she'd dreamt of him that night. Was it that obvious? He'd been there only for Christmas Eve and the following evening. They'd strung the lights on the tree and sat drinking Henry's Bristol Cream sherry long after the Montgomerys had retired. Talking so easily with him, she thought how much he reminded her of Wash Pridgen—how they seemed to finish each other's sentences, how they never ran out of things to say, how much she missed him. She'd given him the small book, and he'd brought her a pair of black jet earrings that he claimed he'd picked up at the last minute. It was the most wonderful Christmas she could ever remember, one that passed far too quickly, but she'd forced herself to put it out of her mind. "I'm not sure how you mean that, Abigail," Maggie said.

"Oh, I just meant I think you need a party," she said, bringing the cream and butter into the pantry and placing them in the icebox. "You know, jazz it up a little, have some fun," she said, sloughing off her previous comment. She began dancing the conga around the dining table in her flowered dressing gown, kicking up her heel, glancing seductively over her shoulder.

Maggie laughed, threw off her slippers, and followed, her hands on Abigail's hips. "One-two-three, *la conga!*" they shouted in unison.

Marcie appeared in the butler's pantry, her stout frame filling the doorway. "Well, I never saw the likes of this at the top of the morning," she said in a deep Irish brogue. "You look like two leprechauns 'bout to get into some mischief."

"That's exactly what we are, Marcie," Abigail said. "Conga on into the parlor with me, darling, and I'll tell you my mischievous plan."

The parlor was a seldom-used room that smelled of polish, old upholstered furniture, and Henry's cigar smoke. There wasn't a speck of dust, but an airless mustiness hung over the room. "Mother never allowed the windows to be opened, summer or winter. She hated the dust and the noise from the street. I think that's why she loved our little cottage in Raleigh. It was so much quieter and cleaner there."

Maggie sat on the piano stool waiting while Abigail stretched her legs out on one of the burgundy velvet sofas. Without her makeup, she was more like the college professor giving a lecture. "First of all, you need some glad rags," Abigail said. "You know, something to do the Charleston in."

"I don't need any more clothes, Abigail. I've already spent some of my advance."

"Look dear, gather ye rosebuds while ye may. If you ever go back to North Carolina, you'll wish you had."

"I feel guilty enough as it is," Maggie said. "With all you've given me, I won't need new clothes for years."

"It's a pity Mother's gorgeous gowns are out of style," Abigail said, ignoring Maggie's protests. "Nothing has a waistline anymore. We'll need to get you one of those darling cloche hats."

"But it'll all be wasted. When I go home, I won't need fancy clothes and hats." *When I go home.* Yes, the thought was there; it came and went, but she tried her best not to listen.

"Put going home out of your mind. You need to shimmy and shake," her friend continued. "Let me think. Yes, that's it! Henry told me this morning that Birch Austin is having a reception for that new writer, Cavenaugh Cummings, on the twenty-third. He's sure we'll be invited."

"I haven't heard of him," Maggie said.

"Well, Henry says everyone is talking about him. Evidently he spent quite a bit of time in Hollywood, and his friends give him the fodder he writes about. I understand he's quite handsome."

"That sounds like mighty high cotton to me."

"Oh, he's probably as ordinary as you or me, but just you wait until we finish on Newbury Street. They'll think you're from Hollywood too."

———

THE BIRCH AUSTIN HOUSE ON DARTMOUTH STREET was said to be one of the most elaborate in Back Bay. They had taken a cab and were disembarking beneath a porte-cochère with elaborate wrought-iron gates on either end. Henry said he had known Birch since they were boys at Andover. "Congressman Austin named all of his sons after trees on the property," he explained.

"Isn't that strange?" Abigail commented.

"Not if you'd known his old man," Henry said. "He was quite the botanist. Wrote several books on the subject."

"But he made his fortune in paper mills. Isn't that ironic?"

"Yes, dear. Birch is an enigma also. When he inherited this house, we thought it was ridiculously large, but he added a four-story tower and put in an elevator," Henry said. "The entrance used to be around on the other side, but Birch had John Sturgis design a new one so he could bring guests up the elevator to the second floor."

"Why on earth would he do that, Henry?"

"You'll see."

They arrived on the second floor, where three different maids took their coats. Henry gave two cards to the butler, who escorted them to a grand staircase that descended into a large tiled hall. Maggie looked out over the crowded floor below, the beaded and bejeweled gowns reflecting the light from three huge chandeliers. "Mr. Henry Marchand Montgomery, escorting Mrs. Montgomery and Mrs. William Tate Ryan," the butler called out loudly. Maggie almost fainted, until she realized that hardly anyone turned to look.

As they descended the staircase, a distinguished-looking gentleman parted from the crowd and made his way towards them, extending his hand to Henry. "Henry, old boy. I see you've brought your daughters along."

Henry took his host's hand and slapped him on the back. "Flattery will get you nowhere with these lovely girls. They are much too modern to fall for that old line." Maggie burst out laughing. It had been so long since she had been called a girl that it struck her funny bone. "I take that back, Birch," Henry said with mock sincerity. "Obviously, you have amused Mrs. Ryan."

"My dear, welcome to our humble abode," Birch said, kissing her hand and making a deep bow.

Maggie stifled another giggle and made a slight curtsy. "I'm pleased to make your acquaintance, Mr. Austin."

"Birch, my dear, just Birch." He turned quickly to Abigail, taking her hand. "You are lovely this evening, Abigail. Just as lovely as your mother in her prime. Welcome."

As they made their way around the room, Abigail whispered to Henry. "You didn't tell me he knew Mother."

"Everyone knew Vanessa Burchart, darling. And, he speaks for them all when he says you are equally lovely."

Maggie gazed about, hoping to spot the illustrious guest of honor. Small tables surrounded by elegantly dressed men and women dotted the floor of the grand ballroom. At the far end of the hall a band of twenty or more musicians played jazz tunes continuously. Wearing the new amethyst-colored silk dress purchased on her shopping spree with Abigail, Maggie captured her share of glances from the men in the crowd. Beaded all over with a fringe of matching beads along the hem, it clattered softly when she took a step. Her pumps and the cloche hat matched perfectly. Abigail had chosen a dress of black and silver sequins featuring a deep cowl neckline in the back. "Everyone's staring at you, Maggie," Abigail said. "Would you like a cigarette?"

"What?"

Abigail laughed. "I thought that would make you smile."

"I declare, Abigail. I thought you'd lost your mind."

The orchestra returned from a break and began tuning up. "Pretend you're at a hoedown in Onslow County, just having fun," Abigail whispered. "Maybe someone will ask you to dance."

"My stars, I'd die if they did, but it's not likely with a jazz band. Don't they know how to play a waltz?"

"I doubt it in this day and time," Abigail said, perusing the room of tastefully dressed literary aficionados, looking for someone notable to point out to Maggie. "There's one of Henry's favorite agents—the best in New York, he says." Suddenly, she saw Henry's nephew coming down the steps, waving off the butler. "Henry, there's Jonathan."

"Yes, I believe it is." Henry caught his nephew's eye and gestured to him to come over. "Look here, Jon, we didn't know you were back in town. You could have joined us for dinner."

"Sorry, Uncle Henry. I came back yesterday. Saw Mrs. Austin in the hospital corridor today and she insisted I come. I thought you'd be here, but it was too late to let you know I was coming."

"Well, we've been waiting to hear you've finished your residency. You remember Maggie Ryan?"

"How could I forget?" he said, approaching Maggie and Abigail.

"Jon, dear. Give us a kiss," Abigail said. "We had no idea you were back."

He kissed Abigail, then turned to Maggie, surveying her costume in one long glance. "Wow," he said, before taking Maggie's hand to kiss. "The loveliest ladies north of the Mason-Dixon line, to be sure." He bowed slightly to each. "*Doctor* Jonathan McNamara, at your service."

Maggie blushed, feeling like a schoolgirl. Jon was even more attractive than she'd remembered. He smiled as they shared a secret of Christmas past. "It's nice to see you," she said, smiling back. What was it about him that made her want to take his arm and lead him away from the crowd, to be completely alone with him? She'd felt it then, at Christmas. It wasn't a sexual feeling, at least not one she'd ever experienced before. She simply felt a oneness with him, as if they'd known each other for a very long time— as if they'd shared other things, unspoken things. It was a wonderful feeling.

"I was afraid you'd have finished with your work and gone home," Jon said.

"Never," Abigail interceded. "We prolonged her stay until you returned."

Jon was still holding Maggie's hand, staring into her eyes as if to read her thoughts. He looked freshly scrubbed, but carried none of the shaving scents that were so popular among men in Boston. "Abigail did promise to keep you until I came home. I would have been heartbroken had she not," he said in a beguiling tone.

Maggie gently pulled her hand away, glancing at Abigail. "And I thought you were keeping me here to work on my revisions," she half-teased. "I'm much obliged either way, Doctor McNamara."

"Have you forgotten so soon that I gave you permission to call me by my given name—fine doctor that I am now?" He laughed at his own joke, a trait Maggie remembered from their Christmas meeting. She tried not to stare, but on several occasions when he'd invaded her thoughts, she couldn't recall the exact color of his eyes. Yes, they were hazel, and his hair more blond than she'd remembered.

"Have you finished your surgical residency, my boy?" Henry asked.

Jon turned attentively to his uncle, giving Maggie further opportunity to observe him. "I'm finished at Johns Hopkins. Next week I begin a stint at Massachusetts General. Who knows where I'll go from there." Exuding confidence, he folded his arms and rocked a little as if meditating on his good fortune at being in their presence.

"My goodness," Maggie said. "I thought a doctor went into practice as soon as he finished medical school."

Jon grinned. "No, it's a little more complicated today. There's so much going on in medicine. But I want to know about you. Look, I know a great little place not far from here where we can all sit at a quiet table and talk."

"No, no, my boy," Henry said. "I'm in no mood to spend the night in the jailhouse. They've been raiding those speakeasies left and right. Haven't you heard?"

"Darling, that's the fun of it," Abigail piped in.

Jon studied Henry, obviously noting his pallor. "Another time, Uncle Henry, when you're feeling better."

"Now don't go practicing your profession on me. I feel perfectly fine."

Jon looked skeptical, but he turned to Maggie again. "So, tell me, how are things going?"

"Not much to tell right now. I'm still working on revisions."

"Henry's really excited about Maggie's novel," Abigail said. "Aren't you, Henry?"

"Yes, yes, excited, dear," he said with a brief bow. "Now, if you'll excuse me, I'm going into the billiards room and smoke my cigar. Jon, would you get the ladies a cup of punch? That blasted juice is sickeningly sweet. Needs a good shot of brandy."

The two men took off in different directions. "Listen, they're playing the Charleston," Abigail said. All eyes turned towards a man and woman descending the grand staircase, both attired completely in white. "Mr. Cavenaugh Cummings and Miss Gracie Gabor," the butler called out. Every eye turned towards the couple.

"He looks a little like Rudolph Valentino, doesn't he?" Maggie said. "Who is the woman?"

"I've never heard of her," Abigail said, "but she looks like a movie star."

Cummings and Miss Gabor were instantly surrounded by a

crowd, each person carrying a copy of his book. The young woman looked overwhelmed until someone took her arm and led her away. "One of those silent stars, I imagine," Abigail commented. "They usually aren't very good with the press. These things are managed carefully to get the most attention possible, but only the right kind of attention." She looked around for the publisher's book table. "We'd better get our books. You watch, he'll slip out in an hour or so."

"I was wondering why everyone rushed over to him before he had a chance to visit a little."

Abigail squeezed her arm. "Take some notes, dear. One of these days *you'll* be signing books." The comment took Maggie aback because it was one of the first really encouraging things Abigail had said about publishing her book since she'd arrived in Boston.

Jonathan disappeared shortly after he'd brought their drinks, leading Abigail to surmise that they might find him asleep in a chair. "Poor darling, he's always exhausted."

"I guess so," Maggie said, taking a sip of her punch. "He told me he seldom sleeps in his own bed at night. It's usually a cot at the hospital."

"Did you notice?" Abigail asked, smiling.

"Notice what?"

"He's spiked our punch."

———

MAGGIE WAS INTRODUCED TO ONE DIGNITARY after the other all evening, but they hadn't gotten anywhere near Cavenaugh Cummings. She'd just about given up when she saw the author excuse himself from a group of admirers and make his way towards her. She glanced over her shoulder to see if his attention was on someone else. No—he was coming directly towards her. Abigail was oblivious to his approach, engrossed in conversation with a woman she knew from college days.

"Hello, there. I just wanted to come see how y'all are doing ovuh heayuh, Miss Maggie Lorena," he drawled, offering his hand.

Maggie smiled. She knew he was making fun of her Southern drawl, but since she'd been in Boston, she learned to laugh along with the funmaker. "Mr. Cummings, I can't believe it's y'all coming over here to a poor little country girl from North Carolina. Are we acquainted?"

Cummings laughed loudly and brushed a black curl away from his forehead. "I'm sorry, Mrs. Ryan. Henry Montgomery was just explaining your reason for being in Boston. I couldn't resist the urge."

"I reckon I thought you were an actor instead of a writer," she quipped.

"Forgive me," he said, making a slight bow. "My mother was from South Carolina and that Southern twang comes quite naturally."

"Twang?" she asked, deciding that this overdressed mannequin was a smart aleck as well.

To her surprise, Cummings took her elbow and leaned in closer. "Montgomery says he hopes to publish your novel within the year. Congratulations, but I wanted to give you a little advice. Don't let any of those old fogeys like Evelyn Armstrong get hold of it. They'll tear it to pieces."

Maggie shrank back a little. "What makes you say that?"

"Oh, just something I overheard Henry Montgomery say."

"Thank you kindly, Mr. Cummings. I believe I can trust Mr. Henry to do the right thing." She held out her copy of his book. "I'd be much obliged if you'd sign my copy."

Cummings reached into his pocket for a handkerchief, carefully wiped his hands, and retrieved an expensive-looking fountain pen from a pocket inside his coat. When he had signed his name in an elaborate scrawl, he snapped the book shut. "Remember what I said."

———

HENRY, A COPY OF CUMMINGS'S BOOK IN HAND, came to announce that it was time to leave. "Wait," Abigail said, "I didn't get to talk to him. I want him to sign my book."

"They've gone now, but I have one for you." He opened the book to the frontispiece. "See, just for you, dear."

"Thank you, darling. I'm afraid I missed half of the party while talking with Barbara. We hadn't seen each other since Radcliffe."

"If you ladies don't mind, I have an early appointment tomorrow and I don't want to oversleep." Henry said.

"All right, dear, but we should say good night to Jon."

"I've asked him to dinner tomorrow evening," he said, taking them each by the elbow and leading them toward a door on the lower level. "Come, the cab is waiting."

Once they were all bundled into the taxi, Maggie had a chance to quiz Henry about her encounter with the author. "I told him about you, Maggie. He's quite fond of the South. Said he might settle in North Carolina one of these days."

"He doesn't have a very good Southern drawl."

"Don't tell me he pulled that one on you," Abigail said.

"He really is rather unpleasant," Henry said. "I suggested that he send an inscribed copy of his book to Evelyn Armstrong. She *is* the grande dame of American writers at present, even if she is living in Paris. He said it would be far too modern for her. Hrrumph! Evelyn is as modern as they come. He'd do well to have her endorsement."

"The party was rather boring, wasn't it, dear? If I hadn't seen Barbara and Jon hadn't been there, Maggie and I wouldn't have known another soul."

"These things are always rather boring," Henry said glumly.

"I imagine it doesn't take much to bore Mr. Cummings after Hollywood," Maggie said. "Do you think he lives the life of a movie star? He certainly dresses like one. And Gracie, whoever she was." Henry did not reply.

"Henry?" Abigail said. "Maggie asked if you think Cummings lives the life of a movie star?"

"That's all right," Maggie said. "I think he's asleep."

When they reached Upton Street, Abigail patted Henry's face, trying to rouse him. "Darling, wake up. We're home."

"Maybe Jon spiked his punch, too," Maggie laughed, unaware of the magnitude of Abigail's concern.

"No, I think he's passed out."

Maggie reached for Henry's hand. "He's cold as ice."

The driver pulled the cab up in front of the Montgomerys' brownstone. Conscious of the conversation and the rustling about in the back seat, he turned and asked the ladies if something was wrong. "My husband has passed out. Please, take us to 612 Union Park."

"Somebody probably slipped him a mickey. He'll just have to sleep it off, lady."

"No, that's not it at all," Abigail snapped. "Just take us to Union Park."

I 4

Too Many Puddings

WITH THE HELP OF THE TAXI DRIVER, Henry Montgomery was put to bed in his old room. "Jonathan says no one else has slept there since Henry moved out and he moved in," Abigail said. In the parlor, she sat down in a chair covered in gold brocade fabric. The decorative trim around the bottom was torn into shreds. Abigail laid her head back on the chair and closed her eyes. "I can't believe this is happening," she said.

"Don't worry. I'm sure Henry will be all right," Maggie said.

"No, Jonathan said it was a stroke. There's not much he can tell until Henry comes around." Abigail leaned forward, putting her head in her hands. She had removed her shoes, and the black beaded dress was twisted and rumpled. "I don't know what to do. I telephoned Marcie." She looked down distractedly at the torn fringe. "Look at this chair. Henry's beagle, Charlie, did that when he was a puppy."

"What happened to Charlie?"

"Henry said he was a carriage chaser first, then it was automobiles. He was run over by the man across the street. On purpose, Henry said. That man hated Charlie because he always chased his car."

Their conversation seemed mundane and pointless under the grievous circumstances. Abigail was beside herself with worry, and Maggie did not know how to help her. "I'm not doing you a bit of good just sitting here," Maggie said, getting out of her chair. "I'll walk over to the Upton Street house and change clothes—bring you something comfortable to put on."

———

IT WAS AFTER MIDNIGHT WHEN MAGGIE RETURNED. The streets had been very dark, lit only by a feeble gas jet in widely spaced streetlamps, and she'd had the feeling that someone was following her. Safely back in the house, she listened for Abigail, for voices, hoping that Henry was resting and Jonathan with her. She heard noises in the kitchen downstairs and found her way to where Jonathan was making coffee.

"Come in, Maggie. I'll have a pot ready in just a few minutes. I think I must have coffee in my veins, I drank so much in med school."

"How's Mr. Henry?"

"He's resting. Abigail lay down across the bed and fell asleep. I left her there. She's going to need her rest too."

"Do you know what happened?"

Jonathan turned toward her, and in the bright overhead light of the kitchen he looked older than she'd thought. His face was deeply lined, and there was very little hair on the back of his head. "Uncle Henry's had a pretty bad stroke. I don't know if he'll come out of it at all," he said, all business now, something she had not seen before.

"He hasn't looked well, but . . . "

"I recognized that something was wrong earlier this evening. I'd planned to take a better look at him—ask some questions when I came over for dinner. Too late for that now," he said, apparently regretting the lost opportunity. He poured Maggie a cup of black coffee and offered her sugar and milk. "These things don't just happen all of a sudden. There are symptoms that lead up to it."

"He was seeing Dr. Conrad right regularly," Maggie said.

"Oh, yes, Dr. Conrad. That old fogey wouldn't recognize a case of chicken pox if he saw one!"

"Really, Jon, I think Abigail would have done something if . . . "

"No one could tell Uncle Henry anything. He is as hardheaded as they come," he said, reflecting momentarily. "It runs in the family."

Maggie smiled at his attempt to lighten the situation. "Are you sure it was a stroke?"

"Oh, yes, no doubt. I imagine a clot broke loose and went to his brain." He took a long sip of his coffee and put the cup in the sink. "Look, please make yourself comfortable. I have to get back up there. Try and overlook my kitchen mess. I haven't hired a housekeeper yet."

"You go on," Maggie said. "Don't worry about me, but please call me if there's anything I can do."

When he'd left, she discarded her coffee and filled a kettle with water for tea. Adding hot water and some powdered soap to the dishpan in the sink, she recalled the dishwashing chore in the camp house. The water was always cold before she finished, and the strong soap made her hands red and raw. She had nice fingernails now, polished and filed smooth.

Something caught her eye on the sill of the small window above the sink. A man's wedding band. Maggie dried her hands and held the ring to the light. The inscription on the inside read *Forever yours AJM. Forever,* thought Maggie. Forever was a long time.

———

ABIGAIL PADDED INTO THE KITCHEN in her stocking feet, looking somewhat dowdy in the cotton house dress Maggie had brought from home. "I'm sorry, Maggie. I fell asleep. You must be exhausted. You haven't had a wink of sleep."

"I'm wide awake, Abigail. Would you like some tea?"

"No, but let me look in Jon's icebox. I'd love a glass of milk." She opened the bottom of the icebox and turned her head in disgust. "Whew! Jon needs to do something here," she said, closing the door quickly.

"He said he hadn't had a chance to get a housekeeper."

"Poor Jon, his wife died in childbirth. The baby, too. That's when he decided to go into medicine."

"I wondered—he seems a little old to just be getting out of med school. But I didn't want to pry."

"I think Jon's about forty, but I'm not sure," Abigail said, drawing a glass of water at the sink. She took a few sips and set the glass down and turned to Maggie, suddenly tearful. "I don't know what this means, but Jon says that Henry may never recover completely."

Maggie was on her feet, her arms around Abigail. "Yes, he will. I know he'll be just fine," she lied. "I just know it."

Neither of them had heard Jon's footsteps. "No," he said, almost as softly as his quiet approach. "I'm afraid not."

The two women looked at him but said nothing. The doctor assumed his clinical tone again. "Uncle Henry has passed. There was nothing else I could do." He held his arms out for Abigail, who swooned into them just as he'd expected.

"Oh, Jon," Abigail sobbed. "It can't be. He was going to the Greenbrier to rest. He had so many things he wanted to do."

Tears were in Jon's eyes, and Maggie closed hers, refusing to witness the pain they both were experiencing, afraid of conjuring up her own pain of losing Wash, then her Yancey. She tried to picture Henry as she'd last seen him only hours ago. He'd appeared to be irritated, disgruntled. She'd thought it had to do with some unpleasantness in his business.

Jon sat Abigail down in a kitchen chair while Maggie drew her a glass of water. "I need to get in touch with Dr. Conrad. He was out when I called last night."

"Marcie will go for him. She knows where he lives," Abigail said, somberly. Turning to Maggie, Jon asked if she would mind going to break the news to Marcie.

"No, I want to see Henry, then I'll go with Maggie," Abigail said. "Let me tell Marcie. I think she loved him as much as I did."

———

AFTER THAT ABIGAIL WAS IN A STATE OF SHOCK for days, unable to eat or manage the slightest chore other than bathing and dressing. Marcie treated her like a child, cutting her food into small bits, preparing only the foods Abigail preferred the most. "She'll go t'pieces like she done when her poor mother died, if I don't. She's not as strong as she looks," Marcie said.

Unaccustomed as she was to burial services in the city, Maggie found herself in charge of most of the arrangements. Henry's mother had been Catholic, attending Mass every day of her life at the huge Cathedral of the Holy Cross on nearby Washington Street. His father had come from a staunch Baptist family who had been generous contributors to the Concord Baptist Church just off Montgomery Street, where Henry was born. Although they were married in the Baptist Church, Jon said, his great-aunt and uncle had an understanding: she could go to her church, but the children would be raised as Baptist. A strong Irishwoman, Henry's mother had taught him and his sister their Catholic prayers anyway, and how to say the rosary. She saw to it that they learned their catechism by forbidding them to leave their rooms on Saturday morning until they could recite their lessons. Henry's father was none the wiser, according to Jon. "I often heard him say after his father died that he was as much a Catholic as a Baptist," his nephew said. "And I don't think there's ever been any question as to where Uncle Henry's funeral would be held or where he'd be buried."

"At least I'm familiar with the Baptist hymnal," Maggie said to Jonathan. "I'd die if I had to make plans for a Catholic funeral."

"You wouldn't have to worry about a thing in the Catholic church," Jon said. "Mass is Mass, and the priests do it their way regardless."

"Your mother was Henry's sister?"

"Yes, the tenth child. 'Immigrant Irish,' they called us." He smiled. "We have the reputation of coming into the South End and taking over."

"I don't know much about Catholics," Maggie said. "I've never met one before."

Jonathan roared with laughter. "Well, we won't bite you. Although I'll bet you've heard that our priests do all kinds of things."

"I declare, Jon. You make us sound so backward."

"I'm sorry, Maggie. I couldn't resist. I was in Raleigh once and attended Mass at the Sacred Heart Cathedral. It's the smallest cathedral in the country. A beautiful little stone church with only a handful of parishioners, compared to the Catholic churches in Boston."

"I went to school in Raleigh—a long time ago," Maggie said. "My sponsor, Mr. John Pullen, took us by the wagonload to the Fayetteville Street Baptist Church."

"I know. Abigail told me you were one of her students."

"What were you doing there?"

"I was at Davidson College. One of my classmates invited me home for the holidays," he said, reminding Maggie of her brief but full days at BFU—of Wash Pridgen. Jon perked up, smiled at her. "I wish I'd met that pretty little red-haired girl riding in a wagon then," he said.

"You probably wouldn't have looked twice. There were lots of girls at BFU prettier than me—more your age, too. How old are you, anyhow?"

Jon laughed. "Does it matter?"

"Not really, I reckon. But I think I've got a few years on you."

"Do tell. I should have known, I've always been attracted to older women."

Maggie studied him. He was tired, no doubt, but she suspected that the deep lines in his face were more likely due to heartache. "There's been a lot of water over the dam for both of us since then, hasn't there?"

"Abigail told you about my wife?"

"Yes, and . . . "

"The baby. Yes, the baby."

"I lost my little boy," Maggie said. "He was seven." They stood looking at one another, acknowledging feelings too unpleasant to voice.

Maggie straightened her dress. "I'll go and get Abigail. The funeral car will be here in five minutes. You'll ride with us, won't you?"

"Of course I will. Uncle Henry was my benefactor. I could never have gone back to medical school if it hadn't been for him."

Wash Pridgen had said the same thing about his uncle in Wilmington. "We all need someone to give us a little push," Maggie agreed. "Aunt Mag did that for me."

"Sometimes we need more than that. Sometimes we need someone to walk with us, to keep us company," Jonathan said, taking her hand in his. "Come, let's go and get Abigail."

———

THE DAY WAS TYPICALLY BOSTON, with gray skies and a cold wind. When they returned to the brownstone following the service, Marcie put out an elaborate luncheon in the dining room. Maggie was introduced to cousin after cousin, plied with question after question, until she felt compelled to escape to the kitchen with Marcie. Genie was there too.

"I don't know how much longer Miss Abigail can manage up there with the likes of those stuffed-shirt Montgomerys," Marcie said. "Mr. Henry was the nicest one o' the whole lot of 'em. Of course his dear mother was a saint." She crossed herself and continued stirring a pot of stew.

"Maggie, you look a bit worn," Genie said. "Why don't you sit down and I'll fix you a cup of tea."

Maggie slumped into a chair at the kitchen table. "I'd be much obliged, Genie."

Genie reached for two china teacups from the breakfront. She spooned loose tea into a matching teapot, and Marcie waddled over to pour in boiling water. "There's teacakes in the jar there. Give her a couple of those, dearie," she said.

They sat at the table and stirred milk and sugar into their tea. "I wish I could go up there and snatch Abigail away and bring her down her with us," Maggie said. "A cup of tea in the kitchen with her women friends is just what she needs."

"She sure looks worn to a frazzle, doesn't she?" Genie said.

"What did you say?"

Genie looked puzzled. "I said she looks worn to a frazzle. Don't you know that word?"

"Of course I do," Maggie laughed. "But I'm surprised that you do. Sounds like something I'd say."

"My grandmother was from the South, honey chile. Why do you think Mr. Henry wanted me to edit your manuscript?" Genie had slipped off her shoes and propped her feet up on one of the wooden kitchen chairs. She leaned back and looked at Maggie. "I could have been your Lizzie's daughter."

"Never," Maggie said, amusing them both for different reasons. "Lizzie wouldn't have put up with you for a minute."

"We've still got a lot of work to do, but without Mr. Henry, I don't know where to begin."

Maggie was startled. "What?"

"Mr. Henry *was* Warren-Montgomery. Mr. Warren hasn't been involved in years, and I don't think Abigail is . . . is up to it." Genie got up and slipped her shoes on. She put her hand on Maggie's shoulder. "Look, let's just get past today. Abigail will know what to do."

Maggie hadn't given her manuscript a thought since Henry died. All of her attention had been turned toward Abigail and making the funeral arrangements. Suddenly, she was overcome with the gloomy realization that without Henry Montgomery, getting her book published was up to Abigail.

"You okay, Maggie?" Genie asked.

"Yes, I'm fine. Do you think anyone will miss me if I just slip up the back stairs and go to my room?"

"No, honey, go on. Jonathan is with Abigail. I'll take this tray up and check on her. You get some rest."

Literary Jargon

"I'LL BET YOU'RE TIRED OF EATING OFF THIS TRAY,"
Maggie said, delivering Abigail's breakfast to her for the third
morning after the funeral. Abigail had refused to come downstairs,
even for her meals. "I'm going to open these drapes now and you'll
see that the sun is shining. Maybe we'll walk downtown to the
office today."

"No, I couldn't bear to look at Henry's desk," Abigail said. "I've
asked Genie to manage without me until my spirits improve."

"How long do you think that'll be?" Maggie knew she was
sounding like Aunt Mag, but that tone had always worked for her.
"You can't just stay closed up in this stuffy bedroom. Here, I'll open
a window." She barely cracked the window when she felt the icy
spring air.

Abigail sat up in the bed and smoothed her tousled hair. "Please
don't lose patience with me, Maggie dear. I couldn't bear it. What
would I have done without you? You have brothers and sisters. I
have no one since Henry is gone."

"Jonathan is someone. All of Henry's family seem to adore you."

"Jon is a dear, but he's a man and he has his work. Medicine is
not the easiest thing, you know. Not today."

Maggie thought of Dr. Bayard back home, of the endless miles
he rode in his buggy to care for everyone from Colly to
Elizabethtown. "I ought to take Jon home with me. We could sure
use another doctor in Bladen County."

"Don't talk of going home yet. Come sit here with me," Abigail said, patting the bed.

Maggie did as she asked, wondering where this conversation was headed. In the past few days, she'd become more and more annoyed by Abigail's self-pity. *The worm has turned*, Maggie thought. *I'm getting a dose of my own self-revolving sentimentality*, a term she'd read in one of Henry's books called *Aberrations of the Mind*. He'd loaned it to her one evening when they were discussing melancholia. "You'd do well to acquaint yourself with personality disorders, my dear," he'd said. "Makes your characters more interesting." Maggie had taken the book to her room and been fascinated with the descriptions, some closely resembling aspects of her own personality.

"Aunt Mag says the best way to overcome grief is to get busy," Maggie said.

Abigail lay back on the pillows and pulled the bedclothes over her head, reminding Maggie more of a child than a fifty-year-old woman. "I'd like you to leave Tate and stay with me for good, Maggie."

"What? I can't hear you with the covers up over your head like that."

Abigail flipped the covers back and sat up straight in the bed. "I want you to stay here in Boston with me—permanently."

Maggie was stunned. Not that she hadn't thought about leaving Tate—staying in Boston.

Tears came into Abigail's eyes. "I know I shouldn't even ask . . . not now . . . not until you and Tate have worked things out." She covered her face with her hands. "I don't know what I'm saying, Maggie. I just know I need you . . . with Henry gone, I . . . . Please don't ever leave me."

"You're just upset. You have a bunch of other women friends. I know you do."

"No, I don't," Abigail whined. "I gave them up when Henry and I were married. Don't you see?"

"I declare, Abigail, you should know that your friends will still be there. I know you write a lot of letters. What about Newport?" Abigail reached out for Maggie's hand. "You could come, too. There'd be parties and all sorts of interesting people. You could write . . . "

Maggie looked at her in disbelief. What was Abigail thinking? "Look, I don't know exactly what I'm going to do, but I reckon I need to find out what's to become of my manuscript before I start thinking about going off somewhere. Genie phoned day before yesterday and said a package had arrived from Evelyn Armstrong. It was addressed to Mr. Henry and she didn't want to open it until you felt up to it."

Abigail thought for a minute. "It must be your manuscript." She reached for her brush on the bedside table. "Ring up Genie and tell her to bring it over right away."

"Now, Abigail, I'm dying to know what she said, but if you're not up to it, I can wait."

Abigail hopped out of bed and pulled on a long white chenille robe. "No, let's do it now," she said, tying the belt about her waist. "What Evelyn Armstrong has to say might make a difference." She started for the door. "Come on, I'll phone Genie myself."

———

GENIE ARRIVED AT THE BROWNSTONE within the hour, package in hand. "I didn't want to bother you until you felt better, Miss Abigail."

Abigail snatched the parcel out of Genie's hands. "I know, dear. I appreciate your thoughtfulness, but this is too important for Maggie."

They watched her tear open the brown paper wrapping and pull a cover letter off the top. After reading it, she slipped the letter into her pocket. "Well, that's that! But what does she know? Cummings warned you that she was behind the times." She handed Maggie the manuscript pages. "Let's just forget about Evelyn Armstrong."

Maggie and Genie stared at her. Genie spoke first. "What did she say?"

"Oh, she just said that Maggie's story might be better serialized in the *Ladies' Home Journal* or the *Companion*." Abigail pushed her hair back and glanced in the mirror. "My goodness. I look a fright." She turned back to them. "The letter was to Henry and it contains a lot of literary jargon about trends and such. Here, Genie, take the letter back to the office and put it on my desk. I'll deal with it later."

"May I read it?" Maggie asked.

"Of course, dear. But why not wait for her letter to you? She said she had written. You should have it in a few days."

Before Maggie could protest further, Genie slipped the letter into her bag and put on her coat. "I need to get back to the office and lock up. Come in on Monday, Maggie, and we'll get to work again."

"Why don't you want me to see the letter?"

"That's not it at all, dear," Abigail said kindly. "Evelyn has written to you personally and I'm sure she will give you the guidance you need. It's just that she was rather blunt with Henry and I don't think it's fair to either one of you for you to read her remarks to him."

"I'd like to see what she said."

"You will, dear. But I think you should see what she has to say to you first. That's the natural order of things."

EVELYN ARMSTRONG'S LETTER ARRIVED at the Montgomery residence on Upton Street the following day. Maggie heard the postman ring and picked up the mail as he dropped it through the slot in the door. "I've got it, Marcie. It's only the mailman," she called out.

The envelope was large, the letter itself written in beautiful, flowing script on heavy ivory parchment. A small book was enclosed.

Paris, France
February 28, 1926

Dear Mrs. Ryan,

I've just finished reviewing the pages from your manuscript *"Evangeline"* sent to me by our mutual friend, Mr. Henry Montgomery. I am duly impressed with your sentence structure & word choices, but I feel that you have much to learn about story-telling. I say this by no means to discourage you, but to guide you. There are many elements to story-telling and the story itself is but one. There were times when I was reading your script that I was truly absorbed in your prose; so much so that I actually forgot where we were in the story.

I suspect that *"Evangeline"* is memoir encased in a happy-ever-after fairy tale. But Love is never so simple, is it? The prince is seldom all charm and wit: sometimes he remains somewhat of a *"frog."* I have been accused of being *"old fashioned,"* of portraying my heroines in a subjective light, subjective to the men in their lives, subjective to society. On the other hand, my dear, with your pen you have dissolved a poor marriage and created a perfect union with such a minimum of angst, that I am afraid only the most naïve romantic would find it believable. From experience, I tell you that nothing contains tighter knots than a poor marriage. No, my dear, a poor marriage is a monster that must be taken by the tail and cast into the sea, but only after one has wrestled it to the ground.

In *"Evangeline,"* you have made the *"thing"* your pet, smoothed its scales & talked sweetly to it. Where is the misery, the wretched pain, the *"breaking"* of the spirit that occurs before the *"thing"* can be tamed? My dear Maggie Lorena, you must try and sell *"Evangeline"* to one of the ladies' magazines, or better still, set it aside as an exercise in learning & begin anew. Something tells me that you have experienced quite a bit in life. Henry says that he & his lovely wife have taken you under their wings for a prolonged stay in Boston. Perhaps their purpose is to free you from the moral coil that entangles you. Trust me, my dear, until that happens, you will never be able to express yourself fully.

I invite you to send me your first three chapters when you have made a new start. To help you along your way to a successful literary endeavor, I *have enclosed my guidebook, "Write It Right the First Time".*

Yours truly,

Evelyn Armstrong

———

MAGGIE FOLDED THE LETTER SLOWLY and replaced it in the envelope. Sun was streaming in the window of her room on the back of the brownstone. In the narrow courtyard below, daffodils were pushing up through the dark soil. She pulled her desk chair over to the window and propped her feet up on the sill, staring out at the mulberry tree, whose swollen buds held the promise of spring. She should be angry. She should be upset, wailing and wringing her hands. Instead she felt calm, at peace with Evelyn Armstrong's words. Hadn't she known all along that *Evangeline* was a fairy tale? Neither Abigail nor Genie would say it, but they knew. Even Henry couldn't be that blatant, couldn't tell her that her book did not have the depth and substance to be on his list. He'd asked Evelyn Armstrong to tell her because it would be impersonal, objective. Armstrong's offer to instruct would soften the blow. Maggie chuckled to herself. Did Henry Montgomery really believe that she was so naive?

Outside, the sky was blue and cloudless, and across the rooftops she saw ships in the harbor. Up till now a journey between Wilmington and Boston would be made by ship or train. Soon it could be by airship. Just yesterday, an article in the *Globe* predicted regularly scheduled airplane flights between Boston and New York within a year. What would it be like, looking down from heaven? She smiled, recalling the dream she'd had long ago of flying to Raleigh on the back of a great white heron.

Big ideas, Aunt Mag had said. Yes, Abigail had put some big ideas in her head. But hadn't she always encouraged Maggie? Hadn't she always wanted Maggie to be all that she could be, just as Aunt Mag had done? But until now, Maggie could not see the difference. Why had it taken this complete failure to make her see that it was one thing to encourage a young, unmarried woman to reach for the stars, but a forty-two-year-old woman, one with a husband and two sons was another.

Abigail tapped on her door. "Maggie, may I come in?" Wearing a brown silk dressing gown, her hair freshly washed and curled, she peeked into Maggie's room. "I thought we might take in a show tonight. You haven't been out since Birch Austin's party. Since Henry . . . "

Maggie didn't budge from her position by the window. "Neither have you," she said.

Abigail stood over her. She looked more as she had in Raleigh. The flirtatious manner she used around Henry had disappeared completely, as had her mourning facade. She was sober, sincere. "Are you all right?" she asked. "Marcie said you picked up the mail. I thought maybe you had gotten a letter."

"From Miss Evelyn Armstrong? I sure did. It's right there on my desk. You may read it, if you want to."

Abigail looked concerned. "What is it, Maggie? What did she say?"

"I expect she said the same thing she said in Henry's letter. She told me I should start over."

"I can't believe she would be so cruel. You're not going to, are you?"

"I reckon I will."

Abigail sat down on a footstool, her hands in her lap, more like the instructor with an insolent student. "You're acting peculiar. Now tell me what this is about?"

Maggie took her feet off the windowsill and stood over Abigail. "I just think Evelyn Armstrong is about the most wonderful, honest person I've ever come across."

"And?"

"And she's right. I need to begin again—make a fresh start."

Abigail stood up, reaching for Maggie's hands. "Maggie, no.

You're giving up too easily. All the work you've put into *Evangeline*. You can't just discard it."

Maggie pulled away, marching to the center of the room where she turned to face Abigail. "I reckon I can if I want to. Why couldn't you tell me outright like Evelyn Armstrong did? The book *is* a silly love story."

"Darling Maggie, you have a gift. A good editor can . . . Genie and I can help you."

Maggie sat down in the chair by the window, gazing at a single bud on the mulberry tree. Spring in Boston was still weeks away. "Maybe that's the best I can do. I should have gone back to college, but I married Tate. I reckon I made my bed."

"Maggie, dearest, you don't need a college education to be able to write well," Abigail said, kneeling beside her. "Look at Eleanor Roosevelt. She's a wonderful writer, but she never finished college. Eleanor is the wife of the governor of New York and she teaches school at Todhunter."

"Do you know her?"

"We have lots of mutual friends in the Women's Trade Union League. I was hoping to take you to the exposition this fall. I know Henry's death has set things back for all of us, but we can begin again—just you and I. We'll get your book published and everything will fall into place."

Maggie stared at her. "What'll fall in place?"

Abigail paced back and forth in front of Maggie, the brown satin dressing gown sweeping the floor each time she turned. "You—me. We can move into Henry's house on Union Square. We'll travel. Go abroad. I'll show you everything."

Maggie rose up out of the chair. "Good gracious, Abigail, that's wishful thinking if I've ever heard it. You make it sound so easy." She hugged her friend and softened her tone. "Please don't think I'm not obliged for all you've done already, but I can't rightly stay on in Boston, not now," she said, walking away, her eyes on Abigail's reflection in the mirror. "I reckon you're just about the best friend I have in the world, but it wouldn't be right. I need to get back home. Like Lenny said, I owe Tate that much."

As soon as the words were out of her mouth, Maggie recognized the truth. She'd stayed long after she knew things were not working out. What life would be like when she got home, what she would do with the rest of her life, she had no idea. She just knew she needed to go. "I expect I'd better see about getting a train ticket to North Carolina."

Abigail rushed to her, grabbing Maggie around the waist from behind, talking to her through the mirror. "You can't go back there. You'll never be happy. You never were. You belong here with me!" Like a frightened child, she tightened her embrace even more when Maggie tried to pry her hands loose. "No, I won't let you!" Abigail said.

"Quit that," Maggie demanded. "You know I can't stay."

Abigail's hands fell loosely to her sides and her chin rested on her chest. "I knew you'd leave me . . . just like Mother . . . like Henry," she said, starting for the door.

"What's gotten into you? You knew I'd have to go home some-time."

Abigail straightened up, regaining some of her composure. "Not after Henry died. I didn't think you could go after Henry died."

"Well, I never said anything like that. Matter of fact, I thought you ought to be getting tired of me. What about all your friends you used to talk about?"

Abigail stamped her foot. "Don't you see, you idiot, it's only *you* that I want." She turned and fled down the hall, slamming the door behind her.

Maggie was flabbergasted. Abigail had the devil in her for some reason.

———

MAGGIE PRAYED THAT JONATHAN WOULD STOP BY later that evening. It had become his habit to every few days, but they never knew exactly when he'd come. At Massachusetts General Hospital, sometimes he worked twenty-four hours at a stretch. When the doorbell rang, Maggie and Abigail were in the parlor listening to the evening news on the radio.

"Jonathan, I'm so glad you're here," Maggie whispered. "She's very upset because I'm leaving."

Jon did not look concerned. "That's understandable."

"Maybe you should give her something."

"Is that you, Jon?" Abigail called out.

"Yes, dear," he said, tossing his coat onto the coatrack hook. "I hope you have a fire going. That wind is ferocious."

"Come on in, Jon. We missed you at supper," Abigail said, lifting her face to receive his kiss.

"You're a little pale, dear. Have you been getting enough rest?"

"I'm fine, Jon. Everybody's leaving me. I don't know what I'm to do."

"Well, I know what you need. Doctor's orders. You need some rest. I'll go up with you and get you settled. I brought a bottle of brandy—a little gift from a patient." He looked at Maggie. "I did miss supper. Maybe Maggie could forage in the kitchen and come up with some victuals for a poor starving resident."

Maggie brushed Abigail's cheek with a kiss. "I can do better than that. I'll cook you some corn bread and fatback. That ought to stave off hunger."

Leading Abigail up the stairs, he shouted, "You can heat up some collard greens too. I'm hungry enough to eat a horse."

Maggie chuckled. She didn't doubt a bit that Dr. Jon McNamara liked collard greens. He was just that kind of fellow who would try anything. On the way down to the kitchen, she thought about how she would miss him when she left Boston. She'd seen Jon almost every day for the last two weeks. He'd make a wonderful doctor with his gentle, persuasive manner. If only she could see her future—if she could know—there might be a place for him in her life.

———

"WHAT HAPPENED?" HE ASKED HER after he had tucked Abigail in for the night.

Starting from the beginning, Maggie told Jon how she had been daunted by all of the revisions. "Genie told me how good it was, but she kept making me change all these things. Henry sent it off to Evelyn Armstrong to see what she thought. She wrote back that I should start all over. I just feel like . . . like maybe the only reason Henry wanted me to come to Boston was to please Abigail." Maggie had never admitted this before, even to herself.

"No, Maggie. Uncle Henry wouldn't have had you come and live here—advance you money if he didn't think your work was worthy of publication."

"Henry would have done anything for Abigail."

"Really, you think so?"

"Jon, I don't know how to say this, but something happened today. Something sort of funny." She took his plate and scraped it in the garbage pail before slipping it into the sudsy water. "I can't explain it. Abigail doesn't want me to leave . . . ever."

He came to stand beside her at the sink, leaning against it to face her. "Well, that goes for both of us."

Maggie blushed. "Now don't you go making this any harder for me. I have a husband and children at home in Bladen County and I have to go. I've already written to Aunt Mag to let them all know."

He walked back to the table and cleared it of the remaining dishes. "I'm aware that you have some unresolved issues waiting for you, but something came up in my life today that I wanted to talk to you about."

"What, Jon?"

"Let's sit down a minute." He pulled a chair out for her and sat down on opposite side of the small table. I've been thinking about where I'd like to settle down—you know open up a practice. Since we talked about my time at Davidson in North Carolina, I've had this terrible longing to go back down South." He reached across the table and took one of her hands, holding only the tips of her fingers. Their eyes met. "You've had something to do with that, you know."

"Jon, I . . . "

"No, don't say anything, not yet. I just wanted you to know what I'm thinking about. I've signed up for some extended work in gastrointestinal surgery—medicine is advancing rapidly—new procedures are being developed as we speak, and I want to be on the forefront—on the top if you will," he said, his eyes gleaming.

"Jon, that's wonderful. I can see how excited you are about medicine." *But what does it have to do with me?* she thought.

"I'll work in the clinic here at Mass General for the next year. I'll be on call night and day—there'll be little time for anything else."

"Probably a good thing you aren't married, isn't it?" she said, an attempt to sound objective. *But what was he getting at?*

"Yes, it is, but someday—in the near future, I hope to marry again—have a home and family, a practice in a small town."

"Well, we certainly could use you down our way!" she laughed. "I think old Dr. Bayard is about worn out. He'd welcome you, to be sure."

He slipped in closer to the table, taking both of her hands in his, their knees touching. "I was thinking about Wilmington—not too far from you, is it?"

"Well, no, but . . . "

"They have a new hospital there. My chief says they're sending out letters, searching for staff, touting the beautiful old historical port city, the beaches."

"Oh, yes, you'd love Wilmington, Jon." She looked at her empty cup to avoid his eyes. "Would you like a little more coffee? Let me get it," she said, going to the stove.

He came up behind her and pressed his cheek to hers. "You don't have to commit to anything, but if you go home and find that you can no longer tolerate . . . " He hesitated. "Maggie, I want you to be a part of my life."

Maggie was speechless. Jonathan McNamara in Wilmington, and he wanted—

"You don't have to say anything," he whispered. "I just wanted you to know what I'm thinking about."

What could she say? He was telling her that he wanted to be near her. There must be dozens of other hospitals who were looking for well-trained surgeons. But Jon McNamara was choosing Wilmington, North Carolina—to be near her, among other things. She turned in his arms, put her face on his chest, wanting desperately the kiss she knew would be inevitable if she had raised her lips to his.

1 6

Promises

MAGGIE LEFT BOSTON AT THE END OF THE WEEK. Abigail, her face long and a stiff smile on her lips, stood between Jonathan and Genie on the station platform. Jon opened up his overcoat and loosened his scarf. "It'll be springtime down south. A good time to go home." His eyes met Maggie's only briefly before he continued with the small talk. "Of course when the weather heats things up about July, you'll wish you were back in New England."

"I'm already doing that," she said wistfully.

"Then why don't you just stay?" Abigail pleaded, her eyes anxious, tearful. She reached for Maggie's gloved hand. "I really want you to."

"Now, Miss Abigail, you know she can't," Genie said. "We all want her to stay, but Maggie knows what she has to do." Maggie had spent several hours in Genie's office explaining her feelings, not of rejection, but of renewal. Genie had encouraged her to go home and try what Evelyn Armstrong had suggested. "Maybe that's your niche," she'd said. "People love those serial stories. You've got a knack for writing romance. I'll bet we'll be reading them in the *Boston Herald* before long."

Abigail had been like a child, pouting, making uncalled-for remarks. "You'll be sorry before you get out of the city," she said. Maggie was tired of trying to reason with her.

"There go your trunks," Jon said. "You don't travel lightly, do you?"

Color rose in Maggie's cheeks. She'd heard that remark before. Except that this time, she had two trunks. The old one that still carried the smell of kerosene on its exterior, and a second, even larger one. "I guess not."

Abigail suddenly came to life, a touch of her old self reappearing. "Don't chide her, Jon dear, Maggie needs her things. And I did give her another trunk. Henry would have wanted her to have some of his books, and there were his clothes . . . "

"Tate will love the suits and pants," Maggie said.

"If the boys were a little older, they could wear Henry's shoes. He loved beautiful shoes." She stared blankly at the steam escaping from the railroad car.

"I guess I'd better get on board," Maggie said. "Jon, will you help me with my satchel?"

Abigail turned away, taking a step before Maggie stopped her. "Aren't you going to give me a hug?" At that, Abigail threw her arms around Maggie and sobbed loudly. "Forgive me. I know you must go. It's just that we've been through so much together. I'll miss you so," she cried.

The fur on Abigail's collar tickled Maggie's nose, but she didn't pull away. "I'll come back, I promise."

"Promise?"

"You know I will, and in the meantime you have all your friends in Boston—Genie and Jon, too." Maggie said in a lighter tone. "Maybe the three of you will get in that yellow Buick and drive down to see us this summer." She glanced at Jonathan. "We're not that far from the beach."

"Yes, I'd like that," Abigail said. "Jon, you'll come, won't you?"

"Of course, I'd love to see Wilmington." He picked up Maggie's satchel. "I'd better get you on board," he said, moving towards the train. "I want to make sure you have a decent seat. My footrest was broken when I last came up from New York, and I was miserable."

Maggie followed Jon, taking his hand as she ascended the steps. Passing the open door of the small toilet, she got a whiff of stale urine, reminding her momentarily that she was about to leave a more civilized world. Jon located her seat and placed her bag under it. "Looks like a pretty good seat," he said, wiggling the back and looking for the footrest. He'd insisted on buying her a first-class ticket, saying it was barbaric in this day and time not to have sleeping accommodations on such a long journey. After her trip up to Boston a few months earlier, she'd welcomed the gift.

Except for a few small presents at Christmas, Len's ticket, and her heavy coat and shoes, the advance that Henry had given her on her arrival was almost intact. Abigail would not take it back and Maggie felt badly about it. The Montgomerys had refused to let her spend a cent when she was in their company. Times would likely be hard as always once she got back to Bladen County, and she knew she'd be glad to have her money.

Jon looked the car over, his eyes darting from the mahogany paneling to the rich upholstery. "This is the Florida Special. It only runs November through May. That's when all the 'snowbirds' fly down south. You'll have stops in New York and Philadelphia. Then, you're straight through to Richmond, where you'll change trains."

"I had to change in Petersburg on the way up," Maggie said.

"I don't know how they make out these schedules, but someone has to be a genius to figure them out. After Richmond, you'll probably stop at every crossing between there and home," he said.

"I don't mind a bit. I love seeing all the little towns. And the train stations, some of them are so quaint," Maggie said. "Besides, I'll be numb by then."

They were standing very close together in the aisle. Most of the other passengers in the car were already in their seats. Since he had told her about the possibility of coming to North Carolina, she'd thought of nothing else. Right now, she wanted him to take her in his arms and hold her, kiss her. "You must be worn out from staying up all night," she said. "I don't know how you do it."

"I don't get tired until I stop," he said, moving a little closer. The look in his eyes was unmistakable, the moment electrifying. She should have been thinking of Tate, renewing her marriage vows; instead she knew she was offering herself to this man body and soul. "They haven't made the last call," he whispered. "Let's sit down a moment."

Maggie slid into the seat, and Jon sat down next to her. "I want to kiss you, you know," he said, his breath warm against her cheek. She raised her lips, wanting his kiss more than anything.

A man stopped in the aisle beside Jon, checking his ticket. "Sorry," the man said with a little wave of his hand. "Not my seat. Go on, say your good-byes."

Jon had not even turned around, but the interruption sobered Maggie. "Jon, there are right many things you don't know about me," she said, her eyes on the seat in front of her. "Mostly, that I'm going back home to something I can't change, no matter how much I may want to."

He leaned closer, and she longed to wrap her arms around him. "I'm not asking for anything—not now. I have no right," he said. "I may not be as cloying as Abigail, but at the moment, I feel the same way she does." He glanced out the window. "I can't bear to think you would not be in my future. On the other hand, I know that you can't be—not until you have a chance to straighten things out." He touched her cheek.

"Your hands smell like rubber gloves," she said.

He sniffed his hand. "No, they don't—you're changing the subject."

"Yes, they do. You're just used to it. Now you'd better get off this train unless you want to take a ride down to New York and back today."

Jon laughed. "All right, I was getting too serious," he said, checking to see if Abigail and Genie had left the platform. "Good, they've left without me." He pulled her into his arms. "I will see you again," he whispered.

"I hope so—someday," she said, the words muffled in his collar. He smelled so clean. His neck was warm, and she longed to stay right there forever.

He kissed her on the forehead as he might a child. "I'll find a way to let you know."

———

RAISING THE FOOTREST AND TILTING HER SEAT BACK, Maggie was aware that her lack of sleep since Henry died had caught up with her. But she slept lightly, Jon's remarks lacing her reverie. Why hadn't she said *no* and been done with it? She was a married woman and she had no right to entertain thoughts of a liaison with Jon. But how could she, when Jon had stirred her passions, her desire to be loved—when he was offering her the life she'd always wanted, the life that Wash had once offered her?

She awoke just as the train entered the tunnel underneath Grand Central Station. It had been dark when she'd come through New York on her way to Boston, and she'd missed the sensation of going underground. As the seats filled, she imagined that many of the men smelling of tobacco were salesmen. At the last minute, her hopes of having the entire seat to herself were dashed when a stout fellow, perspiring heavily, sat down next to her. He was well dressed in a three-piece suit and carried a heavy overcoat on his arm. "Whew! I thought I'd missed the train," he said, wiping his brow.

Maggie nodded and turned to look out the window, feeling the jostle of the train as it began to move. She was not inclined to conversation. Maybe Boston had rubbed off on her.

"How're you, Miss?"

"Pretty good, thank you."

"Where you off to?"

"I'm on my way back to North Carolina."

"Well, how 'bout that? Me, too. I'm from Whiteville. Columbus County. Name's Wooten. J. C. Wooten. Betcha never heard of Whiteville."

"I reckon I have. I'm a little further down the line. Near Atkinson. I'm Maggie Ryan."

"Pleased to meet you. Pender County, huh? Just down the road. I remember going through there on the way to Wilmington."

"Actually, I live in Bladen County, but the depot in Atkinson is nearest our place."

"That's even better."

Maggie closed her eyes, dreading the long hours on the train. Thank goodness she'd change trains in Richmond and Mr. J. C. Wooten would go on to Raleigh, where he'd take the Seaboard to Fayetteville, then the old Yadkin Valley Line to Whiteville. That was the long, tedious route she'd taken on the way to Boston. The stationmaster at Atkinson had told her then that there were so few passengers on the route anymore, he was afraid passenger service would be discontinued.

Wooten removed his coat and stored it on the shelf above. Loosening his tie, he put his head back, ready for a nap. Maggie pulled the book Evelyn Armstrong had sent her out of her bag and opened it to the first page. Wooten sat up. "What's that? Lemme see," he said, reaching over and turning the book his way. "*Write It Right the First Time.* Ooo, that sounds highfalutin'. You must be a teacher or something."

"Sort of," she said, determined to discourage him with as little conversation as possible.

"You look kinda like a schoolteacher."

Maggie chuckled. "I used to be a long time ago." She paused a moment. "What does a schoolteacher look like?"

He smiled. "Well, you know, they look like they know everything. Like they don't have much patience with boys."

"Is that the voice of experience speaking?" she asked, warming to him a little.

"I reckon it is. I never wore a dunce's cap, but I sure sat in the corner a lot for messin' with the girls and such stuff as that. I'm a storekeeper now. Own a general store in Whiteville."

"Mmm, that's nice."

"You kin to any of the Ryans over in Onslow County?"

Maggie perked up. "Why, yes. They're my husband's people. Do you know them?"

"My cousin Clara's daughter married a Ryan boy last month. Let's see, I believe his name was Jimmy." Wooten's face brightened. "Yep, that's it, Jimmy Ryan."

"That'd be my husband's brother's son. I can't believe he's old enough to get married," Maggie said, trying to remember when she'd last seen James's children. Probably at Sally Catherine's funeral. Yancey had been just a baby then, and they'd put off going to visit until it was too late for his grandmother to ever see him. Maggie still felt badly about it, even after all these years. Jasper had loaned them his car, and they'd all gone to Onslow County for the funeral. But Aunt Mag said it was what you did for the living that really counted.

———

MAGGIE LOOKED OUT AT THE LANDSCAPE RUSHING past her window. Would she be able to fall back into the old ways? The thought of a tub bath only once a week reminded her of the times Tate had approached her during the night. She hated the rank smell of a man. Only on Saturday nights after he'd fully bathed had she welcomed his attentions. *What will it be like . . . being with him after all these months?* She could only imagine falling asleep in the arms of Dr. Jon McNamara, the thought reviving the desire she'd felt for him. And he had wanted her in the same way—not with the fire of Reece Evans, but with a need to be filled with love. What would it be like to fill that need?

Katie had written not long ago that Tate and the boys had moved into the unfinished house. She couldn't put the image out of her mind. *The roof is on, but the siding's only half up. He's wrapped brown meat paper around it to keep the wind out. I can't imagine you coming home to that after living in Boston. If I were you, I'd stay gone until he finishes the house.* Katie would never know how close she'd come.

———

J. C. WOOTEN WAS SOUND ASLEEP with his mouth open wide, but he stirred when Maggie tried to slip past his knees. "Excuse me," she said, nudging him.

"What?"

"Excuse me, please. I need to go to the toilet."

"Well, good gracious. I do too!" He stood unsteadily and moved into the aisle. "Ladies first."

The stench in the toilet was unbelievable. *Might as well get used to it,* Maggie thought. She washed her face with her handkerchief and pinched her cheeks to bring up the color. Looking into the small mirror, she attempted to smooth her hair, but the rust-colored curls had a mind of their own. As she slipped out and closed the door, Mr. Wooten was engaged in conversation with another gentleman. Overhearing the words *those evolutionists*, she quickly turned in the other direction. She'd heard enough of that from the pulpit last year. "God or Gorillas" had been the motto of most of the preachers, and Governor Morrison had even banned a high-school biology textbook for mentioning evolution. Maggie found the whole topic confusing and she sure didn't want to debate it with J. C. Wooten. The dining car was probably just a couple of cars ahead, and Maggie was determined to find a table before he saw her.

She looked at her watch. A sign said dinner service would begin at five-thirty. It was only quarter past. In the center of the car were two large silver urns and cups for coffee or tea. Turning the small tap on the urn, she remembered the box of Red Rose tea that Marcie had put in her room the day before she left, saying, "You probably won't be able to get Red Rose tea down there in North Carolina. Just write to me and I'll send you a box now and then." Maggie thought she would miss Marcie as much as anyone.

She sat down at a small table for two beside the window, thinking they must be nearing Philadelphia. One of these days, she hoped to drive a car through every state in the Union. She wanted to see the Mississippi River and the French Quarter in New Orleans. She wanted to see the far West, the Pacific Ocean. She tried to picture Tate riding in an open car, flying along at top speed. *He'd never want to do that, but I'll bet I know someone else who would!* The thought perturbed her, and she tried to concentrate on the scenery. Putting Jonathan McNamara out of her mind was going to be difficult.

A Lapse of Memory

PACING UP AND DOWN THE LOADING PLATFORM in Burgaw, Maggie had looked about for Tate, or anyone who might have come to meet her. She'd even thought Aunt Mag might come along for the ride. But there was no one in sight. Inside the station, an agent was busy rearranging freight behind the ticket window. He looked up, wiping his sleeve across his forehead. "Yes, ma'am, can I help you?"

"Someone was supposed to meet me . . . could you hold my trunks in the station while I walk over to Devane's and look for him?"

"Yes, ma'am, but there ain't no need to do that. Mr. Cyrus has already locked up the hardware store. He's probably still jawing with some of the boys over there in that vacant lot next to Harrell's. Want me to send someone over to get him?"

"That'd be nice."

"Just sit on the bench out there. We'll get him for you."

Weary from the long trip, Maggie welcomed the chance to sit outside and breathe fresh air. Spring arrived at least a month earlier in North Carolina than in Boston. Across the street at the courthouse, there were large beds of brightly colored tulips blooming in front of the pink azalea bushes. Burgaw could thank Mr. Hugh MacRae in Wilmington for that. A few years back, he'd bought thousands of acres of land near Castle Hayne, at the edge of New Hanover County. MacRae resettled immigrant families on the land, giving them a chance for a new life in America. Some of them with names like Oosterwyk and Tingla had grown flower bulbs in the low countries of Europe, so flower farming in eastern North Carolina was a perfect fit for them. Now just about every town square in the region had iris, daffodils, and tulips laid out in beautiful beds.

Cyrus Devane was startled to see Maggie when he came around the train station. "Maggie Lorena! What in the world? I didn't know you were coming in on the train." He hugged her, holding her a little closer than she liked. She hadn't forgotten that he'd wanted to marry her at one time.

"I've been up to Boston," she said. "Tate should've been here to meet me. I wrote to Aunt Mag."

"Good gracious, honey. She must not of got your letter," Cyrus said. He'd aged, but Maggie thought he was still a burly, nice-looking man, especially handsome when he smiled. "Don't look so worried, honey. I'll run you over there in my truck."

"I hate to put you to that trouble. I've got two trunks. Why don't I just stay with you tonight until I can get word to Tate? I'd love to see the children."

"What children?" he asked, amused. "You've lost track of time, honey—there's not a one at home anymore except Mary Beth, and she's working over at the café in Wallace. I had to get her an automobile, or she couldn't of done it."

"Then I'd be much obliged if you'd take me as far as Aunt Mag's."

Cyrus looked at her curiously. "You mean you're not going to see Tate first thing?"

"If he doesn't know I'm coming, I'd rather freshen up—get some sleep."

He shook his head, laughing. "You ain't changed much, Maggie Lorena."

"What's wrong with wanting to freshen up a little before I see my husband? I must look a fright."

"If I was Tate, I wouldn't care what you looked like. Probably act like a cave man and drag you into the bed by that curly top of yours."

"I declare, Cyrus. Maybe you need to be thinking about getting married again."

"Humph! All the pretty gals like you I know are already married." She was flattered to think he wasn't entirely joking.

―――――

THE LETTER—AND ONE OTHER—was right where Aunt Mag had put it on the mantel. "I meant to read it, but I forgot," she said.

"What do you mean, you *forgot* to read my letter, Aunt Mag?"

"Well, I knew what it said."

"Aunt Mag, are you all right?"

"Of course I'm all right. What's the matter with you, Missy, coming in here and talking smart to me? Did you leave your manners up there in Boston?"

Maggie had wondered whether something was wrong when Cyrus drove her up to the house well after dark. In the headlights, they saw Aunt Mag in her black dress and starched white apron out behind the house, taking clothes off the clothesline. Or was she hanging them? Whatever, it was strange to see her elderly aunt performing such a chore at that time of the evening.

When he'd unloaded her trunks, Maggie asked Cyrus to go on back to Burgaw. They'd talked all the way and she was worn out. Besides, she had to deal with Aunt Mag, and she'd rather do that on her own.

"Did you forget to tell Tate I was coming in on the train this evening, or what?"

Aunt Mag was already rattled and cross, Maggie assumed from getting caught outside at that hour. Her black dress was loose on her thin body, and Maggie thought something might be ailing her. "I just wasn't in the mood to hear how you were enjoying Boston— about all those shows you were seeing. I was sick of how much fun you were having up there and us missing you and wondering if you were ever coming back."

"Aunt Mag, I can't believe you'd say that."

"Well, I said it, and you heard me."

Maggie checked the urge to say she thought Aunt Mag was losing her mind. Instead, she asked if they could talk about it in the morning. "I'm so tired, I'd just like to go crawl into my old bed and sleep."

"You need some dinner first. I'll fix you a plate. Your brother Zeb bought a side of beef last week. Gave me some meat for stew. I've got some out yonder on the porch in the icebox." She limped towards the door, then turned and gave Maggie a hard look. "I like your hair like that, and you got rid of that dark glass, didn't you?"

"Yes, ma'am, I did, and thank you."

"Why don't you get out of those clothes? Looks like you slept in them."

"I did."

"You want a sweet potato?"

"Don't go to any trouble. I'm really not hungry." *No use arguing with her,* Maggie thought, watching Aunt Mag shuffle off to the pantry, bent nearly double with arthritis. Age was taking its toll. Maggie felt a twinge of guilt. Things hadn't been right between her and Aunt Mag since Yancey died.

Had she really been so awful, Maggie wondered—to everyone? So inconsolable and selfish? As much as she hated to admit it, she knew she had. Getting away to Boston had helped, but she didn't intend falling right back into the same old rut. She was a new woman now. That might take some getting used to on everyone's part.

Even hers.

———

THEY SAT IN THE DIM KITCHEN talking until midnight. The whole house carried the scent of kerosene from the lamps, reminding Maggie that there would be no electricity at her home down the road, either. She'd dozed on and off on the train, but she'd had so much tea that she was wound up. Aunt Mag, perched on the edge of her seat, was running her fingernail over the embroidered tablecloth, tracing the design over and over. She'd never needed much sleep. "I'm sorry I said that about your letters, Maggie Lorena. I was just being spiteful."

"That's not like you. What were you doing out there at the clothesline after dark?"

"Cousin Maybelle had stopped by here, running on about something she'd heard at the store. I plumb forgot there were clothes on the line."

"I thought your mind was going."

"Well, it may be, but I figured you'd get Cyrus or somebody to bring you here, whenever you made up your mind to come back. You know there's nothing I ever wanted more than for you to go places and see things. I wouldn't take anything for all I saw and did with your Uncle Archie. We even went to the White House one time." Her eyes watered up. "But I missed you." She took a deep breath, punctuated with a sob. "I wish I could have gone with you."

Maggie reached across the table for her hand. "Next time we'll go together. Abigail wants me to come back. Actually, I think she wished I'd stay up there with her and never come home."

"That doesn't sound like Abigail Adams either. Always acted like she thought a lot of Tate."

"I think her mind snapped a little when Mr. Henry died. I know how that feels."

"Are you all right now? I mean, are you back to stay?"

"I'm back. I reckon I'm here to stay. Don't really want to go back to Boston any time soon. Maybe I'll look into writing stories like they have in the *Wilmington Star*. You know, the ones that run for several weeks."

"Now you're talking, Missy." Aunt Mag slapped her knees with both hands. "I can hardly wait until the paper comes when they've got one of those romance stories running." She retrieved a handkerchief from her sleeve, blew her nose, and wiped her eyes. Aunt Mag aged considerably in her absence. The lines in the old woman's face had deepened, and the hair above her lips and on her chin had turned white and beardlike.

"Let me put up those dishes, Aunt Mag. They should be dry by now."

"No, that'll wait. There's something I need to tell you about Tate." She scooted her chair closer to the table and tried to lean back, but her twisted spine kept her forward. "You know that old saying, *while the cat's away the mice will play?*" Maggie listened intently, a puzzled look on her face. "I waited until you came home to tell you this 'cause I wasn't sure what was going on, and I didn't want to stir something up and have it stink."

"What?"

"You never knew the Jackson folks up there near Cotton Cove, did you?"

"I don't think so."

"Well, they had this daughter that ran off from home when she was thirteen or fourteen. Her daddy and mama never heard a word from her until the daddy died two years ago. Well, that girl's about thirty or forty years old now, and she came back home after she'd heard he died to see what her pa had left her. Her mama wouldn't let her in the house. Next thing we got wind of was she'd run off with one of the McBryde boys and he'd married her."

"Eva McBryde's boy?"

"No—no, her sister Kathleen's boy. You know those O'Kelly girls married McBryde brothers."

"I never knew Kathleen, but Eva O'Kelly and I went to Salemburg Academy together. We're kin to the O'Kellys, aren't we?"

"Yes we are, on the Moreland side. But after what I'm about to tell you, you might not want to claim kin. The boy shot and killed his mother-in-law."

"Wait a minute. I remember—last spring, right after Yancey died."

"That's the one."

"What happened to him?"

"Hold on now, it's getting rich. Remember those O'Kelly girls had a brother they called the Judge because that's what he was, out in Oklahoma working with those Indians?"

"Yes, I do remember. I sent him a copy of *Little Pearl*. He was so appreciative."

"Listen up now, don't get me off track," Aunt Mag said. "Well, the Judge came down here last fall—must've been right after you left—and he got that boy plum off the murder charge."

"You mean he went scot-free? Where is he now?"

"Wait just a dang minute, I'm trying to tell you. There wasn't a thing about it in the *Bladen Journal*, but at Homecoming, the Judge was there sporting this great big Indian headdress—you know, one of those long feather things like the chiefs wear. I went up to speak to him and he recognized who I was. I asked him what happened to the boy. Well, sir, he cut me down right then and there. He says real polite to me, 'Cousin Margaret, we've put all that behind us to enjoy this beautiful day of our Lord.'"

"My heavens, what did you say, Aunt Mag?"

"Not a word. I just bid him adieu, and I found Maybelle and I asked her."

"And?"

"I declare, you are impatient. She told me that the jury decided he ought to be sent to the insane asylum in Raleigh to get straightened out."

"There must be more to it than that."

"I reckon there is, but if you can find anybody to tell you any more, I'd like to know who it is," she said emphatically.

"What happened to the girl—his wife?"

Aunt Mag pushed her chair back and hobbled over to the kitchen sink, where she worked the pump handle up and down until cool water streamed out. "She wasn't exactly a girl. I told you Patty Sue Jackson is twelve or thirteen years older than Davy McBryde."

"Well, what happened to her?"

Aunt Mag took a long swig of water. "Ahhhhhh. I was about to thirst to death. All this jawing. I'm by myself most of the time. Go days without speaking a word." She pulled her chair back up to the table. "Now, where was I?"

"You were going to tell me what happened to the girl." Suddenly, Maggie's head was reeling, and not just from lack of sleep. "Aunt Mag, what in the world has this got to do with Tate?"

"Hold your horses, Missy. I'm getting to it." She blew her nose in her handkerchief and tucked it back inside her sleeve. "They say she left way before the trial—went off, nobody knows where—but she showed up again about a month ago. Seems like she's operating some kind of trucking business—got three or four trucks. Your William keeps them running for her. Well, sir, she gets to talking to Tate one day about how he's having a hard time finishing up the house before you get back." She cut her eyes over to Maggie. "If you ever do."

"Did he tell her that?"

"I don't know what Tate told her, Maggie Lorena. But the next thing I hear, she's doing some painting for Tate while William works on her truck."

"Did you say anything to him about how that looks?"

"Oh, he won't let me say a thing. Neither will William. They think she's the nicest person they ever knew. And she may be, but I don't like it one bit."

"You say she's older than the McBryde boy?"

"That's what I heard."

"But younger than me?"

"I reckon, by eight or nine years."

"What does she look like?"

"I've never seen her. William told me she was real pretty. Paints her face up and all that, but she drives a tractor and works like a man."

"Aunt Mag, tell me the truth, you don't think Tate would . . . do anything?"

"I don't know what Tate would do, but I can tell you this, you oughtn't go off and leave a man so long."

"Listen, Aunt Mag, I didn't go off and leave Tate. We had an understanding. He knew I needed to go and get my book published. He was all for it."

"Was he now, Missy? That's not the way I heard it. He told me that day we put you on the train for Boston that he had a feeling you might never come back." Aunt Mag's words stung, and Maggie knew she'd intended it that way.

"Well, I never said any such thing."

"You didn't have to," Aunt Mag continued relentlessly. "Even a blind man could see you had your sights set on getting out of Bladen County. Your letters didn't say anything about coming home either, not until that one there on the mantel." She was wound up now, like Maggie hadn't seen her since she'd railed against Reece Evans years ago. Her final salvo cut Maggie to the quick. "That's why Len went up there—to get you to come home."

"He did not. I invited him to come up and see what a big city was like. I thought he might want to go to school up there. Henry Montgomery offered to send him."

"Hmmph. That boy had sense enough to know he would've been a fish out of water."

Maggie half expected her to say, *and you should've known too!* "I don't understand, Aunt Mag," she said in a pitiful voice. "You always wanted so much for me."

"Boys are different. They find their own way if they've got gumption. Lenny's going to make something of himself, but it's going to be something of his own making. William will probably be right here the rest of his life."

Maggie's uneasiness increased with each minute that passed. She thought *she* would come home a changed woman and find everything just the same; instead, everything was topsy-turvy. On the train, she'd gotten her thoughts together, decided she'd stay with Tate—at least until she could establish herself as a writer for the newspaper. She had a little money—maybe she'd buy a car. Aunt Mag was watching her, aware of something unfamiliar going on in her mind. "If you're telling me all this about Tate to get me riled up," Maggie said, "all I asked you to do was tell Tate I was coming home."

Aunt Mag knew she'd made her point, and she wasn't one to inflict more pain than was needed to make Maggie sit up and listen. "Yes, you did, and the reason I didn't tell him was that I wanted to forewarn you. Didn't want you to be blindsided," she said, not unkindly. "Might just be an old woman's imagination."

———

MAGGIE WAS UP BEFORE DAYLIGHT. Many times in the Boston winter she had longed to sleep on the warm goose-down mattress at her old home place, but last night the ticking had smelled musty and the rough, dried sheets scratched her cheeks. After six months of sleeping on fine ironed linens, she could feel the difference. Thoughts of the inconveniences at home had almost turned her back a time or two.

"Do you want to go with me?" she asked Aunt Mag after breakfast.

"I reckon you don't need me along. I'll go if you want, but I'm not able to get around much without a stick, and I'm liable to hit that woman over the head with it. I'll get Uncle Freddy to bring me up there in a day or two after you've settled the dust."

Maggie hitched up the buggy and took off towards Colly, trying to imagine how much of Aunt Mag's tale might have been exaggerated. Len had been right about her acting peculiar. But this business about Tate was probably just a lot of talk. Talk could do that, get everyone all worked up, imagining the worst. She just might have the nerve to ask Patty Sue Jackson McBryde what she was doing hanging around her husband. That'd give them all something to chew on.

Maggie had awakened during the night, remembering the other letter on Aunt Mag's mantel. Quiet as a mouse, she'd slipped downstairs to retrieve it. Hurriedly, she'd read the letter and slipped it back into the envelope to savor later. The mission at hand was much more important.

1 8

Something Less Than Friendly

M AGGIE FLICKED THE REINS AND URGED THE HORSE
on a little faster. She hadn't made much progress when a road
grader came rumbling towards her, smoothing over the furrows in
the surface, and she had to pull over to the side. There were deep
drainage ditches full of weeds on either side, and she maneuvered
over nervously, afraid that Aunt Mag's Nellie would rear up on
account of the noise. She recognized Jess Porter and threw up her
hand in greeting. He tipped his hat, but there was something less
than friendly in the way he looked at her. Was everyone talking
about Tate and the Jackson woman? She flicked the reins again,
more urgently now.

The first thing different Maggie noticed as she pulled into the
lower drive through the oak grove was a large red-and-white Coca-
Cola sign with RYAN'S GARAGE painted on it in bold letters. All
along the drive were tractors and junk car parts, one or two old
trucks with their engines missing, and an assortment of farm
machinery. The serene lane had changed into a gauntlet of rusting
metal in a space of six months. Attached to the old camp house was
a long shed with a faded blue truck parked beneath it. Wrenches
and other tools hung along the wall and littered a workbench that
ran the full length of the shed.

To her right, the new house loomed far larger than she'd
expected. Maybe it was the brown meat paper that curiously
matched the wood-shingled roof, but it looked right pretty sitting

there in the oak grove with the sturdy little magnolia tree making a comeback at one end. Tate had tried to show her the plans after Aunt Mag's house burned, but she'd had the devil in her then and acted as if she didn't care. Later, she'd sneaked a peek and seen that there were three bedrooms, a kitchen and dining room combination, and a large screened in porch on the back. The place could never compare to Aunt Mag's gracious old house, but she had to admit, she liked its pert little dormers set into the roof.

Tate, his back to her, was sitting on a section of sawed-off log, sharpening a plow. She felt a tingle of familiarity in the curve of his back beneath the muslin work shirt, his rough hands working the whetstone. Her mind sprang immediately to the soft hands of Jon McNamara and his starched lab coat—and just as quickly, she reproached herself for her thoughts.

The jingle of the horse's livery caught Tate's attention, and he turned around and gaped at the approaching buggy before Maggie waved to him. "Well, I'll be damned," he said as she pulled up the reins and led the horse to a stop several feet from him. "Maggie Lorena. You've come home."

"I'd planned to wait until you'd finished the house," she called out. "Looks like I should've stayed a little longer." She stepped down from the buggy, looking around. Tate reached for her, took her in his arms, and held her tightly for a long time. She could almost hear his mind whirling, trying to find the right words to say to her.

"I missed you, honey. You were gone so long."

She pushed him away to where she could see his eyes. "Did you?"

"You know I did. Why didn't you tell me? I would've met the train."

She walked towards the shed looking for her sons, and he followed a step behind. "I wrote to Aunt Mag two weeks ago, but she said she didn't get the letter. Cyrus drove me to her house last night."

He looked hurt. "You stayed there last night instead of coming on home?"

"It was late," she explained. "I wanted to get a good night's sleep."

Grabbing her hand, he stopped her in her tracks. "Why'd you do that?" he said, reaching up and touching her bobbed hair.

"Don't you like it?"

"I liked it the way it was."

"It was old-fashioned. Nobody in Boston wears their hair like that anymore." She peered over his shoulder towards the garage. "Where're the boys? I saw Will's sign."

Will slid out from under a truck, a wrench in his hand, his face smeared with grease. It took him a minute or two to realize who she was. "Mama, you're home!" He rolled off his mechanic's trolley and jumped to his feet. "When d-d-did you g-g-get here?" Will might have grown nearly to manhood, but he hadn't outgrown his childhood speech impediment. "We didn't know you was . . . w-w-were coming."

"My goodness, is that a mechanic or is it my boy?" She reached out to hug him.

He backed away. "No, I'm all g-g-greasy. Lemme go wash up."

"All right, Bud, but hurry up. I missed you."

Will grinned, looking down at his feet. "Nobody's c-c-called me that since you left."

"Nobody's called you *Bud* since I left? Good gracious. Well, Mama's back now and I'm going to call my William Bud from now on."

"He's not a little young'un any more, Maggie Lorena," Tate said. "Folks around here think he's a pretty good mechanic."

"Well, I can call him Bud if I want to. I'm his mama." She looked at her son. "You don't mind if Mama calls you Bud, do you, son?"

William kicked at the black sand with the greasy toe of his shoe. "I don't care what you c-c-call me, Mama, I'm j-j-just glad you're home."

"Where's your brother?"

"He's over yonder in the lower field dipping water over the tobacco plants," Tate said. "We just set them out yesterday. He'll be home directly. Lizzie brought over a pot of turnip greens and corn-meal dumplings this morning. You know Len, he's got that Ryan stomach," he added, smiling. "Has to be fed."

"Is it Ryan or Corbinn?" she asked, pulling Tate along by the hand. "Come on, show me the house. Len said you'd gotten right much done."

Tate lit up like a Christmas tree, and she knew she'd said the right thing. "I added a couple of rooms on the back. One's a little bathing room, the other one is just for your things—you know, for your writing and all."

She was genuinely moved. "Why, Tate Ryan, that's just about the nicest thing I can think of."

"Well, it wasn't exactly my idea. Patty Sue said you'd probably like a bathroom more than a screened-in porch all the way across the back of the house. Then I said what you'd probably really like was a little writing room, so we—"

"Patty Sue?"

"Wait, M-M-Mama. I'll get her," William said, tossing aside the shop towel he'd used to wipe his face and setting out towards the new house.

"She's here now?"

Tate shifted from foot to foot. "Sure, honey. That's her truck William's working on. I forgot you didn't know her."

William returned, followed by a woman wearing a pair of paint-spattered men's overalls and a red flannel shirt. Coarse, bleached hair peeked out from under a scarf tied around her head. "Mama, this here is Miss Patty Sue."

Maggie had to bite her tongue to be civil. "I'm Maggie Ryan. Pleased to meet you, Miss . . . ?" she said coldly, without offering her hand.

"McBryde—*Mrs.,* that is—but please call me Patty Sue. I've

been looking forward to meeting you." She wiped her hands on her overalls. "You just get here?"

"She came in last night on the train," Tate said. "Spent the night with her Aunt Mag."

"Oh, I see." Patty Sue looked at Tate. "You didn't tell me." She turned back to Maggie, a touch of caution in her voice. "I offered to help Tate while William's been working on my truck. Just with the painting. I hope you'll like the colors."

Maggie took hold of William's arm, glancing back at Patty Sue. "Come on, show Mama your new shop."

"Don't you want to see the house first?" Tate called out.

"In a minute, after Miss Patty Sue leaves. We won't be needing her help now that I'm home."

Tate turned apologetically to Patty Sue. "She's kinda high-strung. You probably heard about that."

"I hear lots of things, Tate, but I've been around long enough to know that only about half of what you hear is true." She walked towards the house. "I'll clean up my brushes and get on back home as soon as *Bud* finishes with the truck." Just the way she said it let Tate know her feelings were hurt—and it wasn't hard to see that he'd have hell to pay with Maggie Lorena, too.

———

THE FIRST TIME TATE HAD SEEN PATTY SUE, he'd come back to the camp house for a bite to eat, hot and tired after being out in the field all morning. She was nailing up cypress siding on the new house, wearing overalls and a flannel shirt. At first he took her for a small man, but when she turned around, there was no mistaking she was a woman.

"Hey," she'd called out to him. "Your son's working on my truck and I had to have something to do." Patty Sue could smile real sweet.

Tate had reached over and taken the hammer from her hand. "You don't need to be doing that. It's man's work."

"Pshaw! A woman can do anything a man can do. Let me have that hammer back, and I'll show you."

Humoring her, Tate sawed a few boards and watched her nail them up. After a while he'd taken a seat on an overturned bucket, indicating another for her. "Sit down a minute. I feel like I'm taking advantage of you. You're as good a carpenter as any man I ever saw."

Patty Sue sat down opposite him. "I can do a lot of things better than most men," she said, a smile barely curling her lips. "Of course, some men are better than others."

Tate had felt the heat rise to his face and a stir in his privates. He'd seen that look before, but it had been so long since a woman came on to him, he hardly knew how to act. "You never know what you can do until you give it a try," he said. Her eyes wandered over him again, locking on his. She ran her tongue over the edge of her teeth as if calculating another retort.

Will had come up from the shop then. "Looks good, Papa," he said.

"You can say that again, thanks to your new customer here."

"Yes, s-s-sir, M-M-Miss Patty Sue said she knew how to n-n-nail up siding. I f-f-figured you could u-u-use all the help you c-c-could get with M-M-Mama coming home s-s-soon and all."

Tate spat out a stream of tobacco juice and smiled. "You were right about that, son."

PART III
Colly, North Carolina
1926

The 1919 Chandler Six

19

Strawberries and Butterbeans

SUMMER HAD ARRIVED FULL FORCE IN COLLY, with sun-scorched days, midafternoon thundershowers, and yellow flies that drew blood with their vicious bites. Maggie was thankful that a month earlier Tate had finished putting wire screening on the doors and windows, and she would not have to spend another summer sharing a half-built house with every species of fly and mosquito in Bladen County.

The insects weren't the only irritation that summer. The first day she'd seen one of Patty Sue McBryde's trucks come rolling up the lane, Maggie was fit to be tied. She'd left a washpot of clothes bubbling away and darted behind the wash shed at the back of Will's garage. Maggie was already out of sorts because Lizzie should've been out there doing the wash. But as soon as Maggie had come home, Lizzie had gone off for a few days to visit one of her daughters—for spite, Maggie was convinced, because she'd been away so long on a mission Lizzie hadn't approved of. Her hands chapped and raw from the lye soap, Maggie wished for the hundredth time that she was back in the city.

With one eye up to a crack in the board wall of the garage, Maggie watched Patty Sue step out of the truck, barefooted and wearing a blue-flowered print dress that buttoned down the front. She sauntered over to Will. "How're you doing, Bud?"

Maggie almost choked to hear the woman call her son by her own pet name for him. William fidgeted with his hair, hitched up his britches. "D-d-doing f-f-fine, Miss Patty Sue. How are y-y-y'all today?"

"I'm doing fine, honey. But that ol' truck over there is acting mighty poorly, burning oil like it was going out of style. Have you got time to take a look at it for me?"

"T-t-to be sure, Miss P-P-Patty Sue."

Patty Sue started towards the truck, hustling along in front of him, her rear end swishing from side to side, the blue flowers keeping time. "That'd be swell. Let me get the baby. I'll sit up there on the porch and nurse him, if you don't think your mama'll mind." Behind the shed, Maggie's ears perked up. *Baby?* Aunt Mag hadn't mentioned a baby!

"No, ma'am, she won't mind a-tall. She's out b-b-back doing the w-w-wash. Won't me to go tell her you're here?"

"Nope. I think it's just a gasket. Shouldn't take long."

It really galled Maggie that Patty Sue knew a lot about cars. Will said she could always tell *him* what was wrong. All he had to do was fix it. Spying quickly through the crack first to make sure they weren't looking, Maggie scurried across the yard and into the house through the back door. She'd closed up the front of the house earlier that morning to keep out the midday heat. Peeping out through the lace curtains Aunt Mag had provided as a housewarming gift, she watched Patty Sue plop down in one of her rocking chairs.

Tate had been stringing up new chicken wire around the vegetable garden all morning, and it wasn't long before he came sashaying around the house with a big grin on his face. "Morning, Miss Patty Sue. I thought that was your truck," he said. "How're y'all doing today?" He was all smiles, sort of prancing in front of her where she sat on the porch.

"Morning, Tate. Thought I'd better get that truck down here first thing this morning. I'm gonna need to load it up this evening," she said.

Tate glanced at the nursing baby, then looked off towards the garage, where Will was working on the truck. "I declare, Colin sure is growing," he said, still looking away.

"Yes sir, he's Mama's big baby boy and he's starving," she said, jiggling the baby, her breast partially exposed. "You don't reckon Miss Maggie Lorena will mind if I sit in her new rocking chair up here on the porch, do you?" she asked innocently. "I nursed him before I left home, but he just can't seem to get enough of his mama." She glanced around, as if to see who might be within earshot.

"Oh, no, not a-tall," Tate said. "She's out yonder in the back yard stirring the washpot. I'm sure she'll be around to speak to you in a minute or two."

"You ought to know better than that," Patty Sue said, a bit under her breath, while behind the curtain, Maggie fumed. "Of course, if she doesn't want Bud working on my trucks, I could always take them over to that Keith boy in Atkinson."

"Oh no, don't you be doing that," Tate said. "You bring those trucks right here. Will's a lot better mechanic than Johnny Keith."

"I think so too, but I don't want to cause any trouble."

"How's your business going?" Tate asked, his foot on the step, leaning on his knee with one elbow.

"Pretty good, if I do say so myself. We're hauling strawberries from Chadbourn this week. Brought you a crate in the back of the truck. Don't forget to get 'em out."

"Yes, ma'am! That'll sure please Maggie Lorena."

"Thought it might," she said, grinning. Next thing Maggie saw was Patty Sue pulling the baby off her nipple and putting him on her opposite shoulder to burp.

Tate turned red as a beet and quickly averted his eyes, but he didn't budge. "Baby sure is growing," he said. "How old is he now?"

"He's nearly six months, Mama's big boy, aren't you, Collee?" she said, nuzzling the baby's neck. A loud burp was forthcoming, and Patty Sue shifted Colin to the other breast, only slightly rearranging her dress.

From inside the house, Maggie's view was quite different from Tate's, but the look of entrancement on his face made her cringe. Either he saw the slight movement behind the lace curtain, or his conscience got the better of him, for he slipped his foot off the step and without a backward glance walked off towards William's garage. "Better get those strawberries," he said.

———

ALL SUMMER MAGGIE HAD BEEN WRETCHEDLY melancholic. She'd told Aunt Mag that Tate was happy to see her upon her return, when in fact, he was not—not like he should've been. After all she'd given up to come back to him, he'd actually said he thought it was terrible that she didn't stay in Boston until her book was published. "You might never get this chance again," he'd suggested. "Maybe you ought to go on back while things are still fresh on your mind."

And Aunt Mag hadn't helped things a bit when she found it necessary to dwell on the situation every time Maggie saw her. Like when Len brought her down to spend the afternoon with Maggie one Saturday. "Wonder if Jasper noticed that woman was hanging around here?" she asked.

"You're probably the only one who'd think anything about it," Maggie said.

"Probably. But I'm closer than most," her aunt said, undaunted.

Maggie hadn't wanted to talk about it. She'd tried to change the subject. "I made some of your cheese straws to take to prayer meeting tonight. Try them. I think they're just as good as yours." She handed Aunt Mag a small plate of crest-shaped cheese cookies.

"Did you ask Tate about it? Tell him how it looked?" Aunt Mag persisted. "I'm an old lady, but I declare, he ought to know that people talk."

"I think you got carried away with your imagination. Probably thought it looked a whole lot worse than it was," Maggie said,. "Tate couldn't have been happier to see me."

"Humph! Caught him red-handed! I notice you paint your face up for him now," Aunt Mag said, working her jaw up and down, macerating the cheese straws between her sparse teeth. "And look at that dress, it's practically up to your knees!" she'd sputtered.

"I declare, Aunt Mag, you are so old-fashioned. I'm not going to go back to wearing those drab old dresses down to my ankles after being in the city."

"Well, you look like a hussy to me. It's one thing to dress like city folk when you're in the city, but this house is still a long way from being finished, and you sitting here rocking away in a dress showing your fanny, like you had nothing better to do."

"Aren't you a crotchety old thing? I invited you down to set a spell in my new rocking chairs, and all you can talk about is—"

Aunt Mag had sat up straight and shook her finger at Maggie. "Don't you be calling me an 'old thing,' Missy. I'm liable to turn you over my knee." She broke out in a toothy grin, and they both liked to have died laughing. That's the way it had gotten. Now that Aunt Mag had lost the agility to get up and swish around, her bossiness had lost some of its punch. "I declare, I don't know what gets into me," she sighed. "Treating you like you were a child. I reckon you've wised up a little. You don't need me telling you what to do."

"Oh, go on, say what you want. I'm not as high-strung as I used to be."

"You are, too. William told me how you acted that day around Patty Sue McBryde. He said you pure-tee embarrassed him."

"I did not. I'm going to jerk a knot in that boy for saying that."

"No, don't. He won't ever tell me a thing again. The boys need a confidante. You used to tell *me* everything," Aunt Mag said, rocking to beat the band.

"Not everything," Maggie said. She stood and straightened her skirt. "I'm going inside to get an apron. Somebody gave William a bushel of butterbeans. I thought you might help me shell them."

"Where'd they get butterbeans? Cold weather set mine back—everybody else's around here that I know of."

"I didn't ask him."

She'd spent the rest of that afternoon with Aunt Mag, quietly shelling the butterbeans, aware that her life had changed drastically in the months she was away, though not in the way she'd anticipated. Now and then thoughts of Jonathan McNamara had crept in, and she was glad she'd never breathed his name to Aunt Mag. She'd never told Aunt Mag about Reece Evans either, not about what had happened. But Aunt Mag knew.

"You never did tell me what that other letter said," she piped up out of the blue.

"What other letter?" Was Aunt Mag reading her thoughts?

"The one from that woman over in Onslow County. You know who I mean."

"Emily McAllister, and *you* know her name."

"I do not. I just know she's the sister of that man."

"Aunt Mag, you do have a knack for bringing up the darndest things."

"What do you expect? All I have to do most of the time is sit around and think. Answer my question."

"Emily McAllister is one of the finest women you'd ever want to know. I taught her children in school. Her husband owned the general store in Jacksonville. In fact, one of the things she told me in her letter was that she'd bought Miss Tucie's Hat Shop, and now she's opened up a second store, in Wilmington. Her daughter, Jeanne, manages Miss Tucie's in Jacksonville now."

"I declare, that must be the girl Lenny met on the train. Said she knew you from Jacksonville. One of Eva McBryde's girls was with her. Said she told him you had two house fires."

No, it was Reece's daughter, Agatha, Maggie thought, reaching for a handful of butterbeans, dreading the answer to her next question. "What did you say?"

Aunt Mag said she'd told Len the truth. "That old trunk of yours was the only thing they got out of both houses before they burned to the ground."

Maggie had kept her eyes on the pan in her lap. "What did Len say?"

"Len told me that's what she said."

"Folks just won't let it alone, will they?"

"You ought to write a story about what you've been through. Make a good one."

No. Never again! Maggie thought. There were other stories to be told. Stories that would delight her imagination instead of dredging up the past. Emily's letter, so warm and friendly, had started her thinking.

I'm sending this to your Aunt Mag's house because I don't want to stir up any unpleasant memories for Tate, she'd written. *But I must tell you how thrilled I was that Agatha met your Len on the train. She thinks he is adorable. Since Duncan died last year and I sold Evanwood, Agatha and Mandy have made my new home in Wilmington their home. They had no desire to live at Cranewood, much less in Onslow County.*

Another coincidence has prompted me to write you after so long a time, Emily's letter had continued. *We have become acquainted with the family of one of your cousins. You probably know that Eva McBryde and her husband, Rob, moved to Wilmington from Bladen County. They own a beautiful old home on Princess Street, which they unfortunately must rent out to boarders. One of their girls, Millie, who is about the age of your Len, works for me in the hat shop, and my girls and I have become great friends with her and the rest of the family.*

You simply must come to Wilmington. Bring the boys, and Tate, too, if he'll come. I have a cottage at Wrightsville Beach and you may stay there anytime you like. Wouldn't it be wonderful for all of our youngsters to get acquainted?

Yes, Maggie would certainly go to Wilmington. But she had other things in mind—and they didn't include Tate and the boys.

"Well, are you going to tell me what she said or not?" Aunt Mag pressed.

"Emily invited me to come to see her, and I intend to do just that as soon as we have a car and someone gives me driving lessons."

"Going off gallivanting again, huh?"

"Do you call going to Wilmington gallivanting? I declare, Aunt Mag, you are so far behind the times. Jasper drives back and forth to Wilmington two or three times a week. Just because I'm a woman . . . "

"I never knew you were so hepped up about learning to drive," Aunt Mag interrupted.

"Well, I am. Maybe I'll even buy me a new car with all the money I'm going to make on the stories I'll be writing for the *Star*."

"Counting your chickens before they hatch, aren't you, Missy?"

———

NOT LONG AFTERWARD TATE HAD COME HOME with a big roll of wire screening, saying that Mr. Shaw at the general store in Atkinson had given it to him on credit. "I hadn't figured on getting the screening for the porch until after we'd sold a little of the tobacco," he told Maggie. He got his ladder and a hammer from the barn and began unrolling the screen in the yard. "He said maybe we'd bring him a dozen eggs every week or so."

"Well, that was real nice of him," Maggie said from her perch on the gazebo rail. Her hair had started to grow out again, and damp red curls were pasted to her forehead. She'd spent the morning pulling wire grass out of her rose bed, the only things that had survived the fire and her neglect the past year. "I can't believe you're counting on those old laying hens, Tate. You're buying an awful lot on credit," she said, cutting suspicious eyes towards him. "I hope you're not planning on using any of that little bit of money I've saved up. My advance was hard-earned, especially since my book didn't get published."

Tate was concentrating on cutting the wire screening. "What're you saving it for?" he asked, not stopping to look at Maggie.

"I'm thinking I might buy us a car, a real nice car we could go places in."

"Horse and wagon out there is all I need," Tate mumbled. He was up on the ladder now, tacking a piece of screen under the eaves, struggling to keep it straight against the tug of the heavy roll on the ground.

"How's that?"

He turned around and glared at her. "I said, we didn't need a car as long as we had that horse and wagon out there in the barn."

While she had his attention, she glared right back. "Well, that's an ugly thing to say. You might think about me sometime. Maybe

I'd like to have a car to go places in even if you wouldn't."

Tate turned back to his work. "How come?"

"How come, what? Everybody's getting cars these days. We could go to town now and then, see one of those moving picture shows, go to the beach or even the lake." Just the sound of doing those things excited her, and she walked over closer to him. "Doesn't that sound like fun?"

He stepped down off the ladder and looked at her. "Can't you ever be satisfied with what you've got? You're always trying to be something you're not, Maggie Lorena." He walked off, slapping the dust off his hat against his pants leg.

Chagrined, she went to the gazebo and stretched out in the swing. There was no use in arguing with Tate. Nothing she said or did made him happy anymore. His oatmeal was too hot, or the biscuits were cold, or her strawberry jelly was too runny. Most surprising of all was the absence of that little lopsided smile after he'd had a tub bath on Saturday night. She'd come to expect that, even after all these years.

———

MAGGIE WAS SO CAUGHT UP IN ALL that was going on, she'd completely forgotten about her conversation with Mr. Wooten on the train. "Your brother James was too bad off to even go to Jimmy's wedding," Maggie said when she finally remembered to tell Tate.

"I reckon somebody would of written to us—told us if he was in real bad shape," Tate said.

"When's the last time you wrote somebody a letter?" Maggie asked, her tone indignant to the point of ridicule.

"You know I don't write letters, but one of my sisters should've—"

"Tate Ryan, you need to go see about your people. Those sisters of yours can't keep taking care of you like they used to. They've got their own lives."

"I guess you're right. Maybe when William gets that old jalopy running, I'll go."

"What *old jalopy?*"

Tate's look turned sheepish, and he shifted from side to side. He'd never been a good liar. "Ah . . . that one out there. He's been working on it for a long time. Ah . . . somebody brought an old wrecked truck in here—William salvaged the motor."

Does he think I'm blind? Maggie thought. She'd seen one of Patty Sue's trucks—she knew everyone of them by now—come in hauling a wrecked vehicle of some sort. A rough-looking man, a stranger, got out of the truck and spoke to Will. When she asked her son about it later, he said Patty Sue thought he could use the parts. The motor was perfectly good, he said.

"I thought you said that old horse and wagon out there was all you needed."

"Well, I just might've changed my mind," Tate said, standing up to her. "You've done that a time or two yourself."

"And you might be too late, like you were when your mama died," Maggie retorted, even though she wasn't particularly happy with the thought of Tate being out of her sight for two or three days.

———

FIRST IT WAS STRAWBERRIES, then the butterbeans—then the truck engine and God only knew what else Patty Sue was bringing in there all summer. But Maggie chose to ignore it because times were hard. It took every cent they could scrape together to buy seed and fertilizer, not to mention the store account. Tate was working as hard as she'd ever known him to work. In good weather, he was out in the tobacco fields almost all day. Like most of the farmers around them, he grew corn mostly for his own use—tobacco was the paying crop.

But before Will even finished piecing the vehicle together, Tate had built a new shed on the side of the barn for the jalopy, which was assembled from an old Model T sedan frame with the top removed. Will had torn out the old engine, replacing it with the newer one from the salvaged truck. He'd then welded the truck bed onto the car so Tate could haul things in it. The ongoing project kept them busy most evenings after supper, while Maggie worked on her stories until she could no longer hold her eyes open. Sometimes late at night she'd hear Tate out there revving up his engine.

———

AT THE END OF JULY MAGGIE HEARD BACK from Mr. Edmund Brown, the editor of the *Wilmington Morning Star,* who had accepted the two sample stories she'd sent him and engaged her to be their new romance writer. Mr. Brown said he was quite happy with the prospect of having a local author to provide the serialized stories his readers seemed to enjoy even more than the comics, which were his own favorite. *But I must have at least two complete stories to run five weeks each before I'll accept your proposal. That's the way the syndicates do it. For good reason, I might add.* When she'd completed the stories, she'd sent them off and received a resounding *Congratulations! You're hired, Mrs. Ryan. Please come and visit me in my office when you're in town. I'd be happy to meet the lovely lady who's written these stories in person.*

Maggie set to work at a steady pace, turning out a story a month and always staying a month ahead. The writing energized her again, kept her mind off her troubles at home. Each story ran two columns, with a bold title across the two columns at the top, including her byline and a drawing of the head of an attractive woman whose long tresses formed a border along the edges of the text. For each story Maggie received five dollars, plus she was given a free subscription to the *Star.* And soon Maggie discovered how easy it was to lose herself in her stories. Turning to fiction, she could escape her melancholia, reside instead in a world of fantasy. Each day her fervor increased, spurred on by thoughts of going to Wilmington to meet her editor, to visit with Emily McAllister and Eva McBryde. And who knew what else might come up between now and the time when Dr. Jonathan McNamara settled into his new practice in the Port City?

20

Death and Taxes

TATE RYAN'S LITTLE BLACK JALOPY HAD MEANT MORE to him than he could or would ever say. How could he have known what it would be like to have a car of his own? But Patty Sue knew. She'd seen him looking at the trucks she brought in. A time or two, she'd offered him one of hers to drive, but he'd been afraid he'd make a damn fool of himself. It took some practice to learn to drive, but that didn't keep him from wondering what it would feel like to haul buggy down the road in a vehicle at sixty or seventy miles an hour.

Patty Sue left something almost every time she came by the Ryan place, never making a big to-do about it. She said she'd found that roll of screening on the side of the road. Tate never questioned her about it, but one of the drivers told Will that she did a lot of bartering in her trade. Bartering was something everybody did when money was tight. And Patty Sue had never asked Tate for anything in return—except to ask him a time or two not to mention where he got something. Especially to Maggie.

———

WHEN JIMMY CAME FOR TATE, THE JALOPY was almost finished. "Doc says Pa's eat up with cancer, Uncle Tate. He's been asking for you," his nephew said. Jimmy had driven James's old tin lizzie over from Onslow County, offering to drive Tate back. But

Tate was hell-bent on trying out his little automobile on the road. This was his chance—or was it an excuse?

"No, son, I'll be over there tomorrow," Tate had said. "Need to get my ducks in a row." The following day, Will put the last spark plug in place, tightened the belts, and greased the chassis. Tate washed from head to toe and put on a suit that had been Henry Montgomery's. He slicked down his hair and splashed bay rum on his freshly shaven face. "You look more like you're going courting than to your brother's deathbed," Maggie had said. She'd wanted to go with him, but he'd told her he'd borrow somebody's car and come back and get her and the boys if James passed.

Tate stayed gone for four days. James had died the same day Tate arrived. He hadn't seen all of his sisters together in several years, and they'd begged Tate to stay and spend some time with his pa, Bill Ryan, who was on his last leg too. When Tate finally did come home, Maggie got the devil in her, railing on him no end. "What will your people think of us—not going to your own brother's funeral? You ought to be ashamed. I'll bet you just wanted to be off by yourself."

Yes, maybe I did, Tate thought. Once he'd gotten behind the wheel of the little jalopy, felt the horsepower of the engine, the wheels hardly touching the ground, he'd thought about keeping on going. Even after they'd buried James in the family cemetery out behind the house, he'd had it in the back of his mind. Then his pa, who lay bedridden in the log house he and Sally Catherine had built, wanted to talk to him. *Won't be much longer for me neither, son. It's up to you now to carry on the Ryan name. You've got Will and Len. Don't let anything happen to those boys.*

That's what had brought him back.

Although they were both about grown—Will eighteen and Len sixteen, going on seventeen—they still needed their pa around to keep them straight. Neither had finished high school yet, but Tate intended to see that they did. Maggie Lorena might think she was the only one who cared about education, but she wasn't. He'd never had the opportunity in Onslow County that his children had now in Bladen County. The high school at Cotton Cove had a teacher for every grade, and a bus picked children up and brought them home. There wasn't much excuse for not getting an education anymore.

———

YES, HE'D COME BACK HOME THEN. But all that summer, the lust in his heart near about ruined him. At night he'd dream about Patty Sue, with Maggie sleeping right there beside him. One night Maggie accused him outright.

"I don't know what you're talking about, Maggie Lorena. I must've been having a bad dream."

"You were moaning her name. Over and over," Maggie cried, accusing him of the worst sorts of things. After that, Maggie told him she didn't want to see Patty Sue anywhere near the house again—"or that young'un either," she said. Maggie had never had much patience with small children, except her own.

"Maggie Lorena, I can't tell Patty Sue not to come down here to Will's garage," he said. "We need the money for taxes. She already knows there's another mechanic over yonder at Atkinson."

"Well, I'd just better not see her hanging around my porch, sitting in my rocking chairs," she said, gritting her teeth. Maggie Lorena had stopped fixing her face up like she did when she first came home, and she could look right mean sometimes. Why couldn't she be kind and sweet to him? he thought. There was nothing that warmed his heart more.

———

THAT WINTER NEITHER WILL NOR TATE saw Patty Sue McBryde. Tate feared that Maggie had offended her—sent a hateful letter or said something insulting. He wondered if the baby had pneumonia, worried that Patty Sue had the flu. Maybe Johnny Keith was working on her trucks—something was keeping her away.

Along about the end of February, once the weather began to warm, concern for Patty Sue took a back seat when Tate's mind turned to his chores at hand. There was no end to the things a farmer had to do in preparation for spring planting. Will had helped him re-chink the tobacco barn; now it was time to turn the seed beds over and dress them with chicken manure. He built two new sleds and traded Mr. Lyon a tow sack of shelled corn for a roll of gauze to cover the tender seedlings. He sharpened his hoes and greased the cultivator, made a new supply of tobacco sticks, and overhauled the oil burner. At night, he fell exhausted into bed with but one thing on his mind: readying his farm operation for a new season. Their very lives depended on it.

Then Patty Sue started showing up again. Every time he turned around, there she was. "Business must be picking up," he said. But Patty Sue wasn't much for small talk.

"Yep, sure is." That's all she said.

Tate found more and more excuses to hang around the shop when she was there. Colin was growing fast, going on two now, and the cutest little fellow he'd ever seen. Tate had missed him, and he'd missed Patty Sue too. But when Maggie began to take notice of them again, making snide remarks about what a hussy Patty Sue was—how she dressed her child all wrong, or some such mess as that, it made him mad as a hornet. What was a man to do when his wife acted so contrary? Tate was sure it wasn't because Maggie knew Patty Sue excited him. He kept that hid.

———

—WILMINGTON. Dr. Jonathan McNamara, a native of Boston, Mass., arrived in the Port City today to set up his practice as a general surgeon associated with James Walker Memorial Hospital. Dr. McNamara is currently a guest of Mrs. Sarah Langley, who is giving him her undivided time, escorting him about the city and introducing him to Wilmington's most prominent citizens.

Dr. McNamara told this reporter that he couldn't be more pleased than to be back in North Carolina, where he completed his undergraduate work at Davidson College. He is forty-seven years old and a widower. We welcome Dr. McNamara to the city of Wilmington. —*Morning Star, June 1, 1926*

———

21

Romance Writer

M AGGIE HAD KNOWN FROM A RELIABLE SOURCE about Jon's arrival in Wilmington some time before the article appeared in the paper. Abigail Adams had finally gotten over the huff she'd been in when Maggie left. Her letters were infrequent, but friendly and newsy. She'd sold the publishing company, and she and Genie had spent the winter in the south of France. There Genie had met a gentleman, an artist who'd followed her home to Boston. In her last letter, Abigail had written, *It was disgusting to see the two of them lolling about in steamer chairs on the ship, staring into one another's eyes. Yes, I'm disappointed in Genie. I had high hopes for the girl. She has a book or two in her and I could have helped her.*

Yes, Maggie thought, *like she helped me!* But it was the news of Jon that had thrilled her. Abigail always mentioned him—how he was working diligently, how tired he looked on the few occasions he'd stopped by the brownstone. *I begged him to take a sabbatical,* Abigail said, *just leave it all behind and come to France with us. You know, Jon's quite wealthy now with his inheritance from Henry. He could travel, see the world—but he says he wants to marry again, settle down in a small town, practice in a community where he can make a difference. I believe he has his sights set on Wilmington. I know that delights you since you two became such good friends.*

They had certainly become good friends, perhaps more. But almost a year had passed. How would she feel now? When they'd cooked Christmas dinner in Abigail's kitchen, working closely at the sink, their hands only inches apart, she'd felt an overwhelming desire to strip off her clothes and stand before him, to be ravished right there on the kitchen floor. Occasionally this dream still woke her at night, and she was overcome with desire. Maybe she should be ashamed of those feelings. But as in her stories, being married to one man did not mean a woman could never feel aroused by another. She had learned that from experience. Giving in to those feelings—that might be a different thing.

Maggie had written in turn to Abigail, sending her regards to Jon. *Please tell him that I am delighted that he's thinking of settling in Wilmington. Maybe one day I'll go to the hospital clinic and see him. Tell him I need to have my ingrown toenails operated on. That should give him a laugh.*

———

KATIE WAS THE FIRST PERSON SHE'D TOLD of her scheme— at least part of it. Winter had been hard on everyone in the country, but especially on Maggie's sister, Katie. Two of Katie's children had almost died with pneumonia. Her husband, Roy, had taken Len off with him on a big job down in South Carolina, and Katie had the full burden of feeding and caring for the sick children as well as the healthy ones. In January, Will had hitched up the mule and wagon so Maggie could go and visit her sister, taking along a jar of chicken soup and a head of collards. "You don't know what it's like to have your man gone all the time," Katie said. "You can count the number of times he's been home since we've been married by counting the heads," she said, spoonfeeding one of the youngest children.

"I declare, you need to get a car," Maggie said. "*I'm* going to." She reached into her pocket and pulled out a folded advertisement for a new Model A Ford. "See that? One of these days, I'm going to have that car."

Katie studied her older sister for a minute. They could be twins, the way their coloring matched. Tarred by the same stick, Papa used to say. Katie was a little trimmer, burning up energy chasing after her five children, whereas Maggie was more sedentary, spending hours at her writing table. Maggie might be a little more educated, but Katie had always thought of herself as more level-headed. Now she was sure of it. "I didn't know you were getting so rich writing those stories. New cars cost seven or eight hundred dollars."

"No, not anymore. See, look here," Maggie said, pointing to the advertisement. "They'll be rolling Model A's off the assembly line any day now in Detroit for two hundred and ninety-five dollars. Roy ought to get you one. Len says he's making plenty of money."

"It's all tied up in those big well-drilling rigs," Katie said with dismay.

———

BUT MAGGIE KEPT THE ADVERTISEMENT in her pocket, and every week or so she counted the money she was putting away in her trunk. By the summer of 1926, she'd made almost two hundred dollars, enough for a down payment on a new car. Tate would never in a million years approve of her buying a new car—she'd have to do it on her own. And before she could do it on her own, she'd have to learn to drive. The big question was how to get to Wilmington without raising questions.

She hadn't yet worked that out when Tate drove up one spring day in the old 1919 Chandler Six. Miss Bessie Bloodworth had sent word to him about the antiquated automobile that her sister in Burgaw had stored in her barn since her brother-in-law's death two years ago. Will had taken some tools, a new battery, and an air pump, and they'd gone to Burgaw and gotten the vehicle running. Tate was driving when they came rattling down the lane with the top down, chugging like an old locomotive. In the boot he'd found a pair of goggles and an old driving cap, and Maggie thought she was seeing things until they both got out of the car laughing.

"Well, Maggie Lorena, you've been harping on learning to drive," Tate said, doubling over with laughter. "So here's your new car, shug." He was enjoying himself immensely. "A few more dents won't hurt it."

Maggie was furious. She'd hardly mentioned her wish to him. He'd had no way of knowing what else she was planning, how much money she'd saved—yet he was making a pure-tee fool of her.

William saw right off that the joke had not set well with his mother. "He's just teasing, Mama. It n-n-needs a lot of work, but I'm going to fix it up for you. It's just dirty and hasn't been run for a long time."

Maggie stared at the rusted old heap, with one headlight hanging by the wires and its bumper tied on with rope. "Thank you. That's mighty nice of you, Will." She turned around and went back to the porch, where she was writing a love story in which the heroine got *all* that she wanted, *when* she wanted it.

22

Learning to Drive

WILL STOPPED EVERYTHING TO WORK ON the old car, so badly did he feel about hurting his mama's feelings. But after she'd given it some thought, Maggie had decided that the venerable machine was just what she needed. She'd seen quite a few Chandlers in Boston, not all of them new, either. An automobile that had been around for a while was a testament to its quality. Besides, the money she'd tucked away would come in handy when she was out on her own. Will would fix it up like new. He was good at that, and if he had to, he'd put a new engine in it. Hadn't he done that many times for his current benefactor?

Mice had gotten into the car's upholstery, but Maggie had patched it with her father's old army blanket, which was in shreds anyhow. She'd used Will's wire brush to clean the rust from the bumpers and polished the painted surfaces to high heaven with kerosene, a trick her son had shown her to brighten the faded paint. One of her favorite things about the old car was the wooden wheel spokes, something you never saw anymore. She'd taken sandpaper to them and ordered a can of varnish from the Sears and Roebuck catalogue. They looked like new. Will had cautioned her. "You'll have to be real c-c-careful with them w-w-wheels," he'd said. "If you run over something and b-b-break one, m-m-might not be able to find another one ar-r-round here."

Tate hadn't taken much interest in the Chandler, preferring to drive his jalopy just about everywhere, even out to the fields over

Lyon Swamp where a road ran along the new drainage ditch. After Will had gotten the old Chandler running good, Maggie had asked him to bring the automobile up close to the house where she could admire it. "I'd like you to give me a lesson or two when you get time, son."

"I w-w-will, Mama, but I'm s-s-so far behind in the garage, m-m-maybe we better w-w-wait till L-L-Len comes home."

She'd been thinking about asking Tate, as much as she disliked the idea, when Jasper stopped by to visit her, bringing a string of fish. Jasper was her favorite brother and she didn't care who knew it. She thought him to be about the handsomest man she'd ever known, with his dark hair and angular chin that jutted out stubbornly when he was confronted. He was the most like her father, George Washington Corbinn, whose eyes could read a person like a book. If he didn't like what he saw, he'd turn his back on you.

"Well, now, that's a mess of catfish if I ever saw one. You'll stay and eat with us, won't you?" Maggie asked.

"No, honey. I can't wait to get home and fry some of those suckers for myself. I know you and Tate don't eat until late. I'm pretty near perished right now, just thinking about the fish I left in my truck."

"Where'd you get them?" Maggie asked, knowing that Jasper was a fisherman—but today he was dressed in good clothes.

"Stopped by to see some friends of mine. They're having a big fish fry on the river tonight. Wanted me to stay, but I thought you and your crowd might like some for supper."

"We're mighty obliged, Jasper. Won't you sit a spell?"

"No, Sister, I just want to take a look at that automobile out yonder. Where'd you get it?"

She walked out as far as the porch with him, telling him the story, watching him circle the solidly built old car and admiring every crack and cranny of it. "Tate brought it home sort of as a joke, but he couldn't have done me a bigger favor," Maggie said.

"How come you've taken such an interest in it, sister?"

She snorted resentfully, adjusting the long house dress that she wore with an apron. "Because I'm going to learn to drive it," she said.

"Damn, that's a good-looking car." He stepped back, admiring the lines of the Chandler. "Don't make 'em like that anymore." He shook his finger at her. "Don't you *ever* let Tate get rid of this car without talking to me first, you hear me!"

Maggie was taken aback. Jasper really liked the old car. "Will said parts are almost impossible to find," she said, "but I guess beggars can't be choosers."

"You let me worry about those parts. I'll find 'em, if need be." Maggie was thrilled that her brother, who characteristically set store by valuable old things, appreciated the car. Jasper continued to circle the car, rubbing his hands over it, inspecting the tires and the wooden spokes. "I can't picture you learning to drive, not as high-strung as you are. You're liable to wreck it, and that would be a damn shame."

"And I can't believe you'd say that to me, Jasper Corbinn," she said, lifting her skirt and stepping off the porch, getting right up in his face. "I'm a woman now, a woman who's seen a bit of the world beyond Colly Swamp. Why wouldn't I want to be able to drive a car and go places?"

"Where'd you want to go?"

"I declare, can't I have some hopes and dreams without you asking me for specifics?" she stammered, her hands on her hips. "You're the galvantingest member of the family—going off to Florida, down to Wilmington. Nobody knows where you are half the time."

"Damn, Maggie Lorena, I'm a man!" he said, looking a lot like her father, the old Civil War captain whose flashing eyes and snarling lip had fended off many a disgruntled soldier. "And I don't have nobody at home every evening waiting for me to fix his supper," he said, wagging his finger again in her face.

She backed off. "My stars, you'd think I was talking about leaving home for good. I just want learn how to drive so I can go down to Wilmington and deliver my stories to the paper now and then. May I have your permission, big brother?"

"Wouldn't be the first time," Jasper said.

"First time, what?"

"You know what I mean." But a smile creased his face and he started towards the car. "C'mon, I'll show you a few things while William changes my oil."

Jasper thought he was going to have a heart attack every time Maggie shifted the long stick and the car ground into gear. "Hell, Maggie Lorena, you're going to strip out the whole goddamn gearbox!" He reached down and put his hand on her foot. "Let the clutch out real, real slow until you feel the gear start to grab." The car lurched forward. "Shit! Come over here and I'll show you," he said, getting out of the car and snatching a sheet of paper off her writing table.

"You see, you've got these little wheels with wedges cut out of them. When you're in neutral, they're not touching each other, but when you shift, they move together so they're touching—except they slip together between those little cutout places." He demonstrated with his fingers. "That makes the drive shaft turn and . . . " He realized that Maggie wasn't listening when he looked up and saw Patty Sue McBryde pull her truck into the drive.

"Look at that brazen strumpet," Maggie said. "I just as good as told her I didn't want her coming around here, but she keeps bringing those old trucks to Will to fix."

"Yeah, I heard about that," Jasper said. He'd heard a lot more than that concerning the McBryde woman, but he wasn't about to tell Maggie that she was running whiskey. His sister's family badly needed the money William brought in.

————

ON THE THIRD OF AUGUST, a formal announcement of Wilmington's newest medical practice arrived at Katie's for Maggie.

In a careful hand, along the bottom of the stiff card, was the note *Clinic hours are 12–4, MWF.* The addendum was not signed, but Maggie recognized Jon McNamara's hand.

"He's Henry Montgomery's nephew, for goodness sakes, Katie. I helped him with the funeral arrangements," Maggie protested when her sister handed her the card with raised eyebrows. "I asked him to let me know when he arrived in Wilmington, but I thought it might not look right. I gave him your address."

"Why not, you've become such a *new* woman, driving a car and all that."

"Now, Katie, there's nothing to it. It's just that Tate has been behaving so strange since I came home from Boston. He's just downright cantankerous."

"The pot calling the kettle black?"

"I reckon I've changed a lot in that department, Katie. I just want to write my stories." That much was true.

———

EVERY DAY MAGGIE DROVE THE CAR to the mailbox, up the road to Katie's house, to Aunt Mag's to check on her or carry her some soup—anywhere she could until she felt confident enough to tackle the long drive to Wilmington by herself. The day before she planned to go, she drove down to Jasper's new house on a ruse to show him her new skills. "Come down off that ladder and get in. We'll drive to Zeb's and back."

Jasper reluctantly ambled over to the car. "You're not going to jerk a knot in me, are you, Sister? I ain't got time to be laid up a week or two with a crick in my neck."

Maggie smiled, figuring she'd show him a thing or two. "Get in, Jasper."

"Oh, hell, here I go torturing myself," he said, slamming the car door.

Maggie eased out the clutch and shifted smoothly into first gear. "Well, I'll be dammed, that was not bad." She got her speed up and shifted into second gear, then third, as smooth as you please. Jasper smiled, confident she'd picked up the procedure so easily because he'd explained the mechanics behind the operation of the gearbox. "I might have to start me a driving school," he said.

"If I was to want to go to Wilmington by myself, do you reckon I could find the way?"

Jasper eyed her curiously. "Going by yourself, huh?"

"Yes, I really want to do it," she said, her chin set stubbornly.

"Don't want me to drive you over there? I've got some business in Wilmington."

"No, I don't. Just give me some directions."

"You know how to get to Paul's Crossroad, don't you?"

"I reckon."

"Well, just get on the highway there. It'll take you straight to town."

She got back in the car and closed the door. "Your house looks real pretty," she said. "I see the barn's about finished too."

"I'm right proud of it."

She started the engine. "Jasper?"

"What?"

"You won't tell anybody I'm going to Wilmington, will you? If I make a fool of myself, get lost or something, I'd never hear the end of it. I'd appreciate it if you'd keep it to yourself."

"I reckon I could do that," he said, wondering what she was up to, knowing there was more to it.

23
A Foolish Trek

B UT MAGGIE HAD THOUGHT BETTER OF going off without announcing her intentions to Tate. If something happened to her, or to the car for that matter, he'd be the first one they'd come after. She told him very matter-of-factly that she'd be driving to Wilmington on Friday—by herself. "If I leave early, I'll be back well before dark."

Tate wasn't happy about it, just as she'd figured. "I know you're going to do as you please, Maggie Lorena, but I think you're mighty foolish making that trek to Wilmington, no longer than you've been driving."

"Tate, you're about as old-fashioned as Aunt Mag. Other women drive all over the country, and their husbands don't say a thing about it."

"How long have you been planning on it?"

"Why, I've just been waiting until I felt more confident about driving. Remember when I rode to town with Jasper that time he took Aunt Mag to the hospital? I know right where to go."

"That was more'n a year ago."

"You don't reckon they've moved it, do you?"

"You know what I mean. Besides, you're not going to the hospital, are you?"

That had taken her aback. "I'm just going as far as the newspaper office. Mr. Brown has been after me for a whole year to come by and see him. It's about time I did."

They were sitting on the porch, enjoying a cool evening that had been ushered in by a thunderstorm earlier in the day. "'Bout time the weather cooled down," Tate said. "I'll be going to the tobacco market in a week or so. Anything you want while I'm in Whiteville?"

Maggie was darning socks by what little light there was left before evening set in. "You might go by Mr. J. C. Wooten's store and get some socks for you and the boys. He talked like they have just about everything anybody'd want."

"Anything else? Something for yourself, some dress goods, maybe?"

Maggie kept her eyes on the hole in the sock. She couldn't imagine Tate buying any dress fabric for her. He never had. "That's kind of you, but I reckon I'll do a little looking around in Wilmington tomorrow. I need a pair of house shoes. That's about all."

"Well, let me know if you change your mind," he said, rubbing his thick hands together, then rocking back, intertwining his fingers across his stomach.

"Rheumatism bothering you?"

"No. I was just thinking, Len'll be home. We'll have to borrow a truck."

Maggie threw the darned sock into her sewing basket, stood and straightened her dress. "Well, I'm sure you know someone you can borrow one from." She turned on her heel and went inside, slamming the screen door behind her.

———

MAGGIE WAS UP BEFORE DAWN, BATHING and dressing, carefully examining her outfit, sniffing her blouse, anxious that she not carry with her any of the scents associated with country living, like kerosene and fried meat. She was glad the weather had remained cool. The crisp white blouse she'd chosen would stay fresh, and among working women, at least, her long skirt was still fashionable. She wanted to present herself to her editor, Mr. Edmund Brown, as a modern woman, driving her own car.

"You be careful you don't hit anything," Tate said, waving to her as she steered out of the driveway. She'd asked him to put the top up on the car against the sun and the wind, which she knew would play havoc with her complexion as well as her hair. Her red curls were cut short again with a new pair of scissors she'd ordered with a coupon out of the oatmeal box, and she'd pinched it into waves the way she'd worn it in Boston. Throwing up her hand, she waved to her husband, watching him in her side-view mirror. He'd asked her twice this morning if she was sure she didn't want him to go with her.

———

MAGGIE CROSSED THE RIVER ON THE FERRY *John Knox*. Walking along the rail as the vessel plied the Cape Fear River, she marveled at the difference between this mud-colored waterway and the Black River that had been so much a part of her life. It was the Black River she'd crossed so many times, coming and going to Onslow County. She'd been baptized in the Black River at Longview and had swum in it at Point Caswell. The dark water was actually brown with tannin, a stain given off by the cypress trees that lined its banks and the swamps along the river. It was a lazy river, unhurried through Sampson, Bladen, and Pender Counties until it converged with the mighty Cape Fear just above Wilmington, where it became a burnt-caramel confluence rushing headlong towards the sea.

As she cranked up the automobile and drove off the platform at the foot of Market Street, Maggie received her share of glances from men who stood on the dock watching the ferry unload. She pretended not to hear the whistles or the naughty remarks, but she was glad when she'd left the Dock Street area. Mr. Edmund Brown had given her precise directions to the newspaper office some time ago, and she was delighted when she found herself directly in front of a sign at Front and Chestnut that read THE MORNING STAR.

"May I help you?" a receptionist asked, looking Maggie over when the silver bells above the door chimed. Her hair was coal black—bottle-black to be sure—and she was smacking a wad of chewing gum that appeared in the corner of her mouth when she spoke.

"I'd like to see the editor, Mr. Brown, if you please."

"Who's calling?" the woman asked in a Northern brogue, ducking her cigarette in an ashtray full of lipstick-coated butts.

Maggie launched into a long description of who she was and why she was there, evidently too much information for the receptionist, who proceeded to file her fingernails until Maggie had finished. "He's not here," she responded.

"Oh, shall I wait?"

"Not unless you want to wait all day and into the night when we put the paper to bed. That's when Mr. Ed'll be here."

"Not until tonight?"

"That's right."

Disillusioned and disappointed, Maggie left her next story with the receptionist and bid her adieu, thinking how foolish she must have seemed to call on the editor without an appointment. An ominous thought, considering that she also did not have an appointment at her next destination either.

———

THE JAMES WALKER MEMORIAL HOSPITAL at Ninth and Rankin Streets looked more like a fine hotel than an institution, its wide porches and covered drive-through side entrance lending a graceful ambience to a place where life and death began or ended for many of its patients. She'd heard that black or white, it didn't matter, you could get medical care at James Walker.

She parked the car and walked the perimeter of the building until she found the entrance to the clinic. A white-uniformed nurse stood like a sentry at the door. "May I direct you, my dear?"

"Yes, I'm looking for the surgical clinic. I'd like to see . . . "

"This way," she said, pointing down a long corridor. "Turn left and it's the third door on the left."

Maggie tiptoed down the antiseptic-smelling hall, aware of the loud tapping her modest heels made on the white tiled floor. She entered a large room with chairs lining all but one wall. Another nurse sat at a small table. "Your name, please, and the doctor you're seeing."

Maggie looked about the room at a dozen or more waiting patients. They all stared at her. "I'm really not here to see the doctor—I mean, I am," she stammered, "but I'm not a patient. I wanted to see—"

"If you don't have an appointment, I don't see how we can . . . "

"I wanted to speak to Dr. McNamara. He's an old friend . . . from Boston . . . and I just wanted to say hello."

"Your name, Miss?"

"Maggie Ryan."

"I'll tell Dr. Jon, but he's seeing patients right now, and he has a very full schedule."

"Yes, I understand. I'll sit over here and wait a little while."

"It may be a long while, my dear. He usually doesn't finish until after four o'clock."

"Oh, yes. It's quite all right, I'll just wait."

———

THANK GOODNESS SHE'D BROUGHT THE BOOK Abigail had sent to her. Without Pearl Buck's *So Big* to read, she'd have been even more nervous watching the slow migration of patients go through the door as they were called somewhere into the catacombs of the hospital. If Jon only knew she was in this room, he would have moved mountains to see her. But she had the feeling that the formidable nurse had likely not mentioned *who* was waiting for the doctor. Several times Maggie thought she'd heard his voice as he walked a patient to the interior door, but he never appeared.

Overcome with drowsiness, Maggie dozed on and off sitting straight up in the uncomfortable white metal chair, opening her eyes now and then to glance at the large clock on the wall. At four o'clock, there were still several patients waiting, and a different nurse staffing the desk. Hesitantly, Maggie stepped over to the table and inquired as to whether or not Dr. McNamara was still seeing patients.

"Why no, Miss. He was called to surgery about an hour ago." She looked down at the list on the table. "Let's see who'll be seeing you." But by the time the attendant looked up Maggie had exited the building, blinded by tears of embarrassment. *I should never have come!* she cried to herself. *Foolish, foolish woman!*

The ferryman had warned her to be in line by four-thirty if she wanted to make the ferry. She'd spent eighty-five cents on a round-trip ticket and she had no intention of missing it, nor of driving the lonely road back to Colly in the dark. The visit had been premature, her plan ill-considered. Jon McNamara would have to wait until another time.

Tired and dejected, Maggie drove the thirty-five miles home, arriving in time for supper, a meal she was obliged to fix for her husband and son. The day was supposed to be a culmination of all that she'd prepared for in the last year. Tate had been right, it was a foolish trek, but not because she hadn't learned to drive.

Cal's new Model A Ford

2 4
Coming of Age

EVA MCBRYDE WAS NOT UNHAPPY WITH HER new life in Wilmington. Despite the heartache over leaving her country home, all her doubts and misgivings had been smoothed over by the good that had come of it. By 1927 the boardinghouse on Princess Street was a success, making a respectable home which her family could not have afforded otherwise. Hugh and Calvin had good jobs at the Coast Line, Harry had finished law school, Rebecca was in her last year of nursing school, and Belle would finish business school as soon as she completed a shorthand course. Millie, a sophomore at New Hanover High, worked after school at Beau Monde, Miss Emily McAllister's hat shop on Front Street. The youngest children, Rodney and Vera, walked each morning to Hemenway Elementary School on Fifth Street, a blessing in itself when Eva thought about the long bus rides they would have taken in Bladen County.

The McBryde family had joined the First Baptist Church at the corner of Fifth and Market, where Eva had made new friends and become a member of a women's circle. Church socials and beach trips, moving pictures and boat rides in Greenfield Park added elements to their lives they'd never have known in the country. Yet the sorrow brought on by Davy's incarceration at Dix Hill still hung over Eva like a pall. She had headaches and long sleepless nights when she'd go over and over the situation, figuring how she might have prevented this terrible thing from happening. She felt as if she'd somehow let Kathleen down.

Hugh, believing that managing the boardinghouse was taking a toll on his mother, arranged for a housekeeper to come in twice a week to do the cleaning chores. Dr. Randall saw Eva once a month to measure her blood pressure, and he'd put her on a new medicine, a blood thinner that was supposed to make it easier on her heart, prevent another stroke. But the headaches came more frequently, and she'd found that she couldn't go without a nap in the middle of the day. After supper, it was all she could do to get to her bed.

Eva praised God that He had known that someday she would need a daughter like Millie, one who saw a thing wanting to be done and did it without being asked. Even after work, Millie came home to tidy up the house, fold clothes, put the ironing away, and stock clean towels in the bathrooms. She read stories to the younger children and laid out their clothes for school the next day, all things her mother had done in the course of a day when she was feeling well.

But Eva was careful not to impose on Millie, encouraging her to go to the movies on Saturday afternoons and attend church socials where she'd be in the company of other Christian young people. She'd urged her to get a job in a nice shop where she'd meet elegant women with good manners. Though Eva was a country woman, she was aware of the advantages of knowing the right people and being exposed to the finer things in life. Her own father had been a Congressman until he had met a tragic death, along with her mother, when their house in Cotton Cove had burned to the ground.

Richard O'Kelly, Sr., had taken his three children to Washington, D.C., often, to acquaint them with the nation's capital. They were required to shake hands and curtsy—to be seen, not heard. Their days were spent with grown-ups in the halls of the capitol, their evenings at plays and musicales. O'Kelly's plan was that his children, Dick, Eva, and Kathleen, would garner the attention and approval of his most respected associates, thereby setting them up to marry well. Before Richard O'Kelly's untimely death,

Dick was awarded a full scholarship to Wake Forest College and became engaged to Lilibeth Hanover, a debutante from Oklahoma. While his son was set for life, his daughters, Kathleen and Eva, found themselves orphaned in Bladen County with only a small general store and their inherited land as their dowry. Eva had never regretted her marriage to Robert McBryde, but she had often wondered what might have been different had their father and mother lived.

Eva McBryde couldn't afford to buy her daughter expensive clothes, or a preparatory school education, but she could see to it that Millie became associated with women like Emily McAllister. Eva had met Emily at her church, where the congregation included many of Wilmington's old society. Just after Thanksgiving, she'd worn her best dress and the black fur-trimmed coat Harry had bought her recently at Farrell's, walked downtown to Beau Monde, and asked to speak to Mrs. McAllister.

The shop girl had been gracious, but informed her that Mrs. McAllister came into the shop only three days a week. She would be there the following day. "Would you have her telephone me?" Eva asked, leaving her name and number written on a small note card.

"Of course, Mrs. McBryde."

The proprietor called the next day, and Eva asked if she might have a job for a young apprentice. "As a matter of fact I do," Mrs. McAllister said. "My business has picked up considerably with the holidays and I need someone right away." It had been as simple as that.

MILLIE MCBRYDE TOOK THE SHORTCUT between Market and Princess Streets on her way home from New Hanover High School, cutting through on the narrow lane that ran between Mr. Hugh MacRae's house and his sister's. Ordinarily Millie went straight to the little hat shop on Front Street where she worked, but today she had some exciting news to tell Mama and she couldn't wait until she got home. Besides, it was the prettiest day she'd ever seen in Wilmington, and it felt good to be outside in the May sunshine.

In April, on either side of the lane, blossoms on little apple trees had filled the air with a sweet perfume. In September there'd be tiny red apples that would drop to the ground, scattering like marbles all over the lane. Mr. MacRae's sister, Agnes Parsley, had said she didn't care who picked them up on her side, but old Mr. Hugh was tighter than Dick's hatband. He had his cook pick them up daily in season to make his apple jelly. If he saw anybody snitch a single one, he'd come out there chasing you with his walking stick.

Millie ran up the steps of her Princess Street home two at the time. She loved the elegant old house that had once been the home of Marcus E. Ainsley, a wealthy industrialist who'd made a fortune off cotton after the Civil War. When her brothers had bought it, they'd researched the history of the house and found out that Mr. Ainsley died in the influenza epidemic of 1918. His wife had lived there until just a few years ago when she died, and the house was eventually put up for sale by the bank for taxes.

At school Millie had made friends with Mrs. Ainsley's great-niece, Mary Avis Caine, whose mother remembered Christmas dinners and playing in the dark attic of the enormous old house when she was a young girl. One day Mary Avis and Millie had climbed the stairs to the attic and found Mary Avis's great-grandmother's trunk with her name painted on the end. Instead of the treasure they had hoped to find, the trunk had been full of musty old curtains.

———

ON THE PORCH, RODNEY AND VERA WERE PLAYING checkers at a wicker table. "Hey, y'all," Millie said. Vera looked up at her big sister through thick glasses. She'd been born with crossed eyes and poor sight. The first thing Hugh had done when they moved to Wilmington was take her to a specialist at Bullocks

Hospital. The doctor had operated on Vera a few weeks later and prescribed glasses.

"I beat Rodney twice at checkers," Vera said, jumping up and dancing across the porch.

Rodney had obviously been given the responsibility of entertaining his little sister for the afternoon and was none too happy about it. "Anybody can beat somebody at checkers. You couldn't beat me at marbles," he said.

"Mama won't let me play marbles. She said I'd get my dress dirty."

Millie put her arms around her sister. "Well, it's not ladylike to play marbles, but one of these days, maybe your brother will show us how so we can be smarter than the other girls."

"You'd have to put on a pair of pants," Rodney said, laughing.

"I'm sure we could find some around this house, with all of you boys."

"Where's Mama?"

"She's resting on my bed," Rodney said.

Millie opened the heavy door with its full-length oval beveled glass, shut tight daily against the soot from the Coast Line's nearby freight yards. Careful not to slam the door, Millie adjusted the lace curtain and turned to see her father coming down the stairs carrying his shoes. She hugged him and gave him a kiss on the cheek. "Is it time for you to go to work already, Papa?"

"Almost, Sister. Your mama's resting. I'm going to get me a bite to eat before I go down to the winery."

"Oh, I wanted to tell her something."

"Can't you tell me, shug?"

Millie blushed. "No, sir, it's kind of girl talk." She put her books on the hall table and followed him to the kitchen, where she washed her hands at the sink. "Want me to pour you a glass of buttermilk before I go? I see Mae left a piece of corn bread over there on the stove."

"Don't you want it?"

"No, sir. I've got just enough time for a cherry soda at Brantley's."

"You go on, Sister, I can take care of myself. Won't do to be late for work. Not this day and time with jobs hard to get."

She hugged him again, kissing him on the cheek. "I know, Papa. I'll hurry."

"Take this nickel," he said, digging into his pocket. "Let me buy that soda for you."

"Thanks, Papa. Tell Mama I'll see her when I get home."

———

MILLIE RAN OUT THE BACK DOOR, crossing the narrow yard that enclosed the grassy area where her mother hung out sheets and towels several times a week. She loved to take the laundry down for Mama, loved crushing the fresh linen against her face. Hugh had bought Mama a new electric washing machine that sat on the lattice-enclosed back porch. The first time she'd used it, Millie had begged to help her put the clothes through the wringer attached to the side of the washer. She'd mashed her fingers pretty badly before Mama jerked out the plug.

Slipping through an opening in the board fence, Millie paused to admire the purple and yellow iris that hugged the base of the fence. A large azalea bush in the corner rose above the fence and draped its orchid blossoms on the other side, and the climbing rose trailing across the back porch would soon be covered in red blooms again. On a vacant lot near the corner, Papa had already plowed his garden, planting a row of cut flowers for Mama, who always took a bouquet and a pound cake to a sick friend.

———

MILLIE COULD HARDLY WAIT UNTIL SCHOOL WAS OUT. Miss Emily's nieces, Agatha and Mandy Evans, were arriving in Wilmington in two weeks, and she'd invited all of the McBryde girls to come for the weekend at her Wrightsville Beach home. There'd be a slumber party on Friday night, a bridge luncheon on Saturday at noon, and dancing at Lumina that evening. Miss Emily had spent the last month running back and forth between her home on Market Street and the cottage at the beach, meeting workmen and decorators who were renovating the fifteen-year-old cottage in preparation for the summer.

Belle McBryde had met the Evans girls the previous summer at Lumina, where she and Agatha Evans spent most of their evenings. Big bands like Tommy Dorsey and Stan Kenton played at Lumina almost every night, and guys formed a line to dance with Belle and Agatha, who knew all the new dance steps. Although they were two years different in age—Belle was eighteen and Agatha twenty— they were two of a kind, free spirits with a little bit of devilment thrown in.

Everything Belle earned at her job waiting tables at the Oceanic went for clothes. To look at her out on the dance floor, anyone would think she'd been brought up with a silver spoon in her mouth—just like Agatha, who also waited tables, but not because she needed the money. Waiting tables was what girls did in the summer at the beach—that or clean cottages, keep children for the beachgoers, or any other excuse to spend the summer by the ocean. It was part of belonging to the crowd, a way of meeting life-guards and busboys—anyone of the opposite sex who migrated to the coast every summer for the same purpose.

The day before, Belle had stopped by the hat shop on her way to Rehder's Department Store. "Why did she have to ask that old fuddy-duddy Rebecca?" Belle asked Millie in a whisper.

"Because she likes Rebecca. Agatha and Mandy do, too."

"Agatha is my friend first."

"Don't be so selfish, Belle. I love Rebecca like I love you. We're all sisters." Miss Emily said sisters were like that sometimes, but one of these days they'd probably be the best of friends.

———

MARY AVIS WAS WAITING FOR MILLIE at Bellamy's Drugstore on the corner of Front and Market. "Where've you been?" she hissed. "He's right over there."

"Where?"

"Don't look now."

Millie was facing Mary Avis, straining to see out of the corner of her eye the group of young people sitting around one of the small tables in the drugstore. "Has he seen you?"

"I don't think so, but he's looking over here now," she said, handing Millie a cherry Coke. "The ice has melted."

"I would have gotten it," Millie said. "Here's a nickel. Papa gave it to me."

"Forget it. I had to have something to do while I was waiting for you," she said, glancing over Millie's shoulder. "Uh-oh, here he comes."

"Hi, Rusty," Millie said. Rusty O'Reilly was a senior at New Hanover High School and assistant editor of the yearbook, *Cat Tales*.

"Hey, Millie. I saw you come in. You always come here after school?"

"Sometimes. I work around the corner in the hat shop."

"At Miss Emily's? My mom's in the Sorosis with her."

"I finished the layouts," Millie said. "They're on the desk in the workroom."

"Yeah. I saw them before I left school. Look nice."

"Thanks."

"Well, I just wanted to tell you that." He glanced at her friend. "Hey, Mary Avis."

Millie thought Mary Avis was going to fall off her chair. "Hey," she replied, taking a sip of her soda.

"See you tomorrow, Millie. We go to the printer on Friday."

"Okay. See you."

Mary Avis swooned. "Did you see the way he looked at me?"

"I thought you had a crush on Bobby Renfrow."

"I do, but he's just a sophomore. I can dream, can't I?"

"Look, I've got to go. I'm going to be late for work."

"You can't leave me here by myself."

Millie started for the door. "Come on out with me then, silly."

"You know what I think? I think it's *you* he likes."

"Who, Bobby?"

"No—Rusty."

Millie didn't have the heart to tell Mary Avis that Rusty had asked her to the prom that very morning. Besides, Mama might not let her go.

2 5

Beau Monde

T HE BEAU MONDE SHOP ADDED A TOUCH of high fashion to Wilmington's Front Street. While Miss Tucie's establishment in Jacksonville had been one of eastern North Carolina's finest millinery shops when Emily McAllister bought it from her, Wilmington had a different clientele. Many of Emily's customers were senators' and doctors' wives who had second homes on the sound or the beach. Some came to Banks Channel in yachts, just to watch the sailboat races. These women found great pleasure in discovering a specialty shop in town where they could purchase unusual hats to take home to Boston or New York.

Emily's daughter, Jeanne McAllister, managed Miss Tucie's Hat Shop in Jacksonville, whose name they'd retained because of the former owner's reputation for fine hats. Jeanne had hired one of Miss Tucie's protégées to continue her work when the old woman developed senility. The protégée, a young Swedish woman, turned out to be a godsend for the shop in Wilmington as well. Today, Jeanne was in Beau Monde to bring some of the Swedish milliner's creations from Jacksonville.

Smoothing her blonde hair back behind her ears, she tried on a white felt hat with scrolls of tiny black beads covering the crown and brim. "Will you look at this, Mother? The handwork is perfect."

"Tedious, to be sure. Beautiful on you, but I know just the customer who will die for it."

"Good, I'll be back in a week or two with a couple more originals," Jeanne said, slipping into her long spring coat. Emily thought her daughter to be unusually striking. Tall and slender, with golden hair, she wore the current fashions like a Parisian model. But even on trips abroad when she'd more than once been mistaken for a movie star, she chose to ignore the limelight, preferring instead her own world aloof from the fast crowds and lavish parties. Sleek cars, good clothes, and valuable jewelry were her style, but there was nothing gaudy about her. In many ways she was much like her Uncle Reece.

"Millie should be here soon," her mother reminded her.

Jeanne, who sometimes spent the night with her mother, was in more of a rush than usual. "I'd love to see her, Mother, but I can't stay. I really don't like to drive at night."

"Remember, the McBryde girls are spending the first weekend in June with us at the beach. I need you for a fourth at the bridge luncheon on Saturday."

"I wouldn't miss it for the world."

"I've also asked a few of our friends out on the beach to the lunch. I want it to be a real welcoming party for Agatha and Mandy."

"The McBryde girls would have been enough. I've never seen anything like the way they get along with Mandy and Agatha. You'd think we were kin," Jeanne said, packing some supplies into a large canvas bag. "I feel like we have a real family now, don't you?"

"Yes, I do. I know there wasn't much for you in Jacksonville, but your father and I tried to—"

"Oh, Mother, I didn't mean it like that," Jeanne said.

But Emily had regretted those years she'd spent providing a home for her brother, Reece, at Evanwood while her husband, Duncan McAllister, lived alone most of the time in Jacksonville. It had seemed the right thing to do at the time, and she freely admitted that she'd enjoyed living in the home where her grandparents had raised her. Emily and Reece had been close after their parents died. Still, she knew that her own children had longed for play-mates. When Jeanne and Darcy went away to college, there'd been only a few friends who came home with them for the holidays.

"I know you didn't mind, but I realize now how cloistered you were," Emily said, straightening the hem of her daughter's coat. If I'd raised you in Philadelphia, you'd have had so much more family around. Perhaps like Amanda, you'd marry someone from a fine family. You're witty and well educated."

"Mother, will you stop fussing over me! You've said it yourself, I'm more like Uncle Reece. I don't need that," Jeanne continued, primping in front of a full-length mirror. "But if the hat shop in Jacksonville gets any more boring, I may just decide to do something else." She flipped her storybook-blonde curls up over her coat collar. "Wonder if Charlie Lindbergh would like a little company on his next flight to Paris?"

"Jeanne, really, he's a married man."

"I didn't say I wanted to have an affair with him, I'd just like to have the thrill of accompanying him." She opened the shop door and looked out. "Where on earth is my car? That little mechanic at McMillan and Cameron said he'd deliver it."

"Millie will be disappointed."

"I'll see her at the beach. I want to get back to Jacksonville in time to look over Darcy's books. He thinks his manager has been doing some juggling," she said, pulling on a pair of beige leather silk-lined gloves.

Emily kissed her daughter on the cheek. "History repeats itself, doesn't it?"

"What do you mean?"

Emily smiled. "You're looking after your brother like I did your Uncle Reece."

"Yes, but Darcy pays me, Mother."

Emily opened the shop door. "You're almost twenty-five, darling. Perhaps you should concentrate more on finding a hus-band."

Jeanne laughed. "I've yet to meet anyone I'd like to spend the rest of my life with. And I certainly don't need a man to buy me pretty things." She held out a dainty wrist to her mother. "Look, I've made a killing in the stock market and I'm treating myself to pretties."

Emily looked at the diamond-encrusted watch and band. "Jeanne, you didn't! I have several beautiful watches. I would have given you any one of them. Your Uncle Reece had a fetish for watches, you know."

"Please don't think me ungrateful, Mother. I have my own taste—and nothing gives me more pleasure than walking into Tiffany's, selecting the most expensive watch in the shop, and paying cash for it."

Emily slipped into a chair and began working on a hat, stifling a chuckle. "Really, Jeanne, your behavior is shocking, even to me."

Jeanne sat down directly across from her at the work table. "Look at me, Mother. Can you honestly say that you haven't felt the same pleasure?"

Emily smiled, looking up from her stitching. "I might have done that once or twice," she said. "But I never would have admitted it. In my day, women were less blatant."

Jeanne peeked out the window again and saw the lean young mechanic pull her car up at the curb. "Finally! Look at him slicking his hair back with that comb. I bet he thinks he's the cat's meow, driving my LaSalle." She straightened the seams in her stockings and adjusted her coat so that the collar draped a little in the back. Emily followed her to the door.

"Drive carefully, darling."

"Righto," she said, kissing her mother on the cheek. The mechanic, propped against the car with the driver's door open, lit up a smoke as Jeanne brushed by him. "How sweet of you to bring my car, Jamie. Get rid of that cigarette and I'll take you back to the station."

———

WHEN MILLIE ARRIVED, EMILY GREETED HER with a hug. "You just missed Jeanne."

"Oh, I'm sorry. Am I late?"

"No, you weren't late, dear. Jeanne was in a rush as usual."

"Oh. I wanted to thank her for that box of clothes she gave me. Some of them look like they've never been worn."

Emily laughed. "I'm afraid Jeanne is a spendthrift when it comes to clothes. She has more than she needs. Makes her feel less guilty if she passes them on."

They walked through a bead curtain that separated the displays from the workroom. "We're not going to get into anything too involved today. I'm closing the shop a little early. Amanda's train arrives in less than an hour. Will you come with me?"

"Gosh, I'd love to. How about Agatha?"

"Agatha won't be here for another week. Amanda only arrived in Philadelphia Monday on the Queen Mary. Lord, that girl can really spend money. There's no telling what she bought for her trousseau in Paris."

"Just think, she could have flown back across the ocean with Charles Lindbergh."

Emily laughed. "Yes, wouldn't that have been wonderful? Someday we'll fly back and forth across the ocean in airships."

Millie cringed. "I'd be terrified. What if Lindbergh had run out of gas? They'd never have found him in the Atlantic Ocean."

"Well, he didn't, and I guarantee you, *I* won't be afraid to fly to Paris one of these days."

On the work table, Emily had assembled trim for a fuchsia-colored cloche. Several decorative pins and a long feather lay on the work table. "That feather would be nice on it," Millie said.

"It's for your Aunt Lilibeth. She sent me a swatch of a dress and asked me to make her a hat to match. She said they'd be at the beach next month, and she'd pick it up then. I thought you might like to trim this one out, just for her."

"That'd be fun, but maybe you'd better not tell her. She might decide not to buy it."

"Of course, she'll buy it. Why do you say that?"

"Oh, I don't know, she and Uncle Dick are used to the best that money can buy. She might not like something that her poor relation put together."

"Listen to you, Millie! I'd trust your taste with my best customers anytime. You've such a good eye for combining things, and your sewing is absolutely perfect."

———

AFTER WORK, MILLIE USUALLY ARRIVED HOME in time to help serve the boarders supper, but Amanda's train had been over an hour late. Emily McAllister had driven Millie home after they'd loaded Amanda's bags into the car. Most of the men were in the living room listening to the fights, and Eva had already retired to her bedroom when Millie slipped in the back door.

"Your mama was worrying 'bout you, chile," said Mae. "Where you been?"

"I'm sorry, Mae. I went to the train station with Miss Emily, and you know how trains are."

"I sure do, honey. My sister come down from New York on the Florida Special last year and I waited and waited until my feets was about to fall off." Mae reached into the oven and pulled out a plate of country fried steak and mashed potatoes, dipping a ladle of rich brown gravy over the potatoes. "Sit right here and I'll get you a glass of milk."

"Has Mama already gone upstairs?"

"Yes'um, you'd better see 'bout her when you goes up. She has one of dem headaches. Tell her I'll be here 'bout the usual time. I wants to be sure we get some of the vegetable man's garden peas and tiny new potatoes."

"I'll tell her, Mae. Thanks for saving me some supper."

———

MILLIE FOUND HER MOTHER STRETCHED OUT across her bed, the shades pulled down tight against the late afternoon sun. One arm was across her forehead, and a foot hung off the bed. She was completely still except for the foot that twitched once, then twice.

"Mama, are you asleep?" Millie whispered.

"Is that you, Millie, darling?"

"Yes, Mama. Are you all right?"

"Just a little headache. Come lie down with me."

Millie snuggled against her mother. "Does you head hurt bad?"

"Badly."

"Does your head hurt . . . badly, Mama?"

"I'm better now," Eva said, loosening her deep auburn waves, spilling them out across her pillow. Millie thought she was the most beautiful person in the world, except for the large brown mole that sat in the small crease between her nose and right cheek. As a young child Millie had resisted the urge more than once to reach up and pull it off. Her mother twisted one of Millie's thick black curls around in her fingers. "Imagine, I had nine children and not a single one with my red hair."

"You said it would come out in the grandchildren."

"Oh, it *will* come out in the grandchildren. You mark my words." She pulled Millie into her embrace. "I wouldn't change a single one of you. Not a single one."

Millie propped herself up on one arm. "I got invited to the Junior-Senior Prom today."

"You did?" Eva hugged her again. "That's wonderful! But tell me who? Was it the McCoy boy?"

"It was . . . is . . . oh, Mama, Rusty was so cute."

"Rusty O'Reilly who goes to our church?"

"Yes, that Rusty." Millie sat up on the bed, crossing her legs under her. "I thought I'd die. You know we've been working together on the annual. He came up to me at lunch and asked me if I had a date to the prom. I said no, and he said he'd like for me to go with him. I said I'd have to ask you and Papa, but I wanted to go. Then I saw him at Bellamy's. Mary Avis almost fell off her chair when he came over to our table." They both laughed, and Millie flopped back on the bed.

"He's a senior, isn't he?"

"Yes, ma'am. He's going to Carolina next year."

"Do you like him?"

"Yes, ma'am. But he's sort of conceited or something. The bad part is that Mary Avis has a crush on him. I just couldn't tell her today at the drugstore that he'd asked me to the prom."

"When is it?"

"Next weekend."

"You'll need to tell her soon. She's your best friend, isn't she?"

"What should I do?"

"Just be truthful. But, honey, I'm not sure Papa will like you going out with a senior in high school."

"Aw, Mama, he's not that old. Lots of girls my age are going with boys that are seniors."

"I know, but you're a little young to . . ."

"But this is the Junior-Senior prom."

"All right. I'll ask your papa. And we'll have to start thinking about what you'll wear."

Millie hugged her mother. "Thank you so much, Mama," she said, taking a deep breath. "There's something else. You know, Miss Emily has invited Rebecca and Belle and me to spend the weekend at the beach with Agatha and Mandy right after school is out."

"Yes, that is so nice. I'm glad they want you to come along."

Millie dreaded the next part—her mama and papa, she felt, were sort of old-fashioned. "Well, Belle said they want to go to Lumina on Saturday night 'cause the Lady Bucs are sponsoring a dance and Miss Emily has contributed one of the prizes, and—"

Eva frowned slightly. "Hold on a minute, honey, you're just sixteen. Rebecca and Belle are closer to the Evans girls' ages. They may want to go to Lumina, but I'm sure Miss Emily wouldn't want to take you there. I hear it has gotten a little rough in recent years."

"No, Mama, Miss Emily says lots of families still go there. She's seen little children dancing with their parents."

"Well, if Rebecca and Belle are there, I guess it will be all right. It's just that the Evans girls are so much older."

"Mandy is only twenty-two. Agatha acts like she's about my age."

"How old is she?"

"I think she's twenty."

"Twenty? Why, she's as old as Rebecca."

"I know, but we're all like sisters. Remember *Little Women*? We're like Jo, Meg, Beth, and Amy, except there's one more of us. Me."

"I understand. Who wouldn't love my girls? Agatha and Mandy grew up without much of a family. We should have them all here sometime. Maybe for dinner that Sunday?"

"Could we, Mama? I'll help."

"Of course we can, and we will." Millie loved it when her mother set her chin. The tired look disappeared, and she seemed years younger. "But I'll mention Lumina to Papa, see what he says. There's always that other element, the college boys who . . . " She pulled Millie up by her arms. "They might try and take advantage of a pretty little girl like you."

"No, they won't. I'll dance right away from them," Millie said, hopping off the bed. "Look, I can do the Charleston." Humming, she kicked up her heels and bounced across the floor.

"Look at you, you *can* do the Charleston." Eva said, clapping.

Out of breath, Millie sat back down on the bed. "I don't want to worry you, Mama, but I really want to go to Lumina. If they all go, I couldn't stay at the cottage by myself."

"Wouldn't Miss Emily be there?"

"She likes to go to the dances, too. You'd like to go, wouldn't you, Mama?"

"Yes, now that you mention it, I guess I would." Eva stood up and slipped off her ankle-length dress. "Show me how to do that Charleston thing."

"Wait, Mama. Let me tie your hair back. We'll pretend you've bobbed your hair."

In her slip, Eva practiced the dance with her daughter until she had mastered the steps. "We need some music," Millie said. "I'll go get the Victrola."

Eva's face was red and her breath coming in short rasps when she suddenly sat down on the edge of the bed. "No, honey. That's enough for now. I'm out of breath."

"Are you all right, Mama? You look sort of funny."

"Just a little winded. If you'll get me a drink of water, I'll be fine."

2 6
Little Women, Old Men

THE FIRST WEEKEND IN JUNE EMILY HAD suggested that she'd close the shop on Friday at noon so she and Millie could both get their things ready for the beach. She was not oblivious to the fact that Millie had chores to do for her mother that would be much more important than the few customers who might stray into Beau Monde on a beautiful Friday afternoon. Besides, just about everybody else in town would be heading out Wrightsville Avenue the first weekend school was out, and she intended to be among them. Besides, she needed to stop at the city market for fresh vegetables and the fish market for crab.

Millie spent most of the afternoon at the sewing machine in her mother's room, putting the finishing touches on dresses she'd made for herself and Belle. Rebecca did her own sewing, but Belle couldn't sew a stitch. Not that she'd ever tried. Eva had made all of their dresses until Rebecca and Millie learned to sew. When Rob had closed up the store on Bandeaux Creek, Eva had begged him to let her have all of the bolts of fabric for the girls, anticipating the day when they would want new dresses for every occasion, but as usual, Belle wanted something different.

"I saw this dress in Efird's window on Front Street for ten dollars, Millie. I just know you could make it. Please go down and look at it."

Millie had studied the blue-and-white tissue gingham dress in the window until she was sure she could put it together. "Mama said you could have the rest of that blue dotted Swiss. It's almost the same."

Belle had screwed up her face at the suggestion. "No way. I hate dotted Swiss. It's so babyish. I want gingham and I'll buy it." She was so happy with the dress that she'd brought Millie a bottle of Evening in Paris perfume from Rehder's. But Mama had made Millie leave it unopened on her dresser, saying that only hussies wore perfume.

———

JUNIUS JONES, THE MCBRYDES' NEXT-DOOR NEIGHBOR on Princess Street, insisted on driving the girls out to the beach. Rebecca had been encouraging his attention for the last few months and her younger sisters, Millie and Belle, were not happy about it. "He's old enough to be your father," Belle said. "I saw you out on his porch shaving him yesterday."

"Oh, don't be so such a prude. In nurses' training we have to learn to shave patients. Mr. Jones said I could practice on him."

"Do you really have to shave old men in the hospital?" Millie asked.

"Mr. Jones is not old. He's only forty . . . something."

"Humph! He sure isn't young," Belle said. "You don't even call him by his first name."

"I just started out calling him 'Mr. Jones' and he likes it. Look, he's as nice as he can be. He's gone a lot, working for the Coast Line. When he gets home, he just wants some company."

"I'll bet!" Belle retorted.

"Shut up, Belle. You're just jealous. I think it's real sweet of him to offer to take us to the beach. You can ride the beachcar if you don't like it."

"I thought Calvin might take us after work," Millie said.

Belle was touching up her bright red nail polish. She held up her index finger and blew on it. "Calvin's going up to Raleigh to see Davy tomorrow at the insane asylum."

"Davy's no more insane than I am," Rebecca said.

"We're not supposed to talk about Davy. Mama said—"

"Hush, Millie. You're such a little tattletale. What Mama doesn't know won't hurt her."

"Why aren't we even allowed to say his name?

"Because your Uncle Angus said so," Belle said, rolling her eyes.

"Y'all do it anyway, and Cal gets letters from him at his office." Rebecca's hand went up to her mouth. "He does?"

Belle picked up her brush and smoothed her hair, obviously pleased with her appearance in the mirror. "I knew that."

"Cal said Davy was writing a journal for the psychiatrist," Millie said. "But he's going to give it to Cal in case he never gets out of Dix Hill."

"He might get out of Dix Hill, but he'd probably go straight to the electric chair."

"Belle, you are *so* cruel," Rebecca said. "Don't you even *think* such a thing. Come on, I hear Mr. Jones cranking the car." She grabbed Belle by the arm. "And don't you say a word about me shaving him."

Belle responded with a sly grin. "Now why would I do that?"

———

REBECCA HAD LIKED JUNIUS JONES from the very first time they'd met in the alley between their houses. He'd been out polishing his car and she'd picked up a rag and helped him. About twenty years her senior, Junius Jones was a widower, having lost his wife to cancer shortly before the McBrydes moved in next door. He was a conductor on the Coast Line, making the run from Wilmington to Petersburg and back twice a week with a day off in between. Another time, she'd stopped by and knocked on his door and he'd called her to come in. Looking sick as a dog, he was on his sofa in his undershirt and trousers. "I must've eaten something on the train that was spoiled," he said. Rebecca had gotten soup bones from her Uncle Murdoch's butcher shop and made him a pot of broth. Mr. Jones said that meant a lot to him.

———

"I CAN'T LOOK," REBECCA SAID AS MR. JONES SLOWED the car to make the turn onto the bridge across to the Hammocks. They were passing the ruins of Dr. Sidbury's Babies Hospital. Not long ago, the quaint little hospital had burned to the ground.

"They're going to build it back," Belle said. "It'll probably be a lot prettier than that old wooden building. It was nothing but a fire-trap."

Rebecca was tearful. "It was a beautiful, wonderful little hospital and Dr. Sidbury loved it," she said.

"Aw, honey, don't get upset. I read in the paper where it's going to be much nicer," Junius said. "It's gonna be brick—have lots of beds—private rooms and all that."

"I know, but it just broke Dr. Sidbury's heart."

Belle was making faces in the back seat. "They got everyone out. He ought to look at it as a blessing. I went there one time with Mama to see a little girl in our church who was dying. The place was so drab—looked awful to me."

"You have to overlook the facility sometimes, Belle. It's what goes on in the hearts of the doctors and nurses that counts."

Belle winced. "Oh, brother. Here goes Florence Nightingale again."

"Stop it," Millie said. "It's such a beautiful day to be together."

Belle sat back in her seat and leaned against the window. "Present company excepted," she mumbled, nodding her head towards Rebecca.

———

MR. JONES PULLED HIS 1923 PACKARD TWIN SIX up on the coarse grass that grew between the cottage and the sandy ruts on the lane beside it. Beneath the McAllister cottage, part of the criss-cross lattice work that had enclosed the pilings had been removed to allow for parking. In addition to Emily's Buick, there was Jeanne McAllister's brand new LaSalle V-8 and a Nash 400 that Millie recognized as belonging to Elizabeth Cowell, whose father owned the Nash dealership in Wilmington.

"I'm going to have me a car like that someday," Belle said, referring to Elizabeth's vehicle.

"I wouldn't have a Nash if they gave it to me," Mr. Jones said. "Packard is my kind of car. I bought this one used for my wife just before she died." He cocked his ear towards the engine, expecting the girls to do the same. "Listen to them sixes. Never miss a lick."

Rebecca rubbed her hand over the polished wood trim on the car door. "Me either. I like older models that have been well-preserved," she said, casting a seductive glance his way.

"Oh, brother," Belle said under her breath. "Come on Millie, let's go inside before I get carsick."

Their driver hopped out of the car and ran around to open Rebecca's door, while Millie and Belle climbed out of the back seat on their own. Each had a small satchel that Mr. Jones retrieved from the boot of the car. "What time do you want me to come after you, Becca, honey?"

"I was thinking I might not spend but one night. That is, if you wouldn't mind coming back for me tomorrow afternoon."

His eyes lit up. "Well, yeah! We could go for a boat ride or something. Maybe stop somewhere and have some shrimp." He pulled his watch from his pocket and flipped it open. "Yeah, that'd be good. What time, honey?"

"Four o'clock ought to be fine, Mr. Jones. I'll have had enough girl talk by then."

Belle and Millie missed seeing the peck that Rebecca gave Junius Jones on the cheek, or his hand slide around her waist. Both thought he was a poor catch compared to the good-looking boys that were drawn to the beach in the summer. Rebecca didn't care what her sisters thought. She loved the attention that this older man poured on her, and the fact that he practically ignored her younger, more fetching sisters. She held his hand a moment longer. "I'll miss you," she whispered.

To Be Sure

EMILY MCALLISTER HAD REMODELED her cottage on
Wrightsville Beach extensively following the opening of the
new causeway in June of 1926. Located on the sound side just past
the Oceanic Hotel, it was one of the newer cottages on the north
end, but it had seen some rough wear by a large family. Emily had
put in tiled bathrooms, completely renovated the kitchen, and
closed in one end of the wraparound porch to make a small solarium with a view over the sound.

Prior to the roadway across Banks Channel, when beach access
had been possible only by boat or the electric beachcar, beach house
owners from Wilmington and surrounds drove out as far as the
Hammocks, where most rented a slip at the dock on Harbor Island
near the convention center. Emily had not wanted the responsibility of a boat, choosing instead to hire the dock owner to ferry her and
her groceries and other supplies across Banks Channel.

———

FRIDAY EVENING, AFTER DINNER AT THE OCEANIC, Emily
retired early, fully aware of a sleepless night ahead of her if the giggling girls stayed up all night. But as it turned out, the house was
quiet by midnight and stayed that way until ten the next morning.
Emily had also invited to the luncheon Elizabeth Cowell, her
mother, and three other girls who'd spent last summer at the beach
with Mandy and Agatha.

Millie was the first of the overnight guests to rise and dress, and Emily put her to work tying down the corners of crisp white tablecloths to three small tables on the sound side of the screened porch. Agatha came sailing around the corner of the porch in hair curlers, barefoot and still in her dressing gown. "Oh, goody! You're out here. Aunt Emily is in such a swivet. The flowers haven't been arranged yet and the caterer is on his way. Maybe you can calm her down."

Millie laughed. "She's okay. I was just in the kitchen and she looked to have everything under control." Millie had come to know Emily better in similar circumstances than her nieces did. Under pressure, Emily was a dynamo, whether it was putting trim on a hat at the last minute or getting ready for a fashion show at the Orton Hotel.

"Where's Belle? I need some help with my hair," Agatha said, in a panic. "I asked Rebecca to greet the other guests in case they come before we're ready. She's gone for a walk on the beach. If you see her, tell her to hurry. Liz always comes early." Agatha went running off, mumbling, "Oh, where is everybody when I need them?"

Back in the kitchen, Emily was calmly arranging stems of freesia and miniature roses in three delicate green glass vases. She was dressed in a powder blue linen frock with a white sailor collar. "Agatha said you were in a 'swivet,'" Millie said, laughing.

"Oh, that girl! *She's* the one in a swivet. Imagine, she was still in her gown with curlers in her hair, looking for Belle to help her. What on earth does she do when she's away at school?"

"I imagine she finds someone else who's willing. I just love Agatha."

"I wish she were more independent, like Mandy. I think she will always be a damsel in distress."

"I'll finish the vases if you need to do something else," Millie said.

"Oh, you are a dear. There's more fern in the sink. I do need to give the maid some instructions," she said, drying her hands on a towel. "She's liable to get the silver all wrong." She slipped eight napkins into silver rings and departed for the porch.

Millie was in heaven in the beautiful surroundings that Emily had created. Someday—*someday*—she hoped that she could have a fine home. Not necessarily at the beach, mind you, but a fine home somewhere. To be like Emily McAllister in any way would be a dream come true. The clothes she wore, the way she wore them. Her manner of speaking—so gentle and polite, with carefully chosen words that expressed her exact meaning. *That's what Mama wanted for her too,* Millie thought.

She worked with the arrangements at a large white enameled table in the center of the modern kitchen. When Emily had renovated the kitchen, she'd purchased the latest electrical appliances, seeking the help of a restaurateur who selected a six-burner stove with separate ovens and a large two-door refrigerator. The sink was massive, and there were counters all the way around the room. Wallpaper, hand-stenciled with colorful fish and stems of seaweed, extended from the countertops to the nine-foot ceiling. In one corner stood an electric washing machine. Overhead, an ocean breeze, artificial but nonetheless inviting, wafted from the ceiling fan. Millie thought of the fun she'd have in such a kitchen, entertaining her friends and family with lavish meals. She imagined going down to the dock in the early morning and purchasing shrimp and flounder. She'd spend half the day making fancy sauces and such.

When she'd finished the four flower arrangements, she found a tray and took them to the porch, where Emily was engaged in a conversation with a young man. He glanced at Millie, acknowledging her with a slight lift of his chin.

"I'd ask you to stay for lunch, Len, but I don't think you'd be very comfortable with a gaggle of young women," Emily said.

"No ma'am, I couldn't stay anyhow. Uncle Jasper's waiting for me," he said, tossing his dark red hair back with a slight twist of his head. He was a good-looking guy, tall and well built, not the least bit awkward like some of the boys her age. "Just tell Miss Agatha that I stopped by. She said for me to look her up if I was ever down to the beach."

"Well, that's really nice of you, Len. I'd go and get her, but we're having a lunch party in about twenty minutes and she's still getting dressed. Can you come back later?"

"No, ma'am. Not today. I rode down here with my Uncle Jasper to pick up some flounder. Said he was tired of fishing in those jack holes in Colly, he wanted some real good fish for a fish fry he's having tonight at his new house."

"I'm Agatha's Aunt Emily, and this is Millie McBryde. Millie, this is Len Ryan. His mother used to teach school in Onslow County."

"Did you know Mama, Miss Emily?" Len asked.

"Of course. She taught my children in school."

"I guess you know my pa, too."

"Not very well," she said, hesitantly. "Millie, if I remember correctly, you two are distant cousins."

Millie placed the last flower arrangement on the table nearest her hostess. She blushed and smiled. "We are?"

"I think I'd remember," Len said.

Emily hastily put the last napkins on the table. "Well, while you two sort it out, I really need to get back to the kitchen. Len, I'll tell Agatha you were here." She extended her hand. "Please give your mother my regards, and do stop by again to see us."

"Yes'um, I will." Millie followed Len to the door of the screened-in porch, holding it open for him. "I didn't know I had a cousin like you . . . I . . . mean a girl like you. I mean a girl cousin like you," he said.

"Don't you have any girl cousins?"

"Well, sure. I mean I didn't know I had *you* for a cousin. Aw, shucks. You know what I mean."

Millie was usually shy, but something about Len and his country ways put her at ease. "You have any idea exactly how we're kin?"

"I met your sister Belle on the train. . . " —he scratched his head and looked off into the distance, anxious to get his facts right—"let me see, I think it was in February a year ago." He looked back at Millie and smiled. "Yeah, that's right, it was when Miss

Agatha was on spring break and your sister had been up to Boston to see her." He was getting into far too much detail, but Millie was enjoying watching him. "You see, they were coming home to Wilmington and I was coming back from visiting Mama, who was staying at Mrs. Henry Montgomery's house on Upton Street."

She could see that he was thinking about going into even further detail, so she began to rearrange the silverware, hoping he would get to the point before the rest of the party arrived for lunch. "Anyhow, I asked my mama about it," Len said. Millie looked up at him, and he turned beet red. Sawing back and forth, he gestured with his hands. "She said it went pretty far back. I guess everybody down our way is some kin or another."

"Oh," Millie said. "Is that all?"

"All what?"

"All the kin we are?"

"I guess so," he said. "Look, I'd better get on back to the pier. Uncle Jasper's waiting for me."

She smiled. "And I'd better go help Miss Emily," she said. "Maybe I'll see you at a family reunion sometime."

"To be sure, to be sure," he said, grinning from ear to ear. "I'll tell Mama I saw you."

She watched him take the steps two at the time and walk briskly down the lane, his hands in his pockets. *Yes, to be sure*, she thought.

———

For the luncheon, Emily had made a cold fruit soup for the first course, using fresh strawberries and Georgia peaches that she'd bought at the market that morning, followed by Crab Louis on a bed of bright green lettuce. From a bakery on Front Street, she'd ordered a cream-filled chocolate torte with fresh raspberries in the filling. They played bridge in the solarium after lunch, sipping sweetened iced tea with sprigs of mint and munching on peanut brittle and cheese straws until the sun got too hot on the glassed-in porch.

All but the Evans and McBryde girls, Liz Cowell, and Jeanne had excused themselves, more than likely to head to the beach. In the living room, plans were made for dinner that evening at the Oceanic Hotel and dancing afterwards at Lumina. "Don't count on me," Liz said. "I have a date tonight with a gorgeous hunk I met at the Sorosis Ball last week."

By the door, Rebecca watched for her escort. "I wish you'd stay, Rebecca. I'm sure we'll have a grand time at Lumina," Emily said.

"I expect Mr. Jones will be here most any time, Miss Emily. Thank you so much for inviting us. Lunch was delicious."

Millie jumped up. "Oh, Becca, we almost forgot. Mama wants everyone to come for dinner after church tomorrow," Millie said.

"Oh, my! That's too much on your mother." Emily said.

"No, it's not, Miss Emily," Rebecca said. "I'm going to help, and Mama really wants you to come. She doesn't serve meals except for the family on the weekend. Even at that, my older brothers go to the beach or the boat races with their girlfriends."

"Rebecca is a good cook," Millie said, smiling at her sister.

"It won't be anything fancy like lunch today, but we won't let you go away hungry."

"We'd love to come," Emily said.

Before Mr. Jones's car was out of the driveway, Belle let loose a diatribe that she'd held back all day. "What in the world does she see in that old man? He's not even attractive. Did you notice the way he rolls his shirtsleeves up and wears that corny hat?"

Millie was embarrassed. "Mama says he's not that old, Belle, and Becca really likes him. You shouldn't be talking about him like that."

Belle shot Millie a withering look. "Millie, you are *so* sweet. You don't like him either and you know it!"

Millie didn't want to argue with her sister, not here, not now. "Maybe he just looks old."

"Beauty is in the eye of the beholder," Emily intervened. "We never know why people are attracted to one another." She rose from her chair. "Now, who would like a glass of lemonade?"

———

LATE IN THE AFTERNOON, EMILY REMEMBERED to tell Agatha about Len Ryan stopping by. "Oh, I remember him," Agatha said. "He helped me get my bag down on the train. Remember, Belle? He was from Bladen County."

"I remember."

"He's Maggie Ryan's son," Emily said. "Maggie used to live in Onslow, taught Jeanne and Darcy in school. I've asked her to come and see us sometime."

Jeanne sat up on the edge of her chair. "Really, Mother? *That* Maggie Ryan?"

"Yes, *That* Maggie Ryan."

"My old schoolmarm," she said, falling back into her chair.

"I thought I recognized her at the train station in Boston," Agatha said. "Papa knew her. We saw her in Raleigh one time. He looked at her like he could eat her with a spoon. Mandy and I thought they would have been so perfect for one another. I told Papa, but he said she was already married."

"Yes. Well, enough of that," Emily said, afraid of where the conversation might lead.

"Did you meet him, Millie?" Agatha asked. "He's cute as pie. About your age, maybe a little older. Tall, good-looking."

"We spoke out on the porch. That's about all."

"Don't waste your time on country boys, Little Sister," Belle said. "You'll meet some real guys tonight."

"I think Len's a real guy."

"Millie, you are so naive. Just shows what you know about boys."

So sweet, so naive, Millie thought. But that was just Belle, and she'd been that way as long as Millie could remember. How could sisters be so different?

2 8

Lumina

EMILY LED HER ENTOURAGE OF FIVE YOUNG WOMEN to Station One, where they boarded the beachcar to ride the short distance to Lumina at Station Seven. The Tide Water Power Company had built the enormous dance hall at the end of the line in 1905, illuminating the exterior with hundreds of incandescent light bulbs. In its heyday in the early part of the century, Lumina's six-thousand-foot dance floor would have been filled with elegantly clad youths, but in recent years the dress code had relaxed considerably.

The stars were bright over the Atlantic Ocean as the beachcar skimmed along towards Lumina. They could easily have walked from the McAllister cottage along the boardwalk that edged either side of the trolley tracks, but Emily had insisted that they save their feet for the dancing. When Millie was a little girl, she'd been afraid the waves would come up over the tracks and wash the train away. With friends joking and laughing, it now seemed like a much safer trip. Even Emily was gay and silly, talking of all the new dances she'd read about in her magazines.

The girls had pressed their dresses, wearing the same ones they'd worn earlier in the day for the luncheon. Emily had changed into an apricot-colored silk sheath belted below the waist. Her bobbed hair was loose and windblown, giving her a more youthful appearance. At Station Four, she pointed out the Carolina Yacht Club, closed for renovations since a kitchen fire. "But let's talk about tonight. I want you to dance to your hearts' content and not worry about me. I'm sure I'll see some of my set. And Charlie West's Carolinians are playing," she added excitedly. "I can hardly wait."

"Oooo, listen to Aunt Emily. I think she's got her dancing shoes on," Mandy said.

"Of course I do. I love to dance as much as any of you. And it's much more fun here on the beach than at those stuffy old dances in town."

"Don't worry about Mother," Jeanne said. "Just watch. She'll dance every dance if she wants to."

"What's the plan if we get separated?" Agatha asked, as if she didn't know.

"I don't see how that could happen, but if you should, just take the trolley back to Station One. All of you know the way to the house," Emily said, suspecting that when the clock struck twelve, Agatha and Belle would likely find themselves "separated" from the group.

————

THERE WAS ALWAYS AN OLDER GROUP of beach cottage residents who came to Lumina for the sheer entertainment of watching the younger crowd gyrate and jump with the lively music. Emily left the girls to find their friends, while she located a table near the shell-shaped bandstand where wooden shutters had been lowered around the perimeter of the dance floor to block the wind. On summer nights the breeze was welcome, but in early June, the Gulf Stream had not yet warmed the ocean enough to make it pleasant.

Tonight's promotion featuring the Lady Bucs, a popular Wilmington girls' basketball team, would likely draw hordes of young people from towns where they'd played their games during the last season. There would be prizes galore donated by local stores to promote the event, Beau Monde among them. Emily didn't care much for these promotions, but it was more or less expected that store owners would contribute to the cause. Early in the week, she'd donated a simple straw cloche that might be worn on the beach.

Emily was pleased that she'd gotten in with the right crowd early on when she bought her cottage at Wrightsville Beach. Doubtful she'd ever be asked to join the Carolina Yacht Club, whose membership was exclusive and often passed down in families, she'd made the Oceanic her club in a way, finding it as many of her friends did to be very elegant for socializing. Lumina, however, was sort of neutral territory, a fun place to go to dance, or listen the big bands and watch others enjoying themselves.

Tonight Emily was here more for the girls, but she was sure that sooner or later someone she knew would come along and join her or ask her to join them. She didn't have to wait long. Sarah Langley, chairman of the North Carolina Sorosis, was making her way towards Emily through the tables and chairs.

"There you are, dear Emily. I'll be so glad when the Yacht Club reopens. This place is way too crowded. Come sit at our table—I want to talk to you about the Greenfield Park project," she continued, without stopping for a breath. "Carl's here, and Commissioner Wade is supposed to come. You'll help us, won't you, dear?"

Emily greeted her friend warmly, remembering Sarah's many kindnesses when she first came to Wilmington. Mrs. Langley was fifteen or twenty years older than Emily, but her fine features and beautifully coifed hair helped defy her age. Tonight she was wearing a stylish dress with a lowered waist in copen blue silk.

"Oh, dear," Emily said. "I've promised the Merchants' Association that I'll help with the Feast of the Pirates parade they're starting this year. I'm not sure how well I can do both."

"Emily McAllister, we simply cannot do it without you."

"My goodness," Emily said.

"Please, dear, you must. We can't have a bunch of men running the whole show."

"All right—since you put it that way! I'll help as much as I can," Emily replied.

"Of course, I knew you would," Sarah said, as they made their way back to the table. "We'll talk more later. There's someone I'd like you to meet." She approached a man from behind and tapped him on the shoulder. "I found her, Jon. Emily, may I present Dr. Jonathan McNamara. Jon is staying in our carriage house until we can find him a home."

Emily smiled at the youthful but distinguished man who stood before her. He was very tall and slender and wore a well-trimmed salt-and-pepper beard. "If I've been discussed, I hope it was flattering," she said, extending her hand.

"I'll say, and Sarah was none too shy about it, Mrs. McAllister."

"Emily, please."

Taking her hand, he bowed slightly. "Emily, Jonathan McNamara, at your service."

Since her husband's death, Emily had been introduced to more men that she could keep track of by well-meaning friends; so far, there had been no one who'd held her interest. When Duncan died, she vowed she'd never marry again—never risk being saddled with the wants and whims of another man when she had her children and Reece's lovely daughters to make her life interesting. No, she was content. Unless . . .

"I knew you two would hit it off," Sarah said. "I should have introduced you sooner. Emily, I'll ring you up next week."

Although he was almost bald on the top of his head, Emily guessed the man before her to be in his early forties—a bit younger than her. "Your accent gives you away," she said to him. "Are you from Boston?"

He laughed. "How did you know? I haven't used the words *car* or *park*."

"Oh, I can just tell. I know some people from Boston."

"Really? Well, I know a few people from North Carolina. We could play *Do you know?* But I'd rather dance with you."

"You would? I mean, I'd like that, too." *Wow, I'm acting like a schoolgirl,* she thought. "As long as it's not the shimmy or the Charleston."

"You don't have to worry about either with me. I was deep in the throes of med school when that craze came out. I'm afraid you'll find my dancing a little old-fashioned. I'm still trying to master the fox-trot."

They hardly sat down all evening except when the youngsters took over the floor with their wilder dances. Several times she caught one of the girls watching her, and she gave them a little wave as if to say *Never mind me, I'm having fun too.* Agatha and Belle would look after Millie, and Jeanne was with Mandy and the college crowd, who preferred the lower terrace of Lumina beneath the dance floor. Below, they were away from parents who might disapprove of their smoking, or the bottle that made its way among them. Before the evening was over, they'd likely take off their shoes and walk along the beach, splashing and chasing one another in the ebbing tide.

———

AGATHA AND BELLE NEVER LEFT THE DANCE FLOOR either, finding themselves the focus of boys they'd met at the beach. Belle was fully enjoying herself as usual, sometimes dancing with two boys at a time. Millie was invited to dance several times by a boy who introduced himself as Skipper, but he'd always deposit her back to where she'd stood when he'd found her, saying "See ya!" She wandered back and forth from the refreshment stand to the terrace, wishing she had Mary Avis or someone else her age to hang around with. Tonight, all the boys seemed so much older, and she was sure she'd smelled whiskey on Skipper's breath.

Several times during the evening, Millie had recounted the few minutes she'd spent with Len Ryan. That's who she'd like to be with right now. Would she ever see him again? Mama had told Belle that her Corbinn cousins lived up in Colly, which wasn't too far from

Bandeaux Creek. Maybe next spring he'd come to the family reunion.

Across the dance floor, she watched for Emily, hoping to catch her alone for a few minutes. Emily would help her get over this terrible feeling of being a wallflower. Millie was ready to go back to the cottage, but each time she glimpsed Emily, she was dancing with the same attractive gent who never seemed to take his eyes off her.

Millie looked at the watch Calvin had given her on her last birthday. It was ten o'clock and the crowd was starting to thin. She went to the ladies' room and combed her hair. When she came out the restroom door, Agatha grabbed her arm. "There you are! We've been looking all over for you. Come on, we're going on an adventure."

"Where to?"

"Never mind where to, just come. It'll be more fun if you don't know. Hurry, Belle and the guys are waiting for us."

Millie sorted through the crowd until she found Belle and made eye contact. *Come on!* Belle mouthed.

"You're not going back to the cottage?" she asked Agatha.

"No, not yet."

Belle stomped across the floor. "Hurry up! The guys are waiting for us." Millie protested, to no avail. "Come on, Millie," Belle pleaded. "I told her. She knows Skipper's parents. The other guys are from around here, too. All she said was to be in no later than midnight."

"It's all right, really," Agatha chimed in.

"Midnight? Mama wouldn't like it one bit and you know it!" she hissed at Belle.

Belle grabbed her by the arm and jerked her around. "Look, don't embarrass me. Skipper wants you to come with us. If you don't come, I can't go."

"I promise it's okay," Agatha urged.

Millie hesitated, trusting Agatha a little more than Belle. "All right, I'll go," Millie said, momentarily enjoying the power she felt over her sister.

"Yippee!" Agatha shouted. "Hurry, they're waiting for us down by the dock."

"We're going in a boat?"

"Look Millie, will you stop being such a drag," Belle said. "Yes, we're going in a boat."

2 9

Temple of Love

SKIPPER PURRINGTON AND RIVERS HENSON were waiting for the girls on the dock. Woody Chestnut was in his
father's boat, filling the tank with gas from a metal can. After they
climbed aboard, Woody started the motor and slid the boat into
reverse, quietly backing out of the slip. When they hit the open
water of the channel, he pushed the throttle forward and they went
full speed towards the other side of the sound.

Skipper had slipped in beside Millie, putting his arm up on the
seat behind her. When she shivered and pulled her dress down over
her knees, without a word he put his arm around her and pulled her
towards him. Woody didn't cut his speed until they reached the
drawbridge. A tugboat had just gone through, and he followed in its
wake until he saw his destination. Cutting across the wake of the
tug, he headed for a dark pier behind what they all knew to be the
old deserted lodge called the Bungalow.

Bungalow was hardly the word for the Italianate mansion that
loomed before them. Pembroke Jones, a Wilmington native, was a
mill owner and a wealthy rice planter whose rambling resort home
on Wrightsville Sound known as Airlie was surrounded by gardens.
In contrast, the Bungalow was a hunting lodge set in a dense forest
of oak, pine, and magnolias, and it had stood empty since Mr.
Jones's death in 1919. They'd all heard the stories about it being
haunted, and more than a few young people had been caught by the
night watchman when they went to explore the old place.

"Keep really quiet," Woody said. "My dad knows the watch-man, but it would be mighty embarrassing if we got caught. He's probably asleep at the front gate because that's usually where we sneak in. If he hears us, he'll come looking."

Agatha and Belle had the silly giggles, but Millie was fright-ened. Up on the dock, Woody pulled a bottle out of his jacket and passed it to Rivers. "I think we need a little nip before we venture into the unknown." Rivers passed the bottle to Skipper, who took a sip and passed it to Millie.

"No, thank you," Millie said.

"Well, give it to me then," Belle said, reaching for the bottle and taking a long swig.

Agatha took a turn and looked at Millie. "It won't hurt you, honey. Take a little sip. This is good Canadian whiskey, not white lightning." They'd all heard the stories of illegal whiskey that had been known to poison people.

Millie reached for the bottle and took a tiny sip, feeling the whiskey burn all the way down to her stomach. "It's good," she said weakly.

Skipper grabbed her hand. "Come on, I'll watch out for you, lit-tle girl."

"Just keep quiet and follow me," Woody said. "We'll go through old Pembroke's temple o' luv first," he said, wiggling his eyebrows and grinning. Agatha held onto him and Belle followed, hanging onto Rivers. Skipper brought up the rear, guiding Millie along the overgrown path strewn with pine needles and brown magnolia leaves. Suddenly they came upon a circle of four wedge-shaped pools with a stone pergola in the center. Millie was sure it had once been very beautiful, but now the coquina walks were so littered with leaves and trash, she could hardly make them out. In the cen-ter of the temple, a bronze statue of a little naked boy held a dol-phin, but the pool beneath it was dry as a bone. She ran her hand over the sides of the smooth stone bowl.

"My mother used to come here to parties when she was a young girl," Skipper said. "See that hole in the dolphin's mouth? She said the fish spit water into the center of the pool."

"Okay, everybody, time for another nip of hooch. We've got to be brave," Woody hissed. "And that's not all. You can't pass through the temple o' luv without a smooch. That's the rule. So get busy, boys." He took a swig and handed the bottle off to Rivers, while grabbing Agatha around the waist and kissing her deeply.

Rivers took a turn at the whiskey. "I've been waiting for this all night, baby," he said to Belle.

Skipper took the bottle out of Rivers's hand. Hesitating, he whispered to Millie, "You don't have to do this if you don't want to." She smiled and reached for the bottle and took a small sip. "I don't mind," she said. Skipper pulled her closer, kissing her softly at first. Then, his tongue was in her mouth and she tasted the warm whiskey. She pushed him away.

Embarrassed, Skipper wiped his mouth with the back of his hand. "I'm sorry. I shouldn't have done that. How old are you, anyway?"

Millie blushed, thinking she must seem like such a child. But before she could answer, Woody called out in a loud whisper. "Watch out for the cannon, it might go off any minute!"

Startled, Millie put her hands up to her ears. "He's just messing around," Skipper said. "There's an old Gatling gun mounted on the terrace." He pointed to the bridge that crossed over to the house. "Pembroke's idea of guarding the place," he laughed.

"Shush," Rivers said. "I hear something." They ducked into the oleander bushes and watched a raccoon waddle over to a fish pool and sip the stagnant water.

Entering the house through a broken French door, they came into a huge solarium with a glass ceiling. Moonlight seeped through the dead leaves and vines that covered the glass above splattering on the littered floor. Stepping into the next room, Woody turned on a small flashlight and shone it on the vaulted ceiling. "And he called this a bungalow," Rivers said.

"There's more," Woody said, leading them into a huge room with stone fireplaces at either end, each supported by marble figures. He played the flashlight over the nude female torsos. "In my wildest dreams," he mused.

"Take the flashlight away from that pervert," Rivers said.

Belle grabbed his hand. "Hey, y'all, let's dance," she said, humming a tune as she twirled around the room, Rivers in tow. Glass and paper were strewn about over the hardwood floor, but they danced over it, coming too close to a tall marble pedestal. The crash was deafening.

"My God, now you've done it!" Woody said. "Let's get out of here."

They were on the small bridge leading to the gazebo when the night watchman came running out of the house with a broad-beamed flashlight that he shone in their direction. "Who's there?" he called out, leaning over the rail and peering into the darkness. "I see you scoundrels. You'd better get out of her before I fire this old cannon," he shouted. "I'll bet you didn't know old Pembroke left it in good working order," he taunted. "You better run. I'm calling the police." There was no doubt in their minds that he was fooling around with them, but they ran to the dock and jumped in the boat, taking off without looking back.

———

EMILY WAS WAITING UP FOR THE GIRLS, dreading that they would come in past the designated hour and dampen her euphoria over the evening. A little after midnight, she heard them clamber up the cottage steps, giggling and carrying on. Only Millie stopped in the parlor to say good night. "I hope we didn't keep you up too late," she said.

"No, in fact, I'm surprised you're here on time. Agatha usually pushes the point on curfews."

"She asked me to tell you she'd be down in a few minutes. She had to go to the bathroom. Wanted to brush her teeth."

"Millie, what is it? You look uncomfortable."

"I'm fine. Just tired."

Emily got up from her chair and walked closer to Millie. "Did something happen tonight?"

Millie tried to laugh, but she was near tears. Appointed as the one to face Emily by Agatha and Belle, she wanted to wring their necks. "No, we just went for a boat ride. I'm cold, that's all."

"Well, I can fix that. Come into the kitchen and I'll make some hot chocolate. Would you run upstairs and tell Agatha and Belle?"

Both girls were sound asleep, still in their rumpled dresses. Millie closed the door, glancing in the mirror just before turning off the light. Did she look different? Skipper had kissed her—her first real kiss. On second thought, she wondered if that was really a kiss, or was he just fooling around with the whiskey in his mouth?

"They're sound asleep, Miss Emily. I hate for you to go to all this trouble for me."

"Trouble? A cup of hot chocolate?" Emily poured the steaming drink into large mugs. "Besides, I'm wide awake and I was hoping you girls would get home in time to gab a little. At least you haven't let me down." She sat down at the kitchen table across from Millie. "Now tell me about the boat ride."

"We just went for a ride—across the sound. It was dark. I couldn't tell where we were exactly."

"Oh, so that's it. You went to the Bungalow. I warned Agatha. Woody Chestnut's mother said that was her son's favorite 'adventure.'"

"You mean it's okay? You don't mind?"

"I'd rather you girls not have gone there, if that's what you mean. But I know those boys, their families. I guess all's well that ends well." She sipped her chocolate, her mind more on her own evening's adventure. "Was it fun?" she asked, purposely refocusing on Millie.

"Yes, I guess so. Skipper Purrington was nice."

"Skipper Purrington? Do you know who he is?"

Millie laughed. "Skipper Purrington."

"I mean did you know he was a flier?"

"He didn't brag about it or anything, but I guess he was sort of a daredevil. They all were."

Emily gathered the cups and put them in the large sink. "Oh, he's a good boy. A real nice fellow, but a little too old for you, as you probably found out. I'm not sure your mother would approve your getting involved with him."

Millie laughed. "I don't think we have to worry about that. He didn't ask to see me again."

"Don't be surprised if he does, darling. You're an attractive young lady already. You'll knock them all dead in a couple of years."

Millie blushed. "How about you? I saw you dancing."

"Yes, thank you. I had a delightful evening dancing. With a friend of Mrs. Langley, a young doctor, new in town. Much too young for me, but a delightful chap from Boston, I believe." She turned off the kitchen light and walked arm in arm with Millie up the stairs. "What time is your mother expecting us tomorrow?"

———

AGATHA BROUGHT UP THE SUBJECT AT BREAKFAST the next morning. "Aunt Emily, you haven't told us about your evening."

Emily came to the table carrying a plate of blueberry pancakes. "I don't think I could top your *adventure*." The girls looked at one another. "Now eat these pancakes before they get cold."

"Just tell me who you were dancing with all evening," Agatha teased.

Emily had just placed a forkful of pancakes in her mouth. She held up her finger while she swallowed. "Someone Mrs. Langley introduced me to." She turned to Jeanne. "You remember her, she's bought several of the Swedish woman's hats."

"Mother, tell them *who* he is," Jeanne demanded politely.

"*He* is Mrs. Langley's house guest. She needed some help entertaining him. Mandy, please pass the syrup."

Jeanne picked up her plate and went to put it in the sink. "Mother, if you won't elaborate, I will. Jonathan McNamara is a new physician in town. He's currently working at James Walker Memorial Hospital, and he may or may not settle in Wilmington and open up a private practice. I think he was quite taken with your auntie."

"Jeanne, for heaven's sake, he was no such thing. Jon is just a wonderful dancer and we thoroughly enjoyed the music, but I hardly think he—"

"Oh, I see. *Jon,*" Agatha said in a teasing tone.

"Really girls, you're taking advantage of me." She busied herself removing dishes from the table, returning with the coffee pot. "More coffee, anyone?"

To rescue her hostess, Millie changed the subject. "Jeanne, did you run into some of your college friends? I saw you on the terrace with a bunch of people."

Jeanne scooted her chair in. "As a matter of fact I did. We're all going to the boat races in Banks Channel this afternoon. Anyone want to come along?"

"Mrs. McBryde has invited us to lunch, dear. I was hoping you would join us."

She gave her mother a kiss on the cheek. "Love to, but I promised. Besides, I have to get back to Jacksonville tonight, and those back country roads are treacherous after dark. I need to leave early this afternoon. Millie, please give your mother my regrets."

30

Young Moderns

REBECCA HAD TRIED TO HUSTLE HER MOTHER OFF to church, volunteering to do all of the preparations herself for the dinner for Emily and her nieces. "I want to do it, Mama. I hardly ever get in the kitchen any more and I need to practice."

"For what?" Eva asked.

"Oh, you know, someday I'll get married and . . . "

"Not anytime soon, I hope."

Her mother was baiting her, and Rebecca had no intentions of biting. "Please go on to church, Mama. Papa's waiting for you."

"Just let me finish the chicken and pastry. Papa likes the way I do it."

"Don't you think I know how?"

"Of course you do, but sometimes your pastry falls apart. I want everything to be perfect today."

But Rebecca was as good a cook as her mother, and much more efficient with the electric stove. Eva had a wood stove mentality, starting preparations well before daylight, anticipating the long, slow cooking that had been her way throughout her life. Rebecca had eagerly jumped into the new age, taking a four-day cooking class sponsored by the *Wilmington Morning Star* in which Mrs. Edna Riggs Crabtree, a nationally known cooking expert, directed young moderns in sessions designed to teach them how to make their homes beautiful and efficient. In addition to the cooking demonstrations, there were home fashion shows and exhibits of new products and appliances. Rebecca had come home with a notebook filled with recipes and household hints.

"You should've stayed on at the beach with the rest of the girls, Rebecca," Eva said. She had lifted the stewing hen out of a large pot and was dropping long strips of pastry into the boiling broth.

"I didn't want to, Mama. Mr. Jones took me out to eat shrimp. That was a lot more fun than going to Lumina."

"You used to love to go to Lumina."

"No, I didn't. Not really. I just went along because everyone else did. Belle's the one who loves to dance. I think she'd live there if they'd let her."

"I wish you two wouldn't fuss so much. You're old enough to appreciate each other—be friends."

"We are, Mama. We really are. You just don't pay any attention to us when we're being nice to each other."

"Ummm, maybe you're right." Eva put the last strips of pastry in the pot and covered it with a lid. Rebecca had deboned the chicken and cut it into chunks, readying it to go back into the pot when the pastry was done.

"Please go now, Mama. Papa's waiting for you."

"I ought to stay and help you."

"No, I want to do this by myself. Mrs. Crabtree said putting a pretty as well as delicious meal on the table should be the goal of every young woman anticipating marriage."

Eva had observed the little romance that was going on between her neighbor Junius Jones and Rebecca, but she hoped it was platonic. "You keep mentioning that. Is someone we know anticipating marriage?"

"Well, someday."

———

WHEN THE HOUSE WAS EMPTY, Rebecca brought the new electric Victrola Mr. Jones had given her into the hallway and placed a recording by Duke Ellington on the turntable. Mrs.

Crabtree had proposed playing jazz while doing housework, explaining that the quick-step action led to the earlier completion of tasks. There were so many things to remember from Mrs. Crabtree's course that Rebecca had to refer to her notebook from time to time. She was to wear a colorful smock or apron while doing housework. *No need to be drab and down at the heels because one's work is in the kitchen*, her notes said. She was not to refer to herself as a *housewife*, but as a *homemaker*.

Most of all, Rebecca loved Mrs. Crabtree's new way with foods. Mama's chicken and pastry would be the main dish, but Rebecca had made a carrot and raisin salad and a bowl of cole slaw using a bright green cabbage that she'd bought at a roadside stand on the way home from the beach. For dessert, she used Mrs. Crabtree's recipes for apple charlotte and gingerbread with lemon sauce. She'd already tried them out on Mr. Jones, and he'd asked her to make them again today.

In the dining room, Rebecca put away the oilcloth table cover that Eva used during the week for the boarders. She dusted all the knickknacks and photographs on the mantelpiece, wiped off the chairs, and used the Hoover on the rug. In the back yard, she'd cut sprays of mock orange and blue hydrangea from the tall shrubs that bordered the Jones property and placed them in a large cut-glass bowl for the center of the table. She thought the arrangement looked as if it had been made to order to go with Mrs. Ainsley's Limoges china. Under Eva's bed, Rebecca had found the wooden chest of silver that had been given to her mother when she married Robert McBryde. Mama polished it once a year at Christmas, then stored it under the bed, saying it was too good for boardinghouse use.

Junius Jones walked to Grace Methodist Church on the corner of Fourth and Grace every Sunday morning. He'd often asked Rebecca to accompany him, but Mama and Papa frowned on her appearing in public with the older man. Little was said about it, though Rebecca knew how they felt. Everyone thought Mr. Jones was too old for her—but what they didn't know was that he was anything but old in *that* department. He'd been begging her to marry him before she got caught slipping out at night. But getting married would complicate her life even more—nurses weren't supposed to get married until after they'd finished training.

She pulled up her stockings and checked her makeup in the hall mirror, reminding her that Mr. Jones thought her to be the prettiest of the McBryde girls. He'd told her so just last night. She knew it didn't matter one bit to him that she wore a size eleven shoe, or that her eyes were slightly slanted, a trait Papa said she'd inherited from a Chinaman way back in his line. It was a joke, but Mr. Jones said he liked everything about her just fine. He'd promised to slip out of church service a couple of minutes early to get to the McBryde home in time to help her do some rearranging. Mae would have done her usual cleaning, but Rebecca wanted the room to look like a real living room, not a boardinghouse with everything centered around the big Philco radio where the men sat glued to the fights.

She'd opened the windows early that morning, letting fresh air in, and placed a vase of wygelia in the center of the pie-crust table. Everything had to be set when Mama and Papa walked in the door. For Rebecca, this lunch was as much to show off for Mama and Papa as it was entertain Emily McAllister and the Evans girls.

————

ONE LOOK AT JUNIUS JONES IN HIS SUNDAY BEST suit and she almost cried. He was so handsome, such a gentleman. How could her sisters, or anyone else, fall for those immature boys with their knickers and wild socks when there was a real man like Mr. Jones around? "I thought you'd never get here," she said, putting her arms around his neck.

He ran his hands over her buttocks and up her back, lifting her rayon dress above her knees. "Missed me, did you?" he mumbled into her hair, his hands making further progress towards her breasts.

She pulled away. "Don't, sweetheart, not now. Mama and Papa will be here any minute. I need a little help moving the sofa." As she took his coat, he grabbed her around the waist and tried to kiss her. She pushed him away. "Wait, sweetie, we have to hurry."

"Aw, Rebecca. I thought after last night you'd forget about lunch and just be with me."

Rebecca blushed. "Last night? I shouldn't have . . . " She stood at one end of the sofa. "You take that end. We need to move it to the center of the room just long enough for me to run the Hoover behind it."

"Why do you need to move it? Can't you just vacuum around it? Nobody can see under it."

"Mr. Jones, I can't believe you would say that. Mrs. Crabtree said that not cleaning underneath things was the height of laziness. It's like . . . like wearing dirty underwear."

———

WHEN THE PARTY FROM THE BEACH ARRIVED, Rebecca insisted that Eva, Rob, and Mr. Jones entertain Emily and the Evans girls in the living room while she and her sisters put the finishing touches on dinner. Belle opened the refrigerator. "Yuck! What's that in the blue bowl?"

"*That* is our first course. It's carrot and raisin salad, if you want to know."

"I don't want any."

"I don't care whether you eat it or not, but would you please serve it up on those small plates and put them on the table?"

"Hummph!"

"Don't forget to put a lettuce leaf on first."

"Yes, boss."

"I'll help," Millie said.

"No, you fix the iced tea."

Belle looked up. "Did Mama make it?"

"No, I did."

"I don't want any of that either. You make the worst tea!"

"Belle, why don't you just go sit down in the living room," Rebecca snapped. "You're getting on my last nerve."

Belle flung the piece of lettuce in her hand down on the table. "Fine. Just fine. I don't want to ruin your little show."

"Good riddance."

"I wish y'all wouldn't do that. It makes other people feel so bad," Millie said. "Especially Mama."

"Well, don't say anything to Mama and she'll never know. Belle is such a pill. It's Harry's fault. He spoiled her rotten, always telling her how cute she was."

———

AT THE DINNER TABLE, REBECCA FELT LIKE a real home-maker, just as Mrs. Crabtree said she would when her house was in order and a beautiful meal was on the table. Eva was pleasantly surprised that the dinner had turned out so well. Even Belle ate her carrot and raisin salad.

Millie was sure that Emily McAllister's fresh and youthful appearance today had something to do with the tall doctor who'd been her dancing partner at Lumina. She was especially gay, conversing with Eva and Robert McBryde as if she had always known them. "There are times when I think I'd like to live in the country again," she said.

"You'd be bored silly, Aunt Emily," Mandy said.

"I never found the country boring," Eva said. "Quiet at times, but never boring."

"We had too many young'uns to get bored," Rob said.

As if on cue, Rodney interrupted. "Mama, may Vera and me be excused?"

"Vera and I. Yes, you may, Rodney. You can have your desserts later in the kitchen."

The youngsters hurriedly left the table and Emily continued, "I loved the restful pace of country life. Now, with the telephone and radio, there's no need to ever be bored anywhere."

"Don't forget trains," Mr. Jones said. "Trains got a lot of people out of the country."

"Of course, Mr. Jones. Where would we be without trains?"

Rebecca rose and began to remove their dinner plates. "You have a choice of dessert: gingerbread with lemon sauce, or apple charlotte."

"Apple who?" Belle asked, stifling a laugh. Agatha caught her eye and they both burst out laughing.

"Belle, your sister has worked very hard to fix two lovely desserts," Eva said. "Which will you have?"

"I'm sorry, Mama. Agatha and I just get tickled about things." She looked at Agatha and started to laugh again.

But Agatha had regained her composure. "Yes, we are the silliest things. I apologize, and just to show Rebecca I mean it, I'm going to have one of each."

"Well, all right! Me, too," said Junius Jones.

Agatha rose from her chair. "Come on, Belle, let's help."

———

WHEN THE DISHES WERE DONE, Agatha followed Belle up to her room to listen to the radio, while Millie and Rebecca joined the rest of the party on the porch. Vera and Rodney had engaged several other neighborhood children in a game of street tag. "Wherever do they get the energy?" Eva asked. She and Emily sat on either side of Rob in the large rocking chairs that had come with the house. Rebecca slipped into the swing beside Mr. Jones on the other end of the porch, and Millie and Amanda perched on the porch rail. The day had turned quite warm, but a swift breeze blew up from the Cape Fear River. "I believe we might be in for a storm," Rob said.

"Papa always knows when it's going to rain," Millie said,

"He ought to get a job on the radio," Mr. Jones piped in. "I can count on my corns better than those radio announcers. They always get it wrong."

Rob propped his feet up against a porch post and puffed on his pipe. "A farmer just naturally knows. Part of being a farmer."

"There's times when I wish you were still a farmer," Eva said, her eyes watering up a tiny bit. "Maybe you will be again someday." Rob's reply was a puff of smoke from his pipe.

"That was a wonderful lunch," Emily said. "I dare say you'll make someone a good wife, Rebecca."

The young nurse blushed, and Mr. Jones squeezed her hand. "I just love cooking and making things pretty, if that's what it takes."

An automobile pulled up in front of the house behind Emily's Buick. "Oh, goody, there's Calvin," Millie said, starting down the steps to meet her brother. "Hey, Calvin! Will you take us for a ride in your new car?"

Calvin McBryde slipped out of the car and waved to Millie. "Hi, honey. Let's wait a little while for a ride. I need to tell Hugh something. Is he home yet?"

"No, but come meet Miss Emily."

With his long legs, Cal took the steps two at a time. He was wearing a vested suit, his custom day in and day out. The only time they ever saw him in anything else was when he went squirrel hunting. Even then, he wore a hunting outfit that most men would have thought good enough for church. Cal stepped quickly to Emily's chair and took her extended hand. "Pleased to meet you, Mrs. McAllister."

"My pleasure, Calvin."

"And this is Amanda."

Calvin could suppress neither his smile nor his blush. "Miss Amanda," he said taking her hand very briefly. "The girls have told us a lot about y'all."

Emily glanced out to the street. "I see you have the new Model A. Sure is pretty."

"Yep, I couldn't resist it. Ford prices have come down to less than three hundred dollars. Got it on time, too. It'll be paid for in another six months."

"Better watch spending money 'fore you get it," Rob said, smoke from his pipe wreathing his head.

"No, Papa, you don't understand. That's part of the deal."

"What's gonna happen if you can't make the payments?"

Cal glanced over his shoulder at the women, uneasy talking about money in front of them. "Don't worry about that, Papa. I do all right at the Coast Line."

But his father was persistent. "How come Hugh doesn't have one and he's over you?"

"Hugh doesn't want a new car. He likes driving your old Crow-Elkhart."

"Don't make 'em like that old car anymore. I remember I brought it home right after Millie was born."

"Have you had your dinner, Calvin?" Eva asked. "I'm sure there's something left on the stove. Isn't there, Rebecca?"

Before Rebecca could answer, Cal said that he had eaten and was anxious to talk to Hugh. "There's a meeting going on over at the Armory. Union men. Hugh ought to go. A bunch of trainmen— all the boys from the yard are there."

"Don't be getting your brother all hepped up about that, son," Rob said. "His dog ain't in that fight."

"But his men are involved, Papa. Mr. Baldwin told us to keep our eyes and ears open. He says the Union men are agitators. No telling what—"

"You're looking for trouble, mark my words," Rob warned. "Ought not to get involved in that."

It wasn't like Calvin to talk back to his father, but he was passionate. "Hugh has a lot of friends in the yard. He can't just turn his back on them."

"A man can't always do what he'd like to do best. Sometimes a man has to put his family first." He gazed out into the street, watching his two younger children dodge the ball. "Of course, Hugh may think he only has himself to think about."

—WILMINGTON, N.C. Miss Amanda Elizabeth Evans and Mr. Thomas Kennedy Bouvier III were united in marriage in a lovely ceremony by the Right Reverend Ian McDevitt in the sanctuary of Saint Mary's Catholic Church on Ann Street. The red brick interior and vaulted ceiling of the magnificent church lent themselves well to the autumn theme chosen by the bride. Miss Evans was resplendent in a French-inspired ivory satin gown with insets of Alençon lace, richly embroidered with seed pearls and sequins. She was attended by her sister, Miss Amanda Ann Evans, maid of honor. Mr. Bouvier was attended by his father, the honorable Judge Franklin J. Bouvier of Philadelphia.

For her ten bridesmaids, Miss Evans selected ballet-length dresses with velvet bodices and tulle skirts, creating an illusion of autumn leaves floating down the aisle. Massive vases of fall flowers mixed with silk autumn leaves were placed on the altar by Mrs. Duncan McAllister, aunt of the bride, in memory of her brother and the father of the bride, the late Augustus Reece Evans.

After the ceremony, Mr. and Mrs. Bouvier greeted guests at a lavish reception at the Cape Fear Hotel. Immediately after the reception, the bride and groom left for a wedding trip to the Greenbrier Hotel in White Sulphur Springs, W.Va. After their wedding trip, they will reside in Philadelphia. The bride's aunt, Mrs. McAllister, is one of Wilmington's most active socialites.—
Morning Star, Sept. 26, 1927

31

The Prettiest One

AREN'T YOU TIRED OF ALL THIS WEDDING STUFF?"
Rusty asked Millie as they sat in the swing on her front porch
the Saturday before Mandy Evans's long-anticipated nuptials. He'd
been her escort for a round of parties for the engaged couple all
summer. "How about just you and me going to the beach on Sunday
afternoon?"

"Maybe. I'll have to ask Mama. We're supposed to eat supper
with Miss Emily tomorrow evening. Tom's parents are here and she
wants us to come and meet them."

"I'm sick of Tom Bootiay, or whatever his name is."

"Bouvier."

"Okay, whatever his name is. He is such a snob. The same age
as me and he looks down his nose at me like I'm a little pesky kid."

Millie laughed. "Don't be silly, Rusty. He's just from
Philadelphia. I guess they act like that up there."

"A bunch of snobs," he snorted.

"Rusty O'Reilly, you're acting like a jealous teenager, not a college man."

Rusty laughed. "You're right. Just because I'm eighteen doesn't
mean I have to act like it." After the Junior-Senior prom, Millie had
been sure that Rusty would never ask her out again. The evening
had not gone well. Rusty did not like to dance, and they'd sat out
most of the dances at one of the tables in the gymnasium. But the
following week he stopped by Beau Monde twice, and that Saturday

evening, he'd dropped by her house to sit on the porch with her family. "I believe our Millie has herself a beau," Rob had said to Eva as they retired that evening.

"She could do a lot worse," Eva said. "His father is a banker. Rusty has three older brothers, and they've all been to college, or are going."

"Must be nice to have that kind of money."

"He says he wants to be a newspaper man, or maybe write books."

"I'd think a little more of him if he wanted to be a doctor or a lawyer."

"He's got red hair. Maybe we'd have some redheaded grand-children," Eva said. She rolled over to give Rob a good-night kiss. "Listen to us, Rob. You'd think Millie was going to marry him. This is just her first boyfriend."

"I was yours, wasn't I?"

———

PLANS FOR MANDY'S AUTUMN WEDDING had dominated Emily McAllister's thoughts since early spring. She was the closest thing to a mother that Mandy had, and she'd assumed most of the financial responsibility and coordination of the nuptial events. It pleased her no end that Mandy had decided on Wilmington, rather than Philadelphia, for the ceremony.

Arrangements were made to have the wedding at St. Mary's Catholic Church since the groom's family were staunch Catholics. The ornate Spanish Renaissance church had been originally intend-ed as the cathedral for the Diocese of North Carolina, but when the diocese was formed in 1924, a much smaller church in Raleigh was designated. Now, St. Mary's rivaled many of the Catholic churches in Philadelphia.

Thomas Kennedy Bouvier, the third, arrived in Wilmington six weeks before the nuptials for premarital instructions from Father

Ian McDevitt. By the time his parents arrived in September, Tom and Mandy had been honored at a round of parties that included an oyster roast on Wrightsville Sound and a luncheon on the terrace of the Orton Hotel overlooking the Cape Fear River. At her beach house, Emily hosted one of several bridge luncheons, and the McBryde girls had given a kitchen shower at their home on Princess Street.

———

THE WEDDING GUEST LIST NUMBERED four hundred and fifty. Included were a train car full from Philadelphia, relatives on both sides, a crowd from Onslow County, and the many friends Emily and her nieces had made in Wilmington in recent years. In her invitation to Maggie Ryan, who had yet to come pay her that visit at the beach, Emily had added a personal note. *You and Tate simply must come! There will be so many here from Onslow County who would love to see you. Please bring both of your sons. I especially would like to see Len again since I was in such a rush at the beach when he stopped by.*

But Tate had not come. Maggie had asked him, knowing that the last place in the world he'd want to be would be among Reece Evans's kin. She didn't ask twice. Besides, Maggie and Len made a handsome pair, and she was anxious to show off her son to the young folks. Would Agatha and Mandy remember her? Maybe not—but she remembered them well, especially the precocious Agatha, who'd asked to try on her glasses with the dark lens. Maggie was also anxious to see the little storybook-blonde Jeanne and to meet the McBryde girls.

There was also someone else Maggie hoped she might see. Since her ill-fated trip to Wilmington last August, Maggie had resigned herself to the hope that Jonathan McNamara would find a way to contact her—if he really wanted to. She had not liked the feeling that she was running after him when she went to the clinic that day. No, a chance meeting would be much better, and just by chance, he might have been invited to this wedding. A wedding would be a fine time to introduce a new doctor around town to its most prominent citizens. To provoke his memory, she'd intentionally worn the lilac beaded dress she'd worn to Cavenaugh Cummings's reception in Boston two years ago. More than once, Jon had commented on her appearance that evening. Perhaps that had been precisely when he'd fallen in love with her.

———

ON THE DAY OF THE WEDDING, it would have been difficult to determine which of the Ryans was feeling the greatest measure of anticipation—Maggie, resplendent in the lilac beaded dress, or Len as he parked the car along Ann Street a block from the church. The Chandler was gleaming with a shiny new chrome bumper and a pair of matching headlights that had appeared mysteriously in a mail-order box a week ago. Will had put them on the car before he even told her. "Just a little present from me, Mama," he'd said.

Len's eagerness might even have outdone his mother's. While away on the job in South Carolina he'd written to Millie McBryde, and they'd exchanged several letters, just friendly letters calling each other *cousin*, and such as that. But something led Len to ask his Uncle Roy on the way home to stop in Charleston, where he'd bought a new beige cotton suit—nothing fancy, but it fit him better than stout old Henry Montgomery's hand-me-downs. He'd gotten even taller, and his shoulders were much broader, thanks to the strenuous work of hauling cast-iron pipe and maneuvering the big drill.

Ascending the broad steps up to the church entrance, Maggie surveyed the crowd, half hoping her hunch might be correct. She was instantly gratified to see a familiar figure at the top, shaking hands with a gentleman. *As I live and breathe, that's him!* she thought. She tugged at Len's elbow. "Wait, son, I see someone I want to speak to. Len held back a little, letting his mother lead. As they approached, the doctor turned and caught her eye in disbelief. For a moment, she let him take her in. "Hello, Jon," she called out.

"Imagine seeing you here at a wedding in Wilmington, North Carolina."

"Well, hello. Yes, imagine," he said, looking as if he'd seen a ghost. But his eyes swept over her, silently acknowledging the depth of feeling they'd shared on her departure from Boston. "Maggie, how wonderful to see you," he said, a smile brightening his face. He glanced at Len. "Don't tell me this young man is your son?"

"Yes he is. Len, this is Dr. McNamara, Mr. Henry's nephew."

"Pleased to meet you, to be sure," Len said, extending his hand, sensing something between the doctor and his mother that he couldn't quite put his finger on.

"You must know Emily, or Amanda," Jon said. "Shall I guess, from Onslow County?" He was suddenly casual, as if they had only recently met. But the thing that jarred her most of all was the neat salt-and-pepper beard, giving him a totally different look, that and the formal dress that identified him as a member of the wedding party.

Maggie was—well, discombobulated, as Aunt Mag would say. There was so much to tell him . . . so much to ask, but not here and now. "Abigail said you'd settled in. Of course, I saw the announcement too . . . in the paper." She turned to Len. "Go on in, son. Wait for me in the vestibule." Len did as she asked, casting a puzzled look her way. She took hold of Jon's sleeve and pulled him aside. "I stopped by the hospital one time. You left before I could speak to you."

"When was that?" he asked, seemingly astounded.

"Oh, it was a long time ago—maybe a year or so. It doesn't matter, does it?"

"Of course it matters, Maggie." He nodded to several women as they passed. "When?"

"You were in the clinic—where you said you'd be on that card. Remember *MWF, 12–4*?" She was pushing the point, feeling very foolish.

"I often get called away." He shook hands with a guest, nodded to another. "Look, we need to talk, Maggie, but this isn't a good time. Will you be in town again soon?"

Before Maggie could answer, an older woman waved to Jon from the top step. "Jon, there you are. Please come. They're waiting to seat us."

"I'll be right there, Sarah. Come with me," he said, taking Maggie's elbow. "I want you to meet Mrs. Langley." They made their way into the vestibule, where Jon introduced her.

"Delighted to meet you," Mrs. Langley said, looking admiringly at Maggie's stylish dress and hat. "Are you from Boston?"

Maggie took Mrs. Langley's extended hand. "Pleased to meet you, too. No, I'm from Bladen County. My husband is from Onslow County."

"Well, Jon, let's go on in before they start the music. Toodleloo, Mrs. Ryan."

Len was waiting for her in one of the recesses of the vestibule. "Did you know Mr. Henry's nephew was in town, Mama?"

"Yes, son. I'll explain later. We need to take our seats."

————

THE YEARS HAD BEEN KIND TO EMILY MCALLISTER. Her peachy complexion glowed against a lovely gown of emerald green silk chiffon. Escorted down the aisle by the brother of the groom, she was seated next to a man in the front pew. From her seat toward the back, Maggie thought she was more breathtaking than the bride. Only her slightly graying hair peeking out from under an emerald-green hat had given away her age. It was hard to believe so much time had passed since they'd last seen one another.

Amanda had ordered the bridesmaids' dresses from an exclusive shop in Philadelphia after she'd seen them in a Balanchine ballet in Boston. She'd sent a picture to Emily, who'd wholeheartedly approved and promptly sent the store a deposit. Within days Emily had sent the measurements of the girls in Wilmington, and Amanda had done likewise for the Philadelphia girls. Just as they'd planned, the effect of the array of autumn colors was stunning as the bridesmaids glided down the long aisle.

The last of the ten bridesmaids, Millie descended the aisle carrying her bouquet of American Beauty roses mixed with silk autumn leaves. Rusty had teased her, told her he'd sit on the aisle seat and pinch her as she went by—but she was more worried that she'd trip or turn her heel, as she often did in high-heeled shoes. As she neared the midway point down the long aisle, carefully putting one foot in front of the other, she caught the eye of a young man who turned all the way around in his seat and nodded to her. *Oh my gosh! Len Ryan.* Making a slight misstep, she reached out and touched the end of the pew to get her balance. A soft *oh* went through the congregation as she got in step to the music again. So distracted was she that she completely missed Rusty O'Reilly's nod as she passed the fifth row from the front.

Millie had known that Len would be at the wedding, but she'd tried to put him out of her mind. After all, he was kin to her. No one seemed to know exactly how close. Eva McBryde had lost touch with Maggie Ryan over the years, and Millie was reluctant to press her mother for details, mostly because she didn't want to let on that she was the slightest bit interested in Len. But that day at the beach, she'd known she was.

———

AT THE RECEPTION IN THE FESTIVELY DECORATED Cape Fear Hotel, Millie stood in the receiving line next to Belle. "Did you see Len Ryan in the church?" she whispered.

"What's he doing here? Mandy's never even met him."

"Miss Emily is from Onslow County. Remember? Len's daddy is from there. I think his mother taught school in Onslow and lived with Len's grandparents."

"Speak of the devil," Belle said, nodding towards Maggie and her son proceeding down the receiving line.

Millie tried not to stare, but he seemed more handsome than

she'd remembered. He was bigger—taller, and his ruddy complexion now a deep tan. When he reached them, Millie timidly held out her hand. "Hey," she said.

"Hey, Millie. This here's my mama."

"Well, I declare, Eva O'Kelly's little girl," Maggie said. "You sure are pretty. Isn't she pretty, Lenny?"

"The prettiest one."

"I'm pleased to meet you, Mrs. Ryan."

"Oh, honey, call me Cousin Maggie. Didn't your mama tell you?"

Len was staring at Millie, and she wished she'd checked to see if her lipstick was smeared. "Yes ma'am, she did. This is my sister, Belle."

"I declare, one's as pretty as the next," Maggie said. "I can't wait to see Eva and tell her how nice her girls are."

Belle greeted Maggie and turned to introduce her to Rebecca. "You almost made me fall," Millie said to Len.

Len was aghast. "How in the world?"

"Looking at me like that."

"Well, you were the prettiest one," he teased, his eyes lighting up.

"The *bride* was the prettiest one," she quipped.

"That's a matter of opinion," he said, moving along to take Belle's hand. "Well, cousin Belle, it's a pleasure to see you again, too." He nodded to Millie. "I'll see you later."

32

Disappointment and Disaster

EVA AND ROB HAD TAKEN A SEAT ALONG THE EDGE of the ballroom, balancing crystal plates filled with tiny chicken salad sandwiches and petit fours on their laps. A server came by and offered them sparkling grape juice. "Put it on the windowsill," Rob said. "I don't know how they expect folks to eat without a table to sit at." He ran his finger around his collar. "I said I'd never wear a starched collar again and here I am doing it."

"You look so nice," Eva said, her eyes wandering over the crowd. She was very elegant in a lavender chiffon gown Lilibeth had sent her for the occasion, her auburn hair piled on top of her head. *Just some old thing I had in my closet, Eva dear, but perfect for that wedding*, she'd said in her letter. "Look there, Rob. I think it's Maggie Ryan. Must be her son with her." She caught Maggie's eye and waved her over.

In the beaded dress she'd worn to the Cummings book signing, Maggie created an impression far from that of a country woman. With Len in his new suit, they made a handsome pair. Maggie held her arms out to greet her cousin. "Eva, honey. I haven't seen you since we were schoolgirls, and here we are meeting at a wedding like this more than twenty years later. This is my son, Len." She turned to Rob. "And you must be Robert McBryde," she said, a chill running through her at the mention of the McBryde name.

"It sure is good to see you, Maggie Lorena," said Eva. "You know, Millie works for Emily McAllister. She told her y'all were invited. Who would've thought we'd all come together like this in Wilmington?"

"'Scuse me," Len said. "I need to go find somebody."

"I've been meaning to write to you," Maggie said. "Ever since Len told me he'd met Belle and Millie, but I didn't have your address."

"We're living over on Princess Street right now. The boys bought a boardinghouse, wanting me and Rob to run it for them." She glanced at Rob, but he was watching some of the young crowd dancing in front of the orchestra. "It's worked out pretty good while the younger children have been in school."

"At least you're not stuck in Bandeaux Creek."

Eva shook her head. "I'd give anything to be back there. I envy you, Maggie."

Maggie really wasn't giving Eva her full attention. All during the ceremony, her thoughts had churned, recalling past events and conversations she'd shared with Jon McNamara. He'd asked her when she'd be in town next. He wanted *her* to come to *him*. He had not known she'd come to the clinic. Until today, maybe he thought she no longer cared. But she *did*, and she intended to arrange a meeting with him before . . .

"Won't be long now," Rob said. "There goes Mandy up the stair-case." They all turned to watch the bridesmaids line up, their hands over their heads. Rebecca caught the bouquet, and the girls squealed with laugher. "Oh, dear, I hope there's not a lot of truth in that old adage," Eva said.

"Does she have a beau?" Maggie asked.

"I reckon you could call it that. That's him over there talking to Dr. Jon."

Maggie looked around. "Oh, where? I've been looking every-where for him."

"Mr. Jones?"

"No, Jon," Maggie said a bit impatiently.

"Dr. Jonathan McNamara. Are you acquainted?"

"Yes, in Boston. I wanted to chat with him before we go," she said, wandering off towards the two men.

"Imagine that, Rob. She met Dr. Jon in Boston."

"Might be we'll see her at *that* wedding too."

———

JUST AS MAGGIE STARTED ACROSS THE ROOM, the orchestra began to play, and the floor promptly filled with gyrating couples. "Jon," Maggie called out. "Dr. McNamara." But Jon was shaking Mr. Jones's hand and bidding him farewell. "Oh, wait, please," she cried, struggling to reach him, but Jonathan had been swallowed up in the crowd that surrounded the dance floor.

Len, who was dancing with Agatha, touched his mother's arm as she went by. "I'm dancing with you next, Mama."

"Don't worry yourself about me, Len. I'm trying to catch up with Dr. McNamara."

"Dr. Jon?" Agatha asked.

"Yes, I saw him just a minute ago, but he seems to have disappeared."

Agatha beckoned Maggie to come closer. "He had to sneak out and get the car for Mandy and Tom," she whispered in her ear. "It was a trick. Everybody thought it was going to be one of the groomsmen. Dr. Jon sure fooled them."

"Yes, I reckon he did," Maggie said. "Do you think he'll be back soon?"

"Oh, I doubt it," Agatha said. "Aunt Emily was dead on her feet. Dr. Jon will probably take her home."

Maggie recovered quickly, putting aside a twinge of confusion and dismay. "Oh, no! I haven't had a chance to visit much with either one of them."

Agatha leaned in even closer. "I think they're in love," she whispered.

"What?"

"In love—you know, sweet on each other," Agatha said. "And

why shouldn't they be? They're both widowed. I think it's wonderful, don't you?"

"Yes, wonderful," Maggie said.

———

RUSTY O'REILLY HAD SNATCHED MILLIE'S HAND when the receiving line dispersed and pulled her into a circle of his friends, where a bottle was being passed. "Rusty, I'd like to dance," Millie said, eying the alcohol that was coming her way.

"No way, Millie. Besides I've had about enough of this Bootiay crowd. We're all going out to the beach in my car. You coming?"

"No, I can't. Mama and Papa are here. They wouldn't like it a bit, you know that."

Rusty grabbed hold of her arm and turned her aside, whispering in her ear. "Look, if you don't go, this is it. I'm leaving next week for Carolina. I thought we'd go out on the beach. I've got a blanket in the car."

"Well, I'm not going," Millie said and walked off. Belle had warned her that once these college boys went off to school, they'd ditch the high-school girls in a heartbeat. Millie was right proud of herself as she walked across the ballroom floor in her high-heeled shoes, feeling very grown-up.

Agatha and Belle had entertained Len most of the evening, teaching him several dances. Millie thought he looked to be having a grand time, with the girls making over him. She was sure that Len would never give her another thought.

But she was wrong. "I saw your boyfriend leaving. Want to dance with me?" Len asked, catching up with her as she made her way to the powder room.

"He's not my boyfriend anymore," Millie said.

"Well, then, cousin, let's go dance."

"I was about to come and tell you goodbye, but you were so busy dancing," Millie said, not meaning to sound petulant, but she knew she had.

"They wouldn't let me go!" he said, out of breath. "They're going out to Lumina after this—wanted me to go."

"I'm sorry, but Mama and Papa are ready to leave. We're waiting for Cal to pick us up. I've already called him."

"Let's go ask them," Len said, leading her to where Eva and Rob waited in the lobby of the hotel.

"Go on and dance, honey," Eva said. "We'll wait for you."

Millie looked at her father. "Go on, Little Sister. Just don't you go running off with him to the beach."

"Oh no, sir," Len said. "Mama and me have gotta get on back to the country. She's waiting for me right now in the car. Said she was overheated, needed some air."

Eva looked concerned. "Millie, honey, maybe you should go see about Cousin Maggie."

"Oh, no ma'am," Len said. "Mama's just fine. Just between you and me, she likes to go off by herself like that. C'mon, Millie. That dance is going to be over if we don't get going."

———

IT WAS WELL AFTER DARK BEFORE LEN AND MAGGIE started home. Len was full of talk about all the people he'd met, but Maggie hardly listened. All she could think about was Agatha's offhand comment. Jon and Emily in love—how could that be? Jon McNamara was in love with *her*. They had plans. *She* had plans. Emily had no right . . .

"Mama, you sure are quiet. Didn't you have a good time?" Maggie appeared not to hear him. The dim lights on the dashboard cast only faint light on the passenger side, where she had slumped against the door, dozing. Len leaned across to see her. "Mama, are you asleep?"

"What?" She bolted upright and was startled to see a large buck standing in the middle of the sandy road. He was proud and tall, and in his red eyes a dare compelled her to shout, "Len, watch out!"

But Len had taken his eyes off the road a moment too long, and the brakes on the old car grabbed and sent them spinning across the road and into the ditch. When the car came to a stop, Maggie thought that her heart had stopped, too. "Oh, God, Mama. Are you alright?"

"I t-t-think so. It was a deer. I saw him. His eyes were like fireballs. Where did he go?"

"I don't know, but thank God I missed him. We'd be worse off than just in a ditch."

Len pushed against his door, but finding it jammed, climbed into the back seat and out the rear door. The Chandler was almost on its side in the ditch, and he had to jump from the running board to the dirt road. After he assessed the damage, he broke the news to Maggie. "The wheel's busted and broke plum off the axle. We're going to have to walk to find some help. Come on, I'll help you get out."

Maggie reached around with her right arm and took hold of the back of her seat to pull herself in position to climb over. The pain was so sharp she thought she might've been shot in the shoulder by a stray bullet. "I can't," she cried. "I've hurt my arm, Len."

Len found a lug wrench in the boot and began to beat on the door handle on the driver's side. One way or the other, he knew he had to get Maggie out of the car. When he had succeeded in knocking the handle completely off, he pried the door open. With the car at such a steep angle, Maggie was able to turn herself around so that she was prone on the seat with her head towards Len. He slipped his hands under her arms and pulled until he had her part way out of the car so that she was able to assist herself. Their clothes were covered in grease and black mud, their hair was askew, and Maggie's arm was bruised and beginning to swell.

"I'm sorry, Mama. I didn't know you were hurt," he said, wrapping her in a quilt he'd retrieved from the boot. "Can you walk? We're not far from Uncle Zeb's."

"I reckon I don't have much choice, son," she said, tears streaming down her face. "Just show me the way to go home."

Patty Sue's Ford truck

33

Slow to Heal

THE OLD CHANDLER SAT UP ON BLOCKS FOR MONTHS, its wheel broken off at the axle and some of the wooden spokes busted out. Will put the word out right away to try and find a replacement for the wheel and its odd-sized tire, but several years back the newer models had gone to metal spokes and wider tires. Nothing showed up in the automobile mechanics' magazines that listed used parts, either. His best hope was to find another ten-year-old Chandler stored away in a shed somewhere, but even if they found one, money was more scarce than ever.

Dr. Bayard had told Maggie her arm was broken just below the shoulder. "The best I can do is tie your arm up in a sling, Maggie," he said. "It's just a fracture, but it's going to give you some trouble until it heals." Maggie had protested that maybe she should go to the clinic in Wilmington to see the new doctor, with whom she was acquainted, but Dr. Bayard assured her, somewhat testily, that he'd been practicing medicine a lot longer than Jonathan McNamara and he ought to know how to treat a broken bone.

Maggie's mental health following the accident was as slow to stabilize as her arm was to heal. For the first week she was in a state of drowsy confusion, dosed up with paregoric and aspirin. "I'd give her laudanum if I had any," Dr. Bayard told Tate. "But the government's made that illegal, too." He pulled him aside. "If you can get hold of a little whiskey, make her a toddy. That'll help some."

Eventually Maggie was weaned off the narcotic and slowly returned to her senses, but sobriety brought with it a renewed feeling of rejection and loss. The automobile had been the key to her future. Seeing her stories published in the *Star* and learning to drive had given her the confidence to go and do as she pleased—which she'd decided was all she'd ever really wanted. The isolation of living in the country was driving her mad. Her stories had been but one way she'd escaped. Maggie longed to associate with other women and men who had been to interesting places and done exciting things. Jon McNamara had held that promise for her. Now that she couldn't drive *or* write, she felt truly thwarted.

————

WILL'S BUSINESS HAD SLOWED DOWN CONSIDERABLY, except for Patty Sue's trucks. Tate felt sure she knew how badly they needed that income. Without the cash that Will contributed to the family, Tate would've had to hire himself out—not that any of the farmers in the immediate area had any more money than he did. Most couldn't afford to keep their old tractors and trucks running, much less hire help. And now that Maggie's savings were used up, and she wasn't able to write, they were even more dependent on Patty Sue's business. Tate didn't like the feeling, but he felt sure that Patty Sue knew it and she was looking out for them. *Kind of like that Robin Hood fellow*, he said to himself. She didn't want credit for it.

Will was a little skeptical. "She brought me a truckload of tractor parts," he told his father. "I can't help but wonder where she got them."

"She told me one of the men who works for her is a salvage dealer," Tate said. "Comes across all kinds of good stuff mixed in with the junk."

Will took off his cap and scratched his head. "Scrap parts? Some of them looked almost new." He'd read about what they called the *black market*, kind of like bootleg whiskey, he reckoned. But he knew his pa wouldn't want to hear anything about that.

"Don't look a gift horse in the mouth, son. Maybe we ought to ask her if she could get a wheel for the Chandler."

"Mama would s-s-sure be obliged," Will said. "She hardly c-c-comes out of her room anymore. I think losing her c-c-car was almost as bad as Y-Y-Yancey dying. She liked to have g-g-gone crazy then."

Tate stepped a little closer to Will and cautioned him. "Look here, don't say anything to Mama about getting that wheel. I reckon she won't be driving anymore for awhile anyhow."

WHEN COLD WEATHER FINALLY SET IN FOR GOOD, and Tate arranged their first hog killing of the year, Maggie announced that he'd have to do it without her assistance. "You know I'm practically helpless," she reminded him.

"I'm not expecting you to help, honey. Maybe you could just sit over to the side there and tell the ladies how we like our sausage seasoned and all."

"No, it's too cold. If I get neuralgia in this shoulder, I might never get over it." But Tate decided this was one time he knew best, and he bundled her up in a heavy shawl and wrapped her feet and legs in a woolen blanket, arranging her at a table near the sausage makers.

Katie was wearing a pair of heavy britches that belonged to Roy, and she'd tied a long apron on over his old hunting coat. "Look at her over there," Katie said, speaking to Zeb's wife, Sattie, low enough for Maggie not to hear. "You'd think it was the end of the world."

Sattie agreed. "She used to be right pretty—liked to fix herself up, go to church, play the piano," she said. "I declare, I don't think she's been out of the house since that wreck."

"I know she hasn't," Katie said, her breath turning to mist in the cold winter air. The two women were stuffing sausage into casings and hanging them over a line to dry. Hog-killing time was as much a social event as a time for preserving meat. Most days, farm women worked alone in their kitchens with children at their feet. Chances to meet with other women and gossip a little were few and far between.

"Tate ought to get that automobile fixed for her," Sattie said. "If it was Zeb, he'd buy me a new one."

"She was saving up her writing money for a new car before Tate brought the old Chandler home. I expect that's gone now, too."

"New or old, wouldn't do her any good now," Sattie retorted. "She couldn't drive it."

Katie tied another casing onto the sausage stuffer and pushed the ground seasoned meat into the small hopper with a wooden mallet. Lost in her thoughts, she tried to recall the number of times in her life that she'd wondered at the differences between her and her sister. Maggie was lovely and talented, well-liked in the community, but she'd always had some kind of secret life that went on in her mind. Or *was* it only in her mind? To Katie's knowledge, Maggie had only been to Wilmington alone one time, but Katie was sure as shooting that it had something to do with Dr. Jonathan McNamara. Before Thanksgiving, another letter from him had arrived for Maggie, in care of Katie. She'd held onto it for a week or more before she decided to throw it into the stove, saying nothing about it to Maggie. Someone had to reign her sister in—and it might as well be her.

Aunt Mag took a different approach. If Maggie Lorena had her mind on something—or someone—other than her husband, she thought she knew the best cure. While she was stirring the cracklings in the lard pot, she motioned to Tate to come over to her. "Better not get too close to that fire with your long skirt, Aunt Mag," Tate said, pulling her back by the shoulders. Aunt Mag shrugged his hands away.

"Listen up, I've been meaning to tell you something," she said, giving Tate a piece of advice that surprised even him. "This is one time you need to baby Maggie Lorena. She's helpless, you know."

"*Baby* her? Aunt Mag, I wait on her hand and foot!"

"Oh, I'm not talking about waiting on her, Tate. You do that anyhow. I mean be real sweet to her—pet and pamper her—you know." She raised her eyebrows, smiled and twinkled her eyes.

"Oh, that," Tate said.

———

MAGGIE HAD THOUGHT SHE WAS KEEPING her melancholia hidden by staying in her room as much as possible, letting Tate or Will bring her meals on a tray. Tate had been particularly kind, helping her bathe and dress. Twice he'd fixed her a tub bath, bringing kettle after kettle to fill the big galvanized tub. Under her direction, he'd poured in glycerine and lilac water, swirling it around before she stepped in. At first she was shy, keeping herself covered. She'd even asked him to leave the room. But the second time—it was on a Saturday night and he'd already bathed on the porch. After she'd settled into the warm bath, she'd called to him.

He rushed in, looking apprehensive. "You didn't try to get out by yourself, did you?"

Maggie smiled, thinking he cared more than she'd given him credit for. "No, I just wanted you to come sit with me."

Tate thought she looked like a picture he'd seen in one of the children's books of a fairy sitting with her ankles crossed on a lily pad. Steam rose around her in the chilly room. "Are you warm enough? I can get some more hot water," he said, anxious to please.

"I don't believe you could get much more than a cupful in, without it running over."

Tate was trying not to look, but he'd always loved her big breasts. She kept them hid most of the time. Was it out of spite? He couldn't remember when he'd last seen her naked. He stared, unabashed, at her full breasts floating like balloons on the surface of the water. "Want me to soap you down?" he asked.

Maggie was blushing—or was it the heat from the water? "Soap me down?"

"Yes."

"If you want to."

"I reckon I do. Mighty bad," he added, getting down on his knees, gliding the soap over her back and neck. "Reckon that's enough suds?" he asked.

"Maybe, but I need a little more washing."

Tate dropped the soap into a dish and began to massage her back. Soon his hands found their way to her breasts, and then . . .

Tate sometimes wondered if Maggie had forgotten the pleasure a man could bring a woman—and how much she could bring to him. But if she had, it all came back to her, right there on the floor of her little writing room that Patty Sue had helped him paint.

3 4

A Fine Little Boy

THE WINTER OF 1927–1928 WAS ONE OF THE COLDEST on record in Colly. Ice formed in the horse trough and stayed there, which was not unheard of, but highly unusual. Accustomed to mild winters, most farmers and their families planned their work and outings for the afternoon when the sun had warmed the sandy soil and the frame houses enough to be tolerable. But the winter wind of twenty-eight had kept up a steady howl, and the stoves had burned continuously day and night, barely keeping up with the need for heat. With all the doors to his shop closed and only a small window in the back to let in light, Will couldn't see to work on the few vehicles awaiting his attention. He spent most of the day inside the house with Maggie and Tate, huddled around the Acme stove.

Occasionally, when Maggie would slip out of the room to relieve herself, Will and Tate would light into their favorite subject.

"Wonder what she does in the winter? She sure hasn't been bringing those trucks in like she was," Will said. They both knew who he meant by *she*.

Tate looked up over his reading glasses. "I reckon she's holed up like the rest of us," he said. "Paper says we can expect some snow before the week's out. Can't run a trucking business when the roads are bad."

"Len hasn't been home since Christmas. I'll bet he's snowed in somewhere in the western part of the state." Will got up out of his chair and closed the French doors that separated the dining room and kitchen from the front parlor. Maggie could be heard rattling around in the kitchen. "Pa, Len told me he thought Patty Sue might be into something illegal—like whiskey running."

Tate put his paper down and took off his glasses. "Len ought not to be speculating on something he has no way of knowing is true."

"Well, I just thought I'd tell you what he said."

They could hear Maggie shuffling along towards the closed door. "Better keep it to yourself, son," Tate warned him.

———

THE WEATHER FINALLY WARMED ALONG THE MIDDLE of February, and with it, traffic in Will's garage picked up again. One of the first customers was Patty Sue, bringing Colin with her.

"Well, I declare," Tate said, swinging the boy up into his arms. "Look here, what Mr. Tate made for you." He pulled a wooden bird whistle from his pocket.

Will had seen his father working on the whistle from time to time, and was amused, though slightly concerned, by how much enjoyment Tate got out of knowing Colin. "Uncle Will's got something for you, too," he said, approaching a large wooden box in the corner of the shop. He pulled out a three-wheeler that he'd pieced together.

Patty Sue let out a big laugh, something they seldom heard from her. "Is that what you fellows have been doing all winter while I was working?"

"Got to keep busy," Tate said.

Colin was almost three now, and both Tate and Will had made over him as long as Patty Sue had been bringing him to the garage. "He talks about you guys all the time. I figured I'd better bring him down here to see you," she told them. "He doesn't have any friends his own age, so I guess you'll have to do."

Tate picked Colin up. "Let me run him over to the house and

show Maggie how much he's grown. That arm's given her a fit in this cold weather."

"Sure, I don't mind, but Miss Maggie Lorena might," she said with a smirk.

"Oh, Maggie loves little children, don't she, Will?" But Will had disappeared under Patty Sue's truck, where no one saw his grimace.

———

"I CAN'T BELIEVE SHE DRAGS THAT LITTLE snotty-nosed young'un all over hell and high water," Maggie said.

"He's not snotty-nosed, Maggie. She keeps him real clean."

"Well, he is to me. That woman ought to be ashamed."

"I feel sorry for her, she don't have any family and her husband's locked up in the insane asylum." Tate pulled out a handkerchief and wiped the child's nose. "Little fellow can't help that," he said.

"Why doesn't she get a girl to keep him at home?" Maggie said.

"I don't know. Will just wants to help her out a little," Tate said.

She glared at Tate. "What about you? What's your excuse?"

"Now, honey, you know how much I love children, especially little boys like . . . like Yancey." As soon as it was out of his mouth he knew he shouldn't have said it.

Maggie's hands went up to her face, covering her eyes. "Don't you ever compare him to my son again," she cried.

Patty Sue made matters worse by tooting her horn when she came in the driveway and pulling her truck up right between the garage and the house. She'd call out to Tate if he was in the barn and tell Colin to run over and give Papa Tate a hug. Maggie was bound to have witnessed the scene from her writing room which was on the back corner of that side of the house. He wondered if Patty Sue might do it on purpose.

As a regular thing, she started coming on Saturday mornings, dropping Colin off to play in the shop while she made the run to Atkinson to pick up parts at the train depot for Will. On one particular Saturday, Tate had decided to watch for her and motion to her to park on the other side of the garage. But when Patty Sue came, Tate had stepped down to the outhouse with a bodacious stomachache. By the time he'd gotten his pants buttoned up and made his way up the path, Patty Sue was long gone and Will was petitioning Maggie to keep an eye on the child.

"S-s-she was in a terrible b-b-big hurry, Pa. Had to go to Burgaw to take care of some b-b-business. She'll pick up the p-p-parts on the way b-b-back. S-s-said maybe you'd take the b-b-baby for a ride in the jalopy, but I thought M-M-Mama might watch him so's you c-c-could help me in the s-s-shop."

Out on the porch, Maggie was fuming. Her arm was about healed, but she held it by the elbow with her other hand out of habit. "No, I can't. You take him out yonder to the barn. He'll have to play with those cats," she said. "My nerves can't stand young'uns anymore, and your pa's got chores to do, haven't you, Tate?"

"Maggie Lorena, you know we can't just leave that baby at the barn," Tate said.

"Well, he can't stay in here, getting into my things," Maggie said.

"I'll just take him with me," Tate said, swinging the toddler up on his shoulders. "I've got to fill in a little washed-out place near the drainage ditch. He can play there in the sand with his cars and trucks Uncle Will made him." He ducked as he went through the doorway. "You and Mr. Tate are gonna have a good time playing in the dirt, aren't we, son?"

Uncle Will? Son? Maggie worked her mouth around like she was chewing nails. "Just make sure you're back before his mama is," she called out, her eyes on Tate's departing backside. "I reckon she'd come looking for you." She plopped down in a rocking chair on the porch and closed her eyes. Patty Sue didn't deserve a little boy like that.

Tate hadn't said a word to Patty Sue about Maggie's state of mind as far as she was concerned, but Patty Sue must've figured it out for herself when he wasn't around the garage much anymore. Occasionally she'd come in the back way, across Lightwood Knot Road, finding Tate in the field and bringing a jar of whiskey with her. Sometimes she'd stop at Miss Maybelle's store first and pick up a slab of cheese and some saltine crackers. He'd see that old blue pickup bouncing down the lane and his heart would skip a beat. She always brought Colin with her.

In his daydreams, he'd imagine her kissing him and getting him all fired up. But, really, all she wanted to do was talk. They'd have a couple of drinks out of tin cups while Colin played in the sand. He could tell she liked him. She'd run her fingers over his arm, sending sparks flying. "I don't want to hurt you, Tate," she said. "You've been like a brother to me. We're both married to crazy people, you know." Once Tate had asked her if her husband was really crazy. She shot him a dirty look and said, "He's in the insane asylum, isn't he?"

Another time, she asked him how he felt about Colin. "I know you like him, Tate, but do you *really* like him?" Tate had no idea what she was getting at, but the look on her face told him she wanted-ed a straight answer. He'd never seen her mouth turned down like that, her eyes sort of tearful.

Tate stood up and brushed the sand off his pants. "Well, he's a fine little boy," he said, reaching for Colin and picking him up. The child sat in the crook of Tate's arm, comfortable like he belonged to him. He reached out and touched Tate's nose, saying "boink." Tate returned the gesture. "Boink, yourself," he said, laughing.

"He really loves you, Tate."

What about his own grandfather? Tate started to say, but thought better of it.

Patty Sue stood up beside him. "Let me ask you directly. If something happened to me, would you take care of Colin?"

"No! I mean, nothing is going to happen to you." She was star-ing at him now, a hard stare like she dared him to say no again. "But, if it did," he said softly, "I'd see about the boy—make sure he . . . "

"That's all I wanted to know." She reached out for Colin. "C'mon, son. Mama's got some business to take care of. Throw Papa Tate a kiss."

35
The Queen of England

A S HER ARM HEALED, MAGGIE'S DISPOSITION improved
likewise. She found that by stacking up cardboard shoe boxes
with a pillow on top, she could support her arm enough to take the
strain off, and she was able to use her typewriter again. She'd been
pondering a story and she wanted to get started on it. Mr. Brown
had re-run two of her romances, but she was afraid his patience was
getting short. He'd sent her a note in the mail asking when she
thought she'd get back into production. *I've had several letters from
some of your followers and they're anxious for your return. Please send me a
brief synopsis of your next story and I'll run the little teaser to hold their
interest.*

That part was easy. Within a few days Mr. Brown had his item:
"Beginning next week in the *Morning Star*, a completely new story
by romance writer Maggie Lorena Ryan." *It was a snowy Christmas
Eve in Boston, Massachusetts, when they first met. Upstairs in the parlor, a
gay party was going on, but in the downstairs kitchen, two lonely, star-
crossed lovers found one another. He was free, she was not. Bound by the
shackles of an unhappy marriage, she goes back to her husband only to find
him in a web of deceit. Will fate bring the lovers together again?*

She'd given the story quite a bit of thought while recuperating.
If Agatha was wrong—and she *must* have been—then Jon was still
in love with her. He would be waiting to hear from her. At the wedding, she'd seen the look in his eyes. He still wanted her. Now that
she was able to use her typewriter again, she set out to write

"Lovers' Fate." Why had she not thought of it before? Jon could read *their* story in *The Morning Star*.

————

WILL'S CRUSH ON PATTY SUE DISSIPATED SOON AFTER he found that having money in his pockets made him much more interesting to the girls at Cotton Cove High School. Over the winter, Will had built a flatbed truck from various junk parts, and he was using it almost every weekend to take a crowd up to Singletary Lake. More often than not, there'd be twice as many girls as boys.

"I don't like it one bit," Maggie said to Tate. "It's not near warm enough to go swimming. There's no telling what they're doing up there at the lake."

"You ought not try to keep him tied to your apron strings," Tate said. "Just because he's quit school don't mean he's not grown up."

"He didn't quit high school, he's just trying to get a little money ahead so he can keep us afloat." She cut her eyes towards him in that accusing way of hers. "It's a good thing he's got that much gumption."

"There's no harm in it. They're just doing what boys are going to do."

"I suppose you think it's all right, too, if one of those Colvin boys takes a jar along."

"Now, what in the world makes you think they'll be drinking? They're just boys. Patty Sue told them to stop by her place and pick up a tractor tire she's been holding onto for Will. He's going to patch up the inner tube and they can use it at the lake this summer." Once again, he regretted the mention of that name.

"Now that really galls me," she said. "She's always giving Bud something—always! Last week she brought him a whole set of wrenches. I tried to tell him it doesn't look right for a woman to give a boy presents like that. Especially a woman like her," she added under her breath. "But he's just like you—he bows and scrapes like she's the queen of England bestowing knighthood on him."

Tate was finishing up his supper. He sopped up the last of his gravy with a piece of corn bread, wiped his mouth, and cleared his throat. "You know, Maggie, if you're gonna keep harping on Patty Sue like that, I just might leave you." He said it without thinking, but somehow he wasn't as afraid of her wrath anymore. Right here lately, there hadn't been a day when she didn't throw something up to him. In fact—he'd given it some thought—she'd never been happy with him, and he sure as hell wasn't happy with *her* now. It was times like this that he had a prickling recall of his emotions that night when Aunt Mag's house burned down.

3 6

Lost Letter

T HE FIRST WEEK OF MARCH BROUGHT THE PROMISE
of spring to the fields and trees—and the promise of a long-
anticipated visit from Abigail Adams the next month. Abigail wrote
Maggie that she and her traveling companion wanted to see the
famous Airlie Gardens, and the azaleas around Greenfield Lake.
She would also visit friends in the mountains after their sojourn on
the coast, stopping first in Hendersonville, then Asheville. *They're
old friends of mine from Florida who find the summers in the North
Carolina mountains much more to their liking, but they don't arrive until
the end of May, so we'll stay at the beach until then. Jon has reserved rooms
for us at the Oceanic on Wrightsville Beach. Are you familiar with it? He
has a friend who has a cottage there, but when he telephoned, I told him that
I'd prefer the hotel. I think he was disappointed—this sounds like a <u>very
good friend</u>, if you know what I mean.*

*Maggie, you simply must come. I've missed you and you have to meet
Reggie. She's about your age, a darling girl who loves to travel and meet new
people—as I do! We'll enjoy the sun for a few days—maybe even dance at
that wonderful old pavilion they call Lumina. Jon says he'll also arrange a
private tour of some of the gardens in the area. He's obviously settled into
Wilmington quite nicely and has good connections—so important to a successful practice.*

*As I write, I'm so excited to see you! The copies of the stories you sent are
<u>marvelous</u>! You see, I didn't steer you wrong; Evelyn Armstrong knew you*

could do it. I've asked Jon to reserve a room for you at the Oceanic—your own special quarters! You may bring anyone you like to share your space, but I suspect that some time away from the country will be welcomed. We'll dine out every evening, so bring your finery.

Bring her finery? Maggie had to laugh. She had not dressed even for church since Mandy's wedding. Her "finery" might need some alterations, and she hadn't sewn a stitch since she'd broken her arm.

Aunt Mag was none too happy about being called upon to help Maggie put together a wardrobe for her weekend at the beach. "Why doesn't Abigail come here to see *you*? Seems kind of rude to just ignore me and Tate," Aunt Mag said. She'd been handed a needle and thread and was changing the buttons on a cotton dress. "I don't see a thing wrong with these buttons. Why'd you want to change something that was perfectly good?"

"If you don't want to help, let me have it back," Maggie said, reaching for the dress. Her aunt jerked it to the side. "Well, quit fussing, then."

"How're you going to get there? You don't have a car anymore."

"Stop rubbing it in."

"I guess you could drive that old jitterbug out there that Tate calls his jalopy. Like to jarred my false teeth right out of my head bringing me up here."

"Jasper said he'd take me. Oysters will still be in season, and you know how he craves those awful things."

Aunt Mag looked up over her glasses with a twinkle in her eye. "I think it's more than oysters Jasper craves. Katie says he's still seeing that woman who lives at the Cape Fear Hotel. Never have met her," she said, holding up the dress to inspect her sewing.

"I've never met any of his women friends, and I reckon that's the way he likes it," Maggie said.

"At least he's not running around on a wife who's stuck at home somewhere. Some men do that, you know."

"Aunt Mag, you can bring up the darndest things. What made you think of that?"

"Nothing, not a thing. I was just reflecting on human nature."

———

WHEN JASPER DROPPED MAGGIE OFF at the elegant old Oceanic Hotel that many Wilmingtonians thought of as their summer club, he told Maggie he'd pick her up Sunday afternoon. "If you're nice to me, I might even let you drive my new car after we get across the river," he said.

"Why not all the way?" she asked. His answer was a familiar smirk.

Maggie's old friend was waiting for her in one of the rockers on the veranda. Maggie had wondered, even worried a bit, about what to expect. "Darling Maggie Lorena, it has been *too* long. Here you are as young and beautiful as ever, and I have turned old and gray." Abigail was putting on airs again, and Maggie could see why. Reggie had a turned-up nose reminiscent of some of the snobs in the Montgomerys' set. But she seemed to make a delightful companion for Abigail, who needed someone to lean on.

"You look wonderful, Abigail, and I'm so happy to see you, too," Maggie said. "It's hard to believe it's been three years."

"Has it, dear? I hardly realized, with all that has gone on in my life since Henry passed." She took her companion's arm. "And Reggie and I have just begun to travel. I'm already looking forward to a cruise in the Caribbean. Maybe you will come."

Just getting away the short distance to Wilmington had been a chore for Maggie. Maybe she was getting older, but she had lost some of her enthusiasm for going places and doing things. It was too easy to stay home and rattle around in her little room, writing her stories. She had to admit that Jon McNamara was an enticement for this occasion.

"Change your clothes, dear, and we'll go for a stroll on the boardwalk," Abigail said after they'd had tea in the lobby.

"I think I'll be fine in this," Maggie said, mentally reviewing the limited wardrobe she'd brought along.

After the Bostonians had slipped into what they called beach pajamas, causing Maggie to feel a little inferior in her cotton dress, they proceeded to the boardwalk that ran along the beach in front of the hotel. "We have absolutely nothing like this in New England," Reggie said, holding tightly onto her large brimmed hat. Maggie had begun to like her, finding her witty and friendly after all.

"I never saw the ocean when I was up there," Maggie said. "Only Boston Harbor."

"I offered to take you to the Cape," Abigail said.

"I know you did. Maybe I'll come back some day," Maggie remarked.

"Oh, do!" Reggie said. "We'll go to Martha's Vineyard!"

"Let's go up," Abigail said, looking up at the elegant observation tower with its three levels of balconies that overlooked the beach. "The manager said up there we'd have the best view of the ocean between Atlantic City and Florida."

By the time they'd reached the top of the tower, Maggie was breathing heavily and perspiring. She'd put on a bit of weight as a result of her curtailed activities the past months. Still, she was glad she'd devoted the extra effort to tailoring her spring frocks to fit— she felt better about her appearance than she had all winter. "Whew, that was a lot of stairs," she said, sitting down at a small table.

"Yes, but worth every step," Abigail said, looking out across the Atlantic Ocean and down the beach. "Look there," she said pointing to a crowd that had gathered on the north end of the beach. "Wonder what's going on?"

"Let's go see," Reggie said.

Maggie was thankful that going down was easier than the climb up, and she was as excited as the other women to see what the hubbub was about. They kicked off their shoes and began walking towards a large object that had washed up on the shore. The closer they got to it, the more potent the odor became. "Oh, that smells terrible," Maggie said. "Let's go back."

But Abigail and Reggie were fascinated. "I believe it's a sperm whale," Reggie said. "It's bound to be more than fifty feet long." She rushed ahead, engaging another onlooker in conversation. In a few minutes, she came rushing back. "It *is* a sperm whale and it's already been there four or five days. He advised us not to go much closer."

"What on earth will they do with it?" Abigail asked. "Surely they won't leave it there on the beach while it rots."

"That gentleman lives here on the beach, and he said the North Carolina Museum of Natural History was going to come and get it and take it to Raleigh for an exhibit."

"My stars, I don't know how they'll do it," Maggie said, turning back towards the hotel, "But I think I'd rather see it in a museum." She was feeling anxious about getting back to her room to freshen up before dinner. "What time are we expecting Jon?" she asked.

Abigail looked at her watch. "An hour from now, if we're lucky. Dr. Jon isn't known for his punctuality."

"In that case, I think I'll run a bath in that fancy tub," Maggie said. "Looked mighty inviting to a country girl."

"We'll all go up," Abigail said. "I'd like to put my feet up a bit. Tomorrow will be a long day with garden tours and lunch downtown. Jon said that Saturday night is his treat, and he was keeping the place a surprise." Maggie suspected that Emily McAllister would be an invited guest as well, but she was reluctant to mention her thought to Abigail for fear she'd pick up on her resentment.

———

JON BUZZED MAGGIE'S DOOR AT THE OCEANIC FIRST. She opened it and her heart skipped a beat. "Hello, Maggie," he said. She was speechless, simply staring at him as if he was a figment of her imagination suddenly come to life. "May I come in?" he asked.

Pull yourself together, she thought. "Jon, it's so nice to see you again. I keep reading about you in the paper," she said gaily, inviting him in. "Please sit down."

He closed the door and reached out to her, pulling her into his arms without a word. The old feelings returned to Maggie—oneness, belonging. They had been made for each other. But in the same instant, she knew better. Gently she pulled away. "I'm truly glad you've found what you wanted in Wilmington," she said. "Even if it wasn't me."

"It was you, darling Maggie," he protested. "It still is. But when you didn't answer my letter, I knew—"

"What letter? You never wrote to me, Jon."

"But I did! I sent it to your sister's house, just as you told me." he was flustered, confused by her accusation.

"Jon, there was no letter," she said calmly. "I was incapacitated. I'm sure Katie would have given it to me." She paused, considering what had likely happened.

"I don't think it matters now," he said. "You're still married to Tate, and I'm . . . " He'd told her then how he'd asked her to let him know where things stood. His conscience would not allow him to interfere in her marriage in any way if she had gone home and found that she no longer wanted to leave Tate. He'd needed an answer because his life in Wilmington was becoming more involved. When he'd realized that there was a connection between her and Emily, he knew he could not pursue a relationship with Emily until he'd resolved things with Maggie. "If you'd been here in Wilmington waiting for me when I arrived, this never would have happened, but over a year had passed and I'd had no word. My honor would not allow me to pursue you any further."

Maggie stood by the window, looking out at the roiling sea. What a mess she had almost made of her life in this quest for something totally unrealistic. She turned to face him. "Jon, I do love you, but I can never leave Tate. Is that what *you* needed to hear, too?"

He kissed her then, and she felt the wave of desire in it just as in her daydreams. But she pushed him away and slipped a shawl around her shoulders. Her arm had nearly mended; so would her heart, she supposed. "Let's go," she said quietly. "Abigail and Reggie are waiting for us."

————

THE NEXT MORNING, MAGGIE AWOKE WITH a violent headache, brought on—she was sure—by the encounter with Jon. Dinner had been pleasant enough. Jon had even rubbed her knee under the table, but it was more a comforting pat than a romantic gesture. She'd just completed a story where the protagonist was in love with a complete cad—and she decided there was something of that character in Jon.

Still, losing his interest had left her blue. She called Jasper and asked if he might take her home. Her brother was more than willing—something she attributed to the fact that his plans hadn't turned out as well as expected either.

Her brother was quiet on the drive home. Nothing had been mentioned about Maggie taking the driver's seat, not that she could've stood his relentless criticism. Not today. Not after listening to Jon tell Abigail about the new house he was building in Winoca Terrace, one of Wilmington's finest new residential areas. Completely unaware of Maggie's aborted hopes of a life with Jon, Abigail had instructed him on the importance of a "hostess," someone with the correct social skills to manage his residence. She'd never said the word "wife," but then . . .

"What're you thinking about, sister?"

Startled, Maggie sat up and looked around to get her bearings. "Oh, I was about to fall asleep."

"No, you were wishful thinking," Jasper said. "I could tell."

"Was I? Since when did you become a mind reader?"

"Look, shug, there's something I've been meaning to tell you. Going off to the beach by yourself, staying at the Oceanic with those society women. It don't look right."

"What on earth are you saying, Jasper Corbinn?"

"I'm just saying that you and Tate ought to be doing things together. Now that the boys are about grown, you could . . ."

"My stars! There you go talking about other people gallivanting, when you're the—"

"Hush, Maggie Lorena!" he shouted. "I'm trying to tell you something."

Maggie flinched, drew herself back against the door. Jasper, keeping one eye on the road, was glaring at her. "You are one hard-headed woman. Will you just listen to me for one minute? I'm trying to tell you that I don't have what you have—what Katie and my brothers have. You ought to be taking care of it." He lowered his voice. "You ought to be taking care of Tate."

Something told Maggie to get off her high horse and listen. Jasper was serious. What was he trying to tell her? "Are you giving me a lecture about marriage?" She had *you of all people* on the tip of her tongue, but she held it back.

"Yes, I guess I am, sister. You might think I'm not qualified, but I know what I'm talking about. I'd give anything if I'd gotten married when I was younger—had me a couple of boys, a girl." She was staring at him now, not believing her ears. She'd always thought he loved being a sport, a man about town or country with no strings attached. "You and Tate, Zeb and Sattie—the rest of 'em, y'all have got something I can't never have," he said. "Children to pick up where you leave off." She thought he'd almost sobbed.

"Jasper, you could've gotten married a dozen times. Why, I remember that girl at the Moore's Creek picnic when Pa got the medal for being one of the Immortal Six-Hundred, she . . ."

"Maggie, honey. You don't understand what I'm saying. Yes, I could've done a lot of things, but I didn't and I'm sorry, because now I'm getting too old for it. I'm just a used up old has-been like that woman I was with last night, and I don't have a damn thing to go home to."

They were passing the place where the deer had challenged the

Chandler and Len had swerved off the road. In a flashback, she saw the car on its side in the ditch, Len pulling her through the window. "They're good boys," she said.

Jasper looked across the seat at her. "And Tate's a damn good man."

PART VI

Wilmington, North Carolina

1928

Ⅹⵁ

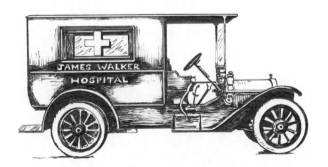

Ambulance, circa 1928

37
Mishap on Smith Creek

H UGH MCBRYDE HAD SPENT THE MORNING in his office at the Coast Line, where he'd been made division manager just a few weeks ago. He didn't have to work on Sundays, but the freight department never really shut down, and he enjoyed the slower pace of a day without all the secretaries and clerks around. Maybe he should've been in church, but he just didn't feel called to go. Hadn't since he'd been out on his own. He left the office shortly before noon and had the forty-cent dinner at the New York Café on Princess Street. He could've gone home for dinner, of course, but a crowd would likely be there and he didn't want to waste a nice Sunday afternoon sitting around on the porch chewing the fat like old folks.

Some of the trainmen were gathering at the Armory about three o'clock and they'd asked him to stop by. As much as he hated to get involved, he knew they needed his support. Right now he just wanted to stroll down to the Custom House on the waterfront to take some pictures. Hugh loved the river and all of the activity that surrounded it, especially the large oceangoing ships from every-where all over the world. He buttoned his jacket. In the springtime the sun could be scorching hot, but the wind off the water coming up any of the streets that ran perpendicular to the river was blustery and cold.

Reaching Water Street, he walked down to the Wilmington pier, where he photographed a Norwegian merchant marine vessel with the small Kodak camera his parents had given him for graduation from Oak Ridge. Up on the deck of the ship, he saw a sailor photographing him. Hugh waved to the crewman, who motioned to him to meet him at the ship's ladder.

After some unsuccessful effort at communicating, Hugh shrugged his shoulders and started to walk away, when the captain of the vessel approached him. "He wants to trade cameras with you," he explained to Hugh in accented English.

"Why would he want to do that?"

The captain turned to the sailor, exchanging a few words. "He says he bought his camera in Hong Kong. It is very complicated and he has never learned to use it. He says he just wants a simple box camera to take pictures for his son in Norway."

Hugh chuckled. "Let me see it." He reached for the camera, and the sailor smiled and handed him a German-made Leica. Although Hugh couldn't read the marks on it, he knew it was one of the best cameras in the world. "I can't give him my camera for sentimental reasons, but I'll buy that one off of him. He can get one like mine, if not better, at the camera store on Front Street tomorrow." The captain translated again. The sailor nodded eagerly. "Ask him how much." They agreed on ten dollars, and Hugh knew he'd made a good bargain.

With his new camera and several rolls of film in hand, Hugh wandered down to the old Sprunt Cotton Company's wharf, where he found two rascally-looking young chaps, slingshots in hand, aiming at the glass windows in the closed warehouse. He chuckled to himself. When he'd first come to work in Wilmington, he and Cal had brought their twenty-twos down to the pier and shot ten or fifteen huge wharf rats. He held his camera up and caught one boy taking aim at the windows. In the same frame, he captured the other boy's surprised expression when he saw Hugh with his camera. *That ought to be a good one*, Hugh thought. *I'd give it to the cops, but they're probably just going to tear these old warehouses down. Might as well let the youngsters have their fun*, he thought, watching the boys scamper away.

Meandering along the waterfront, he paused to take several more pictures, one of a pretty girl looking wistfully down the muddy Cape Fear River. *Probably some lonesome sailor's wife.* The thought reminded him that he had planned to be married by now himself. Twenty-six years old and his career well established, he was past being ready for a place of his own. The boardinghouse had been a perfect solution to help Mama and Papa. So far the house was paying for itself with a little bit left over each month. The extra would be a nest egg for Papa when he could no longer work. And he'd promised Mama that one day he'd make sure she got back to the country. As for himself, he had yet to meet anybody whose bed he'd want to put his shoes under.

Walking back down towards the Coast Line freight yards, Hugh saw a police car and a gathering of men at the gate. *Wonder what that's about?* Coming a little closer, he saw one of the yardmen and several other trainmen. The yardman recognized him. "Mr. McBryde, we lost a man today. Joe Hilburn, one of the switchmen."

"What do you mean, *lost* him?"

"He's gone, disappeared when we crossed Smith Creek."

Hugh nodded to the other men, standing aside while a switchman named Dillinger reported the details to the policeman. "We was out there in the freight yard, switching cars around. Allen, he's the yardman, was operating the engine. Me and Hilburn were pulling the switches. When the train got to the trestle, Hilburn was hanging onto the side of a car. He jumped down like always and pulled the switch when we come to Smith Creek. I saw him swing back up on the flatcar. I seen him do it a hundred times. Then he'd always ride across the trestle, hop off and pull the switch on the other side. But *this* time he didn't pull the switch on the other side."

"When did you realize he was missing?" the policeman asked Allen.

"I had another train coming, so I pulled the brake. I don't know what Hilburn was doing back there. When I started up again, I saw the second switch wasn't thrown. I sent the fireman to see what in the hell Hilburn was doing. That's when we found out he wasn't on the flatcar."

"Do you suppose he fell off when you pulled the brake?"

"How in the hell would I know? Hilburn was the switchman. Nobody ever fell off before."

"How about you, Mr. Pittman? Did you see Mr. Hilburn fall?"

"No sir, I was on the other side of the last car. When the train stopped, I hopped off and crossed over the tracks, expecting to see him on t'other side. But I didn't see him nowhere. I looked down. That's when I seen Joe's cap on one of the girders. I knew then he was in the water. Me and Dillinger, we looked our fool heads off, thinking he was going to pop up any minute downstream."

Dillinger wiped his eyes with a red bandana. "He never did. C'mon, Pitt, let's get back over there. They're still looking for him."

The policeman turned to Hugh. "You in the freight department?"

"Yessir, I handle the paperwork, but I don't run the yard."

"Well, we can't find anybody, it being Sunday and all. Need to go tell Mrs. Hilburn. She lives way out in Winter Park, I believe."

"Yes, sir. Joe Hilburn's son works with me. Maybe we should try and find him."

"It's going to be a terrible shock for the entire family," the policeman said. "Anybody know who their pastor is?"

"That'd be Reverend Hathaway," Dillinger said. "He lives across the street from them."

"Can you show us the way? Tell the pastor what happened?"

"No sir, I can't do that." The switchman wiped his eyes. "I'm just barely able to hold myself together. If I saw his wife Isla, or any of those young'uns out on the street, I just couldn't stand it."

"I'll go," Hugh said. "It's the Coast Line's responsibility."

———

BUT THE ATLANTIC COAST LINE RAILROAD didn't feel responsible, Hugh was pretty sure. Upper management would not admit that the accident was a safety violation—not now, not since the Florida land boom had collapsed in 1925 and freight revenues had been steadily declining. When earnings dropped, new equipment purchases ceased, men were laid off, maintenance lagged behind, and safety measures were not enforced. Directives came down from the president's office almost daily. Maintaining a low accident rate saved on insurance, labor, and relief department costs.

Ordinarily men in the freight yard like Joe Hilburn might see things not being done as they should be, might get unhappy about safety practices, but a job in the Coast Line freight yard was highly regarded, and a man usually did everything he could do to hold his job.

But Hugh was aware that Joe Hilburn and some of the other yardmen had recently joined the Brotherhood of Trainmen. And there'd been a lot of talk in the newspapers about working conditions. Now the unions were getting involved—that was what the meeting at the Armory today was about.

Joe Hilburn had let on to his son that one of the yardmen he worked with on his shift didn't follow the rules, but he demanded his son not say anything. Hilburn had seniority, could have pulled the yardman off his shift, but he didn't want to throw his weight around. On the day he died Joe told his wife that this would be the last shift he would work with that man. *How could he have known?*

———

DOZENS OF VOLUNTEERS FROM THE BROTHERHOOD of Railroad Trainmen walked the banks of Smith Creek, peering into the dark waters for some sign of the lost switchman. A solemn crowd of townspeople followed, hoping to see the body pulled from the cold water. Another of Hilburn's sons worked for the Ethyl-

Dow Chemical plant that operated near the railroad trestle. Some of his co-workers brought small boats to search the still waters. Back and forth they plied the deep stream, thrusting long poles into the water every foot or so. An ambulance, the only sign of hope, followed their progress along the bank.

Hugh couldn't stay away from the tragic site despite the Coast Line position. Mr. Baldwin had cautioned his protégé. "I know you're close to these men, McBryde, but you can't appear too involved. Maybe there was a riff going on between Hilburn and the engineer. We don't know what might've happened."

"His wife says Joe was concerned about safety violations. That'd be the Coast Line's responsibility, wouldn't it?"

"Yes, but we just don't know. Poor fellow might have been over-whelmed with debt—all those children. Might've seen a plunge into the creek as the only way out of his problems."

"Everyone who knew Joe Hilburn say that he would never have jumped into that creek with a thought to ending his life."

———

ON THE THIRD DAY, AFTER SETTING OFF TWENTY-SEVEN charges of dynamite to try and loosen the tangle of logs beneath the surface, the men hooked Joe Hilburn's body with a dragline, ending the harrowing search. The victim's watch had stopped at seven minutes after twelve noon, precisely the time the flatcar had passed over the trestle. The coroner's investigation revealed a deep gash on Joe Hilburn's left temple, confirming speculation that the switch-man had fallen from the car, smashing his head on the girders before he hit the water. How or why, no one would ever know for sure, but Isla Hilburn had her suspicions.

3 8

Most Women Do

O N THE DAY OF JOE HILBURN'S FUNERAL, Eva McBryde had gotten up before light to make a pound cake and fry two chickens. She'd packed the funeral food in a large basket with a jar of Mae's grape preserves and a gallon of tea. It was her standard funeral basket. Black or white, the families of Eva's acquaintance could always count on food and sympathy from her when a loved one passed.

"They're going to have the service right there in the house," she told Millie. "Maybe you could occupy their youngest, a little girl named Susan. I know that would mean a lot to Isla."

"I'd rather do that than sit inside. Funerals are so sad."

Eva removed her apron and hung it behind the kitchen door. "This one certainly is. Imagine your papa going off to work one day and not coming home." She gazed into the distance. "We mustn't take anything or anyone for granted, Millie."

———

OUTSIDE THE HILBURN HOME, A BLACK HEARSE waited under the trees. Millie sat with nine-year-old Susan Hilburn on the sunny back steps, watching a flock of chickens peck at a handful of corn the girl had thrown at their feet. "Daddy always let me take care of the biddies," Susan said.

"Have you had these big old chickens since they were biddies?" Millie asked.

"Most of them," the child said, throwing the last of the corn in her hand to the greedy birds. She pulled her dress down over her knees and rocked back and forth. "One time I was changing their water and I stepped on one and killed it."

"Oh, I'm so sorry. Did your daddy get mad?"

"No, he just said it would go to heaven to be with Anne."

"Who is . . . who was Anne?"

"My little sister that died. She was just a baby. I came after her." She looked up at Millie and smiled. "Maybe to take her place."

"You know, I had a little brother that died, and we got a new sister after that."

Susan looked out over the yard, focusing on a push mower leaning against the side of a shed. "We put the biddie in a little shoebox and buried him right over there."

"That's a nice place."

"Will God send me a daddy just like mine to take his place?"

Millie had to hold back the tears. If only life were so simple. "I'll bet God doesn't have any more daddies as nice as yours."

"Did you know my daddy?"

"No, but my brothers did. Tell me about him if it won't make you too sad."

Susan smiled. "He loved me the best."

"I'll bet he did."

"I was the baby and he would carry me around on his shoulders. Every day when he came home from work, he had a surprise for me in his lunch box."

"He did? What else?"

"Well, he always let me sit on his lap after supper and have the last little bit of iced tea in his glass. Mama made us drink milk at supper, but Daddy always saved me that last little sip of tea."

"He must have thought you were a pretty special little girl."

"Everybody said he spoiled me."

"I'll bet he just loved you a lot. That's what *spoiled* means."

Susan got up from the step and brushed off the back of her dress. Inside, the preacher was saying words they couldn't quite hear. When the singing started, Millie heard Eva's high-pitched monotone—*In the sweet by and by, we shall meet on that beautiful shore.* Mama loved to sing. She said she couldn't carry a tune in a bucket, but she sang anyway.

Susan stood up and pointed. "See that rooster over there?"

Millie had seen the rooster and was keeping a wary eye on it. "Yes."

"He's mean as the devil. Chased me all the way into the house one time."

Millie burst out laughing. "He did? You're bigger than he is. You should have turned around and chased him back."

Susan shook her head from side to side. "Unh-uh. He was flapping his wings and prancing way up high on his old rooster legs," she said, walking on her tiptoes and waving her arms up and down. "I ran as fast as I could and got inside on the screened-in porch. He strutted off like he'd won the race or something."

"I don't care much for roosters either," Millie said, looking about the yard at all the things that indicated the presence of a man. There was a large garden to be plowed, a mule and a cow. The child seemed to sense her thoughts. "My daddy's not coming back. Not ever."

Millie squatted down to Susan's level. "I know. Maybe God needed him to do some work up in heaven."

"They don't have trains up in heaven. My daddy was a railroad man and they don't have trains up in heaven, do they?"

Millie took a deep breath. "I don't know, they might." She was listening to the drone of the preacher praying over the child's father, thinking the service was almost over. "Would you like to go on a picnic?"

"I guess so." Susan started towards the house. "But I want to tell my daddy goodbye first. He's in the living room in a casket. Do you want to see him?"

"I may need to help my mama with the food. Don't you want to stay here in the kitchen with us? I'll fix you a glass of tea."

"No, I want to see my daddy." The child was starting to tear up.

"Let her go," Eva whispered. "They've closed the casket."

"Go ahead, Susan. I'll make us a picnic and we'll take it to Greenfield Lake."

"This is so sad. A man in his prime with a family to feed and clothe," Eva said. "I don't know what Isla is going to do."

"Won't she get his railroad pension?"

"I hope so, but the Coast Line is denying that it was their fault."

"That's not fair, Mama. I heard Hugh say the Coast Line should take responsibility."

Eva had piled a platter high with fried chicken. "Hugh may be trying to do the right thing, but Harry says the Coast Line doesn't take kindly to employees who go against them."

"Will Mrs. Hilburn have to go to work? She can't take care of the children and the house if she has to go to work."

"She'll find a way, honey. Most women do."

———

A FEW WEEKS LATER, MR. BALDWIN BROKE THE NEWS to Hugh McBryde that he was being transferred to the Coast Line offices in Atlanta. Hugh would have to move immediately. The Coast Line had recently picked up controlling ownership of a 640-mile railroad, the Atlanta, Birmingham & Atlantic Railway Company—in a coup of sorts, keeping it out of the Seaboard Air Line's hands. Hugh had been up for a promotion, and Mr. Baldwin had practically promised Hugh that he was next in line for his supervisor's job. Hugh wondered if the sudden transfer was a way of reprimanding him for standing up for Mrs. Hilburn, and for Joe. Maybe it wasn't, but the AB&A was the largest railroad in the country with no union employees, a distinction that did not escape his ire.

Rob and Eva McBryde were devastated. Hugh was their rock. Without him, maintaining their life in Wilmington would be difficult. The boardinghouse was bringing in less money every week. Jobs were hard to find, and more people were leaving the city than were coming there to look for work. Cal assured them that he would find a boarder to take Hugh's room, and he'd keep bringing his co-workers to fill the table at lunch time.

"If you can't make the payments, you'll have to put the Princess Street house on the market," Hugh said. "But things will get better before that happens. I'm sure of it."

39
An Albatross

WITHOUT HUGH TO MANAGE THE BUSINESS END, things didn't get better. The boardinghouse on Princess Street became too much to handle for Rob and Eva. Hugh's letter, which they shared for all to read, dashed any hope that he might return.

Mable is a stenographer in the Coast Line's business office. I know you'll like her. We plan to be married by a justice of the peace here in the city next month. Her folks are too old to travel and neither one of us has any time off. We'd rather get settled into an apartment, then come home in midsummer when we can go to the beach.

Of course, you know this means I'll need my money out of the house on Princess Street. I think it's a good time for all of us to get out. I'd like to put a little money in the stock market—maybe buy a piece of land in Florida. Y'all ought to think about that. Land's real cheap down there now.

Cal, maybe you can find a smaller house for Mama and Papa. We've all known for some time that the big old boardinghouse idea has about played out. You might even think about renting something until the economy settles down.

———

HARRY AND CAL HAD ALREADY DISCUSSED GETTING OUT of the arrangement. *Nothing but an albatross to Mama and Daddy anymore,* as Harry put it. Harry's practice had picked up and he was more and more involved with politics in Wilmington. Several Sundays in a row he'd brought a young woman to dinner, an indication that he was intent on making a good impression on her. He'd been thinking about a small house out on Brookside Drive for some time. Marriage was a natural choice for an ambitious young attorney. As for Calvin, he'd also had his eye on a place of his own for months. The little house had a shed where he could keep his new car.

Rebecca had finished her training at James Walker Memorial Hospital in May and went to work for Dr. Sidbury at the new brick Babies Hospital on Wrightsville Sound. She'd likely want to get an apartment closer to the beach, her siblings guessed. Belle had completed her second year in business school in June and had already announced her plans to move to Washington, D.C. She would live with an ex-roommate of Agatha's who'd arranged a job for her at the Library of Congress.

Calvin and Harry took Hugh's suggestion, putting the Princess Street house on the market after finding a suitable, but much smaller, house on Red Cross Street for their parents and the younger children. Millie would be at home a while longer to help Mama and Papa. She'd enter her senior year at New Hanover High School in the fall, and Emily McAllister had offered her a full-time job at Beau Monde when she finished her diploma. There was no denying it, you couldn't keep young people from following their own stars.

But the timing was not good for Rob, who within a few weeks of the move lost his job at the old Bear Winery when it was sold to make way for a new building. Finding other work at his age was not going to be easy. But Rob had a good laugh when, during demolition, one of the huge casks was found to hold wine instead of water. "Every now and then, when the weather would change, I'd put my flashlight on it and see a drip or two from the spigot," Rob said. "Didn't take a genius to figure there was wine in it."

Harry was charmed by the thought of a whole cask of wine just a few doors down from the courthouse. "Why didn't you tell us? We could've had a huge party down there, and no one would have known the difference."

"Now, son. It'd look mighty bad to have you arrested just before an election."

Harry laughed. "I hate to think of federal agents busting open that vat, letting it run into the river. What a waste."

———

ALL THESE EVENTS LED UP TO a precipitous announcement by Rebecca that she and Mr. Jones were going to get married in the courthouse the following Friday. They would host a small dinner at the Orton Hotel for her family immediately after the ceremony. "I feel terrible," Eva cried. "My eldest daughter being married in a courthouse."

"That's what they want, Eva," Rob said. "No need to get worked up about it." He didn't tell her that before they vacated the Princess Street house he'd seen Rebecca sneaking out the back door in the middle of the night a couple of times, knowing full well where she was going. If Jones hadn't wanted to marry her, Rob might've had a word to say, but it had been obvious to him since they'd first moved in that the man had feelings for his daughter.

Junius Jones stood to make a toast to his bride with a glass of the hotel's best sparkling grape juice. He was not a cheapskate and he wanted the McBrydes to know it. "To my bride, my greatest joy in life, may we live out the rest of our days in perfect bliss."

Rebecca had a funny look on her face. For the first time, Eva thought maybe she realized that Junius Jones was talking about the last half of his life, whereas hers was just beginning. But Rebecca kissed him and said, "I've never been happier in my life."

"As you all know, we'll be right there on Princess Street," Junius said. "Y'all are welcome to come and stay with us if you start missing your old neighborhood."

It was meant to be a joke, but the McBrydes—from Rob and Eva, right down to little Vera—were disconcerted that they'd had to give up the house that had once belonged to one of Wilmington's wealthiest families. It had been a source of pride to Eva that Millie had never been reluctant to tell her friends at school where she lived. Rodney and Vera were leaving playmates they'd known most of their school days.

"We're hardly four blocks away from Princess Street," Eva said. But she knew that those four blocks were the equivalent of miles from the right address.

4 0
Red Cross Street

THE SMALL HOUSE ON RED CROSS STREET had only two rooms to rent out. One had a small kitchenette, which brought in a little more money. Eva had to let Mae go, and they'd cut back to only one meal a day for the boarders. But what really broke Eva's heart was that Millie dropped out of high school to work full-time and help make ends meet. "It's not right, you not being in school," Eva cried. "I'd rather go to the poor house."

"Lots of my girlfriends are dropping out, Mama. I'll go back when things are better. Right now, we have to pull together like Papa says."

"But it's your senior year. Your friends will finish school and you'll be left behind."

"No, Mama, I'm telling you, I'm not the only one. Miss Emily said I could work as many hours as I was able. When things are better, I'll get back in school."

"Well, I'm glad some people have money to buy new hats."

Millie laughed. "You know what they say, the rich get richer and the poor get poorer."

"That's not funny, honey."

"I know, I didn't mean it to be."

———

FINALLY, ROB GOT ON AS A CARPENTER with Worth and Worth, agents for the Cape Fear Steamboat Company, which had built the *A. P. Hurt,* an old iron-hull stern-wheeler he'd seen many a time on the Cape Fear River. "I'm making pretty good money right now," he told his wife. "I always was a good carpenter. The Worths have seen what I can do."

"But if we had a house and a little land up in the country, Millie might live with Rebecca, finish high school. Vera and Rodney wouldn't mind going to school in the country. Wouldn't be any worse than moving here. We could raise our own pigs—have a cow—plant a row or two of corn and some sweet potatoes."

They were sitting in the cramped, airless kitchen of the Red Cross Street house. Eva had given up her electric stove for a wood stove that had seen at least fifty years of use, saying she didn't mind a bit. But she had, and Rob knew it. "Eva, I know how much you want to go back to the country, but we can't move when we're already strapped for cash. Takes money to make a move and I can't ask the boys to help. When that house on Princess Street sells, we'll talk about it. Right now, I think we ought to be glad we've got a roof over our heads and rent money coming in."

In the hall, the telephone was ringing. "Mama, it's long distance," Vera called out.

Eva dried her hands on her apron and pushed back the thick pompadour of auburn hair that framed her face. She took a deep breath. "All right, Rob, but I won't ever stop wanting to go back."

He watched her slowly make her way out the door and through the hall. When she sat down in the straight chair by the phone, all he could see was her foot. Didn't he love her more that life itself? Didn't he want her to be happy? But he couldn't just pick up and move back to the country. Not when he had a job and people were getting laid off left and right. "What?" he heard her say. "You don't mean . . . ?" He got up and walked to the doorway in his stocking feet. Eva's face was snow white and her hand shaking as she held the mouthpiece. "Do they think he was coming here?" She looked up at Rob. "All right. You do that," she said. "Let us know."

"What is it, Eva?"

"That was Geneva. Davy's escaped from the insane asylum."

"Good Lord."

"They think he might be headed this way."

"What on earth for?"

"He told the psychiatrist there that he had a cousin in Wilmington. Someone who'd help him jump on a freighter, get out of the country if he ever got the chance."

"Calvin?"

"I guess so."

CAL WAS DISTURBED BY THE CALL FROM GENEVA, but he didn't want his parents to know just how upset he was. "He'd never come here, Papa. Davy knows it would only get us both in trouble with the law."

"Can't never tell what somebody in his state of mind might do. Don't sell Davy McBryde short, son. Not with the law after him."

"Don't be too hard on him," Cal begged. "Davy probably just said that to throw them off. Why would he come here? Right where they'd be looking for him?"

"Poor child, incarcerated all this time in an asylum because of that woman he married," Eva wailed. "I'm glad he escaped. I hope he goes to California or somewhere they'll never find him."

"Eva, shug, don't be talking like that. We all think this is a terrible thing, but the law's the law." He got up from his chair and went to stand beside her. "We can't help him. You know that, don't you, shug?" Eva would not look at him. "Shug?"

DESPITE HIS DENIALS, CAL KNEW THAT HE'D HEAR from his cousin sooner or later. Davy was a wild card. Not crazy, but you never knew what he might do if a whim struck him. The last time Cal had been to see Davy in Raleigh, they'd talked about something that he knew was eating at him. Davy had been even more despondent than usual. Cal had made the trip to Raleigh at least once a month to see his cousin at Dix Hill, saying nothing to his family in Wilmington. When the weather was nice, they'd eat lunch outside, sitting on a board bench that ran along the side of the brick building where Davy was confined. The narrow, treeless yard, closed in by a high chain-link fence with three rows of barbed wire strung across the top, sat directly beside a gravel road.

That day, his cousin gazed out across the meadow that lay to the west of the insane asylum, a soft breeze rippling through the ankle-deep sweet clover. "I don't belong here, Cal," he'd said. "Look at those nuts over there clawing the fence. They're the crazy ones."

"Must be the main attraction in Raleigh on Sunday afternoons," Cal said, watching the cars on the dusty road pass by in slow procession.

"Coming to look at the crazy people," he said, leering back at them. He picked up his sandwich and took a bite, staring blankly at the grassy meadow in the distance. "You don't know how much it means to me for you to come, Cal. Daddy won't let anybody else come. He's ashamed of me." He'd put his head on his knees atop his crossed arms. When he raised up, he'd had tears in his eyes. "Sometimes I think I *am* crazy, Cal, else how in the hell did I end up in the loony bin?"

"Like you said, you don't belong here."

"Patty Sue knows that. She's knows I didn't kill the old lady on purpose. Patty Sue framed me, Cal. Sure as hell, she set the whole thing up." He slammed his fist against a fencepost, rattling the barbed wire along the top. "If she'd ever been to see me, ever come just one time and asked me to forgive her, I would have—even after all this."

"Have you made any headway with that psychiatrist what's-his-name?"

"Dr. Cameron. I've been writing things down in a journal. He said it would help me figure out what I did wrong."

"Has it?"

"Hell, no, Cal! It just makes me see what a damn fool I was. One of these days, I'm going to get out of here and knock the hell out of her."

"Better not be talking like that."

"I don't mean I'd hurt her or anything. I just want to know why in the hell she did this to me. I was good to her. I loved her. I wanted to take care of her for the rest of her life. I could've done it, Cal. Daddy told me that piece of bottomland near the river had my name on it. I could've cleared it . . . we had that tractor. I could've built us a little house."

That's when Cal had told Davy about Ben Jessup. He hadn't planned to, but after Davy had brought up the subject of the bottomland near the river . . . . Cal would give anything to be able to take it back. It had probably eaten Davy up inside.

———

MILLIE OFTEN WALKED HOME TO LUNCH from the hat shop, to check on her mother if nothing else. Sometimes she'd bring the wash in off the clothesline, or start something for supper. When Eva was sleeping, Millie wouldn't wake her, she'd just go about a few chores before returning to work. Most likely Eva would say something that evening, like *My little fairy princess snuck in here today and did my work for me.* That brought Millie a lot of pleasure.

She heard the phone ringing before she reached the porch. Taking the steps two at a time, she pushed the front door open and grabbed the phone, thinking it just might be for her. "Hello?" There was no response. "Hello, is anyone on the line?" She was about to hang up when the caller whispered her name.

"Millie?"

"Who's this?"

"Hey cousin." His voice was louder now, almost natural-sounding. "This is your ol' cuzzin Davy. You remember me, don't you, honey?"

She spun around, half expecting her mother to be there asking for the phone. "Hey, Davy. How . . . how . . . are you?"

"Fine, honey, just fine. Say, I'm in town for a few days and I need to talk to ol' cuzzin Cal. Is he around?" He sounded like he thought she was still just a little girl.

"Cal's at work, Davy. Where are you?"

"Listen, honey. It don't matter where I am, but I need to talk to your brother."

"You could call him at the Coast Line."

"Could you give me that number, honey? I don't have a phone book handy."

Millie knew the number by heart and recited it to him. "Are you going to call him?"

"I am, honey, I sure am. But listen, I don't want you to tell Uncle Rob or Aunt Eva that I called. Might worry them. I just need to talk to Cal. He can tell them hello for me."

She tried to think of something to say, something grown-up, but nothing clever would come out. "We've been missing you, cousin Davy. Come to see us sometime."

"Well, darlin', I'll do that," he said, sounding like he meant it. When Cal didn't come home for dinner that night, she began to wonder whether she should break her word and tell her mama.

———

DAVY MCBRYDE HAD BEEN ON THE RUN for four days when he dialed the number Millie gave him. Cal had just sat down at his desk after lunch when the phone rang. "Can you meet me at Ward's Corner?"

"*Davy?* Is that you?" Cal whispered.

"Who in the hell do you think it is?"

"Where are you? I've been worried sick."

"Look, Cal. I need some help. I can't go back there."

"Davy, they're looking for you. They know you're going to come here." Cal glanced around to make sure no one was within earshot.

"Just bring me some clothes, Cal. That's all I ask."

"You know I can't do that. Just give yourself up. Dr. Cameron is trying to help you."

"Yeah, help keep me there. Cal, please. I'm desperate. I won't ever ask you to help me again."

Cal hesitated. Maybe if he saw Davy, he could talk him into giving up. "I'll have to wait until after work. Where're you calling me from, anyway?"

Davy sighed. "Mr. Ward's house. He's over at the store."

"You broke into the house?"

"The door wasn't locked. I just needed to use the telephone. Please come, Cal."

"I'll try, but you've got a lot of explaining to do."

Davy breathed a sigh of relief. "Wait till evening. The store'll be closed by then. Just pull off somewhere along the road. I'll be watching for you."

Xo

Sheriff's car, 1928

41

The Escape

May 1, 1928

DEAR DR. CAMERON,
I'm in Fayetteville now, down by the wharves waiting for something to go my way. I'll bet you were real disappointed when you found out I was gone, especially since you said we were making great headway. But I'm going to say this right up front. Every time I talked to you, I came away knowing that we hadn't made any headway at all. You still think I'm crazy as a loon. I know, you said you wanted to save me from the electric chair, but you should've listened when I told you that I wasn't going to pretend I was crazy just so I could stay alive. Not at Dix Hill with a bunch of loonies. No sir, Davy McBryde has other plans.

Here's how it goes—if Patty Sue had been to see me just one time, if she'd ever said she was the least bit sorry that she'd caused me to kill somebody, I might of tried to wait it out. Uncle Dick said after I had treatment, I might be eligible for a retrial. But no, not once in the past four years did she lead me to believe that she wanted <u>anything</u> but to keep me as far away from home as possible.

I know why now. Remember that boy, Ben Jessup, that came to see me? I didn't tell you what he said. My cousin Cal had told me he'd heard some talk—told me who said it—but I wanted to hear it straight from Ben. So I wrote to him and asked him to come to see me, and he did. First thing he told me was that he'd met Patty Sue at the Ryans' place in Colly. He said he was hanging around the shop waiting for their boy Will to work on this old Fordson tractor his daddy give him. Patty Sue was there helping Tate Ryan with some painting in his new house. Now, ain't that something—she can't come see her husband rotting in the loony bin, but she can help somebody with their house painting? Anyhow, Ben says she stepped out in the yard and called him over by hisself under the trees, and she asked him if he knew anything about digging an artesian well and setting up a ram pump.

Well, she asked the right person, because Ben had done a many of them for folks along the river who wanted some sweet water—some in the same business as Patty Sue. He said he agreed to meet her the next day, and she took him directly to my piece of land on the river. Ben knew it was mine because we used to play pirates over there when we were young'uns. I called it my kingdom.

She'd told everyone else she was starting a trucking business, you know, taking produce to markets all around. She has three old trucks and Ryan's son, who's a mechanic, keeps them in good running condition for her. Ben said everybody up our way knew it was a lie. The truth is she's running a liquor still, probably the biggest one in Bladen County, and he ought to know. He said he tapped into that artesian well for her on my land, way down near the river in a tangle of vines and underbrush, a place where the law would never find it.

Ben said he bet she was making up to a hundred barrels of mash at a time. He'd seen the corn hauled in by the truckload. A bunch of colored boys worked for her, shucking and shelling corn. Some came and went at all hours of the day and night, but most stayed there in camp houses, stirring the mash and keeping the fires going. Not knowing we were friends, she asked Ben if he wanted to come work for her, and he said he would, figuring he was going to tell me about it at some point.

Every week, at the end of a run, when the mason jars were filled and put back in boxes, she'd come down to the still after dark and count the boxes before these old rattle-trap-looking trucks would start coming in. Ben said they might look like rattle-traps, but he swore every one had an engine that could outrun the law if need be. Two or three o'clock in the morning, the loaded trucks, with their lights off, would pull out going in different directions about an hour apart. There wasn't any traffic that time of night, and those white sandy roads light up like a shiny ribbon in the moonlight.

The next week, Ben said, those same three trucks would show up again. Patty Sue was clever. She'd bring one truck in on the Elwell Ferry, another by the main road, and another by the old logging road that ran along the earthen dam by the river. By this time there'd be another batch of whiskey. When Patty Sue showed up after dark, they'd hand her sacks full of cash and she'd take the money to an old one-room house she called her office where she'd count it. Then, in the dark of night, the drivers would leave again with trucks full of corn liquor. Ben said he'd seen it done a hundred times. He couldn't imagine how much money must've been in those sacks. After Ben told me, I knew I had to go down there. Here I was rotting away in an insane asylum, and Patty Sue not only enjoying the fact that I was out of her sight, she was making money hand over fist on my land.

I walked right out of the gate Sunday afternoon. I was out in the yard writing in this here notebook, when I saw the super let a car in. Somebody's dog jumped out and ran off when the driver stopped to ask directions. Two or three other people got out of the car and started chasing the dog. So while the super was distracted, I walked through the open gate and ducked into some bushes. No one saw me except maybe one of the loonies.

After dark, I crawled out of the bushes beside the wire fence and commenced to make my way towards the train tracks. I'd heard the whistles blow day and night. When I found the tracks, I followed them until I found just what I was looking for, not far from the Boylan Avenue viaduct. I hoisted myself up on a big flatcar loaded with heavy machinery. All I wanted to do was to get to the Cape Fear River.

I slept most of the night face down under a tarp covering part of the machinery. When I pulled my jacket together, I remembered the bum I'd snitched it from under the railroad trestle. Poor dumb son of a bitch was passed out, drunk as a skunk. Probably woke up and thought the rats had drug his coat off during the night. I slept light, aware of stopping and starting. Not scared or anything, just afraid I'd conk out and miss getting off in Fayetteville.

———

I'm sure the super notified the sheriff when I didn't show up for supper. The law will be after me by now, but I don't care. If I can just get downriver, I could hide for the rest of my life in Bladen County if I wanted to. I know every creek, every swamp, every ditch, and I can run faster than a deer. But I don't want to be an outlaw hiding out in the woods. No sir, when I finish my business with Patty Sue, I intend to hop onto a freighter on the river-front in Wilmington, join the Foreign Legion way on the other side of the world. I've read about somebody doing that.

Don't be thinking you'll tell them where to find me, because I'll be so far gone when I send this to you, they won't never find me. They'll probably look for me at my daddy's place first. The joke'll be on them. No sir, I don't have any cause to go see my daddy. When I was in jail in Elizabethtown, old Angus told me then how much of an embarrassment I was to him. Said I'd ruined any chances for my brothers to be in politics, or anything else respectable in the county. Told me right there in the courtroom that he never wanted to see my sorry face again.

———

Well enough of that, I'm getting off track. Coming into Fayetteville on the flatcar, I looked out through a gap in the tarp, saw it was daylight and chil-dren were waving at the engineer from shanties along the railroad track. I was sure I was on one of those Pullman trains like the Florida Special. Probably bringing a lot of hotshots like Vanderbilts and Astors down from New York, bringing their fancy cars, going down to Florida to sit around in their pink houses under palm trees drinking illegal whiskey. I thought of Patty Sue and wondered what her whiskey tasted like. No telling how many she might've poisoned.

Closed up under the big machine on the flatcar, I could smell my own sweat and the rank jacket that I'd stolen from the hobo under the bridge. I knew the wharves weren't far away. But, being hungry as a wild boar hog, with no money—not a nickel to buy a cracker or a candy bar—was going to be a problem.

When the train jerked to a halt, I rolled over on my shoulder, stared through a gap in the tarpaulin and saw a switchman checking the coupling. He looked up, straight at the gap in the tarp. "You better get the hell off this flatcar, you bum," he said to me. "The yardman's coming and he don't like hoboes, no way, no how."

I stared back, afraid it was a trick. The switchman slapped his hand down on the bed of the car like he was running off a dog. "Git! I said, git!"

I rolled out from under the gearbox on the other side of the flatcar and dropped feet first onto the greasy cinders, losing my balance and toppling into the weeds that smelled like pee and dead rats. When I picked myself up, I ran as hard as I could towards a warehouse near the street. Against the side of the building I caught my breath, wondering which way to go next. As if it was calling an answer to me, a boat horn sounded down by the river. I took off towards the water, knowing I'd be home by dark.

———

Well, Dr. Cameron, this journal is really turning into an adventure story, one I think might be good to send off to one of them magazines. You probably wouldn't want to do it, so I'm asking you now to give it to my cousin Cal if anything happens. Of course, I don't intend to get caught, and in that case I might just give it to him myself. Cal's just about the best friend I could ever have. Daddy used to call us river rats, because as boys, we built more rafts than anybody he knew. We took them across the river lots of times. One time I went off on my own. It was right after Mama died. Went all the way to Wilmington on a raft me and Cal had built while she was so sick and Aunt Eva was with her day and night.

When Aunt Eva called me in and told me Mama had died—she'd already sent Cal home and said I needed to be with Daddy—I think I did go a little bit crazy then. I wanted to run away, and run I did, straight to the river. The raft was on the slope, one end stuck in the mud, but I pushed and pulled until it started to float free. Then I hopped on and shoved off with a long pole, and before I knew it, the river was taking me to Wilmington. I felt so free leaving everything behind me. I wish I felt that way now.

But I sold the logs at the creosote factory, and I turned right around that same day and paid seventy-five cents for a ride home on the Thelma. Even though Mama had just died, when I got back I got a good tanning out behind the woodshed.

Daddy didn't put up with much, especially from his oldest boy who he wanted to be exactly like him. How can you be just like your daddy? Oh, there were things about Daddy that I was like. I was hotheaded, that's for sure. Just ask Mrs. Jackson about that. And, I loved liquor just as good as Daddy. I think a swig of liquor makes a man feel good about most anything. But Mama said liquor made Daddy mean. I sure as hell had seen that side of him.

———

I want to tell you about Oak Ridge too. When it came time for Cal to go off to school at Oak Ridge Institute, Daddy decided it might do me good to go. Hugh, Cal's oldest brother, had gone to the Ridge and he said he didn't think I'd like it. But Daddy had made up his mind. I thought I knew why. He'd started courting again, and I was sure he just wanted to get rid of me. By this time, I was doing a little courting of my own, smoking cigarets and trying out a swig or two of whiskey now and then for the hell of it. Cal wanted me to go with him, but the last thing in the world I wanted to do was to go off to school.

Oak Ridge was way out in the country, up in Guilford County near Greensboro. The little book they sent to Daddy said something like, "Away from most of the temptations to vice and extravagance incident to town and city life." Sounds a lot like jail, doesn't it? But Daddy sent in the $112 for first semester and signed me up for Spelling, English, American History, Science, Arithmetic, and Latin. I near about died, but I still had to go.

Me and Cal left on September the third, right in the middle of the best bird hunting season, knowing it'd be Christmas before we'd get home again. I was sad, real sad, but I didn't let on to Cal. We rode the train, carrying duffel bags full of sheets, towels, and blankets, even window curtains. Aunt Eva had helped me get my mess together, ordering a bunch of stuff like new underwear and socks from the Sears and Roebuck catalogue. She said when

Hugh went he lost about half his long handles and heavy socks to the laundry.

"You be sure and count your things when they come back," she told me. Aunt Eva was real careful about things like that. She'd give you anything she had, but she didn't want anybody being careless.

We got off the train in Kernersville, a tiny little town about the size of Atkinson. The lady that met us at the train told us how much we were going to love being at the Ridge. She was pretty as a picture. The daughter of Mr. Whitaker, the headmaster, I believe. Said her name was Agnes. "Stop by to see me sometimes, Agnes," I said, but she never did.

She dropped us off at our dormitory. The dorm was real nice, steam-heated, and it had electric lights and great big living rooms on every floor with overstuffed leather chairs and fireplaces. Next to the living room was a "study hall" where one of the teachers, Mr. Capps, said we'd spend most of our time. I looked over at Cal and laughed.

Our room was even smaller than the one I've been in at Dix Hill. Two single beds and one great big window. That's all. But I was beginning to feel sort of grown-up, being away from home, having our own place, until he started telling us all the rules. We'd have to go get fitted for our uniforms, which we had to wear all the time. Then he took us into the study hall and told us we had to sign a solemn pledge, saying we wouldn't drink whiskey, play cards, or carry a pistol. I looked at Cal and he looked at me, both of us thinking about how we'd planned on doing some target practice with the old Colt .45 that Daddy had given me last Christmas.

Man, I loved that gun and figured it would be a good thing to have on hand away at school like this. Cal knew better, but Cal never tried to tame me much. He wasn't prissy or anything like that, but he tended to walk the straight and narrow line himself. I think he got a kick out of seeing what a daredevil I was.

The Ridge was perfect for Cal. When it came to studying and following the rules, he just did what he was told. Not me. I hated it. Wearing those old scratchy uniforms was one of the worst parts. And there were all these things you couldn't do. If you got caught breaking the rules, you got demerits. You started out the year with one hundred credits, but every time you missed a drill or chapel, or got caught smoking a cigaret, they slapped demerits on you.

Everybody also had to belong to a literary society, and I got so I liked that. You see, we had these classical books to read and one of the professors told us that we were not much different from the young men in ancient Greece. He said, like them, we'd left our parents for a journey into the unknown to seek a higher form of life—some such shit as that, but it made sense in a way, and it makes even more now that I'm on this journey.

In the afternoon, after classes, we had to play some kind of athletics. There wasn't any getting around being on one team or the other. And we had rifle drills every day, playing around and twirling make-believe guns. Silly looking as all get-out if you asked me.

We only had about an hour after drill before the chow bell rang. That's when I'd take off for the woods and find me some quiet spot, just to clear my head and smell the trees and earth. Wasn't anything like the bottomlands along the Cape Fear River, but it was quiet there in the woods, and the smells were nearly the same. God, I loved to be by myself out there in the woods.

First semester, the worst thing that happened to me was that Mr. Whitaker found the Colt in my footlocker. Our rooms were inspected every morning at seven-fifteen by some brown-noser goon. If you had one single thing out of place, he slapped a demerit on you. Somebody must have told him about the gun because I only took it out on Saturdays when me and Cal would go off campus and shoot at squirrels. Getting off campus wasn't too hard to do. They thought it was kind of nice when you wanted to go down to the five and dime in Kernersville and buy your mama a birthday present or something like that. Me and Cal could think of all kinds of things to tell them at the desk. Then, we'd just hightail it out the back door and take off across the woods with the Colt tucked in my belt.

Mr. Whitaker wrote to Angus and told him that I was on probation for having a pistol at school. I had over fifty demerits already, and he told Daddy I was in danger of expulsion. Didn't take long to make that happen. After Christmas holidays, I brought a jar back, smuggled it in, and hid it under a loose floorboard underneath my bed. The same little son of a bitch that told on me about the pistol, must've told about the jar. Man, I was on the train for home the next day and that was the last I ever saw of the Ridge.

Well, back to my story. You'll have to forgive my messy writing, Dr. Cameron, because right now I'm curled up under a stack of lumber near the city wharf, waiting for some barge or something to go my way. This pencil is about down to a nub, so I might have to go looking for another one somewhere.

The river's not as wide here as it used to be. Believe me, I know. I've been to this dock so many times I can't even count. When the Thelma *used to dock here, a trip upriver to Fayetteville was my favorite thing to do. Daddy or Grandpa were always taking me along. The* Thelma *was about the only riverboat left on the Cape Fear. Nowadays it's mostly gasoline tugs.*

Traffic is starting to pick up on the river, and I'm about to have to wrap this here notebook back up and see if I can hitch a ride on a tug or something. It's getting light, but there's no way I can afford to hide out till dark. I'll have to take a ride on a barge in broad daylight whether I like it or not.

Bandeaux Creek

I'm holed up here now in Uncle Rob's old store, resting and catching up on writing. I about wore myself out getting here, but I was lucky. I kept my eye on this tug pulling two barges, idling near the dock. When I saw two men on the tug cast giant hemp ropes over to the first barge, I knew I'd found me a ride. I was dreading the swim, but I'd have to make the tail end of the second barge if I wanted to travel with them. I waded in, but I got stuck knee-deep in mud and had to fall backwards into the water to free myself. I lost one shoe, so I kicked off the other one and swam as hard as I could for the barge.

The water was damn cold, but I caught hold of a trailing rope and pulled myself up onto a ledge. The acid smell of fertilizer burned my eyes and nose, so I climbed higher to get away from the drift. When I looked back towards the dock, I saw a little boy pointing at me. A man with him yelled, "Man overboard!" We were way out in the middle of the river then, and the tug driver couldn't hear the voices above the chug of his engine. I waved back and pointed like crazy across the river, trying to distract the boy and the man. It worked. They searched the shore, looking for whatever I was point-

ing at, while I slipped around to the side of the barge, praying the noon sun would soon find me and take the chill off my bones.

By the time we reached Elizabethtown, my clothes were nearly dry. As we passed underneath the new McGirt bridge, I realized that I'd never been across it. It was the first bridge to span the Cape Fear River above Wilmington. I'd seen it when they first started construction, but it took them a long time to build it. Every time we went upriver, Grandpa would say something like, "I hope I live to see that big bridge completed."

Grandpa didn't live to see the bridge finished, and I might not have either if I hadn't gotten out of Dix Hill. I just laid there on that ledge and stared up at the concrete pillars and all that steel, thinking how someday I'd come back and drive across it in a flashy automobile.

Bandeaux Landing is only seventeen miles from Elizabethtown. I recognized it by a piece of the wreckage from the steamboat Magnolia *that stood up in the mud fifty feet from the dock. When we came close to the wreckage, I let go the barge, allowing the river to carry me until I reached a stretch of shore on the lower side. Picking a fallen tree to pull myself out of the water, I thought again about Grandpa, who'd taught me how to fish here in the cool shadows along the river's edge.*

I was still four or five miles from Cotton Cove. In a boat, I could have been there in fifteen minutes, but I had to make my way across the slew along the river. A spring freshet had filled it with water, and I had to take higher ground to get over to Uncle Rob's old place, where I was headed first.

There's a clearing here where Uncle Rob and Aunt Eva's house had stood. Old man Wetmore, a surveyor from Lumberton, bought the house and tore it down, saying he was going to build a more modern house with the same solid cypress boards. He never did. But he left the old store and it looked like nobody'd been about it for a long time. The door was padlocked, but I knew where the key was. When I was a boy, Daddy used to send me down there to deliver molasses. He'd told me if Uncle Rob wasn't in the store, I'd find the key on a nail under the steps—and there it still was.

I unlocked the padlock and pushed the wooden door open and smelled the rancid smoked hams that hung from the rafters. Corn meal was scattered all over the floor where mice had gotten into it. I reached around in the bone-dry drink box until I found a hot Coca-Cola with a rusted top. I snapped the top off, gulped it down. It was terrible, but I was dying of thirst. There was a box of Baby Ruths, but when I tore open the wrapper on one, what had been a candy bar was nothing but weevil dust now.

I spent a few minutes looking around the old store, picturing Uncle Rob behind the counter and Aunt Eva sorting the mail into the little cubbies in the back. Many a time, I'd helped Cal unload barrels and boxes down on the river and haul them up to the store in a wagon. Uncle Rob would have had a truck now, if he was still here. I guess old man Wetmore couldn't make a go of it either.

A jar of pickled pigs' feet looked to be in pretty good condition until I dipped my hand in and swished it around. God, I almost puked. Everything in that store was rotten or eaten up already, but I picked up two pencils and some chewing tobacco and stuffed them in my pocket.

———

Before I could give any more thought to finding something to eat, I heard what I thought was a car or maybe a truck coming down the road. Well, it wasn't neither. It was the law, a man on a motorcycle calling hisself a highway patrolman.

When I heard that, I thought I was a goner. But old July Tatum, a colored fellow that's been around since slavery, came up and told him he'd been working around there most of the day and hadn't seen anything. Holding my breath, I kept my ear to the crack by the door jamb and listened as the cop questioned old July. As soon as I heard that motorcycle crank up and head out on the road, I threw open the shutter in the back of the storeroom, heaved myself over the sill, and took off like Blalock's bull on the deer run that me and Cal had used back and forth between our houses. Closing my eyes, I felt like the same fleet-footed boy I was chasing through the thick woods years ago. A boy who'd never killed anyone. A boy who'd become a river pilot or a sea captain. The smells of spring were all around me—yellow jasmine, fresh pine, sweet bay, magnolia. Tears streamed down my face, and I ran and ran until I came to a field where Daddy had already planted his corn.

I reckon Daddy knew I was loose. Might even be worrying that I'd come back home and make some trouble. But I skirted the lower field, didn't look across the pasture, didn't want to see the house where I was raised, the stump where I kept my whiskey. All I wanted was to do was find Patty Sue.

Once I hit the woods again, I was amazed at how soft the forest floor was. All that white sand beneath dry brown leaves. God, it felt good to be walking on sand again. Nothing but red clay up in Raleigh. I guess even the sand burrs feel good when you're homesick.

The family cemetery where Mama was buried was not far from the fields. After checking to see that no one was around, I opened the rusty gate and went straight to her grave. I stood there a long time staring at the stone marker before I fell down on my knees and said a prayer. I told Mama I knew she was up in heaven. I said, "If you can hear me, I want you to know how sorry I am that I've disappointed you. If only the Lord had let us keep you a little longer. I could have grown up like you wanted me to. Maybe been a lawyer like Uncle Dick, or a ship's captain." I told her I didn't mean to kill Mrs. Jackson. "It was a terrible accident," I said. "But I've got to go see Patty Sue, find out why she didn't stick by me." I heard something in the brush and looked up to see the white tail of a doe disappear into a thicket of sweet bay. Back in ancient Greece, a boy might've thought it was his mama.

42

On the Run

CAL WAS LOOKING STRAIGHT INTO THE SETTING SUN as he drove up Highway 421 towards the crossroads where the Wards had a Pure Oil station. He'd stopped there almost every time he went to Cotton Cove, to give old Mr. Ward a little gas business and to reach down into the Coca-Cola box and pull out an ice-cold drink. He'd never be able to go there again if Mr. Ward found out he'd helped Davy. The knot in the pit of his stomach tightened. Maybe he should've told Harry, asked him what to do.

Highway 421 was the main road to all the beaches around Wilmington. Thankful that traffic wasn't as heavy on Thursday evening as it was on Fridays, Cal pulled onto an old farm road within sight of the station. By then only a slice of moon and a few stars lit the evening sky. Two cars passed before a figure wearing a plaid flannel shirt and ill-fitting overalls emerged from the woods. Cal opened the door and watched his cousin race across an overgrown field. "Is that you?" Cal called out in a loud whisper.

"Get back in the car and douse that light!" Davy said, hunching over and slipping into the seat beside Cal, rank with sweat and his dark hair full of brambles. "Damn, I thought every car that passed was going to turn in here," he said, drawing a deep breath.

"What'd you do, join a Wild West show?" Cal said, looking at Davy's feet.

Davy looked down, a smile easing across his lips. "I kinda like these cowboy boots. You'd never guess where I got 'em." Taking another deep breath, he looked at Cal. "I wasn't sure you were coming."

"Shouldn't have," Cal said, sternly. "You're going to get me in a whole lot of trouble."

"I had nobody else, Cal. You gotta know how much this means to me."

No, I guess not, Cal thought, taking a closer look at Davy now that his eyes were accustomed to the dark. Davy had the same sharp features as Hugh and Harry, *the McBryde look*, he called it. Deep brown wavy hair, a broad forehead, and intense brown eyes. Davy's nose was a little different. Instead of the slightly flared nostrils like Cal's had, his was tapered and not too large—more like his mother's. Disheveled as he was tonight, he was still handsome, boyish. "Where've you been?" Cal probed. "Miss Geneva called Mama last Monday. Said you'd escaped. They thought you might be headed this way."

"Cotton Cove."

"Cotton Cove? Did you see Patty Sue?"

Davy nodded his head. "Sure as hell did. Found out what she was up to. Watched her for a couple of days. Saw the liquor still. You won't believe how big that operation is, Cal."

"How'd you get there without anybody seeing you? They say every lawman between here and Raleigh is on the lookout for you."

Davy reached into his shirt pocket and pulled out a crumpled cigarette. "They don't call me river rat for nothing."

Cal returned his smirk. "You came all the way on the river?"

"Wanna hear how I did it?" he asked, tapping his smoke on the dashboard.

Cal backed the car deeper into the trees, where the two men got out and leaned against a gnarled oak, their feet stretched out in the stubby grass. "Did you talk to her?" Cal asked first thing.

"Wait a minute, will you. Let me start at the beginning. I might never have another chance to tell you."

Cal relaxed, waiting for Davy to begin. Something told him his cousin might be right.

———

FOR THE NEXT TWO HOURS, DAVY DRONED ON, sometimes devoid of emotion, reciting events as if they'd happened to someone else. "Everybody in Cotton Cove believes you're innocent as the day is long," Cal said. "Haven't met anyone yet who thinks highly of Patty Sue."

"When I slipped out that day, I knew the law would be after me, but I figured if I could just get to the river, they'd never find me."

"What'd you do, build a raft?"

"I could've. Remember the one we built together?"

"I remember," Cal said. "You stole it from me and floated it downriver to Wilmington and sold it for pulp."

"Aw, you don't still feel hard about that, do you, cousin?"

"Sure do."

Davy hung his head and his voice dropped almost to a whisper. "You remember why I did it, don't you?"

"It was the day your mama died. I was just kidding. I don't feel hard."

"Thanks, Cal. I didn't get but five dollars for it. Daddy took the rest of it out of my hide behind the woodshed when I got home."

"Uncle Angus was always hard on you."

"That's because I was his oldest boy. He never could figure out why I didn't want to do everything just like he said. Like to have killed me when I got kicked out of Oak Ridge."

"You ought to have known better than to brag about having that pistol in your footlocker," Cal said.

Laughing, Davy sauntered off into the woods to relieve himself. "Worked, didn't it?" he called back.

Davy sat down again under the tree, and Cal looked at his watch. It was after ten o'clock. "You better tell me the rest of it."

"Let's see, where was I?"

"You got off the barge at Bandeaux Creek?"

"Yeah, I wanted to go by Uncle Rob's old store before I headed on down to Cotton Cove."

"Why's that?" Cal asked.

"Well, it was the only place I thought I might find something to eat. And I guess I just wanted to see my old stomping grounds again. You probably think that sounds crazy, but I had this weird dream one night about being in Uncle Rob's store. You were there and we were sorting the mail for Aunt Eva."

"We did that one time. Remember?"

"Yep, it was when Mama was dying and Aunt Eva was with her day and night. Uncle Rob said, 'How 'bout you boys sorting the mail?' We thought he was giving us an important job, but he was probably just trying to keep us out of trouble."

Cal closed his eyes and pictured the small store and the cage window in the back where his mother once ran the post office. She was seldom there without the smallest child in the family at her breast and another at her feet. Papa ran the store, but Mama kept his books and ran the postal operation, rain, sleet, or snow.

"You asleep?" Davy asked.

"No, just thinking back. What does it look like now?"

"Run down on the outside, but when I opened the door, the old place looked just like Uncle Rob left it. I was starving to death, but nothing was any good."

"Old man Wetmore gave it up after a year or so."

"I know, Patty Sue was the last postmistress. No telling what she had going on with Wetmore," Davy said, agitated.

"After he tore our house down, I never went back home," Cal said.

"Would've made you sick. Did me—those big old oak trees standing like sentries over nothing but the smokehouse and the barn. Right pitiful-looking."

"Go on with your story," Cal said. "How'd you get in?"

"You won't believe it. As soon as I saw the padlock, I remembered that Uncle Rob always kept the key . . . "

Before he could finish his sentence, Cal said, " . . . on a nail under the steps."

Davy smiled. "Mr. Wetmore didn't change much."

"It's a wonder somebody hadn't cleaned it out."

"No, sir, not with July Tatum keeping an eye on the place all these years."

"You reckon he still does?" Cal asked.

"He saved my life that day, Cal. I was rummaging around trying to find a tin of Vienna sausages—anything to eat—when I heard this loud engine coming down the road. Damned if it wasn't a motorcycle. Pulled in right next to the store. I heard the kickstand go down, and I knew somebody was looking around. That's when I almost shit in my pants."

"What'd you do?" Cal asked.

"Nothing, I didn't have to. Next thing I heard was old July say, 'Howdy, Capt'n. I seen you come up on dat motorsickle,'" Davy said, imitating the old colored man. "'Ain't no gas. Mr. Rob's sto' been closed a long time,' he says. I heard him spit out a stream of tobacco juice. 'But I still keeps an eye on it.'" Davy began to laugh, taken with his own mimickry.

He stood up to act out the other part, deepening his voice. "'I'm Sergeant Lambert, Highway Patrol,' the man says. 'You live around here?'"

"'Yassuh,' July says, 'just over dere in de woods. What's de Highway Patrol?'"

Davy slapped his hand on his knee and laughed. "The guy didn't even answer him, pulled out a picture of yours truly, I guess. He says, 'Have you seen this man?' You know July's about half blind, but he says 'Hmmm,' real serious-like," Davy said, scratching his scruffy beard.

'Would you know Davy McBryde if you saw him?'

'Yassuh, I reckons I would. I seed him almost every day of his life 'fore he left here.'

"The patrolman asked him if he'd seen me around lately. 'Nawsuh. His daddy said he won't never comin' back dis way. I could count on that.' That liked to killed me, Cal—just the way July said it let me know Daddy was sure I'd never get out of Dix Hill."

Davy continued, putting on a little sideshow now, alternating the parts of the patrolman and then July. "'Thass his Uncle Rob's old store, but it b'longs to Mr. Wetmore now. He give it up after a year or so. Gone back up dere to Lumerton.'

"'Got any food in it?'" Davy said, switching his tone and stance to imitate the soldierly patrolman.

Cal was bent double laughing. Davy had a real knack for imitating dialects. "'Won't much when they closed it. 'Magine everything's eat up by rats now.'"

"Well," said Davy, serious now, "I heard steps and I thought I was a goner for sure. But the patrolman started his engine and released the kickstand. 'Ask around,' he said. 'See if anybody's seen or heard from him. I'll be back.' The patrolman roared off down the road, but I knew July was still there, and probably watching the door. I froze against the wall, hoping I wouldn't have to knock him in the head to get out of there."

Cal looked him in the eye. "You wouldn't have done that, would you?"

"I might've done anything at the time. I'd come this far and I wasn't intending on getting stopped before I found Patty Sue."

Cal brushed off his pants and leaned against his car. What wouldn't Davy stop at to be free again? Should he be afraid? His cousin had always been the bigger, stronger of the two—a little rough around the edges—a little meaner when it came to standing up for himself. But he'd never laid a finger on Cal. Never.

"I think July knew I was there. I saw his hand on the knob. But he just pulled the door to, saying, 'If mastuh Davy 'cide to stop down dis way to see his Uncle Rob's old sto' again, I sho ain't gone tell the law about it.'"

"When I felt sure July had gone, I hiked myself up over the windowsill in the back and took off like a scalded dog for Cotton Cove."

"That path saw a lot of wear in the old days, didn't it?"

"Hell, yeah—Mama never knew for sure which ones of us were her kids or Aunt Eva's."

Cal laughed. "I think *my* mama was the best cook."

"I went to see Mama's grave." Davy hesitated, unable to continue for a moment, then stood up and wept, his head against the oak tree.

Cal didn't know what to say or do. Tears were streaming down his cheeks, too, and he wondered where all this would end. Maybe he should help Davy get away. There were ships leaving Wilmington every day.

Davy waited for Cal to pull himself together. "I found the still right where I thought it'd be," Davy said. "Me and Patty Sue had joked about where we might make some whiskey one of these days." He smiled and shook his head. "That girl was brazen as hell."

"It's a shame she couldn't put her smarts on something legal."

"Once I found the still, I headed back towards the Jackson place. I watched it for a while to make sure nobody was home, and I almost passed out from hunger as well as the thought of going into that room where the old woman had died. When Patty Sue didn't show up, I got my nerve up and slipped in. The stove and sink were all cluttered up with pots and dishes, but I found a sweet potato in the cold oven and some corn bread and a pot of field peas on the stove. No telling how long they'd been there, but I was so perished, nothing mattered.

"Later that evening, when I was hid out in the barn, I heard a truck drive up. Sure enough, it was Patty Sue. I about died when she got out of the truck looking like a man in a pair of paint-spattered overalls and a long-sleeved shirt. Her hair was tied up in a red bandana and she didn't look a-tall like I remembered." Davy paused. "But the real thing that shocked me was, she had this little dark-haired boy with her."

Cal's heart skipped a beat. He'd almost forgotten. "Reckon he might have been . . . "

"Look, goddammit, Cal, don't go complicating my life any more than it is already." He marched off towards the woods, then back again. "Yeah, I thought about that. For two solid days. What if the child *is* mine? You think that changes anything? You think that makes it any easier for me to decide what to do?"

"Go on," Cal said, knowing he'd struck a nerve. "Didn't mean to interrupt you."

"I slept up in the barn loft—not much chance of anyone coming across me. Next day, she left again with the young'un. After they'd gone, I went inside and helped myself to some collards and boiled Irish potatoes she'd left on the stove overnight. I drank some buttermilk from a jar in the icebox and ate a handful of store-bought cookies."

"Weren't you afraid she'd know you'd been there?"

"Patty Sue was about as sorry a housekeeper as her mama. I knew she wouldn't miss a thing. But you know what, she'd sure as hell cleaned out anything that'd ever belonged to me. Not that I'd ever taken much there, but she didn't even have a picture or anything to remind her that I'd even been a part of her life."

"You should have known better than to expect that," Cal said.

"I guess you're right, but every step of the way, I was hoping that I'd find something, see some sign that I'd meant something to her."

"Did you find any money?"

"I looked for it. Figured she'd have to hide it somewhere. But all I found in her closet to do me any good were these clothes that belonged to her pa. Ain't these cowboy boots swell?" Davy said, pointing downward. "There was a razor and a strap in the bathroom. I took them along with a bar of sweet soap and had a bath down in the creek. After I got cleaned up, I put the razor and strap back, looked around for any sign that I'd been there and took off across the woods for the still.

"Activity had picked up by then. Colored boys going in and out of the still, filling jars and loading boxes up on the porch. I climbed up in a thick bay magnolia and got where I could see everything that was going on. After dark, up drives Patty Sue in that beat-up old truck that she bought with her daddy's money when we first got married. She was all fixed up, wearing a tight-fitting red dress, her hair piled up on top of her head.

"I watched her light a cigarette, and she looked out into the woods in my direction. There was no way she could see me, but I didn't twitch a muscle. One of the men told her he was ready when she was. She took off her shoes and walked over to the porch of a storage house, and asked the one she called Oree if he had added water to some of 'em. I couldn't believe it. Nothing makes a man madder than to find out the whiskey he's paid good money for's been watered down."

"Wish we had some now, watered down or not," Cal said.

"You and me both, cousin. Anyway, she went up there on the porch and counted the boxes and told the guy he was one short." Davy grinned. "Now where in the hell do you think that box went?"

"You didn't?" Cal said.

"I did, but I had to leave it in the woods. Didn't get to finish but one jar. They've found it by now," Davy said, losing a little of his enthusiasm for his story. "Well, the first truck arrived just after dark, an old Dodge, so fine-tuned that it almost purred. Driver pulls up near the shed where she's sipping her whiskey and says hello. She smiles at him and says, 'Al, honey. Nice trip?' in this voice thick as sorghum molasses. He slides out of the driver's seat and saunters over to her, doesn't bother to close the truck door. Up on the porch, he drops this paper sack on the table and reaches for her hands, pulls her up, talking dirty to her and rubbing his business up against her. She asks him if he'd got a Chandler wheel for her—I don't know what in the hell that was about. Then, she takes him by the hand and pulls him inside the camp house, calling him 'Tiger' and stuff like that. I liked to died." Davy was on his feet again, ranting, shaking his finger in Cal's direction. "You see what she is, don't you, Cal? A whore, just like her mama said she was. A goddamned whore. And I think about that poor kid with her . . . " He walked away, leaned against a large live oak, and took a deep breath. "Look, Cal. I need you to drive me down to Charleston."

"You know I can't do that. You've got to go back to Raleigh."

"Go back? I can't do that. I might've . . . I'll be dammed if I'm going to spend the rest of my life in that loony bin."

"Maybe Harry can get you a new trial."

Davy turned his head. "No, they'll put me there for good. I'd rather go to the chair."

"Aw, Davy, not really."

"Yes, I would. I sure as hell would. So the way I figured it was that if I was going to go to the electric chair anyway, I'd make a run for it."

"Why didn't you just stay there a while longer, Davy? Maybe they'd have let you out."

"Look, Cal. I need to get going. You going to drive me to Charleston or not?"

"I can't. Everybody would know. I have to be at work tomorrow." His jaw set, Cal opened the car door. "I've brought some clothes like you asked. They're in the boot. That's all I can do."

Davy opened the other door and stood with his foot on the running board, looking across the top of the car at Calvin. They'd never had a fuss about anything before this. "I shouldn't have gotten you involved, Cal. I didn't know what else to do."

"Too late to say you're sorry, cousin," Cal said, opening the boot. "They'll find out I helped you one way or the other."

43

My Brother's Keeper

THE SHERIFF ALMOST MISSED THE MAN LYING in the
ditch when he shone his light down the farm road across from
Ward's Corner. Someone had reported seeing a car parked there
around dusk that night. Mr. Ward hadn't thought much about
somebody breaking into his station. As far as he could see, nothing
had been taken; he didn't keep money there anyhow. But the next
morning, when word came about Patty Sue McBryde, the sheriff
went back to look around some more. That's when he saw the
man's legs sticking up out of the ditch, his first thought being that
the escapee had committed another murder.

———

DR. JONATHAN MCNAMARA THOUGHT SO, TOO. But what
had possibly saved Calvin McBryde was that his head lay partially
submerged in the cold, brackish ditch water. The temperature of
the water had helped minimize the swelling around Cal's brain. Jon
was with him when he came to. "You've been out cold, Cal.
Someone knocked you in the head." The doctor waited a few sec-
onds before asking, "You know who it was, don't you?"

"Did he take my car, too?"

"Yes. Did you give him any money?"

"No."

"That's good. The sheriff is waiting to talk to you. Your brother Harry's on his way. You might need some legal representation."

Harry barged into the room. "You fool. You goddamned *fool.*

Don't you know that aiding and abetting a criminal can get you five to ten years?"

"Quit your yelling. I'm not deaf."

"Why didn't you call me? Why'd you go meet him? Davy's been declared an outlaw. You should have known that."

"Davy's my cousin. He's yours, too. He called me to come help him. I didn't know what he'd done. He said he wasn't going to spend the rest of his life in an insane asylum. Said he went to talk to Patty Sue. I think he just wanted to see if she'd change her tune, help him get a new trial."

"Bullshit! You should have known better than that. He was lucky they didn't send him to the chair the first time."

Cal's face reddened. "He didn't mean to kill that old lady. Patty Sue was the only one who knew that—" He put his hand up to his head and fell back across the examining table.

Jon rushed over and felt for Cal's pulse. "Better leave him be, Harry."

Cal tried to sit up again. "Do they know where Davy went?"

"As far away as possible, I imagine."

Cal was as white as a ghost. Jonathan pressed him back down on the table. "Look here, this can wait. What's done is done. Cal, lie down and stay quiet." Jon warned. "Harry, you better let him catch his breath."

"I'm going out to the car. I need a drink," Harry said.

Cal rolled over on the narrow examination table and put his arm across his eyes. His head was splitting, but he knew Davy had done that to protect him. Davy was like that.

"The deputy out there wants to see you," Harry said, coming back into the room. "You need to talk to him."

"Wait a minute," Cal said. "Did they tell you about that big still she was operating?"

"Biggest one ever found in Bladen County."

"She was a hoodlum, Harry. A pure hoodlum. Came down here and took a perfectly good country boy and got him accused of murder, then made money running liquor while he was locked up in Dix Hill."

"I'll go out and talk to the deputy," Jon said. "Give you guys a little time to discuss this calmly. Take it easy," he said to Harry.

Harry walked over to the window, lifted a slat in the blinds, and looked out. "Damn parking lot is full of police." He turned to Cal. "How long have you known about the still?"

"Ben Jessup put Davy onto it. I told Davy he ought to ask him, but I swear to you, Harry, I never thought he would try to escape."

The doctor stuck his head in the door. "The Bladen County sheriff's here. Says he needs to talk to you now, Cal."

Before Harry could step aside, the sheriff pushed past him.

"You Calvin McBryde?"

"Yessir."

Harry took a step forward. "And I'm his brother and his attorney."

"I know your daddy, boys. How's old Rob doing?"

"Fine, sir."

"Say what you've got to say, Sheriff," Harry said. "He's been through a lot. I'd like to get him on home."

"I hear you've been fraternizing with a known criminal."

"Wait a minute. My brother didn't know what Davy McBryde had done."

"He knew he'd escaped from Dix Hill, didn't he? How'd you know that, son?"

"Davy's my cousin," Cal answered with what energy he could muster. "He called me. Asked me to meet him. I thought he was going back. Said he'd been to Cotton Cove—talked to his wife."

"He talked to her all right—with an axe." Cal and Harry both cringed. "Did you give him the use of your car?"

Cal became angry. "No, sir, I guess he knocked me in the head and took it."

"Well, we've got your car back now, holding it for the investigation. My boys caught up with your cousin at the Pee Dee River in South Carolina. He won't be knocking nobody else in the head now. He took two bullets in the back."

———

—MARION, S.C., MAY 13. Davy McBryde, whom officers from Bladen County, N.C., said they had been seeking since Saturday for the slaying of his wife at her home in Cotton Cove, N.C., was shot and killed today on a highway in this county. McBryde was being pursued by a group of officers and others from Bladen County and was overtaken near here. Officers said he attempted to draw two pistols that were found upon the body. He was then shot, it was said, by one of the officers.

According to the North Carolina men, the suspect, who had been away from the home for about three years, turned up yesterday and killed his wife, the former Patty Sue Jackson, with an axe. —*Wilmington Morning Star, May 14, 1928*

———

44

Repercussions

UPON HEARING THE NEWS THAT CAL WAS HURT and Davy shot down by the Bladen County sheriff, Eva went into a swoon that lasted three days. Rob sat by her day and night, while Millie cooked their meals and kept the house running. She'd never seen her mother like this. The doctor had been by and prescribed a sedative, but Rob said that only time would bring her around.

Cal, though recuperating at home, was unable to work. Rebecca had been to see him, but he'd told her he wasn't hurt—just needed to be by himself. Harry had given him a few days to absorb the terrible events before he stopped by Cal's small house and found him sitting on the front porch. "You feeling any better, Cal?"

"Could be worse," Cal said, thinking of Davy.

"This is not going to help my chances in the election very much."

Harry's normally mild-mannered brother glared at him. "Is that all you can think about? We're talking about Davy, *our* double first cousin here—my best friend—and you're worried about your career?"

"Settle down, Cal. I just meant these things have repercussions in the whole family."

"All I can think about is Davy shot in the back like a dog."

"He was trying to get away, Cal. Think about it. He'd murdered his wife. There'd be no getting out of it this time."

"Nobody saw him do it. Could've been one of those bootleggers that worked for her. She carried around a lot of money."

"Why'd he run then?"

"He was already facing going back to Dix Hill—that or the electric chair."

"You defend him after what he did to you. You might've died, Cal."

"I wish I could have helped him more—kept him from . . . "

"You'd better not let the law know that. Like I said, *aiding and abetting* can get you three to five years in the state penitentiary."

"He didn't deserve to die," Cal said.

Harry, chastised, sat down in a rocking chair and lit a cigarette. Cal was right, all Harry had been able to think about was that the McBryde name was going to be mud. "What else did he say?"

"He asked me if we'd talked to his daddy."

"What'd you say to him?"

"I told him no."

"You didn't tell him?"

"I couldn't. No matter how hard he felt towards his daddy, I didn't want to tell him that Uncle Angus was dying. Just would've made things worse."

"You didn't tell him about the little boy either?"

Cal straightened up. "No—I tried to one time, but he didn't want to hear it. And I'm not convinced that child is his either. Knowing Patty Sue, could've been anybody's."

"We'll never know now, will we?"

————

THE SHERIFF BROUGHT DAVY MCBRYDE'S BODY back to Elizabethtown after the Marion County coroner had examined it. Geneva McBryde asked if Cal and Harry would go and identify him. The coroner had looked at the brothers as if they'd been responsible for the whole affair. The death certificate read *Death by gunshot wound to the back.* "Davy would have hated to know they put that on there," Cal said.

"What else could they say? That's how he died."

"But the way they wrote *to the back.* Makes him sound like a coward."

"He was armed and dangerous in their minds, Cal. They found two pistols on him."

"See there? He wasn't shooting at them, though he could've. Doesn't that tell you he wasn't dangerous?"

———

WHEN THEY BROUGHT CAL'S CAR BACK, the deputy handed him a packet of papers wrapped in an old piece of oilskin, secured with rubber bands. "We found this on your cousin. Sheriff called up the insane asylum, talked to that psychiatrist, Dr. Cameron. He said give it to you. Thought your family might like to have it. Won't do that boy no good anymore."

45
An Oilskin Packet

CAL WAITED UNTIL EVERYBODY HAD GONE before he opened the packet, feeling like Davy was standing right beside him. *You wanted me to have this, didn't you, old buddy?* Choking back the tears, he sat down in a rocking chair on his front porch and opened up a Blue Horse notebook. On the lined paper of the frontispiece were penciled the words *To Cal, the best friend a man ever had.* On the opposite page in large script, Davy had written a title: *Bandeaux Creek.* In smaller script below that, *Between the Rivers.*

A capable artist when he put his mind to it, Davy had drawn little pictures all around the perimeter of the page. There was a carefully executed head of a squirrel, the front end of a Model T Ford. On other pages were a stump with a jar sticking out of it, the moon over water, a spiral of copper tubing, pistols and rifles, a boy on a river raft, and all sorts of nature drawings. Cal cried as he skimmed the pages written by his lonely, troubled cousin. How could he have saved him, this boy so like him, but who'd taken one step in the wrong direction and ended up dead?

Cal turned to the back of the notebook. Coming to the last few pages, which were blank, he read the note. *Please give this to Cal when you're finished with it.*

Wednesday, somewhere in South Carolina

Dear Dr. Cameron,

I'm glad you asked me to do this—tell my story. I want to tell it more than anything now because I know that for years to come, people will be talking about me—saying how bad I was. Maybe I am bad, but I don't think so. I believe I am a warrior, on a journey into the unknown. But maybe I got lost along the way. The law is after me for sure now. I saw it in the paper at a store back at the state line. I pulled off under the Pee Dee River bridge not far from Marion to write this so I can mail it to you before I get to Charleston. I don't want somebody else finishing this story for me.

———

The shed where Patty Sue parked her truck was only ten or twelve feet from the barn. Up in the hayloft, I watched her every move. After she cut the engine, she picked up a brown valise off the seat beside her, opened the door, and set it on the ground. Stepping out of the truck, she stretched and looked towards the house. When she leaned into the truck to get her purse, I took a flying leap and landed on the ground right in front of her. The headlights were still on and I knew I'd scared the shit out of her, but she managed sort of a smile and said, "I figured you were around here somewhere."

I bowed, real gentlemanly like, and held the truck door open for her. "You really didn't expect me to stay in that loony bin much longer, did you?"

She put her left hand on the truck door, edging her right hand towards her purse on the seat, and said, "Look here, I don't know what you're doing, but I don't want any more trouble with you."

I grabbed her arm, told her she'd started this. I yanked her away from the truck, afraid she had a gun. "No wonder your mama didn't love you, you conniving bitch," I said to her. She picked up the satchel and was walking away from me when I grabbed her again and jerked her around. "Poor old woman. A mama doesn't turn against her daughter without some cause. Old lady didn't deserve to die so you could get rich."

She asked me what I was talking about. I said, "She didn't have a cent to her name. Had to take in laundry. Your daddy died and left everything to his darling daughter. Bet he thought you were up there in New York working as a waitress or something." She laughed and said, "Oh, really?"

"Your mama knew, though, didn't she?" I said. "She knew you were a whore, running around with gangsters. You set me up to kill her." Then she said something that really made me mad. "Even a dumb country hick like you could figure that out, huh?" She pulled away from me and said, "It worked, didn't it? But you had to go all to pieces. Then that old mailman had to stick his nose in it."

"Why?" I asked her. "You had everything already. She could have gone to live with some of her folks." She sat down on a chopping block by the woodpile, shaking her head. "She was running Daddy's still, stupid. Daddy left her the still."

That got to me. How could I have been such a damn fool? I sat down beside her. "He left me the money and the house," she said, "but what I really wanted was the still." I said I didn't believe her, but she just laughed and said, "You think I wanted to start from scratch?"

I said, "Wait a minute. Your mama was running a still? Why didn't you tell me?"

Patty Sue said I didn't understand. "Mama hated the ground I walked on," she said. Her daddy knew it, and he always wanted Patty Sue to have a place to come back to. He didn't care what happened to her mama. She said that's why old lady Jackson was so mad when she showed up.

You'd of thought we were man and wife, just sitting there talking. I could smell her stale perfume, cigarettes—another man's come. She stood up. "They're going to catch you if you hang around here. I'll give you some money. You can get away. Start over."

For a minute, just a minute, I thought she might have had her reasons for acting like she did. I stood up, too. She looked at me sort of tender like and said, "You were a good boy, Davy. Too good for me." That's when I asked her why she got me involeed. She said, "You got yourself involved, stupid. You and that big dick of yours. All you wanted to do was fuck. Then you wanted to get married so you could legally fuck me. I saw how things might work out for us."

That made me mad as hell. I asked her if that was why she let me rot in jail. She edged towards me, saying, "Look, grow up. It can still work. The new still is much better. I've got connections. You could go up north. Be on the receiving end up there. We could make a lot of money . . . "

That did it. I didn't want to hear any more of her conniving. "No. Stop it!" I said. "I don't want anything to do with you. Ever!"

"Why'd you come here then?" she practically snarled at me. Tears were streaming down my face and I could hardly see her even though the sun was coming up. I said I wanted to know why she let them put me away. Why she never came to see me or wrote me a letter. "You were my wife," I said.

She started back towards the truck, saying, "Well, now you know. Look, I need to get my purse." I just sat there sobbing like a baby, my head in my hands. But when I looked up she was pointing a pistol at me. "You thought you could come back here and take my money, didn't you?" she said.

That sobered the hell out of me right quick. I looked towards the house. "There's somebody up. I saw a face at the window," I said. She glanced towards the house, ever so quickly, but I was like an ancient warrior. In one motion, I picked up the axe and flung it towards her. The brown valise was at my feet.

I never looked back.

He turned to the last page. *Cal, make sure they bury me next to Mama.*

PATTY SUE'S TRUCK HAD BEEN SITTING in the Ryans' garage for more than a week, fixed and ready to go. Tate and Will were both worried; it wasn't like her to leave her trucks that long. By Wednesday, Tate came to the uneasy decision that he needed to go see about her.

Maggie came out of the house onto the porch just as Tate was turning out of the driveway. Walking over to the garage, she found

Will in his newly dug grease pit, a truck sitting above it. "Do you know where your pa's going, Bud?" Will pretended not to hear. "Will Ryan, are you down there in that hole?"

"Yes, m-m-ma'am. I c-c-can't come up right now."

Maggie bent down as far as she could and peered into Will's greasy face. "I said, where was your pa going?"

"H-h-he said he had to r-r-run up to C-c-cotton Cove for something."

"Well, he didn't tell me. What business did he need to tend to?"

"I don't know. I g-g-guess he was in a hurry, M-M-Mama."

———

TATE HAD NEVER BEEN TO THE JACKSONS' HOUSE; in fact, he'd never even heard of the family until the day they said Davy McBryde murdered Gladys Jackson in cold blood. There hadn't been a lot of talk about it back then, not even from Maggie or Aunt Mag, and Tate didn't read the newspaper except on occasion. But today he had a sense that something was wrong, bad wrong.

He found the place easily enough. Pulling into the driveway, he half expected to see little Colin playing on the porch and Patty Sue hanging out clothes or some such as that. Instead, the Bladen County sheriff stepped out from the brush that lined the lane, aiming a shotgun directly at him. "Halt! Get out of the car!" he said, scaring Tate half out of his wits.

Tate cut the engine and stepped out of the car. "Howdy, Sheriff. It's just me—Tate Ryan—coming to check on Miss Patty Sue. Nothing wrong, I hope."

The sheriff eyed him curiously. "Howdy, Tate. What kind of business you got with Patty Sue McBryde?"

"Nothing much. My son Will does some work for her. We haven't seen her in a week or so. Figured something might be wrong with the little boy." Tate hated to lie, but his instincts told him this might be the time for it. "I had some business this way. Thought I'd stop by and check on 'em."

"Nothing's wrong with the little fellow. Leroy's got him over yonder looking at those old bloodhounds in the back of his truck."

"Where's his mama?"

The sheriff lowered his gun and hitched up his pants. He was a strikingly handsome fellow despite a large crooked nose, one Tate had heard was the result of a brawl of some sort. There'd even been talk about him having a girl living with him. "Look here, Tate, we've got a homicide here. You better get on down the road. I wouldn't want you implicated in any way."

"You mean somebody's been killed? Who?"

"Can't say right now. Investigation is underway. We've got an escaped criminal on the loose. Might've been him, might not have."

"Is it . . . Miss Patty Sue?"

"I told you, we got an investigation going on. She's been running a still over by the river. My men are there now trying to round up some of her boys—don't know how many were working it, but we'll find out."

"Patty Sue?"

"Hell, Tate, do I have to draw you a damn picture? She's been murdered by her own husband."

Tate reached out for the car door to steady himself. Blood rushed to his head, thundering in his ears. "Patty's Sue's been killed?"

"You heard me right. Dead as a doornail right out there by the woodpile. Little colored girl who stays overnight with the boy found her this morning. Girl was all to pieces."

Tate looked out across the yard, where the deputy had Colin up on his shoulders walking towards the house. "Colin—her little boy? Did he . . . "

"Oh, he never saw his mama, doesn't know a thing about it."

"Can I talk to the boy?"

"Sure, go ahead. Say, you don't know who's his next of kin, do you? The girl said all the Jacksons were dead or gone as far as she knew. Somebody's got to take him. We can't carry him with us back to the jailhouse."

"I'll take him," Tate said, knowing he'd soon regret giving it no more thought than purchasing a sack of corn.

———

MAGGIE WAS STUNNED, NOT ONLY BY THE FACT that Patty Sue McBryde was dead, but by Tate's gall in asking her if she thought they might take the boy to raise.

"My God in heaven, you must be crazy as a loon, Tate Ryan. I told you how I feel about young'uns, especially this one."

"He's just a baby, Maggie Lorena. I can't see how it would hurt to show him a little kindness."

"He must have some people somewhere. What about the McBrydes? He's part of their clan."

"Sheriff said they don't think so. He plans to find out when he catches Davy McBryde. If he don't claim Colin as his own son, then somebody's got to take him."

"Well, don't be getting your hopes up because it's not going to be the Ryans."

———

IF IT HADN'T BEEN FOR THE BOY, TATE WAS SURE he would have fallen to pieces. Patty Sue had restored a part of him. It wasn't just that she caused him a stir in his privates, it was more than that. She renewed his spirit, the part of him that made him happy to be a man. Farming, tending his livestock, providing for his family, that's what a man liked to do, but a woman to stir his privates, even if she didn't belong to him, was a blessing in itself.

William had been devastated by the news, too. They had both set such store by her. Tate tried to comfort his son, but it was hard to find the right words. There was no way he could tell Will all of what he'd heard. That Patty Sue Jackson McBryde was mixed up with some gangsters up north, keeping the wrong kind of company with the wrong kind of men. "She won't what she seemed, son. I'm as disappointed as you are."

"But how could he kill her, Papa? She was nice as she could be."

Tate hesitated. "The law'll get him, son."

"Len said she operated a big still up there on the river. Only reason she liked us was because I kept her trucks running. You believe it, Pa?"

"No, I don't. And lots of people operate stills in this county. I know some of 'em. I reckon I like a taste of liquor now and then, like most red-blooded American men."

"But Patty Sue was a woman."

"I reckon that don't make much difference, if you know about making shine and selling it."

"That ain't no reason to kill her."

"There was more to it, son. Let's leave it like that."

———

OUT OF RESPECT FOR THE FAMILIES, THERE WAS LITTLE TALK about what had happened. Angus was on his deathbed and Geneva refused to let anyone bring any news, good or bad, to him. "Let him have his peace," she said. "Davy has his now."

In the somber home on Red Cross Street, Millie comforted her mother the best she could. "He made his bed hard, didn't he?"

"Yes he did, from the time he was born," Eva said. "Kathleen used to say he was the most fun of any of her children, but he sure marched to the beat of a different drum. She'd laugh when he got into a little trouble. 'At least he's not a sissy,' she'd say."

"Do you think he's in heaven, Mama?"

Eva brightened up. "Well, of course he is. The Lord loves the sinner as well as the saint." Her smile faded. "Davy was not a bad person. The Lord forgives us when our mind errs. It's what we do from our hearts that counts."

Rob came into the room unexpectedly. He stood in the doorway, absent of words. "What is it, Rob?"

"Jessie Rae called. There's not going to be a funeral service."

Eva sat up in bed, wanting to comfort him. "There has to be some words said over him."

"No, Geneva decided. No funeral service."

Eva was stunned. "There has to be. It isn't right." She took a moment to gather her wits. "No matter what Davy did, he was still part of this family, one of our own."

"Not our place to decide, Eva."

"But they'll bury him in the family plot next to Kathleen, won't they? That's what would matter most to Kathleen." Eva lowered her voice to a hush. "And to me."

Jeanne McAllister's LaSalle

46

A Feast of Pirates

BY SUMMER EMILY MCALLISTER'S LIFE HAD BECOME full to the brim. After Mandy's wedding, she'd plunged right back into volunteer work, chairing six art shows for the North Carolina Sorosis to raise funds for the Greenfield Park beautification. In August she would finish up one more major responsibility— the second annual Feast of Pirates festival—before her marriage to Dr. Jonathan McNamara, assistant medical director of the James Walker Memorial Hospital.

Emily relished the time she had to herself on the weekends at the beach house. She'd installed a telephone and set up a small office. There'd been none of the usual beach parties with all of the girls this season. Rebecca was married and nursing full time and Belle was working in Washington, so Agatha had chosen to stay in Philadelphia.

Millie suspected that her boss didn't mind a bit, since Dr. Jon was taking up most of her spare time. The beach house allowed the couple privacy without a lot of gossip. And Millie wasn't one to talk. She was happy to be enlisted to help Emily with preparations for the Feast of Pirates. Millie spent most of her afternoons typing announcements to newspapers all over the state, touting the celebration built around the privateers that had infested the area in the eighteenth century. Letters were also sent to shop owners on Front Street urging them to create special window displays. Everyone was encouraged to attend in costume. Beau Monde set the standard with a display of buccaneer-style hats for discriminating ladies.

"I'd never have gotten this done without your help, Millie," said Emily. "Not with the wedding coming up so soon."

"You're the organizer. I've just been an extra pair of hands."

"You're more than that, dear. You're a member of my family."

"Thank you, Miss Emily. You've been mighty good to me."

"Have we heard back from the manager at the Cape Fear Hotel? That bandstand is a must."

"Mr. Quarles called today. He just asked that we take it down promptly the next day. The ACL Surgeons are having their annual meeting at the hotel starting Monday and he wants to have the streetfront clear before they arrive."

Emily looked concerned. "Did you assure him that we would?"

"I said I didn't think it would be a problem, but I'm not sure the carpenters will like working on Sunday."

"Remind me to ask Jon if we should offer to pay them extra. Hasn't he been wonderful? There's nothing like a man to carry the voice of authority."

Millie smiled. "I don't remember anyone refusing you."

"Oh, dear. I hope I haven't been too pushy. You know how men are."

"Miss Emily, don't worry. You could charm a snake."

They both laughed. "Now I have to charm someone down at Tide Water Power to let us have a special beachcar for the children. Jimmy MacMillan is going to fix up an old fishing boat like a pirate's ship. He'll take them over to Money Island for a treasure hunt."

"I hope he's planning to bury lots of money. Hugh used to take us over there to dig for Captain Kidd's treasure. We had so much fun."

"All taken care of, thanks to our generous doctor."

"I don't mean to be a smarty-pants, Miss Emily, but I think you're really in love. Your eyes sparkle like all get-out when you talk about Dr. McNamara."

Emily blushed. "Does it show that much? I don't mean to act like a silly schoolgirl."

"You're not silly. Mama says that real love doesn't come along very often."

"How about you, Millie? I haven't heard you say much about Rusty lately."

"I guess I didn't tell you we broke up. He went to both sessions of summer school. I don't hear much from him. I think we're just friends."

"Oh. I thought maybe it was more than that."

"I don't mind. He liked me more than I liked him. I'm waiting for someone to really knock my socks off."

"You're still young, but I have an idea. You need a new look, a grown-up look. Now that you're a working girl, you should buy yourself a couple of dresses, have your hair cut professionally— maybe wear a little more makeup."

"Mama and Papa might not . . . approve."

Emily pulled her into an embrace. "Millie, dear, you're growing up. Your parents know that. Someday, *you* might want to go to college."

"I'll need to finish high school first. Right now, Mama and Papa are having a hard time. I can't even think about it."

"I know, dear. But let's play beauty parlor, just for fun. Come with me, and bring my purse, please." Emily led the way to a small room at the back of the store, a modern addition that had been installed by the building's most recent owner. The construction was shoddy, but Emily had insisted that she needed a toilet to stay in business. "Alva Stanley is coming by with a couple of the Carolina Aces to go over the music for the parade. I want to see what a little primping will do for you."

The first thing out of Emily's purse was a pair of tweezers. "This will make all the difference," she said, as Millie winced with each jerk of her brow. "I'll have you looking like a movie star."

"Ow, I didn't know it hurt this much."

"That's the worst of it," Emily said, unzipping a small bag. "Now for a little rouge and some bright lipstick." Rummaging in her makeup kit, she found the exact shade she was searching for. "Wow, you look great." They both gazed into the hand mirror, but Emily was not quite ready to abandon the makeover. "Would you let me trim your hair?"

"I guess so. I washed it this morning."

"Get me your sharpest scissors."

Emily lifted Millie's dark hair and began to cut, combing and snipping, slowly shaping Millie's shoulder-length tresses into a bob similar to hers. "With all of these beautiful waves, I don't think I'll ruin you."

"Would it help if I dunk my head under the faucet?"

"We only have cold water in the shop."

"I don't mind. Mama used to wash our hair under the pump when we lived in the country."

"I'll get a towel."

When they had finished, Millie couldn't believe her new look. "I wonder what Skipper Purrington would think of me now."

"Forget about Skipper. He's a dear boy, but he was way too old for you." She laughed. "There are more fish in the sea and it's very close by. Here comes Alva Stanley now."

———

MILLIE SCOOTED INTO THE WORKROOM to finish up one of the pirate hats she was making for the members of the band. Emily called out to her. "Millie, dear, would you bring my notebook? Mr. Stanley is here."

Presenting the notebook to Emily, Millie nodded to Alva Stanley. "Hi," he said, his eyes roving quickly over the young assistant. "The rest of the boys will be in after they park the car. Nice shop you got here, Mrs. McAllister."

"Thank you, Al. This is Millie McBryde. Maybe you two have met."

"No, ma'am, I think I'd remember."

Millie smiled. "I'd better get back to work unless you need me, Miss Emily."

"No, stay. You can help select the music. You know more what the young folks would like than I do."

A bell over the door jangled, and the remaining band members sauntered in one after the other. "Where've you guys been?" Al said. "Look who's going to help us."

"Come on in, boys," Emily said. "Millie's going to go over the music with you. I've got to get to the hotel and meet some folks."

"But, Miss Emily, you . . . I . . . " Millie was terrified that Emily would leave her with the eight young men. She'd seen the Aces up on the bandstand at Lumina in flashy jackets and such, but here in person in the shop was another thing. "My sisters and I are real fond of your music," she said, for lack of something more clever. Belle would have clicked her gum, smiled real cute, and done that little wiggle thing she did around boys.

"Fond?" Alva asked with a twisted smile.

Millie blushed. She'd already made a fool of herself. "Crazy about," she stammered.

"Well, that's more like it. *Crazy about* is a lot better than *fond of.*"

"Prunes" Powell, one of the saxophone players, leaned over the counter. "Quit fooling around, Ace. You're making Millie blush. You're going to be there on Saturday aren't you, doll? I'm nominating you president of our fan club."

"Yes, sir. I mean, yes, I'll be there. My friend Cora Lee and I are dressing up like wenches."

"Witches?"

"No, *wenches,*" she said, laughing. "Pirates always have wenches."

Silas Sheets, the piano player, pushed Prunes aside. "Is the other—ah . . . wench as pretty as you?"

"Get outta here, Silas. You're embarrassing Millie," Al said, pushing him aside. "How about costumes, honey? Does Mrs. McAllister want us to wear costumes?"

"You'd better! If not, you'll likely be the only ones there in regular clothes. We've made each of you a pirate hat."

"Well, shiver me timbers, this is going to be a hell of a lot of fun."

———

ON THE DAY OF THE FESTIVAL, no one was more surprised than Emily when Jonathan McNamara showed up outside the hat shop on horseback in full British naval dress.

"My ship has been on the high seas for months chasing these pirate dogs," he said in an officious tone. "I'll have their heads and their treasures before the day is over."

"Jonathan, you look wonderful. You didn't tell me. I thought you'd be at the hospital."

"Wild horses couldn't have kept me away, darling." He did a double-take of her outfit. "Wow," he said, raising his eyebrows. Emily blushed crimson. She had fashioned harem pants out of red striped silk curtains that she'd recently replaced at the Market Street House. Her blouse was white silk with large bell sleeves, and on her head a red silk handkerchief completely disguised her brown hair.

"Just a minute. I have to tell Jeanne and Millie." Emily rushed back into the shop. "Come out and see. Jon's on a horse!"

Jeanne was first in the doorway. "Well, the handsome doctor can ride, too," she said in a sultry voice. "I'm not surprised. You seem to be good at everything."

Jon tipped his commodore's hat. "Madam, you're not in costume?"

"I'm working on it."

Over Jeanne's shoulder, Millie shrieked, "Dr. McNamara! You look wonderful. I wish I had a camera."

"Let me through, girls," Emily said. "I'm tired of worrying about last-minute details—I'm ready to have a little fun too. Lock up when you're done, and I'll see you at the parade."

"Ah, my first pirate wench of the day," Jonathan said, reaching down to scoop Emily up. He set her down in front of him on the horse. "It's off you go to my *boudoir*."

"Jon, behave! People are watching."

"Oh, Mother. Relax—you could use a little ravishing," Jeanne said. "If you can't, I can."

Millie and Jeanne watched them ride off down Front Street. "Aren't they cute together?" Millie said. "I think they're really in love."

Jeanne shrugged. "If you say so."

47

Belly Dancing

CORA LEE WAS WAITING FOR MILLIE AT BELLAMY'S Drug Store. She'd ridden the trolley car into town from her home out in Forest Hills. The two girls had met at a church beach outing early in the summer, discovering a common bond since both had dropped out of school to help their families. Millie and Cora Lee had spent their last two Saturday afternoons working on matching costumes. Cora Lee had made white batiste off-the-shoulder blouses trimmed in embroidered eyelet. Millie had sewn the full skirts, making them out of a bolt of blue-and-white-striped fabric Eva had given them. Calling themselves "the twin wenches," they'd tied their hair up in red handkerchiefs and painted their faces lavishly with makeup.

The streets were crowded with pirates and ladies in costumes of every description. Most carried out the theme, but among the men several Confederate uniforms were sighted, along with peg-legged swashbucklers. Earlier in the day, the parade had been made up of horse-drawn floats and elaborately decorated cars of every make and model loaded with pirates. Afterwards, the costumed revelers swarmed the streets, dancing and frolicking like circus clowns. One man, an honest-to-goodness circus performer, walked a tightrope strung from the second-floor window of one building to another across Front Street.

Up on the bandstand, the Aces played their hearts out while Millie and Cora Lee swayed on the front row. Suddenly, Millie remembered that she had promised to bring her friends to the back of the bandstand at the Aces' break. "I told Jeanne we'd stop by the shop and pick her up," she reminded Cora Lee. "I can't wait to see her costume."

When Millie knocked on the closed shop door, Jeanne opened the curtain just enough to peek out. "Let's go," Millie said. Jeanne slipped out the door and turned the key in the lock while Millie and Cora Lee surveyed her back side. "Oh my goodness, Jeanne, a Turkish harem girl! Miss Emily will kill you!"

Jeanne smiled devilishly. "Mother will love it! Don't you know that mothers live vicariously through their daughters?"

"The *guys* will love it," Cora Lee said, focusing on the skimpy top that was nothing more than a brassiere covered with sequins.

"Where did you get those harem pants?" Millie gasped. "They look like something right out of *Arabian Nights.*"

"I got the idea from Mother. These were some old curtains in the attic at the house in Jacksonville until a few days ago. I found the shoes in that little shop down on Water Street that sells Turkish tobacco."

"Well, we don't have to worry about anyone looking at us—not with Jeanne along," Cora Lee said.

The three girls set off down the street arm in arm. "You'll be my bodyguards, won't you?" Jeanne said, laughing. "I may need protection."

"You will for sure when the Carolina Aces see you," Millie said.

———

THE REVELRY WENT ON ALL DAY and well into the night. The Carolina Aces had played until six then made their way into the street to join the party crowd. Jeanne McAllister was having the time of her life, belly dancing in the street, laughing and carrying on with every man she came across. In office windows above the street onlookers called down to people on the street below, beckoning them upstairs for refreshments. The term *speakeasy* was never used, but no doubt there was alcohol being served. Only illegal liquor could make people let their hair down like that.

———

IT WAS AFTER NINE O'CLOCK WHEN CORA LEE and Millie caught up with Jeanne and two sailors from the Coast Guard cutter *Modoc*. Millie was glad Emily McAllister had left with Jon by then. She'd sent word for Jeanne that she'd leave the porch light on for her. They found Jeanne sitting on the curb, where one of the men was playing a ukulele. "Come on, sugar, do that hip wiggle thing again."

"Not on your life. I've had too much to drink."

The other sailor laughed. "You just need a little hair of the dog that bit you." He pulled her up. "Come on, I know a place down by the water called Sailors' Delight. They take care of Coast Guardsmen like we were their own children."

"Forget it, sailor. I said I've had enough."

Millie took hold of her arm. "Let's go, Jeanne. Come back to the house with us. Cora Lee's spending the night."

"Hey, let me get another buddy and we'll all go," the sailor leered.

"You might have to go a round with one of my brothers. They're both big as prizefighters."

"Ha! Aren't you the sassy one. If y'all don't want to have fun no more, we'll find us some girls that do. Come on, Bugsy."

Bugsy hesitated, looking at the blonde girl who was a little green around the gills. "Wait a minute. Jeanne, honey, we'll take you home. I'm from Wilmington. I know where your mother lives on Market Street."

Jeanne put her arms around him and kissed him on the cheek. "That's real sweet of you, Bugsy, but I think I'll go with the girls.

Call me sometime."

The sailors ambled off down the street without looking back. Millie and Cora Lee each took one of Jeanne's arms. "You're going to stay with me tonight," Millie said. "Your mama would never forgive me if I didn't take care of you."

Jeanne stopped and looked her straight in the eye. "No, honey, I'm soberer than most judges. Just get me to the shop and I'll spend the night on the cot there. Need to be in Jacksonville tomorrow. I'll call Mother so she won't worry."

"Are you sure you'll be all right?"

"All I need is a little sleep. I promised my brother Darcy I'd go to church with him. He's met someone and wants me to check her out. Glad he cares what I think," she mumbled.

"I really wish you'd come home with us."

"No. Just need a little sleep. Then drive on back."

———

JEANNE ONLY SLEPT A FEW HOURS ON THE NARROW COT in the back room of the hat shop. She woke to the sound of gnawing and saw a huge wharf rat in the sink, chewing on the remnants of her mother's lunch. Without changing her clothes, she left through the back door and climbed into her car. "Home, James," she said to the LaSalle. "We're out of here."

———

THE STARS WERE BRIGHT OVER THE BIG SAVANNAH when Jeanne awoke from a strange dream. Her mother was calling her, but her own voice was stuck in her throat. Then the pain hit and she screamed in the night like a wild animal. Her face was covered in wet, sticky blood, her hand lifeless somewhere beneath her. If only she could reach the horn. Someone would hear. Someone would come. Through the torn cover of the car top, she could see heaven. God was up there someplace. God wouldn't let her die.

———

JIMMY RYAN THOUGHT HE WAS SEEING THINGS. A ray of light shone straight up out of the pocosin into the cloudless night sky. He'd seen a searchlight like that at the new air base near Jacksonville, but this wasn't a searchlight and he knew it. He pulled his Model T off to the side of the sandy road and watched until he was positive he was seeing headlights from an overturned car. "Hey!" he called out. "Is anybody there? Are you hurt?" Only the frogs answered him with their incessant chirp.

He knew he'd never make it across the marshy bog without some boards. "Can you hear me?" he yelled again into the darkness. Staring into the black tangle of briars and grass, he saw a faint red glow, bright, then dim. "That's it, hit the brakes." The flare of light brightened and faded again. "You can hear me, can't you?" he shouted. The red glow brightened and ebbed, brightened and ebbed. "Okay, I'm gonna go get some help. I know you're scared, but I'll be back. I promise."

Jimmy was gone at least half an hour. That's how long it took to drive to the sheriff's house over on Stump Sound. He'd had to wake him, then find his way back to the spot on the Big Savannah where the car had left the road. They brought long boards to spread across the scaffold of underbrush. "How do you know this is the right place?" the sheriff asked. "I don't see no lights."

"Battery must've died. I marked the place with that tire iron."

"Well, we'll just have to wait until daylight before we can go in there. You stay here and I'll get some help." He started his car. "Whoever's in that car's probably dead by now anyhow."

48

A Great Depression

TIMES WERE ALREADY HARD FOR TATE RYAN and the
other farmers in Bladen and Pender Counties, and they were
about to get harder. On September eighteenth, a great hurricane
passed over the sandhills of North Carolina, bringing with it a
tremendous deluge that caused the Cape Fear and Black rivers to
overflow their banks and form a solid lake between the two. From
Ivanhoe to Caintuck, late crops were washed away, and every field,
house, and barn stood under water. Chickens, hogs, mules, and
cows, anything that couldn't get its head above the water or find
some refuge atop a raft or roof, drowned in the dark waters. The
only way to get anywhere was by boat.

The water didn't reach its crest until September twenty-sixth.
Until then Tate and the boys built scaffolds to get their possessions
up out of the water. Of course, Maggie's things were at the top of
the list. Motor vehicles simply remained where they had been
parked, the encroaching flood lapping at their running boards, in
due time covering their roofs. For most people, the second stories
of the newer schoolhouses became the only places safe from snakes
and other displaced varmints that were as desperate as anybody to
find a dry spot.

But Aunt Mag refused to go to the schoolhouse, opting instead
to camp out on the second floor of the old home place. "I'll stay
with her," Maggie said. "She's too old to leave home."

"Too ornery, is more like it," Tate said.

"Now, why would you say that? She's never done a thing to you, Tate Ryan, except maybe take up for me."

"I'm not talking about that. I meant she's being contrary. Won't do something unless it's her idea."

"Well, what's wrong with that when you're ninety-two years old?"

Tate threw his hat down on the kitchen table. "Maggie Lorena, you'd argue with a damn doorpost. I just heard her say one time that she was glad she didn't live up north where she'd have to go to school and church with colored folk." He wagged his finger at her. "That's who's going to be up there at the schoolhouse, you know. That's why she don't want to go up there," he said, reaching for his hat. He'd gotten more hard-edged and contrary himself, it seemed to her, after Patty Sue McBryde's death.

"I declare, your reasoning sure is warped. Help me get my satchel in the boat. I don't think my feet will ever dry out."

Tate had paddled a row boat up to the back door. He helped Maggie onto a bench and then into the boat. Just as she stepped in, she turned to him. "They'll have separate bathrooms and all, won't they?"

"What?"

"At the schoolhouse. They'll have separate bathrooms for the white and the colored?"

"Lord help us. That'd be the last thing on my mind if I was going there because I was flooded out of my home."

Maggie sat down on the board seat and wrung out the hem of her dress. Something caught her eye. "Look, Tate. What's that over there? Oh, no, it's one of my pullets," she wailed. "You said you got them into a crate."

Tate pushed off with a pole and headed out towards the oak grove. "I did the best I could, Maggie Lorena."

———

AUNT MAG WAS SITTING ON THE FRONT PORCH in a rocking chair, her bare feet propped up on the railing. Maggie had seldom seen her without her shoes. "I figured I'd better get the soles of my feet toughened up. See there, water's already up to the top step."

Tate swung the boat around so that Maggie could step out onto the porch. "Maybe it'll stop there. Papa said he built this house up off the ground for one reason—so the water couldn't reach any higher than the porch."

"Well, I got the rugs rolled up anyhow," Aunt Mag said. "If you'll give us a hand, Tate, we can drag them upstairs together. I can't worry about that old piano."

"Might be some blocks in the barn," Tate said. "I'll get it up a little higher."

———

BEFORE TATE LEFT, KATIE AND HER FIVE CHILDREN arrived. Tate helped them out of his brother-in-law's fishing boat. "Let's tie it up to the porch rail," Katie said. "If somebody came along and stole Roy's boat, I'd never hear the end of it."

Tate laughed. "He sure does favor his fishing boat. I reckon nobody else has ever been in it except you or one of the children."

"Well, he oughta stay home and look after his things. I'm sick and tired of being left with all these young'uns and having to put up with floods and such."

"I declare, I've never heard such railing," Aunt Mag said. "You ought to be proud you have a husband who can bring a little money in. Farmers round here are suffering. At least Roy's had the gumption to do something else."

Tate thought she might be implying something. Aunt Mag could do that in a heartbeat. "I'd better get on back," he said.

"William's going off somewhere with his friends. I'll stay in the hayloft until the water goes down. I'll come back and get you then."

"Oh, I almost forgot to tell you," Katie said. "Cyrus Devane sent word that he'd be over here this evening. He's got that big boat he takes out in the sound. Said we could stay with him until the river goes down."

———

BUT MAGGIE HAD CONCOCTED ANOTHER PLAN. When Cyrus came for them she told him that she and Katie and the girls were going to Wilmington to stay with Miss Emily McAllister. Said she couldn't bear the thought of staying in the house where Mary Ellen had died. It was a lie, but it served the purpose.

Katie pulled her off to the side. "What in the world have you got in mind, Maggie Lorena?"

"I've been thinking that this might be a good time to go visit Emily. She's been begging me to come to her beach house." Maggie was producing her plan on the spot. "I want you to come with me."

"But I just brought a few things with me. Nothing right for Wilmington," Katie said.

"Oh, come on, Sister. We'll rummage through that trunk of Abigail's dresses. There'll be some things in there that would be nice in town. I haven't worn half of them."

Cyrus looked confused. "Wouldn't it be a lot simpler for you to come to Burgaw and stay with me till the water goes down?" he said.

"Don't think I'm not much obliged, Cyrus," Maggie said. "It's just that a little trip to Wilmington appeals to me now more than Pender County." She pulled her aunt aside. "Call Lenny at this number and tell him to come and get us. I know he will. I don't want to get stuck in Burgaw."

Aunt Mag hugged her, hissing in Maggie's ear, "You don't seem to mind me getting stuck over there."

"You get Cyrus to help you call Len at that number I gave you. The water's liable to start going down any day now."

"My stars! You'd think you were going off on a jaunt of some kind."

———

LEN, WHO'D BEEN WORKING WITH HIS UNCLE ROY up in Rocky Mount, drove one of the huge well-drilling rigs to Wilmington, where he rented a boat with a gasoline motor and set off upriver after the women. At Maggie's suggestion, Len called Emily McAllister first, asking if Maggie and her sister Katie might stay at the beach house, just until the flood waters receded. "I know it's a lot to ask, Miss Emily," he said, "but Mama thought you might help us out. Just about everything we had is going to be ruined."

Emily did not hesitate. "Bring them here to my house on Market Street. I'm honored that she thought of me, Len. Please come and stay, too."

"No, ma'am. Papa will need some help."

"Don't you have a brother who still lives at home?"

"Yes, ma'am. William's there, but at times like this, Pa needs us both."

"Your uncle? He must be worried about his family."

"Uncle Roy had to finish up the job we were on. Only one of us could leave. We were drilling a deep well and running into a lot of rock." Len laughed. "He said he'd rather drill through rock any day than put up with a boat full of women."

———

THERE WAS LITTLE THAT TATE COULD DO until the water receded, but to be honest, he was thankful to have the time to himself. Will spent most of the duration with his friends who lived on higher ground—somebody always had a car or a truck for him to work on.

And Tate wanted to be near the house, gather up things as the water receded. He'd cleaned and oiled his shotgun, keeping it handy for the occasional squirrel that darted through the treetops. Squirrel was mighty fine eating for a hungry man. On the ridge of an old bay, he'd made himself a camp where he built a fire and roasted the skinned squirrel like he'd done as a boy when he and Grandpa had tromped the woods in Onslow County. Grandpa never liked to bring game home. He said it was best right there in the woods or on the bank of the river, closest to God.

After he'd eaten, Tate paddled the small boat to the barn and disembarked only a foot or two below the loft. The hay was dry, and he slept there in peace while the water found its way back home. Not the least of his thoughts were about the boy who'd come and gone out of his life. He'd prayed that God would let him keep Colin, thinking it might make Maggie right again. She'd been at her best, after all, when the children were small. But the Lord wasn't seeing eye to eye with him, and the day after Patty Sue's funeral a woman had driven up to the house in a big black Buick and asked to see Tate.

"I understand you're keeping my sister's grandson. I want him to come with me." She was a strange woman, gnarly like a bent oak. Tate tried to see some semblance of Patty Sue in her, but this woman was hard favored and had a distinct edge to her voice that grated on him.

"You mean you're old lady Jackson's sister?"

"If you're referring to Gladys Jackson, then the answer is yes. Where's the boy?"

"Ma'am, have you got some proof of who you are? I mean, I'm not going to give this little boy over to somebody I don't even know."

"I told you I was Patty Sue's aunt. Now get me that boy!" she demanded.

Tate had refused and he'd caught hell from Maggie. The next day the woman returned with a deputy sheriff, who told Tate the woman had a right to the child as her next of kin. That was the last he'd seen of Colin McBryde—a boy he'd come to love as his own—leaving his sludge-filled heart barren as the flooded fields.

49
A Yellow Brick House

WHEN THEY ARRIVED AT THE MODERN YELLOW brick home on Market Street, Emily welcomed them graciously on the front steps. "My, my," Katie said. "I'll bet Wilmington never saw anything like this before." Maggie was awestruck too, staring at the Spanish-style two-story home surrounded by palmetto palms, very different from the Italianate architecture that was the norm in the city. "It's beautiful, Emily. Did someone build it for you?"

"No, it was built by one of the Coast Line's executives who moved here from St. Augustine. He wanted a house exactly like the one he had in Florida. But he preferred Florida winters after all, so he moved after only a few years in the house."

"Look at those little iron balconies," Maggie said. "Can you go out and stand on them?"

Emily laughed. "I don't think you'd want to. They're only a few inches wide."

———

AFTER EMILY HAD SHOWN THEM TO THEIR ROOMS, Len walked with his Aunt Katie and her daughters as far as Front Street, where he'd parked the big well-drilling rig on an empty lot. "You go on, son," Katie said. "The girls and I want to walk around and go through all of the stores. We'll take the streetcar home. Your mama had some catching up to do with Miss Emily."

"Don't take any wooden nickels," Len said, joking as usual.

"Wooden nickels might be better than no nickels," his cousin Sadie said.

Katie gave her nephew a hug. "You better get going. Cyrus said he'd come and get us when the water goes down. I'm already dreading that mud."

———

MAGGIE AND EMILY SAT IN A SMALL PARLOR on one side of the front hall across from a dining room with a large round table. Maggie recalled another day when she'd had tea with Emily McAllister, in Onslow County. Emily had been the mistress of Evanwood, her grandfather's estate, Maggie desperately in love with Emily's brother and confused by his irrational behavior. Maggie could not believe that the two of them were sitting together again so many years later, under such different circumstances.

"Please tell me about Jeanne," Maggie said. "How is she? I can't imagine one of my boys being almost killed like that."

Emily wrung her hands, obviously distraught by the reminder of how close her daughter had come to death. "I was devastated. If it hadn't been for . . . for her doctor, I don't know what I would have done. But Jeanne has an exceptional attitude. I was afraid that I had spoiled her, but she's been so strong throughout this ordeal."

Emily was pensive. She seemed different, distracted. Maybe just a little older, Maggie thought. "You know, Tate's nephew, Jimmy, was the boy who rescued her," Maggie said proudly.

"Of course, Jimmy Ryan," Emily said. "Thank goodness for his sharp eyes—way out there in the boondocks. I sent him a small reward." Maggie knew about the reward. Tate's sister Betty had written that Emily had sent James a check for two hundred dollars. They were all overwhelmed.

"You've certainly had your share of misfortune, Maggie. Losing a child, two homes burned to the ground," Emily sighed. "Now your new home, your cherished belongings, covered with mud and saturated with river water."

"I try not to think about it too much," Maggie said, glancing around the elegant room. Something was oddly familiar about it. "We are much obliged to you for putting us up like this. I've been wanting to come to see you, ever since the wedding." Her eyes settled on a small round table where she saw the collection of photographs of Emily's ancestors and family. "This is Reece, isn't it?" she said, picking up a picture of a young man in an ornate metal frame.

"Yes, he was a handsome devil, wasn't he?"

"He could be right devilish," Maggie said, recalling his anger the night Reece had burst into the Ryan home.

Emily poured Maggie another cup of tea. "I was so glad to have you there. I'm sorry I couldn't spend time with you. You know how weddings are."

"Mandy was beautiful," Maggie said. "It was the most wonderful wedding I've ever been to. I saw lots of folks from Onslow County." She had no intention of revealing her true feelings—not about Jon.

"Len danced with Millie!" Emily exclaimed. "Isn't she adorable? I wish she was my own daughter."

"Len said she thinks right smart of you too, Emily. I believe they've been corresponding," Maggie said, leaving out the fact that she'd read every one of Millie's letters to Len.

———

THEY'D SPENT THE AFTERNOON REMINISCING about past events and mutual interests. Emily loved living in Wilmington. "You would, too, Maggie. There are art shows and charity balls, plays at Thalian Hall. I'm having a wonderful time, and the hat shop has been quite a success."

"I know, I see your name in the *Star* all the time."

"Speaking of the *Star*, I've been reading your stories," Emily said. "They're wonderful. I can hardly wait for the next week's edition. How on earth do you do it?"

"My head is always churning with stories," Maggie laughed. "Tate can't stand it. He says anybody can make up stories. He'd be happy if I just spent all my time scrubbing floors and doing the wash."

"How is Tate?"

"He's about the same." What else could she say? She couldn't tell her about the boy Tate wanted to raise—or that he left her on occasion, taking off in that old jalopy—gone for days at a time with no explanation. "He's still working on the house, but it's mostly finished. We don't have wire strung in the county yet, so it's about like living in a camp house. I guess we're what you'd call backwoods."

"But you could have a Delco generator. Everyone in Onslow is getting one."

"We were saving for it, but with this flood, I don't know."

"Come to the kitchen with me," Emily said. "We can talk more while I start dinner. I imagine Katie and the girls will be back soon."

"You mean you don't have a cook?"

"Of course not. I haven't had a cook since I left Onslow County," Emily said as she pared a pan of potatoes. "There's a fabulous butcher shop down on Front Street—actually I guess your cousin, Murdoch McBryde, owns it—and we have a wonderful old city market. You never know what they'll have when the trucks come in early in the morning."

"Ummm, what are we having?"

"I thought you might enjoy a roast of beef—I have a special marinade."

"My goodness, yes," Maggie said. "We almost always have pork. The only cow we ever had on the farm was our milk cow. Poor thing, I hope she hasn't drowned."

"I'm sorry, Maggie. I didn't mean to bring up something unpleasant."

Maggie smoothed her hair back and reached for an apron that

hung on the pantry door. "It's all right, I'm not even going to think about that again. Let me peel those potatoes for you."

The two women bustled about in the kitchen preparing dinner until Emily slipped off her apron and untied Maggie's. "The rest of dinner can wait. Let's go sit out on the terrace. I'll fix us a glass of wine—something special. Maybe you'll recognize it." She opened the refrigerator and removed a bottle of wine, holding it up for Maggie to see the label on the dark green bottle.

"*Evanwood?* From your brother's grapes?"

"Yes, dear."

On the terrace, Emily held up her glass. "To Reece."

She took a sip, remembering the picnic by the creek when Reece Evans had tossed her eyeglasses into the stream. "He had a hateful streak when things didn't go his way," she said.

"Didn't I warn you about that?" Emily asked.

"I reckon you did, but it was too late. I was already in love with him."

"I've always wanted to ask you, that time you met him in Raleigh, did you consider staying there—leaving Tate?"

"No."

"I'm sorry," Emily said. "I shouldn't have asked, but Reece came home so happy and excited. He said he'd seen you. I thought maybe you . . . "

"Maybe I did, but that's all in the past, isn't it?"

Emily reached out to take her hands. "You've never had all that you deserve."

"I'm not so sure I deserved any more than I've gotten. I reckon I was young and foolish. Made some bad choices. There always seemed to be a way out, or at least I thought so. I was looking for somebody to make me happy. But Aunt Mag says happiness comes from within. You can't count on somebody else—you've got to find ways of making yourself happy. I've been thinking about that a lot lately."

"What have you found that makes you happy, Maggie?"

"My writing, for one thing. I can make all my characters do whatever I want them to, kind of like playing God."

"You do love to write, don't you?"

"I reckon I do more than anything. I never know exactly where my stories are going. They're like my life, not all good and not all bad. Sometimes things turn around when you least expect it. That's what makes a story interesting. I'm right surprised myself at some of the things that happen in my stories."

"Are you working on a novel?"

"No, I've decided that I'm best at little stories that have a connection. You know, like I'm doing for the *Star*."

"Well, you've certainly found your niche. Jeanne and I are your biggest fans."

"I was hoping she'd be well enough to see me."

"Of course. She's asked for you." Emily was tearful. "You may be shocked. She was hurt pretty badly. Her pelvis was broken. Her arm was mangled . . . they had to . . . "

"Don't tell me. Just let me go see her. Maybe I could read to her."

"That would be wonderful. Here's this week's edition of your story. She'll be thrilled."

5 0

School Marmie

AFTER A LARGE BREAKFAST OF FRENCH TOAST, sausage, and fresh fruit, Katie took the girls on the beachcar out to Wrightsville Beach while Emily drove Maggie to James Walker Memorial Hospital. "I had totally forgotten about my Sorosis meeting this morning. I'll take you to Jeanne's room and be back for you by noon if that's all right."

"To be sure," Maggie said. "Please don't rush. I'd like to walk around the hospital a little."

"Maybe you'll see Jon McNamara. He told me he'd met you in Boston. Abigail Adams was here with a friend last spring. They had nothing but praise for you and your work. Abigail was married to his uncle, wasn't she?"

"Yes, that's right," Maggie said, wondering if that was all he'd told Emily.

"You may see him in Jeanne's room. He's in surgery all day, but sometimes he stops by if he has a break between procedures."

"He's her doctor?"

"Oh my, yes. I don't know what I would have done without Jon. Not only does Jeanne adore him, he's the best surgeon at James Walker." Emily was beaming. Maggie was sure she'd feel the same about a doctor who'd saved her child's life.

———

JEANNE MCALLISTER WAS ALMOST THIRTY YEARS OLD. She'd been a beautiful child with her head full of blonde curls. If she'd become a beautiful woman, it would be hard to tell now with her head bandaged and most of her face covered. Emily said she'd hit the windshield when the car rolled over, leaving deep jagged cuts in several places on her face. Jeanne had survived the crash only because she had not lost consciousness and was able to reach the horn and the brake pedal with her uninjured arm.

Feeling faint from the shock of seeing Jeanne's head and face completely bandaged, Maggie gripped the rail of the white iron bed. "I'm so sorry about your accident. I should've come when I read about it in the paper."

"I haven't felt much like company, have I, Mother?"

"No, you haven't, darling. But Maggie's not company," she said, pulling a chair out from under a small table. "She's just your old schoolmarm here to read to you."

Jeanne managed a slight smile. "You were a good ol' schoolmarm."

Maggie took the chair that Emily offered and sat close to the bed. "Please don't feel that you have to talk. Your mother said I might read to you. Would you like that?"

"If I can stay awake. Rebecca gave me a shot before she went off duty."

Before Jeanne and her mother could finish answering Maggie's question about Rebecca and the other McBryde girls, the drugs took effect. Emily looked over at Jeanne. "Look, she's asleep."

"You go on," said Maggie. "When she wakes up, I'll read to her if she feels like it."

As soon as Emily left, Maggie slipped out the door and went to the nurses' station. "Could you tell me if Dr. McNamara is in the hospital today?" she asked a nurse.

"Yes, I believe he's in surgery. His office is on the first floor if you'd like to wait for him there."

Maggie took a deep breath, not sure how she should reply. "No, I'm here visiting Jeanne McAllister. I only wanted to say hello."

"He should be in to see her before long."

"Oh, yes, I know. I just thought it might be best if I . . . "

"That's the best place to catch him," the nurse said. "He's like a fly on a horse's tail."

———

JEANNE WAS STILL SLEEPING WHEN MAGGIE returned to the room. She sat beside the young woman, letting her thoughts wander. What if Jon should tell her he was still in love with her? *Suddenly something can happen—someone can go out or come back into your life.* She'd written those very lines in her last story, "It's All a Matter of Chance." Maybe Jon had seen it. Maggie was deep into her thoughts, so deep that she dropped off to sleep.

May I come in? Maggie looked up, startled. In the dim light of the hospital room, his features backlit by the bright hall lights, she didn't recognize his face at first. *Maggie, is that you?*

Jon? Yes, it's me, she said, standing to greet him.

He stepped into the hall, motioning to her to follow. Gathering her into his arms, he whispered in her hair. *I thought I'd never see you again.*

Someone had laid a hand on her shoulder, shaking her gently. A familiar voice called her name. She looked around, getting her bearings. "Oh, I fell asleep," she said. Jon was standing beside her, smiling.

"I'm not surprised. Emily says you've been through quite a lot with that flood. I'm sure you're exhausted."

"Jon, is that you?" Jeanne called out.

"Yes, dear, I'm here. Maggie Ryan is here, too."

"I know," Jeanne said weakly, a smile spreading across the part of her pale face that was visible. "She's my ol' schoolmarm."

"Not that *old*, am I?" Maggie said with a little laugh, trying to get a grip on her emotions.

Jon leaned over and kissed Jeanne on the top of her bandaged head. "All the *old* folks are here. Your old teacher, your old doctor . . . "

Jeanne tried to laugh. "You're not old, Dr. Jon. You're just right."

"All right, now, stop flirting with me," he said, standing at the foot of the bed. "That sort of thing goes to my head, and I might forget that I'm here to change your bandages." He began rolling up the bed. "Let's get you in a better position."

"Should I leave, Jon—Dr. McNamara?"

"No, Maggie, unless Jeanne wants you to."

"Where's Mother?" Jeanne asked.

"She had a meeting. She'll be back soon. Maybe you should wait until . . . "

"I don't mind," Jeanne said, closing her eyes. "You can be my marmie."

Maggie stifled a giggle. "Your *marmie?*"

"Please stay," Jon said. "I promised Jeanne we'd do this. I have to be back in the operating room in a few minutes. She may need you."

Maggie sat in a chair, watching him gently pull the bandages away, layer by layer. He handed Jeanne a small mirror. "Brace yourself. You're not going to like what you see, but I promise you that in a week or two, these scars will fade."

Jeanne stared at her reflection in the mirror for a long moment, then turned away, beginning to cry. "I don't want to see any more."

Jon sat on her bed, pulled her into his arms. "I promise you, we'll do everything to make them go away completely. There are new things being done with reconstructive surgery. I'll take you wherever you need to go. We'll . . . " Maggie felt like she was watching an intimate scene in a movie, the doctor kissing Jeanne's forehead, touching her tear-stained cheeks over and over. Jeanne sobbed like a baby while he rocked her in his arms.

51

Disillusioned

EMILY WAS BACK SHORTLY BEFORE NOON, a package under her arm. "This is for you, my darling," she said as she entered the hospital room. "A pretty blue bed jacket to match your pretty blue eyes." When she suddenly realized that she was looking into Jeanne's unbandaged face, Emily burst into tears. "Oh my poor Jeanne, my darling little girl," she sobbed, holding her daughter like a child.

"Don't cry, Mother. I cried enough for both of us. Awful, isn't it?"

Emily wiped her eyes. "No, no, darling. It is just so wonderful to see your lovely face again."

But Jeanne had seen the ragged scars that had turned that lovely face into a caricature. A deep gash across her forehead and a slash down her cheek had created a frown that time might never erase. "Not so lovely anymore."

Emily rocked Jeanne in her arms. "You'll always be my beautiful little girl."

"Jon says the scars will fade."

Emily dabbed at her daughter's tears. "Of course they will . . . just a matter of time," she said, regaining some of her composure. "I'm sorry I missed him. I thought he would have waited until I came back." She busied herself, straightening the bed, rearranging items on the beside table. "I would not have gone to that meeting if I'd known he was going to do this today."

Jeanne tried to smile. "Not to worry," she said in a slurred voice, "my marmie was here."

"Your *marmie?*"

"My old school marmie."

Emily glanced at Maggie. "Yes, your old school marmie," she said, nodding. "Thank you, Maggie."

Jeanne drifted off to sleep while the two women sat near her bed. "I can't believe I missed Jon," Emily said. "I wanted to ask him to dinner tonight."

"I'm sure he's busy," Maggie said.

"Well, it's just too bad if he is. I'm making paella, his favorite dinner."

"I've never had pay-ella," Maggie said, mispronouncing the word. "What is it?"

"Mother makes wonderful paella," Jeanne said, without opening her eyes.

"It's a wonderful Spanish dish with rice, chicken and seafood, seasoned with saffron." Emily stood at the foot of Jeanne's bed. "Here's an idea. If I don't catch up with Jon, I'll send enough over for both of you, Jeanne."

"Jon knows Marmie," Jeanne said slowly, her eyes still closed.

"I know, he told me, darling." She turned to Maggie. "I was saving this for a surprise when we could tell you together, but I'll tell you now. Jon and I are engaged to be married," Emily said, beaming with pleasure. As difficult as it was to hug somebody who you really wanted to hate from that minute on, Maggie hugged Emily, congratulating her the only way she knew how. They said good-bye to Jeanne and left the hospital arm in arm, with Emily bubbling over with excitement about honeymoon plans. "It's months away now. We've postponed the wedding until Jeanne is better. We'll fly to Paris. I've dreamed of doing that. Jon knows a wonderful small hotel. We'll go to the Louvre, eat in little sidewalk bistros. I can hardly wait."

How could Maggie hate Emily? How could she hate Jon? It was her own life that she hated. The old saying came back to her, she'd made her bed hard—now it was hers to sleep in. But while she struggled to overcome her bubble that had burst, something in the back of her mind nagged at her. Yes, it was as plain as the nose on her face, Jeanne McAllister was in love with her doctor, and Maggie suspected that he was a bit more enamored with Jeanne than he should be, considering his pending marriage to her mother.

Tate Ryan's jalopy

52

Home Is Where Your Heart Is

MAGGIE'S TRIP TO WILMINGTON GAVE HER an entirely new outlook. Any hope she had held for Jon McNamara's attention completely dissipated upon witnessing his actions in Jeanne's hospital room. He was a cad—and it was all she could do not to warn Emily McAllister. Had she stayed a few more days, an opportunity might have presented itself, but news had come that the water was receding and Maggie wanted to visit Eva McBryde. Compared to the dire situation the McBrydes were in, Maggie felt fortunate that she had a place to come home to.

Eva had sent word by Millie that she wanted Katie and Maggie to have lunch with her before they returned to the country. By the end of the week, the *Star* reported that the floodwaters were beginning to recede. Unless there was more rain, the news article said, people should return to their homes in two to three days. "I dread like the plague going back, for more than one reason," Maggie said to Katie. "Being here in Wilmington reminds me once again just how behind the times we are."

"Cyrus says they've strung the electric line as far as Burgaw, but it'll be a while before we get power out in the county," Katie said. "Roy's putting in a generator the next time he comes home."

———

WHILE THE HOUSE ON PRINCESS STREET HAD BEEN an elegant home at one time, the McBrydes' Red Cross Street house had never been anything but what it was now, a big two-story box with a porch on the front. Eva had done her best to brighten up the drab living room. She knew how to put on a nice luncheon. She'd ironed her cutwork tablecloth and napkins, set the table with her good china and silver, and snipped a few yellow chrysanthemums from a clump in the back yard to put in a crystal vase. Millie had cooked the chicken for her salad the night before. Early that morning, she'd made a lemon pudding cake and put the salad together. There were a few green grapes left from a sack Cal had brought her on Sunday.

"This looks just like something Miss Emily would do," Millie whispered to her at lunch. She could only stay a few minutes for lunch because the downtown Merchants' Association was having a big promotional event. The shop would be full of patrons most of the day looking to buy one of Miss Emily's fall hats on sale. "Just leave the dishes for me, Mama. I'll do them with the supper dishes," she said, scooting out the back door.

"I declare, every time I see that girl I just love her more," Maggie said.

"She's a treasure all right," Eva said.

"Too bad she's kin to Len. Mama used to laugh and say your mother and she were cousins *twice removed*," Maggie said. "I was never quite sure what that meant, but I know she put great store in the fact that she was some kin to your brother Dick. He's real famous, you know."

Eva smiled. "I don't know what we would do without Dick. He'll be here in a week or two for homecoming."

"He's going to be at church in Cotton Cove?" Katie asked.

"Well, we might have to go by boat, but we'll be there."

"Bud will have a car running by then," Maggie said. "We'll all go together. I'd sure like to see him in that headdress the Oklahoma Indians gave him."

KATIE EXCUSED HERSELF TO TAKE THE GIRLS to the movie at the Bijou, leaving Eva and Maggie to visit the rest of the afternoon. When the dishes were in the sink, Eva covered the table with a large checkered cloth. "I won't have to cook much for supper tonight. We only have two boarders now, and they eat in one of the cafés most of the time."

"I can't imagine renting rooms to people you don't know," Maggie said.

"Oh, it's not bad at all. We've got the nicest little couple in the apartment. She uses my washing machine and does their laundry. The other fellow upstairs takes his laundry out and eats somewhere downtown."

"Do you have a garden?"

"We used to, but so many people have lost their jobs and don't have money for rent, they've put up some shanties on the vacant lot where Rob had his garden. I reckon they need it worse than we do."

Maggie studied her cousin, who was a year younger than herself. Eva's face was drawn to the side slightly from the stroke she'd had when she was only forty years old. Her hair was still a dark auburn and her skin the color of cream, but the corners of her mouth turned down and deep furrows creased her forehead. Maggie seldom regarded anyone's trouble greater than hers, but Eva's life was taking a toll on her. "Everybody's having trouble making ends meet," Maggie said.

"I'm sure we could do a little better in the country. Rob would have his garden, and we could raise a few pigs and chickens."

"I imagine you're better off right where you are," Maggie said. "There's not much to move back to. Especially after this flood. At least you've got electricity and indoor plumbing."

"I wouldn't mind lighting oil lamps again. The soft light from a lamp was so cozy. And I reckon I'm not too proud to empty a slop jar now and then."

They sat on the back porch overlooking a grassy plot with a small grape arbor in the corner. "Rob had to take a job at the gas station. He's too old for that. I want to cry when he comes home black with grease."

Maggie laughed. "I know what you mean."

"I wouldn't tell this to everyone, Maggie, but I think I can trust you. It's all I can do to climb those stairs every night. My heart . . . I think it's giving out."

"Isn't there a room downstairs you could use?"

"Only one, with a little kitchenette. We get more rent from it than we would two bedrooms upstairs."

"Well, it looks to me like you wouldn't be much good to anybody if your heart failed. I'd take the best room myself."

"I had this idea that I might ask you to keep a lookout for us. I know lots of families are leaving the country and looking for work in the cities and towns. Maybe a nice house with a little land will come available."

"Not anymore," Maggie said. "In fact, lots of the young ones haven't been able to make it. They're coming back home."

"Well, something might come up. You'll keep an eye and ear out for us, won't you?"

"Of course I will, Eva, but don't you want to go back up to Bandeaux Creek?"

"Oh, I'd love to, but our old house is gone now. They tore it down. You know as well as I do that a house is not a home. Home is where your heart is."

Yes, Maggie thought. *Home is where your heart is.* Maybe that's why the two houses Tate had built for her never seemed like *her* homes. Her heart was not in their home in Onslow County. And the unfinished place they were living in now . . . well, it may have started out as hers, but Patty Sue Jackson McBryde had tainted it. Maggie could live there, but it would never be *her* home. "I'm sorry about your nephew. Like to've shocked us all to death," she said. "That woman was another thing!"

Tears came into Eva's eyes. "I'd rather not talk about it, but since you mentioned it, all I can say is, I'm glad my dear sister didn't live to see it."

" 'Twould break any mother's heart."

"Davy was the sweetest child on earth," Eva said. "My Calvin's best friend. He just got mixed up with the wrong . . . crowd."

"You can say that again."

"I never knew Patty Sue personally. They ran off to South Carolina and got married right before we left Bandeaux Creek. She was a lot older than Davy."

"Hmmph!" Maggie retorted. "I met her when I came home from Boston and found her hanging around our place helping Tate do this and that . . . getting William to soup up her trucks. She used to run moonshine, you know."

"Do tell, I had no idea you knew her," Eva said cautiously.

"Yes ma'am. The sheriff went in there and busted up her liquor still. Said it was the biggest one he ever saw in Bladen County. I never met young Davy, but I'm here to tell you, he got himself mixed up with an alley cat, as they say up north. The sheriff said you should've seen the room she took those drivers in when they came back from a run. One of the colored fellows that worked for her told Tate that she slept with every one of them, and her a mother, too. There were red satin sheets on the bed and black lace curtains. He said, 'Mistuh Tate, it looked jus' like one o' dem ho houses I seen in Harlem,'" Maggie said.

Eva was shocked by the indelicate remark, but she let her continue.

Maggie slapped her knee and cackled. "If I hadn't run her off, she'd probably have been in Tate's britches before long."

"I wonder what happened to the little boy," she said, hastily shifting the direction of the conversation.

"Some of her people came and got him," Maggie said without emotion.

"That's for the best. He'd never have had a good life here. All the talk . . . "

Maggie was suddenly ashamed that she'd hardened her heart against Colin McBryde. "I guess a little young'un like that couldn't help what his parents did. Or what people believe."

"People can be cruel, Maggie," Eva said, recalling all the talk about Maggie Lorena when the second house burned. "You know about that, don't you?"

Maggie slipped a handkerchief out from her sleeve and wiped her forehead. "I reckon I do, Eva."

————

ABOUT THE TENTH DAY THE WATER BEGAN to recede, taking with it the very substance of Tate's being. Gone were his crops and livestock—drowned, washed away. What little that remained was covered in mud and the stink of dead things. Almost fifty years old and what did he have now to show for all of his hard work and heartaches? He looked around him at the house, the barn, the smokehouse—everything covered in black silt—and he wanted to cry. Not the least of his pain was beneath the shed next to Will's garage where his old jalopy sat, tires flat, its headlamps and windshield broken by floating debris. He was sure it would never run again.

Will and his friends had hoisted the old Chandler up onto the flatbed truck, along with several motors and parts that Will feared would be ruined by the water, and hauled them to higher ground. There wasn't time to come back for Tate's jalopy. Watching the water creep closer and closer to the house, Maggie, who was scared to death of snakes and had never learned to swim, had gone into one of her screaming fits and told him if he left her to move his jalopy to higher ground, he'd never hear the end of it.

After he'd taken her to Aunt Mag's, he'd come back home and studied the situation, wondering if there might be some way he could hoist the vehicle up to the rafters of the shed, but he'd had to give up the idea when he couldn't find enough rope. For more than a week, all he could see was the ragged top just below the surface of the water, put to some good use he reckoned by the rooster that swooped down to it from the rafters now and then.

Maggie had come home from Wilmington, taken one look at the mess in the house, and said they'd have to let it dry out before she'd get into cleaning. Not only were the mattresses ruined, the kitchen stove was filled with sludge. Enlisting Lizzie's help, she scraped out her room and retrieved her typewriter from one of the shelves high over her bed, shelves Tate had made to place her most precious possessions on. After the fire, Dr. Bayard had suggested it. "If she had shelves to place her memorabilia on," he'd said, "maybe the trunk would take on less significance as a receptacle of her losses." Tate had obliged, crafting the shelves from the salvaged picket fence that encircled the gazebo and garden before Aunt Mag's house burned. Tate called them her memory shelves. He'd never told Maggie that Patty Sue had helped him sand the edges of the rough boards.

CAINTUCK, PENDER COUNTY, N.C.
Mrs. Margaret Moreland McFayden died
of natural causes yesterday in her home in
Caintuck at the age of ninety-one. Mrs.
McFayden was widowed some years ago
when her husband dropped dead of a heart
attack at their home in Colly. Since that
time the widow has lived in the home of
her deceased sister, a prominent member
or the community, and her late husband,
war hero and former county commissioner Captain George W. Corbinn. An active
member at the Bethany Baptist Church
until her death, Mrs. McFayden will be
remembered for her generous spirit and
loving service in the name of our Lord. —
Bladen Journal, November 4, 1928

53

Death in the Family

L EN STAYED HOME FOR SEVERAL WEEKS TO HELP with the cleanup, spending a good bit of time helping his great-aunt Mag. "She ought not to be living there by herself, Mama. She can hardly get around anymore, and you should see the things she eats. Nothing much but sweet potatoes and corn bread."

"Well, I can't go down there and wait on her. And she won't come here and stay with us," Maggie said. "She's no worse off than we are, I reckon."

Len thought he could understand why. His mother liked to be waited on, herself. Len got amused at the two women who bent his ear about each other. Just the other day Aunt Mag had said Maggie was spoiled rotten. "Always wanting somebody to see to her needs."

"I reckon you had a hand in that, didn't you, Aunt Mag?" Len retorted.

"No, sir, I did not. I tried to teach her to do everything she could for herself. It's your daddy that waits on her."

———

LEN WAS THE ONE WHO FOUND AUNT MAG sprawled out on the kitchen floor. Evidently she'd gotten up, dressed in her usual black garb with a starched white apron over it, and gone to the kitchen to stoke up the stove. "Looked like she drew a chair up to sit in while she was poking at the coals. Must've fallen off the chair and hit her head on the stove leg."

"Poor old darlin'," Maggie sobbed. "How long did she lay there wishing some of us would come?"

"She was stone cold, Mama. I saw her late yesterday. Remember, she sent you that plate of divinity?"

Maggie reached for a piece of the candy. "She knew how much I loved it."

"I don't believe she could've died more than four or five hours ago," Len said.

Tate stood by the open back door, staring off into the distance. Aunt Mag had told him just a few weeks ago that she wasn't afraid to die, but she sure did dread the *sting* of death. "She ought'n to have stayed there so long by herself. She was one hardheaded woman," he said.

"I'd never seen her without her teeth before," Len said. "Her cheeks were all sunken in and her mouth gaped open like a baby's mouth."

"Oh," Maggie cried. "She'd never let anyone but me and Katie see her without her teeth."

"Aunt Katie went back to her room and found them in a glass of water," Len said. "She gave them to Mr. Bradshaw to take to the funeral home. He said they'd put them back in before she was laid out."

"You told Katie before you came and told me, your own mama?"

Len was somewhat taken aback by the reprimand. "She told me to go get Mr. Bradshaw while she stayed with Aunt Mag."

"Well, I should've been there too," Maggie pouted.

Tate closed the door behind him, mumbling, *Jesus Christ himself couldn't please you, Maggie Lorena.* He thought back over the time he'd known Aunt Mag. She'd looked after him from the day he came to Colly to live in the house she'd given to Maggie. He'd always known that a Ryan from Onslow County was not what she'd had in mind for her favorite niece. But it seemed like the more grief Maggie gave her, the more Aunt Mag sided with him.

The next day Tate went alone to Bethany Baptist Church to dig Aunt Mag's grave. He had situated Aunt Mag's grave next to that of her sister, Ellen, honoring her wishes and that of the family. It was his special gift to her, a final resting place for the old woman whose gumption he admired more than anyone he knew. But all the time he was digging, his mind was on another woman whose bones lay moulding in an unmarked grave in Cotton Cove.

———

THE SUNSHINE WOMEN'S CIRCLE, OF WHICH Aunt Mag had been the oldest living member, had gathered gold and red chrysanthemums for the funeral, filling four large vases to go across the pulpit stage. Reverend Mizelle had bragged on the staunchest member of his congregation for a good twenty minutes, saying how she had been the one he could call on when there was no one else to go to the side of a dying neighbor, to help deliver a little colored child, or pray over a man who had no family. "Margaret McFayden would go in the middle of the night if necessary. She always did what she could, no matter how rich, how poor," he reminded the mourners. "There's probably not a one of you in this church that didn't benefit from her kindness one time or the other." Then he'd prayed over her, that the Lord would use her in heaven as he had on earth. "Give her the little children, oh Lord, that she never had on this mortal landscape."

At this, Maggie and Katie glanced at one another, stifling snickers. Aunt Mag had often confided in them that she and Uncle Archie had decided not to have children. How they'd accomplished that had become a joke between the two sisters.

"I know y'all are sure going to miss her," Reverend Mizelle said when they'd gathered out under the trees for dinner.

"She was like a mother to me. I don't know what I'm going to do without her," Maggie said.

"You hadn't been about her much since you came back from Boston," Tate said when the preacher was turned away.

She glared at him. "I haven't been well. Aunt Mag knew that."

"Sit down, Mama, and I'll bring you a plate," Len said. "Papa, you'd better go rescue Will. Old lady Marshburn's got him cornered talking about her old Model T." Len thought he had done a lot of that lately—rescued Papa from Mama. Why couldn't married folks just get along?

54

Division of Property

THE FOLLOWING SPRING, KATIE CALLED THE FAMILY together to clean out the old home place where they were all born. Len and Will had set up long tables on sawhorses, and Katie had prepared a lunch of fried chicken, potato salad, and pimento cheese sandwiches. As it happened, Maggie's birthday was the following week, and Katie had taken it upon herself to make a large coconut layer birthday cake. "I know it's not your birthday yet, but without Aunt Mag around, you won't likely do much celebrating. I thought this might be a good time with me and your brothers here."

Maggie was seated in front of the cake, and the rest of the family stood or sat around her. She'd gone back to wearing the dark glass in one side of her spectacles, and Katie felt sorrier for her than she ever had. "You shouldn't have done this, Katie, but I'm mighty obliged."

Katie hugged her around the shoulders. "You deserve it, dear sister. It won't be as good as Aunt Mag's, but I know she would've approved of the little celebration."

After lunch, the children of G. W. and Ellen Corbinn stood in the middle of the living room, assessing the contents of the house. Captain Corbinn had left Zeb the land that the house sat on, but Zeb had wanted Aunt Mag to continue to live there as long as she was able. Now he was ready to claim his heritage. "Sattie doesn't want one bit of the furniture, so y'all just divide it up between yourselves," Zeb said.

"I'd like to have Mama's piano if no one else wants it," Maggie said.

"Len put it out in the barn after the flood. I don't reckon it's much good now."

"There's nothing here I want," Katie said. "Aunt Mag kept giving Mama's things away. When she'd emptied out a room, she'd close it off."

"I imagine Uncle Freddy's children got most of it," Ralph said.

"Saved us the trouble," his brother Ernest said.

Zeb started for the door. "Well, y'all take what you want. I don't want another thing. This house itself holds all the memories I want."

"How come Jasper's not here?" Maggie asked.

"He's building a barn out behind his house," Zeb said. "A place to put his old tin lizzie. Said to tell y'all that all he wanted was a couple of those old mule collars out there in the barn, just because they belonged to Papa."

"Well, he should've come to celebrate my birthday anyway."

"I reckon he weighed that option."

"Oh, Zeb, he did not!" Katie piped in. "The birthday cake was a complete surprise to everybody." She patted Maggie on the shoulder. "I'm sure he would've come if he'd known, Sister."

"All right, then. Put them in the wagon, I'll take them to Jasper on my way home," Maggie said. "I've been meaning to see what he's done with his new house. Reckon he's thinking about getting married?"

Her brothers all laughed. "Nope. You can bet your bottom dollar on that," Zeb said.

"Well, he needs somebody to look after him," Maggie said.

"You mean somebody for him to wait on like Tate waits on you?"

Maggie glared at her brother. "You don't know what it's like to lose a child." She turned on her heel and started out the door.

"You've 'bout flogged that horse to death haven't you, Sister?" he called out.

"That's mean, Zeb," Katie said.

"It's the truth, ain't it?" Zeb's sharp tongue was just his way, Maggie knew that. Aunt Mag had done the same thing, jerked a knot in Maggie by pointing out her shortcomings. It had nothing to do with love. Or did it? Without Aunt Mag's steady presence to keep her in tow, Maggie's life was going to be different. Katie would stand up for her to a point, but Aunt Mag had been the one to straighten her out.

When Zeb put the collars in the wagon and handed her the reins, he looked surprised when she hugged him and kissed him on the cheek. "Thank you, Zeb," she said.

"Tell Tate there's an old harrow in the barn. Might be better than the one he has. He's welcome to it."

"I will, Zeb. I'm sure he'd be much obliged. Why don't you and Sattie bring it down this evening and have supper with us?"

"This evening?" Zeb asked, stunned even more by the invitation.

"Yes, I put a hen on to stew before I left. I'll make some pastry."

"I reckon we could, if you're sure you're not too worn out."

"No, not a-tall. I'll ask Jasper to come, too," she said, thinking how proud Aunt Mag would be of her.

CAINTUCK, PENDER COUNTY, N.C. David Jasper Corbinn, of Caintuck, prominent planter and sportsman, died from heart failure at his home here yesterday morning at nine-thirty o'clock in the morning.

Mr. Corbinn served on the Pender County Board of Education for a number of years and was chairman of the Board of County Commissioners for several terms. In his youth, Mr. Corbinn was often found in Wilmington, socializing around among a host of his friends. He was a man with a most genial way, affable humor and good nature. Mr. Corbinn told good stories and told them well, having a vivid recollection of many interesting events reaching back into the past, illustrating men, their peculiarities and surroundings.

Mr. Corbinn was educated at Salemburg Academy and the University of Kentucky, at which he became a very famous football star. He was 59 years old and was never married. Funeral services will be conducted today at two thirty o'clock at the old Bethany Church with the Reverend J. L. Mizelle officiating. He is survived by his four brothers and two sisters.—*Bladen Journal, April 27, 1929*

55
Old Mule Collars

FROM THE LANE, MAGGIE COULD SEE THE BARN, but Jasper was not on the roof as she'd expected. Pulling the wagon around back, she was sure he'd be in his usual chair on the porch. Not finding him there, she got down from the wagon and walked out towards the barn. From a distance, she saw him on the ground. Tiptoeing to where he lay, she thought he might have stretched out on the grass for a short nap. But his form lay oddly between two rusty plows, his neck twisted in a grotesque manner. She went to touch him, brushing the flies from his nose and mouth. He flinched and she jumped back.

"Jasper, get up. I brought you some cake and those old harnesses." Jasper loved antique farm implements—said one of the reasons he was building the barn was to have a place to put all of his treasures. "Get up now, Sister's brought you—" Maggie's heart beat wildly in her chest. Jasper wasn't going to get up. Jasper was dead. Falling back on the ground near him, she looked up at the cloudless sky. God was up there somewhere, but he hadn't been watching out for her brother. Aunt Mag was old, ready to go, but Jasper had some good years left. It wasn't fair. She'd always counted on Jasper.

How she made it back to Zeb's, she'd never know. Passing Katie's house, she'd waved to the children, but couldn't stop— wouldn't stop. Katie would go to pieces and Maggie had to get to Zeb's. He'd know what to do. Zeb always knew what to do.

———

THE PENDER COUNTY CORONER SAID Jasper had suffered a heart attack before falling off the roof of the barn and breaking his neck. Maggie felt the pain as if it had happened to her. After the funeral, she'd gone to bed and refused any consolation. Tate was exasperated and Katie set aside her own grief to come and sit by her sister. Tate met her on the porch. "I just can't take it anymore," he said. "Dr. Bayard said she might not get over it this time."

"Sister's never been quite the same since Yancey died," Katie said. "I thought she'd made a little headway in the last few years — writing her romance stories and all—learning to drive. And you should have seen her that time we went to Wilmington during the flood, you would've thought she was every bit as elegant as Miss Emily."

"Maggie Lorena could act any way she wanted to," Tate said.

"Before Jasper died, she asked me about going to Home Demonstration Club," Katie said, wavering between hope and skepticism. "Said she wanted to fix up the house."

Tate wasn't sure that was such a good idea. "Fix up the house? She's never cared a thing about this house—nothing but her room."

"Now, Tate, this is a good sign. She'd learn to can, put up food. Home Demonstration Club is teaching women to use what they have. You ought to see the chairs Mattie Bloodworth made out of some old wooden crates."

Tate laughed and slapped his knee. "I sure wouldn't want to sit on one Maggie Lorena nailed together."

———

KATIE SPENT THE REST OF THE AFTERNOON with Maggie. They talked about Aunt Mag and Jasper, recalling their strengths and weaknesses. "It's just us now, Maggie," her sister said. "I can't stay long. You're going to have to get up out of that bed and take care of Tate, or you might lose him."

Maggie sat up in bed and stared at her sister. "What?"

"I said, it's time you took care of Tate. Have you seen how poorly he's looking?"

"He can't," she wailed. "I mean, I need Tate to look after me."

"You're going to have to look after each other, Sister."

———

WHETHER KATIE'S ADMONISHMENT OR TATE'S NEGLECT had anything to do with Maggie's quick recovery, no one knew, but within a few days she was up early in the kitchen, demanding that Tate start a fire in the stove and fill the wood box so she could make biscuits. "I'm way behind on my writing," she told him. "As soon as you and Will are off to work, I need to get busy."

Tate kicked the door closed behind him and dumped an armload of wood in the box. "I thought maybe you'd given that up," he said.

"Given up my writing? Why in the world would I do that?"

"With Aunt Mag and Jasper passing so close together, I was afraid you might not be up to it."

"Well, I am, and I may as well start today."

Tate remembered the letter from the *Star* that had come a few days earlier. "You saw that letter on the mantel?"

Maggie worked at the kitchen cupboard, her back towards Tate, blending lard into flour in her biscuit bowl. "It wasn't good news," she said.

"What was it?"

When she turned to face him, he saw her eyes fill with tears. "I didn't want to tell you. My romance stories have been canceled. Mr. Brown says they had to make some cuts."

"But everybody loves your stories!"

"That's not the point. He said it was a matter of money. The *Star* doesn't have any either." She wiped her hands on her apron. "What'll we do without that money coming in?" she cried.

Tate was hesitant, afraid of her wrath if he tried to touch her, but he held out his arms and she came to him. "We'll make do," he said. "It don't take much to hold us together. Don't you worry."

There it was—so simple to Tate. *It don't take much to hold us together.* Comforted by his massive arms, she wondered why she had pushed him away all those years. Why had she been so hard to get along with? She couldn't remember. "The editor said I could write up the neighborhood news if I wanted to," she sobbed. "He said people loved to see their names in the paper. He can't pay me, but he promised he'd take my stories again when things get better."

Tate picked up a dish towel and dabbed at her face. "Well, I'd say that's better than nothing. It'll give you something to do."

She slapped the cloth away. "I've got plenty to do, Tate Ryan. Have you plowed my garden yet?"

"No-mum, not yet, but I can get to it today if you're hankering on putting seed in the ground."

"You just go ahead and get it ready. Sister said the county extension agent is speaking to our home demonstration club next week and he's going to give out seed and tell us about fertilizing and liming the soil."

Tate was indignant. "I know how to do that."

"Well, I don't."

Tate scratched his head and opened the back door. "I'll get right to it," he said, smiling to himself. He'd never understand Maggie Lorena in a million years. But wasn't that what made a man's life interesting?

———

Maggie made her rounds every week, taking turns visiting her neighbors, her sister, and her brothers. She'd arrive mostly at mealtime, sharing the noon meal and carrying a plate home to Tate and William. When she'd collected enough interesting events to write about, she'd close herself up in her room and compose her column, "Rambling 'Round Colly," describing local events from births and deaths, to tongue-in-cheek reports of a sly fox robbing a hen house, or a bear chasing a neighbor up a tree. Weddings and anniversaries were her favorite occasions for recalling times past. "I remember when the groom was just a boy, and he . . ." The topics ranged from humorous to ridiculous. More often than not, her own kin bore the brunt of her jokes, and some were not too happy about it. But times were difficult and a little humor made them forget about their hardships temporarily, and Maggie Lorena Ryan's column was the highlight of their week.

———

WHEN SHE WASN'T WRITING, Maggie would ramble around the house, rummaging through her things. Maybe she'd spend an hour or two in the kitchen, throwing everything she could find into a pot of stew. On one such occasion, she came across Aunt Mag's recipe book in a box of kitchen utensils Katie had brought her. "It was mostly a junk drawer," Katie said, "but there might be something in there that was Mama's you'd want." The old recipes intrigued Maggie because she'd never really learned to cook. She'd had no need. Now, with Aunt Mag gone and Lizzie laid up in bed with old age, Maggie yearned to cook. At hog killing time, she'd even made the liver pudding using Aunt Mag's recipe.

Tate remarked to his sister-in-law about Maggie's spurt of energy . "I don't expect it to last too long," he said. "But I sure am enjoying it for the time being."

Tears came into Katie's eyes. She'd always loved her brother-in-law. He was kind and gentle, deserving of so much more than Maggie had ever given him. But Maggie was her sister, and she intended to stand by her. "Won't you try, Tate?"

He was sitting in a straight chair on the porch of the house that he'd never really finished. Katie had stepped down into the yard. Tate leaned over towards her, his face level with Katie's. He'd been drinking. She could smell it on his breath. "Katie, all I've ever done is try to help Maggie Lorena. I give her everything I had, more than most men give a woman. I put up with more from her than most men put up with." He took a deep breath and settled back into his chair, staring out towards the oak grove. "I reckon I can do it a little longer."

EPILOGUE

A House Between the Rivers

1931

✗

B Y THE TIME 1931 ROLLED AROUND, MONEY was almost nonexistent in the communities between the rivers. People desperately held on to what they had, bartering and borrowing from one another. When cars became "Hoover carts" because no one could afford gas and oil to run them, Will Ryan was forced to go out of business. No one had any doubt that things would get better sometime soon—they couldn't get any worse. So Jasper Corbinn's house had lain vacant for more than a year following his death, accumulating taxes that none of his surviving siblings could afford to pay.

———

EVA MCBRYDE HAD FAITH IN HER LITTLE PRAYERS. She knew God might not always answer them right away. And he'd plain old ignore you if your prayer was self-serving. But just when you'd about given up, something would happen to make you know He was always listening.

In the summer of 1929, they'd moved to an even smaller house on Nun Street, where they had no boarders. The stock market crash a few weeks later robbed them of what little they had in the Princess Street house, which had been on the market all that time.

Hugh and Harry, both married now, along with Calvin sent a little money each month from their Coast Line salaries to help their parents make ends meet. Millie continued to do alterations and work for Emily McAllister. But when Emily abruptly announced that she was closing her business and moving back to Jacksonville, Millie had been as surprised as anyone.

Looking back, Millie thought she should've known something was wrong when Emily confided to her that Jeanne had started to become hostile towards her. "It's almost as if she blames me for the accident," Emily had said.

"She couldn't possibly blame you," Millie said with complete assurance. She'd never revealed to Emily how drunk Jeanne had been the night of the Pirates' Festival when she'd left her at the hat shop.

How it all happened no one could be sure, but soon after Jeanne McAllister was released from the hospital, her mother suddenly called off the wedding, closed up the hat shop, put her home and the beach cottage on the market, and moved back to Onslow County. Soon afterwards there was talk that Jeanne had accompanied Dr. Jonathan McNamara to Durham, where he had obtained a position with Duke Hospital's specialty clinic in a new field called plastic surgery.

Emily's retreat from Wilmington society was met with regret. She had been a bona fide altruist, and Wilmington had loved her. But the talk that surrounded the end of her relationship with the young doctor and the hurt Jeanne had caused her was more than she could bear. Her protégée couldn't have been more understanding. "I'll miss you most of all, Millie," Emily said. "I want you to have all of my needlework equipment. That box of forms and trimmings are for you. Maybe you can make a few hats along with doing alterations."

"Really? You've done so much for me already. But I will admit that I've dreamed about opening my own shop someday. I'd call it Millie's Millinery or something like that."

"That's perfectly wonderful, dear," Emily said, her eyes filling with tears. "If only *you'd* been my daughter." She'd then given Millie a check for one hundred dollars and asked her to use it to help with her parents' expenses, something Millie would have done anyhow.

"I don't ever want Papa to have to stand in that relief line. I walked by the courthouse yesterday, and it was halfway around the block."

"There will be stars in your crown, dear Millie," Emily said as she locked up the hat shop for the last time.

———

WHEN THE LETTER FROM MAGGIE CAME, suggesting that Jasper Corbinn's house could be had for a song—he had no heirs and there was no one with any money left in the county to buy it— Rob asked Harry to look into it. Within days, Harry had negotiated with Jasper's next of kin to buy the house and five acres of land for a great deal less than its worth. Eva's brother Dick happily provided the money to bring his sister back to the country, where he claimed his roots had made him the man that he was. He'd made a fortune in Oklahoma in the oil wells, and he'd been smart enough to invest his money in petroleum, which was fast becoming the most important industry in the world. In addition to the house in the country for his sister, he purchased Emily McAllister's house on Market Street, a house at Wrightsville Beach, and a place in Florida. Dick O'Kelly was ready to retire, himself.

———

IN A CLOSET, ROB AND EVA MCBRYDE FOUND the Modern Homes catalogue from which Jasper had ordered the unassembled home from Sears and Roebuck in 1925. Jasper's carefully recorded notes in the construction manual had documented each staggered shipment of construction materials: first building paper and nails, lumber and frames; then lath, roofing materials, flooring, siding, downspouts, doors and windows, hardware, cabinetry and millwork—everything needed to build the home. Rob spent hour upon hour perusing the thick manual, amazed at the detailed instructions and drawings. "What I can't believe is that he did it by himself," he said.

"I expect you could've done it too," Eva said.

"'Spect I could've, if it'd all been brought to me and drawn out in those pictures."

"His brother said it cost him over nine hundred dollars," Eva said.

"Shame it's not worth that now, not to him anyhow."

———

ONE OF EVA'S FIRST VISITORS WAS HER COUSIN Maggie Ryan, who'd loaded jars of each thing she'd canned during the summer into the wagon along with two dozen ears of Tate's late corn. "We'll have sweet potatoes by cold weather. I'll bring you some after they cure," Maggie said.

They sat out on the front porch, where Eva had just replanted her rose bush beneath the railing. "You are so dear, cousin. I'll be forever grateful to you for finding this place for us. I just feel so bad that Jasper—"

Maggie dabbed at her eyes with an embroidered handkerchief. "The Lord had his reasons for taking him. I'm at peace with it now. I feel like Jasper would have wanted you to have his house." She pointed to the edge of the field nearest the house. "See those peach trees over yonder? They were little switches when he planted them—before he even started the house."

"Rob says they'll be bearing fruit next year."

"I reckon they will," Maggie said, rising from the rocking chair. She looked out across the yard. "I'll give you some of my dusty miller. It'd look real nice along the lane there."

"Everyone has been so good to us. Your sister Katie was here the day we moved in, with a bushel of field peas. They liked to've ruined before we finished them."

Maggie clapped her hands together. "You'll have to come to Home Demonstration Club with me. They'll loan you one of those big old pressure cookers and you can put up a few things before cold weather."

"Aren't they dangerous?" Eva asked. "I'd be afraid—"

"No sirree, they're not a bit dangerous. I put up about a hundred jars this summer, and look at me, I'm still here!"

"Maybe Millie will go with you. She really likes to cook. Does most of it now. I won't ask her yet, though. She's got about all she can do trying to finish high school at Long Creek."

"My Len was asking about her just the other day. He finally finished his schooling this year. He's working with his Uncle Roy full time now, but he gets home right regularly."

"Millie," Eva called out. "Come on out here, honey, and speak to Cousin Maggie Lorena."

Millie pushed open the screen door and stuck her head out. "Hey, Cousin Maggie Lorena. I'll be out there in a minute." The door swung shut.

"She's a right pretty girl," Maggie said. "Has she got a beau?"

"There's a fellow in Wilmington that she writes to."

"Well, I'd say she and my Len might keep some company. They used to write to each other. I know there's a little kin there, but not enough to make any difference."

"Oh, I don't know about that," Eva said. "Soon as Millie finishes high school, she wants to go back to Wilmington. Maybe open her own hat shop someday."

Millie came out carrying two tall glasses of iced tea. "I thought maybe you two would like something cold to drink."

"I declare, aren't you the sweetest thing. I was just saying to your mama that you and my Len ought to get together sometime."

"Yes ma'am, I like Len a lot. He's home now, isn't he?" Of course she knew he was.

———

EVA MCBRYDE LIVED IN THE JASPER CORBINN house only six months. One crisp spring morning before breakfast, Millie had cracked open her mother's bedroom door and noticed her sleeping. She'd closed the door quietly and gone back into the kitchen to finish cooking breakfast. Rob was washing up at the sink after feeding the livestock. "Mama not up yet?" he asked.

"No, sir, she's sound asleep. Didn't even turn over when I opened the door. I guess she's worn out after planting all those bushes yesterday."

"I'd better go see about her," Rob said. Millie followed him back to the bedroom, drying her hands on her apron. She'd thought nothing about her mother's lack of response—as she'd gotten older, Eva was inclined to move a little slower in the morning.

Watching her father cry was the hardest thing she'd ever done. Millie would remember, later, that she'd reacted more to his grief than her own. "Papa, it's all right, it's all right. Papa . . . "

Millie had ridden the horse bareback up to Zeb's house and asked him to send someone to Burgaw to call Harry. Harry would tell the rest of them. He'd find the words that she could never say: *Mama died in her sleep last night . . . at home, between the rivers.*

※

—COLLY, N.C. Funeral services will be held Wednesday afternoon at the residence in Bladen County for Mrs. Eva O'Kelly McBryde, 54, who died suddenly yesterday morning at her home.

Dr. Broadus E. Larkins, of the First Baptist Church in Wilmington, will officiate. Pallbearers will be nephews of the deceased. Mrs. McBryde is survived by her husband, Robert McBryde; four sons, Hugh McBryde, Calvin McBryde, Harry McBryde, and Rodney McBryde; four daughters, Rebecca McBryde Jones, Maybelle McBryde, Millicent McBryde, and Vera McBryde; and one brother, Judge Richard O'Kelly of Tulsa, Okla. The deceased had returned only six months ago to Bladen County, the place of her birth. She will be remembered by many for her generous ways.—*Bladen Journal, March 21, 1931*

This book was composed in the Hoefler Text and
Bernhard Modern faces in Quark XPress 4.1 on the
Macintosh G4 computer.